Major Joachim Steuben's eyes looked blankly through Sergeant "Slick" Des Grieux. "I really think I ought to kill you now, before you cause other trouble," he said softly.

"Sir," said Broglie. "Slick cleared our left flank. That had to be done."

Steuben's eyes focused again, this time on Broglie. "Did it?" the major said. "Not from outside the prepared defenses, I think. And certainly not against orders from a superior , who was—"

The cold stare again at Des Grieux. No more emotion in the eyes than there would be in the muzzle of the pistol which might appear with magical speed in Joachim's hand.

"Who was, " the major continued, "passing on *my* orders."

"But . . ." Des Grieux whispered. "I *won*."

"No," Steuben said in a crisply businesslike voice. "You ran, Sergeant. *I* had to make an emergency night advance to prevent Hill 541 North from being overrun. I don't like night actions, Sergeant," he added in a frigid voice. "It's dangerous because of the confusion. If my orders had been obeyed, there would have been no confusion."

"Wait a minute," Des Grieux said. "Wait a bloody minute!" I wasn't just sitting on my hands, you know. I was fighting!"

"Yes, Sergeant," Steuben said. "You were fighting like a fool, and it appears that you're still a fool. Which doesn't surprise me." He smiled at Broglie. "The Colonel will have to approve your field promotion to lieutenant, Mister Broglie," he said, "but I don't see any problems."

Des Grieux swung a fist at Broglie. Someone grabbed his arms.

Suddenly, Steuben set the muzzle of his pistol against Des Grieux's right eye—so swiftly that the cold iridium circle touched the eyeball before reflex could blink the lid closed.

Des Grieux jerked his head back, but the pistol followed. Its touch was as light as that of a butterfly's wing . . .

From *The Warrior*

Baen Books by David Drake

Hammer's Slammers
The Sharp End
The Tank Lords
Caught in the Crossfire
The Butcher's Bill
(forthcoming)

Independent Novels and Collections
Redliners
With the Lightnings
Starliner
Ranks of Bronze
Lacey and His Friends
Old Nathan
Mark II: The Military Dimension
All the Way to the Gallows

The General series
(with S. M. Stirling)
The Forge
The Hammer
The Anvil
The Steel
The Sword
The Chosen

An Honorable Defense: Crisis of Empire
(with Thomas T. Thomas)
Enemy of My Enemy: Nova Terra
(with Ben Ohlander)
The Undesired Princess and the Enchanted Bunny
(with L. Sprague de Camp)
Lest Darkness Fall and To Bring the Light
(with L. Sprague de Camp)
Armageddon
(ed. with Billie Sue Mosiman)

CAUGHT IN THE CROSSFIRE

DAVID DRAKE

CAUGHT IN THE CROSSFIRE

This is a work of fiction. All the characters and events portrayed in this book are fictional, and any resemblance to real people or incidents is purely coincidental.

A Baen Books Original

Baen Publishing Enterprises
P.O. Box 1403
Riverdale, NY 10471

ISBN: 0-671-87882-4

Cover art by Larry Elmore

First printing, July 1998

Distributed by Simon & Schuster
1230 Avenue of the Americas
New York, NY 10020

Typeset by Windhaven Press, Auburn, NH
Printed in the United States of America

Contents

Mercenaries

MERCENARY SOLDIERS have been around for a long time. During that time, they've been maligned by everyone—even other mercenaries.

There's reason enough for the dislike of mercenaries: they've taken on a job that the people who hire them can't or won't do.

If it's ability that the citizenry lacks—top-of-the-line hardware (whether that means crossbows or aircraft), and the training to use the hardware properly—then the mercenaries are feared. If it's stomach for the job that's missing—the willingness to do whatever it takes to win, to kill and assuredly to die—then the mercenaries are loathed.

Indeed, mercs are loathed in either case.

But that's purely a personal problem. It's never kept rulers and nations from hiring outsiders to do their formalized killing for them.

Why does anybody want the job?

In large measure, because it *is* a job; and its required

Note: A substantially similar version of this essay appeared in the 1988 omnibus volume *The Mercenary*, by Jerry Pournelle, published by Franklin Watts.

skills have very little application to civilian life. Trained combat soldiers know things that civilians don't—

But when the lads who went to become soldiers return, they find they're not as satisfactory farmers, clerks, stone-masons—whatever—as the fellows who stayed home.

The longer a war lasts, the greater the atrophy of civilian skills among the men who've been doing the fighting. By the time Europe had settled down in 1815, there was nothing in England for Wellington's veterans except beggary. Outside England, though . . .

Bolivar and San Martin led the armies that freed South America from the Spanish crown. The men who stiffened those rebel troops in pitched battle (a very different thing from sniping from behind fences, as Americans learned to their cost at Bunker Hill), were paid-off British veterans.

Because they believed in the cause of freedom from the yoke of Spain? Nonsense—they were men who'd battled on behalf of the Spanish Monarchy for the past decade. But fighting was the only work they knew.

So they faced the Spanish regulars as they'd faced the French; and they showed in South America what they'd proved in the Penninsula: nobody in the world knew *their* work better than they did.

The term "mercenary" covers two categories of soldiers: bands of armed men under their own chosen leaders; and individual men, often grouped with other outsiders but organized and led by officers of the nation hiring them.

The first category is rarely a good idea for their employers; often it is a disastrously bad one. Ariovistus' Germans, the Condottieri against whom Machiavelli inveighed, and Les Affreux of Bob Denard are all examples of mercenary units who've proven more dangerous than the threats they were hired to oppose.

In the second category there are more success stories, perhaps more successes than failures.

Mercenaries under local officers have a history of standing when the fighting gets tough. They're more likely to know their job than conscripted soldiers are; and they don't have the option that conscripts frequently have, of running home if things go badly. The Greeks who marched from Cunaxa to the Black Sea were neither the first nor the last mercenaries to learn how far away home can be if the side that's paying you loses.

Not infrequently, the loyalty and skill of mercenaries can have historic consequences. When King David grew old, the national army of Israel deserted him for his son Absalom. Joab led David's mercenaries, many of them Philistines, against the usurper and his Hebrew followers. The mercenaries crushed the revolt; Joab himself slew Absalom as the youth hung from a tree.

David never forgave them for it. But for good or ill, he died a king and passed on his crown as intended to Solomon.

David's mercenaries were loyal to *him*. Sometimes mercenaries give their loyalty to something as simple as duty, to going where the guy in charge tells them to go— even though they don't understand the situation, and they're pretty sure they wouldn't like it if they *did* understand.

That can change the world also.

In A.D. 532 the situation in Constantinople got out of hands of the authorities. Rival street gangs brawled with increasing violence, despite the efforts of the police. Finally the gang leaders combined. What had been a public order problem became an open revolt directed at the government of the young Emperor Justinian.

Mobs burned the police officers and surged through the streets crying, "Nika!—*Conquer!*" Justinian attempted to mollify them by removing unpopular ministers. The riots continued.

The civil authorities could do nothing. Units of the regular army in Constantinople *would* do nothing, standing aside "until matters had worked themselves out." Nobles slipped from the palace to join the rioters—who crowned a young man from an old imperial family.

Two top military officers, Belisarius and Mundus,

chanced to be on business in Constantinople when the insurrection broke out. They were accompanied by their personal bodyguards—mercenaries they paid themselves, most of them Huns.

Belisarius and Mundus were loyal to Justinian, but they couldn't raise any support among the imperial troops in the city. At last—and after a false start—they went out in separate sorties against the rioters, leading only their mercenary bodyguards.

The rioters—the insurrectionists—were gathered in the Hippodrome, the chariot-racing stadium, preparatory to making a final attack on the nearby palace. Belisarius tried to lead his group through the private tunnel to the imperial box, hoping that he could end the revolt by capturing its leaders. A unit of the regular army guarded the door and wouldn't let Belisarius past.

In desperation, Belisarius launched his mercenaries in a sudden attack on the assembled crowd.

Mundus and his men were still stumbling around in the charred rubble left by weeks of rioting. When they heard the sound of fighting, they found their own route into the Hippodrome, through the ground-level gate that served the arena rather than the stands.

The rioters were caught from two directions by bands of mercenaries. Perhaps a few of the citizens tried to fight, but they hadn't a prayer of winning against heavily-armed veterans who knew their only chance of survival was to kill everyone they saw. Most of the crowd tried to run, but there wasn't any place to run, either.

According to Procopius (who was present), the discipline and heavy armor of the mercenaries drowned the Nika Insurrection in the blood of thirty thousand citizens. Justinian ruled for another thirty-three years and died in his bed.

Was it worth it?

Certainly not to the slain. But I've stood in the magificent vault of Hagia Sophia; and I've read portions of the codified and digested Roman law that is the basis of so much of European social interaction. Neither of those monuments would exist today if Justinian had been deposed in A.D. 532.

And it was worth it to the mercenaries, because they were the ones still standing when the day was over. . . .

David Drake
Chapel Hill, NC

The Warrior

PART I

The tribarrel in the cupola of *Warrior*, the tank guarding the northwest quadrant of Hill 541 North, snarled in automatic air defense mode. The four Slammers in Lieutenant Lindgren's bunker froze.

Sergeant Samuel "Slick" Des Grieux, *Warrior's* commander, winced. He was twenty-one standard years old, and a hardened veteran of two years in Hammer's Slammers. He kneaded his broad, powerful hands together to control his anger at being half a kay away from where he ought to have been: aboard his vehicle and fighting.

The incoming shell thudded harmlessly, detonated in the air.

Sergeant Broglie had counted out the time between the tribarrel's burst and the explosion. "Three seconds," he murmured.

The shell had been a safe kilometer away when it went off. The howl of its passage to an intersection with *Warrior's* bolts echoed faintly through the night.

"Every five minutes," said Hawes, the fourth man in the bunker and by far the greenest. This was the first time Hawes had been under prolonged bombardment. The way

6

he twitched every time a gun fired indicated how little he liked the experience. "I wish they'd——"

Lieutenant Lindgren's tank, *Queen City*, fired a five-round burst. Cyan light shuddered through the bunker's dogleg entrance. A pair of shells, probably fired from the Republican batteries on Hill 661 to the northeast, crumped well short of their target.

"*Via*, Lieutenant!" Des Grieux said in a desperate voice. He stared at his hands, because he was afraid of what he might blurt if he looked straight at the young officer. "Look, I oughta be back on *Warrior*. Anything you gotta say, you can say over the commo, it's secure. And——"

He couldn't help it. His face came up. His voice grew as hard as his cold blue eyes, and he continued. "Besides, we're not here to talk. We oughta be kicking ass. That's what we're here for."

"We're here——" Lindgren began.

"We're the Federals' artillery defense, Slick," Broglie said, smiling at Des Grieux. Broglie didn't shout, but his voice flattened the lieutenant's words anyway. "*And* their backbone. We're doing our job, so no sweat, hey?"

"Our job . . ." said Des Grieux softly. *Warrior* fired three short bursts, blasting a salvo inbound from the Republicans on Hill 504. Des Grieux ignored the sound and its implications. " . . . is to fight. Not to hide in holes. Hey, Luke?"

Broglie was four centimeters shorter than Des Grieux and about that much broader across the shoulders. He wasn't afraid of Des Grieux . . . which interested Des Grieux because it was unusual, though it didn't bother him in the least.

Des Grieux wasn't afraid of anyone or anything.

"We're here to see that Hill 541 North holds out till the relieving force arrives," said Lindgren.

He'd taken Broglie's interruption as a chance to get his emotions under control. The lieutenant was almost as nervous as Hawes, but he was a Slammers officer and determined to act like one. "The AAD in the vehicles does that as well as we could sitting in the turrets, Slick," he continued, "and unit meetings are important to remind us that we're a platoon, not four separate tanks stuck off in West Bumfuck."

"North Bumfuck fiver-four-one," Broglie chuckled. Broglie's face held its quizzical smile, but the low sound of his laughter was drowned by incoming shells and the tanks' response to them. This was a sustained pounding from all three Republican gun positions: Hills 504 and 661 to the north, and Hill 541 South ten kilometers southeast of the Federal base.

The Reps fired thirty or forty shells in less than a minute. Under the tribarrels' lash, the explosions merged into a drumming roar—punctuated by the sharp *crash* of the round that got through.

The bunker rocked. Dust drifted down from the sand-bagged roof. Hawes rubbed his hollow eyes and pretended not to have heard the blast.

The sound of the salvoes died away. One of the Federal garrison screamed nearby. Des Grieux wasn't sure whether the man was wounded or simply broken by the constant hammering. The unanswered shelling got to him, too; but it made him want to go out and kill, not hide in a bunker and scream.

"Lieutenant," Des Grieux said in the same measured, deadly voice as before. "We oughta go out and nail the bastards. *That's* how we can save these Federal pussies."

"The relieving force—"Lindgren said.

"The relieving force hasn't gotten here in three weeks, so they aren't exactly burning up the road, now, are they?" Des Grieux said. "Look—"

"They'll get here," said Broglie. "They've got Major Howes and three of our companies with 'em, so they'll get here. And we'll wait it out, because that's what Colonel Hammer ordered us to do."

Lindgren opened his mouth to speak, but he closed it again and let the tank commanders argue the question. Des Grieux didn't even pretend to care what a newbie lieutenant thought. As for Broglie—

Sergeant Lucas Broglie was more polite, and Broglie

appreciated the value of Lindgren's education from the Military Academy of Nieuw Friesland. But Broglie didn't much care what a newbie lieutenant thought, either.

"I didn't say we ought to bug out," Des Grieux said. His eyes were as open and empty as a cannon's bore. "I said we could *win* this instead of sitting on our butts."

Open and empty and deadly. . . .

"Four tanks can't take on twenty thousand Reps," Broglie said. His smile was an equivalent of Des Grieux's blank stare: the way Broglie's face formed itself when the mind beneath was under stress.

He swept an arc with his thumb. The bunker was too strait to allow him to make a full-arm gesture. "That's what they got out there. Twenty thousand of them."

The ground shook from another shell that got through the tribarrels' defensive web. Des Grieux was so concentrated on Broglie that his mind had tuned out the ripping bursts that normally would have focused him utterly.

"It's not just us 'n them," Des Grieux said. Lindgren and Hawes, sitting on ammunition boxes on opposite sides of the bunker, swivelled their heads from one veteran to the other like spectators at a tennis match. "There's five, six thousand Federals on this crap pile with us, and they can't like it much better than I do."

"They're not—" Lieutenant Lindgren began. Cyan light flickered through the bunker entrance. A Republican sniper, not one of the Slammers' weapons. The Reps had a few powerguns, and Hill 661 was high enough that a marksman could slant his bolts into the Federal position.

The *snap!* of the bolt impacting made Lindgren twitch. Des Grieux's lips drew back in a snarl, because if he'd been in his tank he just *might* have put paid to the bastard.

"Not line soldiers," the lieutenant concluded in an artificially calm tone.

"They'd fight if they had somebody to lead them," Des Grieux said. "*Via*, anything's better'n being wrapped up here and used for Rep target practice."

"They've got a leader," Broglie replied, "and it's General Wycherly, not us. For what he's worth."

Des Grieux grimaced as though he'd been kicked. Even Hawes snorted.

"I don't believe you appreciate the constraints that General Wycherly operates under," Lindgren said in a thin voice.

Lindgren knew how little his authority was worth to the veterans. That, as well as a real awareness of the Federal commander's difficulties, injected a note of anger into his tone. "He's outnumbered three or four to one," he went on. "Ten to one, if you count just the real combat troops under his command. But he's holding his position as ordered. And that's just what we're going to help him do."

"We're pieces of a puzzle, Slick," said Broglie. He relaxed enough to rub his lips, massaging them out of the rictus into which the discussion had cramped them. "Wycherly's job is to keep from getting overrun; our job's to help him; and our people with the relieving force 're going to kick the cop outa the Reps if we just hold 'em a few days more."

Another incoming shell detonated a kilometer short of Hill 541 North. The Republicans knew they couldn't do serious physical damage so long as the position was guarded by the Slammers' tanks . . . but they knew as well the psychological effect the constant probing fire had on the defenders.

For an instant Broglie's hard smile was back. "Or not a puzzle," he added. "A gun. Every part has to do the right job, or the gun doesn't work."

"Okay, we had our unit meeting," Des Grieux said. He squeezed his hands together so fiercely that his fingers were dark with trapped blood between the first and second joints. "Now can I get back to my tank where I can maybe do some good?"

"The AAD does everything that can be done, Sergeant," Lindgren said. "That's what we need now. That and discipline."

Des Grieux stood up, though he had to bend forward to clear the bunker's low ceiling. "Having the computer fire my guns," he said with icy clarity, "is like jacking off. With respect."

Lindgren grimaced. "All right," he said. "You're all dismissed."

In an attempt to soften the previous exchange, he added, "There shouldn't be more than a few days of this."

But Des Grieux, ignoring the incoming fire, was already out of the bunker.

A howitzer fired from the center of the Federal position. The night outside the bunker glowed with the bottle-shaped yellow flash. There were fifteen tubes in the Federal batteries, but they were short of ammunition and rarely fired.

When they did, they invariably brought down a storm of Republican counterfire.

Des Grieux continued to walk steadily in the direction of *Warrior*; his tank, his home.

Not his reason for existence, though. Des Grieux existed to rip the enemy up one side and down the other. To do that he could use *Warrior*, or the pistol in his holster, or his teeth; whatever was available. Lieutenant Lindgren was robbing Des Grieux of his reason for existence. . . .

He heard the scream of the shell—one round, from the northwest. He waited for the sky-tearing sound of *Warrior's* tribarrel firing a short burst of cyan plasma, copper nuclei stripped of their electron shells and ravening downrange to detonate or vaporize the shell.

Warrior didn't fire.

The Reps had launched a ground-hugging missile from the lower altitude of Hill 504. *Warrior* and the other Slammers' tanks couldn't engage the round because they were dug in behind the bunker line encircling the Federal positions. The incoming missile would not rise into the line-of-sight range of the powerguns until—

There was a scarlet streak from the horizon like a vector marker in the dark bowl of the sky. A titanic crash turned the sky orange and knocked Des Grieux down. Sandy red dust sucked up and rolled over, forming a doughnut that expanded across the barren hilltop.

Des Grieux got to his feet and resumed walking. The

bastards couldn't make him run, and they couldn't make him bend over against the sleet of shell fragments which would rip him anyway—running or walking, cowering or standing upright like a man.

The Republicans fired a dozen ordinary rounds. Tank tribarrels splashed each of the shells a fraction of a second after they arched into view. The powerguns' snarling dazzle linked the Federal base for an instant to orange fireballs which faded into rags of smoke. There were no more ground-huggers.

An ordinary shell was no more complex than a hand grenade. Ground-hugging missiles required sophisticated electronics and a fairly complex propulsion system. There weren't many of them in the Rep stockpiles.

Ground-huggers would be as useless as ballistic projectiles *if* Lindgren used his platoon the way tanks should be used, as weapons that sought out the enemy instead of cowering turret-down in defilade.

Blood and Martyrs! What a way to fight a war.

The top of Hill 541 North was a barren moonscape. The bunkers were improvised by the troops themselves with shovels and sandbags. A month ago, the position had been merely the supply point for a string of Federal outposts. No one expected a siege.

But when the Republicans swept down in force, the outposts scrambled into their common center, 541N. Troops dug furiously as soon as they realized that there was no further retreat until Route 7 to the south was cleared from the outside.

If Route 7 was cleared. Task Force Howes, named for the CO of the Slammers 2nd Battalion, had promised a link-up within three days.

Every day for the past two weeks.

A sniper on Hill 661, twelve kilometers away, fired his powergun. The bolt snapped fifty meters from Des Grieux, fusing the sandy soil into a disk of glass which shattered instantly as it cooled.

Kuykendall, *Warrior*'s driver, should be in the tank turret. If Des Grieux had been manning the guns, the sniper would have had a hot time of it . . . but Des Grieux was walking back from a dick-headed meeting, and Kuykendall wasn't going to disobey orders to leave the tribarrel on Automatic Air Defense and not, under any circumstances, to fire the 20 CM main gun since ammunition was scarce.

The garrison of Hill 541N, the Slammers included, had the supplies they started the siege with. Ground routes were blocked. Aerial resupply would be suicide because of the Rep air-defense arsenal on the encircling hills.

The sniper fired again. The bolt hit even farther away, but he was probably aiming at Des Grieux anyhow. Nothing else moved on this side of the encampment except swirls of wind-blown sand.

A shell fragment the size of a man's palm stuck up from the ground. It winked jaggedly in the blue light of the bolt.

Warrior was within a hundred meters. Des Grieux continued to walk deliberately.

The hilltop's soil blurred all the vehicles and installations into identical dinginess. The dirt was a red without life, the hue of old blood that had dried and flaked to powder.

The sniper gave up. A gun on 541S coughed a shell which Broglie's *Honey Girl* blew from the sky a moment later.

Every five minutes; but not regularly, and twice the Reps had banged out more than a thousand rounds in a day, some of which inevitably got through. . . .

"That you, Slick?" Kuykendall called from the *Warrior*'s cupola.

"Yeah, of course it's me," Des Grieux replied. He stepped onto a sandbag lip, then hopped down to *Warrior*'s back deck. His boots clanked.

The tanks were dug in along sloping ramps. Soil from the trenches filled sandbag walls rising above the vehicles' cupolas. Lieutenant Lindgren was afraid that powerguns from 661—and the Reps had multi-barreled calliopes to provide artillery defense—would rake the Slammers' tanks if the latter were visible.

Des Grieux figured the answer to *that* threat was to kick the Reps the hell off Hill 661. By now, though, he'd learned that the other Slammers were just going to sigh and look away when he made a suggestion that didn't involve waiting for somebody else to do the fighting.

Kuykendall slid down from the cupola into the fighting compartment. She was a petite woman, black-haired and a good enough driver. To Des Grieux, Kuykendall was a low-key irritation that he had to work around, like a burr in the mechanism that controlled his turret's rotation.

A driver was a necessary evil, because Des Grieux couldn't guide his tank and fight it at the same time. Kuykendall took orders, but she had a personality of her own. She wasn't a mere extension of Des Grieux's will, and that made her more of a problem than someone blander though less competent would have been.

Nothing he couldn't work around, though. There *was* nothing Des Grieux couldn't work around, if his superiors just gave him the chance to do his job. "Anything new?" Kuykendall asked.

Des Grieux stood on his seat so that he could look out over the sandbags toward Hill 661. "What'd you think?" he said. He switched the visual display on his helmet visor to infrared and cranked up the magnification.

The sniper had gone home. Nothing but ripples in the atmosphere and the cooler blue of trees transpiring water they sucked somehow from this Lord-blasted landscape.

Des Grieux climbed out of the hatch again. He shoved a sandbag off the top layer. *The bastard would be back, and when he was . . .*

He pushed away another sandbag. The bags were woven from a coarse synthetic that smelled like burning tar when it rubbed.

"We're not supposed to do that," Kuykendall said from the cupola. "A lucky shot could put the tribarrel out of action. That'd hurt us a lot worse than a hundred dead grunts does the Reps."

"They don't have a hundred powerguns," Des Grieux said without turning around. He pushed at the second-layer sandbag he'd uncovered but that layer was laid as headers. The bags to right and left resisted the friction on their long sides. "Anyway, it's worth something to me to give a few of those cocky bastards their lunch."

Hawes' *Susie Q* ripped the sky. Des Grieux dropped into a crouch, then rose again with a feeling of embarrassment. He knew that Kuykendall had seen him jump.

It wasn't flinching. If *Warrior*'s AAD sensed incoming from Hill 661, Des Grieux would either duck instantly— or have his head shot off by the tribarrel of his own tank. The fire-direction computer didn't care if there was a man in the way when it needed to do its job.

Des Grieux liked the computer's attitude.

He lifted and pushed, raising his triceps muscles into stark ridges. Des Grieux was thin and from a distance looked frail. Close up, no one noticed anything but his eyes; and there was no weakness in them.

The sandbag slid away. The slot in *Warrior*'s protection gave Des Grieux a keyhole through which to rake Hill 661 with his tribarrel. He got back into the turret. Kuykendall dropped out of the way without further comment.

"You know . . ." Des Grieux said as he viewed the enemy positions in the tribarrel's holographic sight. *Warrior*'s sensors were several orders of magnitude better than those of the tankers' unaided helmets. "The Reps aren't much better at this than these Federal pussies we gotta nurse-maid."

"How d'ye mean?" Kuykendall asked.

Her voice came over the intercom channel. She'd slipped back into the driver's compartment. Most drivers found the internal hatch too tight for use in anything less than a full buttoned-up emergency.

"They've got calliopes up there," Des Grieux explained as he scanned the bleak silence of Hill 661. The Republican positions were in defilade. Easy enough to arrange from their greater height.

"If it was me," Des Grieux continued, "I'd pick my time and roll'er up to direct-fire positions. They'd kick the cop outa this place."

"They're not going to bet three-CM calliopes against tank main guns, Sarge," Kuykendall said carefully.

"They would if they had any balls," Des Grieux said. His voice was coldly judgmental, stating the only truth there was. He showed no anger toward those who were too stupid to see it. "Dug in like we are, they could blow away the cupolas and our sensor arrays before we even got the main guns to bear. A calliope's no joke, kid."

He laughed harshly. "Wish they'd try, though. I can hip-shoot a main gun if I have to."

"There's talk they're going to try t' overrun us before Task Force Howes relieves us," Kuykendall said with the guarded nonchalance she always assumed when talking to the tank commander.

Des Grieux's two years in the Slammers made him a veteran, but he was scarcely one of the longest-serving members of the regiment. His drive, his skill with weapons, and the phenomenal ruthlessness with which he accomplished any task set him gave Des Grieux a reputation beyond simple seniority.

"There's talk," Des Grieux said coldly. *Nothing moved on Hill 661.* "There's been talk. There's been talk Howes is going to get his thumbs out of his butt and relieve us, too."

The tribarrel roused, swung, and ignited the sky with a four-round burst of plasma. A shell from Hill 504 broke apart without detonating. The largest piece of casing was still a white glow when it tumbled out of sight in the valley below.

The sky flickered to the south as well, but at such a distance that the sounds faded to a low rumble. Task Force Howes still slugged it out with the Republicans who defended Route 7. Maybe they were going to get here within seventy-two hours. And maybe Hell was going to freeze over.

Des Grieux scanned Hill 661, and nothing moved.

The only thing Des Grieux knew in the instant he snapped awake from a sound sleep was that it was time to earn his pay.

Kuykendall looked down into the fighting compartment from the commander's seat. "Sarge?" she said. "I—" and broke off when she realized Des Grieux was already alert.

"Get up front 'n drive," Des Grieux ordered curtly. "It's happening."

"It's maybe nothing," the driver said, but she knew Des Grieux. As Kuykendall spoke, she swung her legs out of the cupola. Hopping from the cupola and past the main gun was the fastest way to the driver's hatch in the bow. The tank commander blocked the internal passage anyway as he climbed up to his seat.

The Automatic Air Defense plate on *Warrior's* control panel switched from yellow, standby, to red. The tribarrel rotated and fired. Des Grieux flicked the plate with his boot toe as he went past, disconnecting the computer-controlled defensive fire. He needed *Warrior's* weapons under his personal direction now that things were real.

When the siege began, Lieutenant Lindgren ordered that one member of each two-man tank crew be on watch in the cupola at every moment. What the tankers did off duty, and where they slept, was their own business.

Most of the off-duty troops slept beneath their vehicles, entering the plenum chamber through the access plate in the steel skirts. The chambers were roomy and better protection than anything cobbled together by shovels and sandbags could be. The only problem was the awareness before sleep came that the tank above you weighed 170 tonnes . . . but tankers tended not to be people who thought in those terms.

Lindgren insisted on a bunker next to his vehicle. He was sure that he would go mad if his whole existence, on duty and off, was bounded by the steel and iridium shell of his tank.

Des Grieux went the other way around. He slept in the fighting compartment while his driver kept watch in the cupola above. The deck was steel pressed with grip rosettes. He couldn't stretch out. His meter-ninety of height had to twist between the three-screen control console and the armored tube which fed ammunition to the autoloading twenty-CM main gun.

Nobody called the fighting compartment a comfortable place to sleep; but then, nobody called Des Grieux sane, either.

A storm of Republican artillery fire screamed toward Hill 541N. Some of the shells would have gotten through even if Des Grieux had left *Warrior* in the defensive net. That was somebody else's problem. The Reps didn't have terminally-guided munitions that would target the Slammers' tanks, so a shell that hit *Warrior* was the result of random chance.

You had to take chances in war; and anyway, *Warrior* oughta shrug off anything but a heavy-caliber armor-piercing round with no more than superficial damage.

Kuykendall switched her fans on and brought them up to speed fast with their blades cutting the airstream at minimum angle. *Warrior* trembled with what Des Grieux anthropomorphicized as eagerness, transferring his own emotions to the mindless machine he commanded.

A Slammers' tank was a slope-sided iridium hull whose turret, smooth to avoid shot traps, held a twenty-CM powergun. The three-barreled automatic weapon in the cupola could operate independently or be locked to the same point of aim as the main gun. Eight intake ducts pierced the upper surface of the hull, feeding air down to drive fans in armored nacelles below.

At rest, the tanks sat on their steel skirts. When the vehicles were under way, they floated on a cushion of air pressurized by the fans. At full throttle, the power required to drive a tank was enormous, and the fusion bottle which provided that power filled the rear third of the hull.

The tanks were hideously expensive. Their electronics were so complex and sensitive that at least a small portion of every tank's suite was deadlined at any one time. The hulls and running gear were rugged, but the vehicles' own size and weight imposed stresses which required constant maintenance.

When they worked, and to the extent they worked, the

Slammers' tanks were the most effective weapons in the human universe. As *Warrior* was about to prove to two divisions of Republican infantry. . . .

"Back her out!" Des Grieux ordered. If he'd thought about it, he would have sounded a general alarm because he *knew* this was a major attack, but he had other things on his mind besides worrying about people he wasn't planning to kill.

"Booster," Des Grieux said, switching on the artificial intelligence which controlled the tank's systems. "Enemy activity, one kay, now!"

Warrior shuddered as Kuykendall increased the fan bite. Sandy soil mushroomed from the trench walls and upward as the hull lifted and air leaked beneath *Warrior*'s skirts. Des Grieux's direct vision blurred in a gritty curtain, but the data his AI assembled from remote sensors was sharp and clear in the upper half of his helmet visor.

The ground fell away from the top of Hill 541 North in a 1:3 slope, and the tank positions were set well back from the edge of the defenses. Even when *Warrior* backed from her trench, Des Grieux would not be able to see the wire and minefields which the garrison had laid at mid-slope to stop an enemy assault.

Ideally, the tanks would have access to the Slammers' own remote sensors. Conditions were rarely ideal, and on Hill 541N they never even came close. Still, the Federals had emplaced almost a hundred seismic and acoustic sensors before the Republicans tightened the siege. Most of the sensors were in the wire, but they'd dropped a few in the swales surrounding the hill, a kilometer or so out from the hilltop.

Acoustic sensors gathered the sound of voices and equipment, while seismic probes noted the vibration feet and vehicles made in the soil. The information, flawed by the sensors' relative lack of sophistication and the haphazard way the units were emplaced, was transmitted to the hilltop for processing.

Des Grieux didn't know what the Feds did with the raw data, but *Warrior*'s AI turned it into a clear image of a major Republican attack.

There were two thrusts, directed against the east and the northwest quadrants of the Federal positions. The slope at those angles was slightly steeper than it was to the south, but the surface fell in a series of shallow steps that formed dead zones, out of the fire from hilltop bunkers.

A siren near the Federal command post wound up. Its wail was almost lost in the shriek of incoming.

The Reps had ten or a dozen shells in the air at any one time. The three tanks still working air defense slashed arcs across the sky. Powerguns detonated much of the incoming during its fifteen-second flight time, but every minute or so a round got through.

Most of the hits raised geysers of sand from the hilltop. Only occasionally did a bunker collapse or a shellburst scythe down troops running toward fighting positions in the forward trenches, but even misses shook the defenders' morale.

Booster thought the attack on the northwest quadrant was being made by a battalion of infantry, roughly 500 troops, behind a screen of sappers no more than a hundred strong. The eastern thrust was of comparable size, but even so it seemed a ludicrously small force to throw against a garrison of over 5,000 men.

That was only the initial assault; a larger force would get in its own way during the confusion of a night attack. Booster showed several additional battalions and a dozen light armored vehicles waiting in reserve among the yellow-brown scrub of the valleys where streams would run in the wet season.

As soon as the leading elements seized a segment of the outer bunker line in a classic infiltration assault, the Republican support troops would advance in good order and sweep across the hilltop. There was no way in hell that the Federal infantry, demoralized by weeks of unanswerable shelling, was going to stop the attack.

They didn't have to. Not while Des Grieux was here.

"Clear visor," Des Grieux said. He'd seen what the sensors gave him, and he didn't need the display anymore. He tugged the crash bar, dropping his seat into the fighting compartment and buttoning the hatch shut above him.

Warrior's three holographic screens cast their glow across conduits and the breech of the squat main gun.

"Driver, advance along marked vector."

Default on the left-hand screen was a topographic display. Des Grieux drew his finger across it in a curving arc, down from the hilltop in a roughly northwestward direction. The AI would echo the display in Kuykendall's compartment. A trackway, not precisely a road but good enough for the Rep vehicles and sure as *hell* good enough for *Warrior*, wound north from the swale in the direction of the Republican firebase on Hill 504.

"Gun it!" Des Grieux snarled. "Keep your foot on the throttle, bitch!"

It didn't occur to him that there was another way to give the order. All Des Grieux knew was that *Warrior* had to move as he desired, and the commander's will alone was not enough to direct the vehicle.

Kuykendall touched *Warrior* to the ground, rubbing off some of the backing inertia against the sand. She rotated the attitude control of the drive fans, angling the nacelles so that they thrust *Warrior* forward as well as lifting it again onto the air cushion.

The huge tank slid toward the edge of the encampment in front of a curling billow of dust. Size made the vehicle seem to accelerate slowly.

"Oyster Leader to Oyster Two," said Lieutenant Lindgren over the platoon's commo channel. "Hold your position. Break. Oyster four—" Hawes "—move up to support Oyster Two. Over."

The note of *Warrior's* fans changed. Massive inertia would keep the vehicle gliding forward for a hundred meters, but the sound meant Kuykendall was obeying the platoon leader's orders.

"Driver!" Des Grieux shouted. "Roll it! *Now!*" Kuykendall adjusted her nacelles obediently. *Warrior* slid on momentum between a pair of bunkers as the fans swung to resume their forward thrust.

The Federal positions were dugouts covered by transportation pallets supported by a single layer of sandbags.

Three or four additional sandbag layers supplied overhead protection, though a direct hit would crumple the strongest of them. The firing slits were so low that muzzle blasts kicked up sand to shroud the red flashes of their machine guns.

Warrior's sensors fed the main screen with a light-enhanced 120° arc to the front. The tank's AI added in a stereoscopic factor to aid depth perception which the human brain ordinarily supplied in part from variations in light intensity.

The screen provided Des Grieux with a clear window onto the Republican attack. A two-man buzzbomb team rose into firing position at the inner edge of the wire. Instead of launching their unguided rockets into the nearest bunkers, they had waited for the tank they expected.

Des Grieux expected them also. He stunned the night with a bolt from *Warrior*'s main gun.

Des Grieux used his central display for gunnery. It had two orange pippers, a two-CM ring and a one-CM dot for the main gun and tribarrel respectively. The sensor array mounted around *Warrior*'s cupola gave Des Grieux the direction in which to swing his weapon. As soon as his tank rose into a hull-down position that cleared the twenty-CM powergun, he toggled the foot trip.

Because the tribarrel was mounted higher, Des Grieux could have killed the Reps a moment sooner with the automatic weapon; but he wanted the enemy's first awareness of *Warrior* to be the cataclysmic blast of the tank's main gun.

The cyan bolt struck one of the Rep team squarely and converted his body into a ball of vapor so hot that its glowing shockwave flung the other victim's torso and limbs away in separate trajectories. The secondary explosion of the anti-tank warheads was lost in the plasma charge's flashcrash.

Honking through its intakes, *Warrior* thundered down on the Republican attack.

Guns in dozens of Federal bunkers fired white tracers toward the perimeter of mines and wire. Heavy automatic weapons among the Republican support battalions answered with chains of glowing red balls.

The Federal artillerymen in the center of Hill 541 North began slamming out their remaining ammunition in the reasonable view that unless this attack was stopped, there was no need for conservation. Because of their hilltop location, the guns could not bear on the sappers. To reach even the Republican support troops, they had to lob their shells in high, inaccurate arcs. The pair of calliopes on Hill 661 burst many of the Federal rounds at the top of their trajectory.

Instead of becoming involved in firefights, the Rep sappers did an excellent job of pathclearing for the main assault force. A few of the sappers fell, but their uniforms of light-absorbent fabric made them difficult targets even now that Federal starshells popped to throw wavering illumination over the scene.

A miniature rocket dragged its train of explosive across the perimeter defenses. The line exploded with a yellow flash and a sound like a door slamming. Sand and wire flew to either side. Overpressure set off a dozen anti-personnel mines to speckle the night.

There were already a dozen similar gaps in the perimeter. An infiltration team had wormed through the defenses before the alarm went off. One of its members hurled a satchel charge into a bunker, collapsing it with a flash and a roar.

Warrior drove into the wire. Bullets, some of them fired from the Federal bunkers, pinged harmlessly on the iridium armor. A buzzbomb trailing sparks and white smoke snarled toward the tank's right flank. Five meters out, the automatic defense system along the top edge of *Warrior's* skirts banged. Its spray of steel pellets ripped the buzzbomb and set off the warhead prematurely.

The tank rang like a bell when its defensive array fired, but the hollow *whoomp* of the shaped-charge warhead was lost in the battle's general clamor. Shards of buzzbomb casing knocked down a sapper. He thrashed through several spasms before he lay still.

Warrior passed the Federal minefield in a series of sprouting explosions and the spang of fragments which ricocheted from the skirts. The pressure of air within the tank's plenum chamber was high enough to detonate mines rigged to blow off a man's foot. They clanged harmlessly as a tocsin of the huge vehicle's passage.

The tank's bow slope snagged loops of concertina wire which stretched and writhed until it broke. Republican troops threw themselves down to avoid the unexpected whips of hooked steel. Men shouted curses, although the gap *Warrior* tore in the perimeter defenses was broad enough to pass a battalion in columns of sixteen.

Des Grieux ignored the sappers. They could cause confusion within the bunker line, but they were no threat to the ultimate existence of the Federal base. The assault battalion, and still more the thousands of Republican troops waiting in reserve, were another matter.

Warrior had two dual-capable gunnery joysticks. Most tank commanders used only one, selecting tribarrel or main gun with the thumbswitch. Des Grieux shot with both hands.

He'd pointed the main gun 30° to starboard in order to blast the team of tank killers. Now his left hand swung the cupola tribarrel a few degrees to port. He didn't change either setting again for the moment. Not even Des Grieux's degree of skill permitted him to aim two separate sights from a gun platform travelling at fifty KPH and still accelerating.

But he could fire them, alternately or together, whenever *Warrior*'s forward motion slid the pippers over targets.

The tribarrel caught a squad moving up at a trot to exploit pathways the sappers had torn. The Republicans were so startled by the bellowing monster that they forgot to throw themselves down.

Three survivors turned and fired their rifles vainly as the tank roared past fifty meters away. The rest of the squad were dead, with the exception of the lieutenant leading them. He stood, shrilling insane parodies of signals on his whistle. The tribarrel had blown off both his arms.

Des Grieux's right thumb fired the main gun at another ragged line of Republican infantry. The twenty-CM bolt gouged the earth ten meters short, but its energy sprayed the sandy soil across the troops as a shower of molten glass. One of the victims continued to pirouette in agony until white tracers from a Federal machine gun tore most of his chest away.

Fires lighted by the cyan bolts flared across the arid landscape.

Hawes in *Susie Q* tried to follow. His tribarrel slashed out a long burst. Sappers jumped and ran. Two of them stumbled into mines and upended in sprays of soil.

Susie Q eased forward at a walking pace. Hawes' driver was proceeding cautiously under circumstances where speed was the only hope of survival. Halfway to the wire, a buzzbomb passed in front of the tank. It was so badly aimed that the automatic defense system didn't trip.

Susie Q braked and began to turn. Hawes sprayed the slope wildly with his tribarrel. A stray bolt blew a trench across *Warrior*'s back deck.

A Rep sapper ran toward *Susie Q*'s blind side with a satchel charge in his hands. The automatic defense system blasted him when he was five yards away, but two more buzzbombs arced over his crumpled body.

The section of the ADS which had killed the sapper was out of service until its strip charge could be replaced. The rockets hit, one in the hull and the other in the center of *Susie Q*'s turret. Iridium reflected the warheads' white glare.

The tank grounded violently. The thick skirt crumpled as it bulldozed a ripple of soil. *Susie Q*'s status entry on *Warrior*'s right-hand display winked from solid blue to crosshatched, indicating that an electrical fault had depowered several major systems.

Des Grieux ignored the read-out. He had a battle to win.

Under other circumstances, Des Grieux would have turned to port or starboard to sweep up one flank of the assault wave, but the Republican reserves were too strong. Turning broadside to their fire was a quick way to die.

Winning—surviving—required him to keep the enemy off balance.

Warrior bucked over the irregular slope, but the guns were stabilized in both elevation and traverse. Des Grieux lowered the hollow pipper onto the swale half a kilometer away, where the Republican supports sheltered.

Several of the armored cars there raked the tank with their automatic cannon. Explosive bullets whanged loudly on the iridium.

Des Grieux set *Warrior*'s turret to rotate at 1° per second and stepped on the foot-trip. The main gun began to fire as quickly as the system could reload itself. Cyan hell broke loose among the packed reserves.

The energy liberated by a single twenty-cm bolt was so great that dry brush several meters away from each impact burst into flames. Infantrymen leaped to their feet, colliding in wild panic as they tried to escape the sudden fires.

An armored car took a direct hit. Its diesel fuel boomed outward in a huge fireball which engulfed the vehicles to either side. Crewmen baled out of one of the cars before it exploded. Their clothes were alight, and they collapsed a few steps from their vehicle.

The other car spouted plumes of multi-colored smoke. Marking grenades had ignited inside the turret hatch, broiling the commander as he tried to climb past them. Ammunition cooked off in a flurry of sparks and red tracers.

While *Warrior*'s main gun cycled its twenty-round ready magazine into part of the Republican reserves, Des Grieux aimed his tribarrel at specific targets to port. The tank's speed was seventy KPH and still accelerating. When the bow slid over the slope's natural terracing, it spilled air from the plenum chamber. Each time, *Warrior*'s 170 tonnes slammed onto the skirts with the inevitability of night following day.

Though the tribarrel was stabilized, the crew was not. The impacts jounced Des Grieux against his seat restraints and blurred his vision.

It didn't matter. Under these circumstances, Des Grieux

scarcely needed the sights. He *knew* when the pipper covered a clot of infantry or an armored car reversing violently to escape what the crew suddenly realized was a kill zone.

Two-CM bolts lacked the authority of *Warrior*'s main gun, but Des Grieux's short bursts cut with surgical precision. Men flew apart in cyan flashes. The thin steel hulls of armored cars blazed white for an instant before the fuel and ammunition inside caught fire as well. Secondary explosions lit the night as tribarrel bolts detonated cases of rocket and mortar warheads.

Warrior's drive fans howled triumphantly.

Behind the rampaging tank, Rep incoming flashed and thundered onto Hill 541 North. Only one tribarrel from the Federal encampment still engaged the shells.

Federal artillery continued to fire. A "friendly" round plunged down at a 70° angle and blew a ten-meter hole less than a tank's length ahead of *Warrior*. Kuykendall fought her controls, but the tank's speed was too high to dodge the obstacle completely. *Warrior* lurched heavily and rammed some of the crater's lip back to bury the swirling vapors of high explosive.

A score of Rep infantry lay flat with their hands pressing down their helmets as if to drive themselves deeper into the gritty soil. *Warrior* plowed through them. The tank's skirt was nowhere more than a centimeter off the ground. The victims smeared unnoticed beneath the tank's weight.

Warrior boomed out of the swale and proceeded up the curving track toward Hill 504.

The main gun had emptied its ready magazine. Despite the air conditioning, the air within *Warrior*'s fighting compartment was hot and bitter with the gray haze trembling from the thick twenty-CM disks which littered the turret basket. The disks were the plastic matrices that had held active atoms of the powergun charge in precise alignment. Despite the blast of liquid nitrogen that cleared the bore after each shot, the empties contained enormous residual heat.

Des Grieux jerked the charging lever, refilling the ready

magazine from reserve storage deep in *Warrior*'s hull. The swale was blazing havoc behind them. Silhouetted against the glare of burning brush, fuel, and ammunition, Republican troops scattered like chickens from a fox.

Ten kilometers ahead of the tank, the horizon quivered with the muzzle flashes of Republican artillery.

"Now we'll get those bastards on 504!" Des Grieux shouted—

And knew, even as he roared his triumph, that if he tried to smash his way into the Republican fire-base, he would die as surely and as vainly as the Rep reserves had died when *Warrior* ripped through the center of them

So long as Des Grieux was in the middle of a firefight, his brain had disconnected the stream of orders and messages rattling over the commo net. Now the volume of angry sound overwhelmed him: "*Oyster Two, report! Break! Oyster four, are you—*"

The voice was Broglie's rather than that of Lieutenant Lindgren. The Lord himself had nothing to say just now that Des Grieux had time to hear. Des Grieux switched off the commo at the main console.

"Booster," he ordered the artificial intelligence, "enemy defenses in marked area."

Des Grieux's right index finger drew a rough circle bounded by Hill 504 and *Warrior*'s present position on the topographic display. "Best esti—"

An all-terrain truck snorted into view on the main screen. Des Grieux twisted his left joystick violently but he couldn't swing the tribarrel to bear in the moment before the tank rushed by in a spray of sand. The truck's crew jumped from both sides of the cab, leaving their vehicle to career through the night unattended. "—mate!"

Booster had very little hard data, but the AI didn't waste time as a human intelligence officer might have done in decrying the accuracy of the assessment it was about to provide. The computer's best estimate was the same as Des Grieux's own: *Warrior* didn't have a snowball's chance in Hell of reaching the firebase.

Only one of Hill 504's flanks, the west/southwest octave, had a slope suitable for heavy equipment—including ammunition vans and artillery prime movers, and assuredly including *Warrior*. There were at this moment—best estimate—anywhere from five hundred to a thousand Rep soldiers scattered along the route the tank would have to traverse.

The Reps were artillerymen, headquarters guards, and stragglers, not the crack battalions *Warrior* had gutted in her charge out of the Federal lines—

But these troops were prepared. The exploding chaos had warned them. They would fire from cover: rifle bullets to peck out sensors; buzzbombs whose shaped-charge warheads could and eventually *would* penetrate heavy armor; cannon lowered to slam their heavy shells directly into the belly plates *Warrior* exposed as the tank lurched to the top of Hill 504 by the only possible access. . . .

"Driver," Des Grieux ordered. His fingertip traced a savage arc across the topo screen at ninety degrees to the initial course. "Follow the marked route."

"Sir, there's no road!" Kuykendall shrilled.

Even on the trail flattened by the feet of Republican assault battalions, the tank proceeded in a worm of sparks and dust as its skirts dragged. Booster's augmented night vision gave the driver an image almost as good as daytime view would have been, but nothing could be sufficient to provide a smooth ride at sixty-five KPH over unimproved wilderness.

"Screw the bloody road!" ordered Des Grieux. "Move!"

They couldn't go forward, but they couldn't go back, either. The survivors of the Republican attack were between *Warrior* and whatever safety the Federal bunker line could provide. If the tank turned and tried to make an uphill run through that gauntlet, satchel charges would rip vents in the skirts. Crippled, *Warrior* would be a stationary target for buzzbombs and artillery fire.

Des Grieux couldn't give the Reps time to set up. So long as the tank kept moving, it was safe. With her fusion powerplant and drive fans rated at 12,000 hours between major overhauls, *Warrior* could cruise all the way around the planet, dodging enemies.

For the moment, Des Grieux just wanted to get out of the immediate kill zone.

Kuykendall tilted the nacelles closer to vertical. Their attitude reduced the forward thrust, but it also increased the skirts' clearance by a centimeter or two. That was necessary insurance against a quartz outcrop tearing a hole in the skirts.

Trees twenty meters tall grew in the swales, where the water table was highest. Vegetation on the slopes and ridges was limited to low spike-leafed bushes. Kuykendall rode the slopes, where the brush was less of a problem but the tank wasn't outlined against the sky. Des Grieux didn't have to think about what Kuykendall was doing, which made her the best kind of driver. . . .

A tank running at full power was conspicuous under almost any circumstances, but the middle of a major battle was one of the exceptions. Neither Des Grieux's instincts nor *Warrior*'s sensor array caught any sign of close-in enemies.

By slanting northeast, Des Grieux put them in the dead ground between the axes of the Republican attack. He was well behind the immediately-engaged forces and off the supply routes leading from the two northern firebases. If he ordered Kuykendall to turn due north now, *Warrior* would in ten minutes be in position to circle Hill 661 and then head south to link up with the relieving force.

It didn't occur to Des Grieux that they could run from the battle. He just needed a little time.

The night raved and roared. Brushfires flung sparks above the ridgelines where *Warrior* had gutted the right pincer of the attack. Ammunition cooked off when flames reached the bandoliers of the dead and screaming wounded.

Bullets and case fragments sang among the surviving Reps. Men shot back in panic, killing their fellows and drawing return fire from across the flame curtains.

The hollow chunking sound within *Warrior*'s guts stopped with a final clang. The green numeral 20 appeared on the lower right-hand corner of Des Grieux's main screen, the display he was using for gunnery. His ready magazine was full again. He could pulse the night with another salvo of twenty-CM bolts.

Soon.

When Des Grieux blasted the Rep supports with rapid fire, he'd robbed *Warrior*'s main gun of half the lifespan it would have had if the weapon were fired with time for the bore to cool between shots. If he cut loose with a similar burst, again there was a real chance the eroded barrel would fail, perhaps venting into the fighting compartment with catastrophic results.

That possibility had no effect on Des Grieux's plans for the next ten minutes. He would do what he had to do; and by God! His tools, human and otherwise, had better be up to the job.

The sky in the direction of Hill 661 quivered white with the almost-constant muzzle flashes. Shells, friction-heated to a red glow by the end of their arc into the Federal encampment, then flashed orange. Artillery rockets moved too slowly for the atmosphere to light their course, but the Reps put flare pots in the rockets' tails so that the gunners could correct their aim.

"Sarge?" said Kuykendall tightly. "Where we going?"

Des Grieux's index finger drew a circle on the topographic display.

"Oh, lord . . ." the driver whispered.

But she didn't slow or deviate from the course Des Grieux had set her.

Warrior proceeded at approximately forty KPH; a little faster on downslopes, a little slower when the drive fans had to fight gravity, as they did most of the time now. That was fast running over rough, unfamiliar terrain. The tank's night-vision devices were excellent, but they couldn't see that the opposite side of a ridge dropped off instead of sloping, or the tank-sized gully beyond the bend in a swale.

Kuykendall was getting them to the objective surely, and that was soon enough for Des Grieux. Whether or not it would be in time for the Federals on Hill 541 North was somebody else's problem.

The Republicans' right-flank assault was in disarray, probably terminal disarray, but the units committed to the east slope of the Federal position were proceeding more or less as planned. At least one of the Slammers' tanks survived, because the night flared with three cyan blasts spaced a chronometer second apart.

Probably Broglie, who cut his turds to length. Everything perfect, everything *as ordered*, and who was just about as good a gunner as Slick Des Grieux.

Just about meant *second best*.

Shells crashed down unhindered on 541N. Some of them certainly fell among the Rep assault forces because the attack was succeeding. Federal guns slammed out rapid fire with the muzzles lowered, slashing the Reps with canister at point-blank range. A huge explosion rocked the hilltop as an ammo dump went off, struck by incoming or detonated by the defenders as the Reps overran it.

Des Grieux hadn't bothered to cancel his earlier command: *Booster, enemy defenses in marked area.* When his fingertip circled Hill 661 to direct Kuykendall, the artificial intelligence tabulated that target as well.

Twenty artillery pieces, ranging from ten CM to a single stub-barreled thirty-CM howitzer which flung 400-kilogram shells at fifteen-minute intervals.

At least a dozen rails to launch twenty-CM bombardment rockets.

A pair of calliopes, powerguns with eight two-CM barrels fixed on a carriage. They were designed to sweep artillery shells out of the sky, but their high-intensity charges could chew through the bow slope of a tank in less than a minute.

Approximately a thousand men: gunners, command staff, and a company or two of infantry for close-in security in case Federals sortied from their camp in a kamikaze attack.

All of them packed onto a quarter-kilometer mesa, and not a soul expecting *Warrior* to hit them from behind. The Republicans thought of tanks as guns and armor; but tanks meant mobility, too, and Des Grieux *knew* every way a tank could crush an enemy.

Reflected muzzle blasts silvered the plume of dust behind *Warrior*. The onrushing tank would be obvious to anyone in the firebase who looked north—

But the show was southwest among the Federal positions, where the artillerymen dropped their shells and toward which the infantry detachment stared—imagining a fight at knifepoint, and thinking of how much better off they were than their fellows in the assault waves.

Warrior thrust through a band of stunted brush and at a flat angle onto a stabilized road, the logistics route serving the Republican firebase.

"S—" Kuykendall said.

"Yes!" Des Grieux shouted. "Goose it!" Kuykendall had started to adjust her nacelles even before she spoke, but vectored thrust wasn't sufficient to steer the tank onto a road twenty meters wide at the present speed. She deliberately let the skirts drop, using mechanical friction to brake *Warrior*'s violent side-slipping as the bow came around.

The tank tilted noticeably into the berm, its skirt plowed up on the high side of the turn. Rep engineers had treated the road surface with a plasticizer that cushioned the shock and even damped the blaze of sparks that Des Grieux had learned to expect when steel rubbed stone with the inertia of 170 tonnes behind it.

Kuykendall got her vehicle under control, adjusted fan bite and nacelle angle, and began accelerating up the 10° slope to the target. By the time *Warrior* reached the end of the straight, half-kilometer run, they were traveling at seventy-KPH.

Two Republican ammunition vans were parked just over the lip of Hill 661. There wasn't room for a tank to go between them.

Kuykendall went through anyway. The five-tonne vehicles flew in opposite directions. The ruptured fuel tank of one hurled a spray of blazing kerosene out at a 30° tangent to the tank's course.

The sound of impact would have been enormous, were it not lost in the greater crash of *Warrior*'s guns.

The tank's data banks stored the image of bolts from

the calliopes. Booster gave Des Grieux a precise vector to where the weapons had been every time they fired. The Republican commander could have ordered the calliopes to move since Federal incoming disappeared as a threat, but that was a chance Des Grieux had to take.

He squeezed both tits as *Warrior* crested the mesa, firing along the preadjusted angles.

The night went cyan, then orange and cyan.

The calliopes were still in their calculated positions. The tribarrel raked the sheet-metal chassis of one. Ready ammunition ignited into a five-meter globe of plasma bright enough to burn out the retinas of anyone looking in the wrong direction without protective lenses.

There was a vehicle parked between the second calliope and the onrushing tank. It was the ammunition hauler feeding a battery of fifteen-CM howitzers. It exploded with a blast so violent that the tank's bow lifted and Des Grieux slammed back in his seat. Shells and burning debris flew in all directions, setting off a second vehicle hundreds of meters away.

The shockwave spilled the air cushion from *Warrior*'s plenum chamber. The tank grounded hard, dangerously hard, but the skirts managed to stand the impact. Power returned to *Warrior*'s screens after a brief flicker, but the topographic display faded to amber monochrome which blurred the fine detail.

"S'okay . . ." Des Grieux wheezed, because the seat restraints had bruised him over the ribs when they kept him from pulping himself against the main screen. And it *was* all right, because the guns were all right and the controls were in his hands.

Buttoned up, the tank was a sealed system whose thick armor protected the crew from the blast's worst effects. The Reps, even those in bunkers, were less fortunate. The calliope which Des Grieux missed lay on its side fifty meters from its original location. Strips of flesh and uniforms, the remains of its crew, swathed the breech mechanisms.

"Booster," Des Grieux said, "mark movement," and his tribarrel swept the firebase.

The Republicans' guns were dug into shallow emplacements. Incoming wasn't the problem for them that it had been for the Federals, pecked at constantly from three directions.

The gunners on Hill 541 North hadn't had enough ammunition to try to overwhelm the Rep defenses. Besides, calliopes were *designed* for the job of slapping shells out of the sky. In that one specialized role, they performed far better than tank tribarrels.

Previous freedom from danger left the Republican guns hopelessly exposed now that a threat appeared, but Des Grieux had more important targets than mere masses of steel aimed in the wrong direction. There were men.

The AI marked moving objects white against a background of gray shades on the gunnery screen. *Warrior* wallowed forward again, not fully under control because both Kuykendall and the skirts had taken a severe shock. Des Grieux used that motion and his cupola's high-speed rotation to slide the solid pipper across the display. Every time the orange bead covered white, his thumb stroked the firing tit.

The calliopes had been the primary danger. Their multiple bolts could cripple the tank if their crews were good enough—and only a fool bets that an unknown opponent doesn't know his job.

With the calliopes out of the way, the remaining threat came from the men who could swarm over *Warrior* like driver ants bringing down a leopard. The things that still moved on Hill 661 were men, stumbling in confusion and the shock of the massive secondary explosions.

Des Grieux's cyan bolts ripped across them and flung bodies down with their uniforms afire. Artillerymen fleeing toward cover, officers popping out of bunkers to take charge of the situation, would-be rescuers running to drag friends out of the exploding cataclysm—

All moving, all targets, all dead before anyone on the mesa realized that there was a Slammers' tank in their midst, meting out destruction with the contemptuous ease of a weasel in a hen coop.

Des Grieux didn't use his main gun; he didn't want to take time to replenish the ready magazine before he completed the final stage of his plan. Twice *Warrior*'s automatic defense system burped a sleet of steel balls into Reps who ran in the wrong direction, but there was no resistance.

Mobility, surprise, and overwhelming firepower. One tank, with a commander who knew that you didn't win battles by crouching in a hole while the other bastard shoots at you. . . .

A twenty-CM shell arced from an ammo dump. It clanged like the wrath of God on *Warrior*'s back deck. The projectile was unfuzed. It didn't explode.

Only *Warrior* and the flames now moved on top of Hill 661. Normally the Republican crews bunkered their ammunition supply carefully, but rapid fire in support of the attack meant ready rounds were stacked on flat ground or held in soft-skinned vehicles. A third munitions store went up, a bunker or a vehicle, you couldn't tell after the fireball mushroomed skyward.

The shockwave pushed *Warrior* sideways into a sandbagged command post. The walls collapsed at the impact. An arm stuck out of the doorway, but the tribarrel had severed the limb from the body moments before.

The tank steadied. Des Grieux pumped deliberate bursts into a pair of vans. One held thirty-CM ammunition, the other was packed with bombardment rockets. A white flash sent shells tumbling skyward and down. Rockets skittered across the mesa.

"Booster," said Des Grieux. "Topo blowup of six-six-one. Break. Driver—"

A large-scale plan of the mesa filled the left-hand display. *Warrior* was a blue dot, wandering across a ruin of wrecked equipment and demolished bunkers.

"—put us there—" Des Grieux stabbed a point on the southwestern margin of the mesa. He had to reach across his body to do so, because his left hand was welded to the tribarrel's controls "—and hold. Break. Booster—"

Kuykendall swung the tank. *Warrior* now rode nose

down by a few degrees. The bow skirts were too crumpled to seal at the normal attitude.

"—give me maximum magnification on the main screen."

Debris from previous explosions still flapped above Hill 661 like bat-winged Death. A fuel store ignited. The pillar of flame expanded in slow motion by comparison with the previous ammunition fires.

Though the main screen was in high-magnification mode, the right-hand display—normally the commo screen, but De Grieux had shut off external commo—retained a 120° panorama of *Warrior's* surroundings. Images shifted as the tank reversed through the ruin its guns had created. Air spilling beneath the skirts stirred the flames and made their ragged tips bow in obeisance.

A Rep with the green tabs of a Central Command officer on his epaulets knelt with his hands folded in prayer. He did not look up as *Warrior* slid toward him, though vented air made his short-sleeved khaki uniform shudder.

Des Grieux touched his left joystick. The Rep was already too close to *Warrior* for the tribarrel to bear; and anyway . . .

And anyway, one spaced-out man was scarcely worth a bolt.

Warrior howled past the Rep officer. A crosswind rocked the tank minusculy from Kuykendall's intended line, so that the side skirt drifted within five meters of the man.

Sensors fired a section of the automatic defense system. Pellets blew the Republican backward, as loose-limbed as a rag doll.

Kuykendall ground the skirts to bring the tank to a safe halt at the edge of the mesa. *Warrior* lay across a zigzag trench, empty save for a sprawled corpse. The drive fans could stabilize a tank in still air, but shockwaves and currents rushing to feed flames whipped the top of Hill 661.

Des Grieux depressed the muzzle of his main gun slightly. On *Warrior's* gunnery screen, the hollow pipper slid over a high-resolution view of Republican positions on Hill 504.

The mesa on which *Warrior* rested was 150 meters

higher than the irregular hillock on which the Reps had placed their western firebase. The twelve kilometers separating the two peaks meant nothing to the tank's powerguns.

On Hill 504, a pair of bombardment rockets leapt from their launching tubes toward the Federal encampment. The holographic image was silent, but Des Grieux had been the target of too many similar rounds not to imagine the snarling roar of their passage. He centered his ring sight on the munitions truck bringing another twenty-four rounds to the launchers—

And toed the foot trip.

Warrior rocked with the trained lightning of its main gun. The display blanked in a cataclysm: pure blue plasma; metal burning white hot; and red as tonnes of warheads and solid rocket fuel exploded simultaneously. The truck and everything within a hundred meters of it vanished.

Des Grieux shifted his sights to what he thought was the Republican command post. He was smiling.

He fired. Sandbags blew outward as shards of glass. There were explosives of some sort within the bunker, because a moment after the rubble settled, a secondary explosion blew the site into a crater.

Concussion from the first blast had stunned or killed the crew of the single calliope on Hill 504. The weapon was probably unserviceable, but Des Grieux's third bolt vaporized it anyway.

"I told you bastards . . ." the tanker muttered in a voice that would have frightened anyone who heard him.

Dust and smoke billowed out in a huge doughnut from where the truckload of rockets had been. The air-suspended particles masked the remaining positions on Hill 504. Guns and bunker sites vanished into the haze like ships sinking at anchor. The main screen provided a detailed vision of whorls and color variations within the general blur.

"Booster," Des Grieux said. "Feed me targets." *Warrior*'s turret was supported by superconducting magnetic bearings powered by the same fusion plant that drove the fans. The mechanism purred and adjusted two degrees to

starboard, under control of the artificial intelligence recalling
the terrain before it was concealed. The hollow pipper
remained centered on the gunnery screen, but haze
appeared to shift around it.

The circle pulsed. Des Grieux fired the twenty-CM gun.
Even as the tank recoiled from the bolt's release, the AI
rotated the weapon toward the next unseen victim.

"Booster!" Des Grieux snarled. His throat was raw with
gunnery fumes and the human waste products of tension
coursing through his system. "*Show* me the bloody—"

The pipper quivered again. Des Grieux fired by reflex.
A flash and a mushroom of black smoke penetrated the
gray curtain. "Targets!"

The main gun depressed minutely. To Des Grieux's
amazement, a howitzer on Hill 504 banged a further shell
toward the Federal positions. *Warrior*'s AI obediently supplied the image of the weapon to Des Grieux's display as
it steadied beneath the orange circle.

A bubble of gaseous metal sent the howitzer barrel thirty
meters into the air.

With only one calliope to protect them, the Reps on
504 had dug in somewhat better than their fellows on Hill
661. Despite that, there was still a suicidal amount of ready
ammunition stacked around the fast-firing guns. The tank's
data banks fed each dump to the gunnery screen.

Des Grieux continued to fire. The haze over the target area darkened, stirred occasionally by sullen red flames.
A red 0 replaced the green numeral 1 on the lower right
corner of the screen. The interior of the fighting compartment stank like the depths of Hell.

"I told you bastards . . ." Des Grieux repeated, though
his throat was so swollen that he had to force the words out.
"And I told that bastard Lindgren."

"Sarge?" Kuykendall said.

Des Grieux threw the charging lever to refill the ready
magazine. Just as well if he didn't use the main gun until
the bore was relined; but the status report gave it ten
percent of its original thickness, a safe enough margin for
a few bolts, and you did what you had to do. . . .

"Yeah," he said aloud. "Get us somewhere outa the way. In the morning we'll rejoin. Somebody."

Kuykendall adjusted the fans so that they bit into the air instead of slicing through it with minimum disruption. She'd kept the power up while *Warrior* was grounded. In an emergency, they could hop off the mesa with no more than a quick change of blade angle.

The smoke-shrouded ruin of Hill 661 was unlikely to spawn emergencies, but in the four hours remaining till dawn some Rep officer might muster a tank-killer team. No point in making trouble for yourself. There were hundreds of kilometers of arid scrub which would hide *Warrior* until the situation sorted itself out.

And there were no longer any targets around *here* worthy of *Warrior*'s guns. Of that, Des Grieux was quite certain.

Kuykendall elected to slide directly over the edge of the mesa instead of returning to the logistics route by which they had attacked. The immediate slope was severe, almost 1:3, but there were no dangerous obstacles and the terrain flattened within a hundred meters.

There were bound to be scores of Rep soldiers on the road, some of them seeking revenge. A large number might fly into a lethal panic if they saw *Warrior*'s gray bow loom through the darkness. A smoother ride to concealment wasn't worth the risk.

"Sarge?" asked Kuykendall. "What's going on back at 541 North?"

"How the hell would I know?" Des Grieux snarled. But he could know, if he wanted to. He reached to reconnect the commo buss . . . and withdrew his hand. He could adjust a screen, and he started to do that—manually, because his throat hurt as if he'd been swallowing battery acid.

Instead of carrying through with the motion, Des Grieux lifted the crash bar to open the hatch and raise his seat to cupola level. The breeze smelled so clean that it made him dizzy.

Kuykendall eased the tank toward the low ground west

of Hill 661. With a swale to shelter them, they could drive north a couple kays and avoid the stragglers from the Republican disaster.

For it had been a disaster. The Federal artillery on Hill 541N was in action again, lobbing shells toward the Rep staging areas. Fighting still went on within the encampment, but an increasing volume of fire raked the eastern slope up which the Reps had carried their initial assault objectives.

The weapons which picked over the remnants of the Republican attacks were machine guns firing white tracers, standard Federal issue; and at least a dozen tribarreled powerguns. A platoon of Slammers' combat cars had entered the Federal encampment and was helping the defenders mop up. The relief force had finally arrived.

"In the morning . . ." Des Grieux muttered. He was as tired as he'd ever been in his life.

And he knew that he and his tank had just won a battle singlehandedly.

Warrior proceeded slowly up the eastern slope of Hill 541 North. The brush had burned to blackened spikes. Ash swirled over the ground, disintegrating into a faint shimmer in the air.

Given the amount of damage to the landscape, there were surprisingly few bodies; but there were some. They sprawled, looking too small for their uniforms; and the flies had found them.

Half an hour before dawn, Des Grieux announced in clear, on both regimental and Federal frequencies, that *Warrior* was reentering the encampment. The AI continued to transmit that message at short intervals, and Kuykendall held the big vehicle to a walking pace to appear as unthreatening as possible.

There was still a risk that somebody would open fire in panic. The tank was buttoned up against that possibility.

It was easier when everybody around you was an enemy. Then it was just a matter of who was quicker on the trigger. Des Grieux never minded playing *that* game.

"Alpha One-six to Oyster Two commander," said a cold, bored voice in Des Grieux's helmet. "Dismount and report to the CP as soon as you're through the minefields. Over."

"Oyster Two to One-six," Des Grieux replied. Alpha One-six was the callsign of Major Joachim Steuben, Colonel Hammer's bodyguard. Steuben had no business being here "Roger, as soon as we've parked the tank. Over."

"Alpha One-six to Oyster Two commander," the cold voice said. "I'll provide your driver with ground guides for parking, Sergeant. I suggest that this time, you obey orders. One-six out."

Des Grieux swallowed. He wasn't afraid of Steuben, exactly; any more than he was afraid of a spider. But he didn't like spiders either.

"Driver," he said aloud. "Pull up when you get through the minefield. Somebody'll tell you where they want *Warrior* parked."

"You bet," said Kuykendall in a distant voice.

Federal troops drew back at the tank's approach. They'd been examining what remained of the perimeter defenses and dragging bodies cautiously from the wire. There were thousands of unexploded mines scattered across the slope. Nobody wanted to be the last casualty of a successful battle.

Successful because of what Des Grieux had done. Something about the Feds seemed odd. After a moment, Des Grieux realized that it was their uniforms. The fabric was green—not clean, exactly, but not completely stained by the sandy red soil of Hill 541 North either. These were troops from the relieving force.

A few men of the original garrison watched from the bunker line. It was funny to see that many troops in the open sunlight; not scuttling, not cowering from snipers and shellfire.

The bunkers were ruins. Sappers had grenaded them during the assault. When the Federals counterattacked, Reps sheltered in the captured positions until tribarrels and point-blank shellfire blew them out. The roofs had collapsed. Wisps of smoke still curled from among the ruptured sandbags.

A Slammers' combat car—unnamed, with fender number 116—squatted in an overwatch position on the bunker line. The three tribarrels were manned, covering the troops in the wire. Bullet scars dented the side of the fighting compartment. A bright swatch of SpraySeal covered the left wing gunner's shoulder.

A figure was painted on the car's bow slope, just in front of the driver's hatch: a realistically-drawn white mouse with pink eyes, nose, and tail.

The White Mice—the troops of Alpha Company, Hammer's Regiment—weren't ordinary line soldiers.

Nobody ever said they couldn't fight but they, under their CO, Major Steuben, acted as Hammer's field police and in other internal security operations.

A dozen anti-personnel mines went off under Warrior's skirts as the tank slid through the perimeter defenses. Kuykendall tried to follow a track Rep sappers blew the night before, but Warrior overhung the cleared area on both sides.

The surface-scattered mines were harmless, except to a man who stepped on one. Even so, after the third bang! one of the Feds watching from the bunker line put his hands over his face and began to cry uncontrollably.

Three troopers wearing Slammers' khaki and commo helmets waited at the defensive perimeter. One of them was a woman. They carried sub-machine guns in patrol slings that kept the muzzles forward and the grips close to their gunhands.

They'd been sitting on the hillside when Des Grieux first noticed them. They stood as Warrior approached.

"Driver," Des Grieux said, "you can pull up here."

"I figured to," Kuykendall replied without emotion. Dust puffed forward, then drifted downhill as she shifted nacelles to brake Warrior's slow pace.

Des Grieux climbed from the turret and poised for a moment on the back deck. The artillery shell that bounced from Warrior on Hill 661 had dished in a patch of plating a meter wide. Number seven intake grating ought to be replaced as well. . . .

Des Grieux hopped to the ground. One of the White Mice sat on *Warrior*'s bow slope and gestured directions to the driver. The tank accelerated toward the encampment.

"Come on, Sunshine," said the female trooper. Her features were blank behind her reflective visor. "The Man wants to see you."

She jerked her thumb uphill.

Des Grieux fell in between the White Mice. His legs were unsteady. He hadn't wanted to eat anything with his throat feeling as though it had been reamed with a steel bore brush.

"Am I under arrest?" he demanded.

"Major Steuben didn't say anything about that," the male escort replied. He chuckled.

"Naw," added the woman. "He just said that if you give us any crap, we should shoot you. And save him the trouble."

"Then we all know where we stand," said Des Grieux. Soreness and aches dissolved in his body's resumed production of adrenaline.

The encampment on Hill 541 North had always been a wasteland, so Des Grieux didn't expect to notice a change now.

He was wrong. It was much worse, and the forty-odd bodies laid in rows in their zipped-up sleeping bags were only part of it.

The smell overlaid the scene. Explosives had peculiar odors. They blended uneasily with ozone and high-temperature fusion products formed when bolts from the powerguns hit.

The main component of the stench was death. Bunkers had been blown closed, but the rubble of timber and sandbags didn't form a tight seal over the shredded flesh within. The morning sun was already hot. In a week or two, a lot of wives and parents were going to receive a coffin sealed over seventy kilos of sand.

That wasn't Des Grieux's problem, though; and without

him, there would have been plenty more corpses swelling in Federal uniforms.

General Wycherly's command post had taken a direct hit from a heavy shell. A high-sided truck with multiple antennas parked beside the smoldering wreckage. Federal troops in clean uniforms stepped briskly in and out of the vehicle.

The real authorities on 541N wore Slammers khaki. Major Joachim Steuben was short, slim, and so fine featured that he looked like a girl in a perfectly-tailored uniform among Sergeant Broglio and several Alpha Company officers. They looked up as Des Grieux approached.

Steuben's command group stood under a tarpaulin slung between a combat car and Lieutenant Lindgren's tank. The roof of Lindgren's bunker was broken-backed from the fighting, but his tank looked all right at first glance.

At a second look—

"*Via!*" Des Grieux said "What happened to *Queen City*?"

There were telltale soot stains all around the tank's deck, and the turret rested slightly askew on its ring. *Queen City* was a corpse, as sure as any of the staring-eyed Reps out there in the wire.

The female escort sniffed. "Its luck ran out. Took a shell down the open hatch. All they gotta do now is jack up what's left and slide a new tank underneath."

"Dunno how anybody can ride those fat bastards," the other escort muttered. "They maneuver like blind whales."

"Glad you could rejoin us, Sergeant," Major Steuben said. He gave the data terminal in his left hand to a lieutenant beside him. His voice was lilting and as pretty as Steuben's appearance, but it cut through any thought Des Grieux had of snarling a response to the combat-car crewman beside him.

"Sir," Des Grieux muttered. The Slammers didn't salute. Salutes in a war zone targeted officers for possible snipers.

"Would you like to explain your actions during the battle last night, Sergeant?" the major asked.

Steuben stood arms akimbo. His pose accentuated the

crisp tuck of his waist. The fall of the slim right hand almost concealed the pistol riding in a cut-out holster high on Steuben's right hip.

The pistol was engraved and inlaid with metal lozenges in a variety of colors. In all respects but its heavy one-CM bore, it looked as surely a girl's weapon as its owner looked like a girl.

Joachim Steuben's eyes focused on Des Grieux. There was not a trace of compassion in the eyes or the soul beneath them. Any weapon in Steuben's hands was Death.

"I was winning a battle," Des Grieux said as his eyes mirrored Steuben's blank, brown glare. "Sir. Since the relieving force was still sitting on its hands after three weeks."

Broglie slid his body between Des Grieux and the major. Broglie was fast, but Steuben's pistol was socketed in Broglie's ear before the tanker's motion was half complete.

"I think Sergeant Des Grieux and I can continue our discussion better without you in the way, Mister Broglie," Steuben said. He didn't move his eyes from Des Grieux.

The White Mice hadn't bothered to remove the pistol from the holster on Des Grieux's equipment belt. Now Des Grieux knew why. *Nobody could be that fast. . . .*

"Sir," Broglie rasped through a throat gone dry. "*Warrior* did destroy both the Rep firebases. That's what took the pressure off here at the end."

Broglie stepped back to where he'd been standing.

He looked straight ahead, not at either Des Grieux or the major.

"You've named your tank *Warrior*, Sergeant?" Steuben said. "Amusing. But right at the moment I'm not so much interested in what you did so much as I am in why you disobeyed orders to do it."

He reholstered his gorgeous handgun with a motion as precise and delicate as that of a bird preening its feathers.

"You got some people killed, you know," the major added. His voice sounded cheerful, or at least amused.

"Your lieutenant and his driver, because nobody was dealing with the shells from Hill 504."

He smiled coquettishly at Des Grieux. "I won't blame you for the other one. Hawes, was it?"

"Hawes, sir," Broglie muttered.

"Since Hawes was stupid enough to leave his position also," Steuben went on. "And I don't care a great deal about Federal casualties, except as they affect the Regiment's contractual obligations"

The pause was deadly.

"Which, since we *have* won the battle for them, shouldn't be a problem."

"Sir," Des Grieux said, "they were wide open. It was the one chance we were going to have to pay the Reps back for the three weeks we sat and took it."

Major Steuben turned his head slowly and surveyed the battered Federal encampment. His tongue went *tsk, tsk, tsk* against his teeth

Warrior was parked alongside Broglie's *Honey Girl* in the center of the hill. *Warrior's* bow skirts had cracked as well as bending inward when 170 tonnes slammed down on them. Kuykendall had earned her pay, keeping the tank moving steadily despite the damage.

Des Grieux's gaze followed the major's. *Honey Girl* had been hit by at least three buzzbombs on this side. None of the sun-hot jets seemed to have penetrated the armor. Broglie had been in the thick of it, with the only functional tank remaining when the Reps blew their way through the bunker line. . . .

The Federal gun emplacements were nearby. The Fed gunners had easily been the best of the local troops. They'd hauled three howitzers up from the gun pits to meet the Republican assault with canister and short-fused high explosive.

That hadn't been enough. Buzzbombs and grenades had disabled the howitzers, and a long line of bodies lay beside the damaged hardware.

"You know, Sergeant?" Steuben resumed unexpectedly. "Colonel Hammer found the relief force's progress a bit leisurely for his taste also. So he sent me to take command . . . and a platoon of Alpha Company, you know. To encourage the others."

He giggled. It was a terrible sound, like gas bubbling through the throat of a distended corpse.

"We were about to take Hill 541 South," Steuben continued. "In twenty-four hours we would have relieved the position here with minimal casualties. The Reps knew that, so they made a desperation assault . . . which couldn't possibly have succeeded against a bunker line backed up by four of our tanks."

Joachim's eyes looked blankly through Des Grieux.

"That's why," the delicate little man said softly, "I really think I ought to kill you now, before you cause other trouble."

"Sir," said Broglie. "Slick cleared our left flank. That had to be done."

Major Steuben's eyes focused again, this time on Broglie. "Did it?" the major said. "Not from outside the prepared defenses, I think. And certainly not against orders from a superior officer, who was—"

The cold stare again at Des Grieux. No more emotion in the eyes than there would be in the muzzle of the pistol which might appear with magical speed in Joachim's hand.

"Who was, as I say," the major continued, "passing on *my* orders."

"But . . ." Des Grieux whispered. "I *won*."

"No," Steuben said in a crisply businesslike voice. Moods seemed to drift over the dapper officer's mind like clouds across the sun. "You ran, Sergeant. I had to make an emergency night advance with the only troops I could fully trust—"

He smiled with cold affection at the nearest of his White Mice.

"In order to prevent Hill 541 North from being overrun. And even then I would have failed, were it not for the actions of Mister Broglie."

"Broglie?" Des Grieux blurted in amazement.

"Oh, yes," Joachim said. "Oh, yes, Mister Broglie. He

took charge here after the Federal CP was knocked out and Mister Lindgren was killed. He put *Susie Q*'s driver back into the turret of the damaged tank and used that to stabilize the left flank. Then he led the counterattack which held the Reps on the right flank until my platoon arrived to finish the business."

"I don't like night actions when local forces are involved, Sergeant," he added in a frigid voice. "It's dangerous because of the confusion. If my orders had been obeyed, there would have been no confusion."

Steuben glanced at Broglie. He smiled, much as he had done when he looked at his White Mice. "I'm particularly impressed by the way you controlled the commo net alone while fighting your vehicle, Mister Broglie," he said. "The locals might well have panicked when they lost normal communications along with their command post."

Broglie licked his lips. "It was okay," he said. "Booster did most of it. And it had to be done. *I* couldn't stop the bastards alone."

"Wait a minute," Des Grieux said. "Wait a bloody minute! *I* wasn't just sitting on my hands, you know. I was fighting!"

"Yes, Sergeant," Major Steuben said. "You were fighting like a fool, and it appears that you're still a fool. Which doesn't surprise me."

He smiled at Broglie. "The Colonel will have to approve your field promotion to lieutenant, Mister Broglie," he said, "but I don't foresee any problems. Of course, you'll have a badly understrength platoon until replacements arrive."

Des Grieux swung a fist at Broglie. The White Mice had read the signs correctly. The male escort was already holding Des Grieux's right arm. The woman on the other side bent the tanker's left wrist back and up with the skill of long practice.

Joachim set the muzzle of his pistol against Des Grieux's right eye. The motion was so swift that the cold iridium circle touched the eyeball before reflex could blink the lid closed.

Des Grieux jerked his head back, but the pistol followed. Its touch was as light as that of a butterfly's wing.

"*Via*, sir," Broglie gasped. "*Don't*. Slick's the best tank commander in the regiment."

Steuben giggled again. "If you insist, Mister Broglie," he said. "After all, you won the battle for us here."

He holstered the pistol. A warrior's frustrated tears rushed out to fill Des Grieux's eyes. . . .

PART II

Xingha was the staging area for the troops on the Western Wing: a battalion of the Slammers and more than ten thousand of the local Han troops the mercenaries were supporting.

The city's dockyard district had a way to go before it adapted to the influx of soldiers, but it was doing its manful, womanly, childish, and indeed bestial—best to accommodate the sudden need. Soon the entertainment facilities would reach the universal standard to which war sinks those who support the fighters; in all places, in every time.

Sergeant Samuel Des Grieux had seen the pattern occur often during his seven years in the Slammers. He could describe the progression as easily as an ecologist charts the process by which lakes become marshes, then forests.

Des Grieux didn't care one way or the other. He drank what passed for beer; listened to a pair of Oriental women keen, "*Oh where ha you been, Laird Randall, me son?*" (Hammer's Slammers came to the Han contract from seven months of civil war among the Scottish colonists of New Aberdeen); and wondered when he'd have a chance to swing his tank into action. It'd been a long time since he had a tank to command. . . .

"Hey, is there anybody here from Golf Company?" asked a trooper, obviously a veteran but wearing new-issue khaki. His hair was in a triple ponytail, according to whim or the custom of some planet unfamiliar to Des Grieux. The fellow was moving from one table to the next in the crowded cantina. Just now, he was with a group of H Company tankers next to Des Grieux, bending low and shouting to be heard over the music and general racket.

"Hey, lookit that," said Pesco, Des Grieux's new driver. He pointed to the flat, rear-projection screen in the corner opposite the singers. "That's Captain Broglie, isn't he? What's he doing on local video?"

"Who bloody cares?" Des Grieux said. He finished his beer and refilled his glass from the pitcher.

If you tried, you could hear Broglie's voice—though not that of the Han interviewer—over the ambient noise. Despite himself, Des Grieux found himself listening.

"Hey, Johnnie," chirped a woman in a red dress as she draped her arm around Des Grieux's shoulders. She squeezed her obviously-padded bosom to his cheek. She was possibly fourteen, probably younger. "Buy me a drink?"

"Out," said Des Grieux, stiff-arming the girl into the back of a man at the next table. Des Grieux stared at the video screen, getting cues from Broglie's lips to aid as he fitted together the shards of speech.

"No, on the contrary, the Hindis make very respectable troops," Broglie said. "And as for Baffin's Legion, they're one of the best units for hire. I, don't mean the Legion's in our class, of course. . . ."

A fault in the video screen—or the transmission medium—gave the picture a green cast. It made Broglie look like a three-week corpse. Des Grieux's lips drew back in a smile.

Pesco followed the tank commander's stare. "You served under him before, didn't you?" he asked Des Grieux. "Captain Broglie, I mean. What's he like?"

Des Grieux slashed his hand across the air in brusque dismissal. "I never served under him," he said. "When he took over the platoon I was in, I transferred to . . . infantry, Delta Company. And then combat cars, India and Golf."

". . . Baffin's tank destroyers are first class," Broglie's leprous image continued. "Very dangerous equipment."

"Yeah, but look," Pesco objected. "With him, under him, it don't matter. What's he like, Broglie? Does he know his stuff, or is he gonna get somebody killed?"

Near where the singers warbled, "*Mother, make my bed soon . . .*" a dozen troopers had wedged two of the round tables together and were buying drinks for Sergeant Kuykendall. Des Grieux had heard his former driver'd gotten a twelve-month appointment to the Military Academy on Nieuw Friesland, with a lieutenancy in the Slammers waiting when she completed the course.

He supposed that was OK. Kuykendall had combat experience, so she'd be at least a cunt-hair better than green sods who'd never been on the wrong end of a gun muzzle.

Of course, she didn't have the experience Des Grieux himself did. . . .

"*For I'm sick at the heart, and I fain would lie down,*" the singers chirped through fixed smiles.

"Slick?" Pesco pressed. "Sarge? What about the new CO?"

Des Grieux shrugged. "Broglie?" he said. "He's a bloody good shot, I'll tell you that. Not real fast—not as fast as I am. But when he presses the tit, he nails what he's going after."

"Either of you guys from Golf?." asked the veteran in new fatigues. "I just got back from leave and I'm lookin' for my cousin, Tip Rasidi."

"We're Hotel Company, buddy," Pesco said. "Tanks. Why don't you try the Adjutant?"

"Because the bloody Adjutant lost half his bloody records in the transit," the stranger snapped, "and the orderly sergeant tells me to bugger off until he's got his bloody office sorted out. So I figure I'll check around till I find what's happened to Tip."

The stranger scraped his way over to the next table, rocking Pesco forward in his chair. The driver grimaced sourly.

"I don't know if the Hindis are brave or not," said Captain Broglie's image. "I suppose they're like everybody else, some braver than others. What I do know is that their troops are highly disciplined, and *that* causes me some concern."

"C'mon, what about him, then?" Pesco said. "Broglie."

"He'll do what he's told," Des Grieux said, staring at the video screen. His voice was clear, but it came from far away. "He's smart and he's got balls, I'll give him that. But he'd rather kiss the ass of whoever's giving orders than get out and fight. He coulda been really something, but instead . . ."

Sergeant Kuykendall got up from her table. She was wearing a red headband with lettering stitched in black. The others at the table shouted, "Speech! Speech!" as Kuykendall tried to say something.

"Yeah, but what's Broglie gonna be like as an officer?" Pesco demanded. "He just transferred to Hotel, you know. He'd been on the staff."

"Sure, courage is important," Broglie said on the screen. Though his words were mild enough, his tone harshly dismissed the interviewer's question. "But in modern warfare discipline is absolutely crucial. The Hindi regulars are quite well disciplined, and I fear that's going to make up for some deficiencies in their equipment. As for Baffin's Legion—"

Kuykendall broke away from her companions. She came toward Des Grieux, stepping between tables with the care of someone who knows how much she's drunk. The letters on her headband read "SIR!"

"—they're first rate in equipment *and* unit discipline. The war on the Western Wing isn't going to be a walkover."

"Kid," said Des Grieux in a voice that grated up from deep within his soul, "I'll give you the first and last rule about officers. The more they keep outa your way and let you get on with the fighting, the better they are. And when things really drop in the pot, they're always too busy to get in your way. Don't worry about them."

". . . from Golf Company?" trailed the stranger's voice through a fissure in the ambient noise.

Sergeant Kuykendall bent over the table. "Hello, Slick," she said in measured tones. "I'm glad to see you're back in tanks. I always thought you belonged with the panzers."

Des Grieux shrugged. He was still looking at the screen, though the interview had been replaced by a stern-faced plea to buy War Stamps and support the national effort.

"Tanks," Des Grieux said, "combat cars. . . . I ran a jeep gun once. It don't really matter."

Pesco looked up at Kuykendall. "Hey, Sarge," he said to her. "Congrats on the appointment. Want a beer?"

"Just wanted to say hi to Slick," she said. "Me and him served with Captain Broglie way back to the dawn of time, y'know."

"Hey," Pesco said, his expression brightening. "You know Broglie, then? Looks to me he's got a lot of guts, telling 'em like it is on the video when they musta been figuring on a puff piece, is all. Likely to piss off Hammer, don't you think?"

Kuykendall glanced at the screen, though it now showed only a desk and a newsreader who mumbled unintelligibly. "Oh," she said, "I don't know. I guess the Colonel's smart enough to know that telling the truth now that the contract's signed isn't going to do any harm. May help things if we run into real trouble; and we might, Baffin's outfit's plenty bloody good."

She looked at Pesco, then Des Grieux, and back to Pesco. There were minute crow's feet around Kuykendall's eyes where the skin had been smooth when she drove for Des Grieux. "But Broglie's got guts, you bet."

Des Grieux shoved his chair backward. "If guts is what it takes to toady t' the brass, he's got 'em, you bet," he snarled as he rose.

He turned. "Hey, buddy!" he shouted. "You looking for Tip Rasidi?"

Voices stilled, though clattering glass, the video screen, and the singers' recorded background music continued at a high level.

The stranger straightened to face the summons. Des Grieux said, "Rasidi drove for me on Aberdeen. We took a main-gun hit and burnt out. There wasn't enough of Tip to ship home in a matchbox."

The stranger continued to stand. His expression did not change, but his eyes glazed over.

The girl in the red dress sat at the table where Des Grieux had pushed her, wedged in between a pair of female troopers. Des Grieux gripped the girl by the shoulder and lifted her. "Come on," he snarled. "We're going upstairs."

One of the seated troopers might have objected, but she saw Des Grieux's face and remained silent.

The girl's face was resigned. She knew what was coming, but by now she was used to it.

"*The tow and the halter,*" sang the entertainers, "*for to hang on yon tree. . . .*"

The gravel highway steepened by a couple degrees before the switchback. The Han driving the four-axle troop transport just ahead of Des Grieux's tank opened his exhaust cut-outs to coax more power from the diesel.

As the unmuffled exhaust rattled, several of the troops on the truck bed stuck their weapons in the air and opened fire. A jolt threw one of the Han soldiers backward. His backpack laser slashed a brilliant line across the truck's canvas awning.

The lieutenant in command of the troops leaned from the cab and shouted angrily at his men, but they were laughing too hard to take much notice. Somebody tossed an empty bottle over the side in enough of a forward direction that the officer disappeared back within the cab.

The awning smoldered to either side of the long, blackened rent, but the treated fabric would not sustain a fire by itself.

The truck ground through the switchback, spewing gravel. Both forward axles were steerable. The vehicle was a solid piece of equipment, well designed and manufactured. The local forces in this contract were a cursed sight better equipped than most of those you saw. Mostly the off-planet mercenaries stood out from the indig troops like diamonds on a bed of mud.

Both sets of locals, these Han and their Hindi rivals. . . .

"Booster," Des Grieux muttered as he sat in the cupola of his tank. "Hindi combat vehicles, schematics. Slow crawl. Out."

He manually set his commo helmet to echo the artificial intelligence's feed onto the left side of the visor. Des Grieux's cold right eye continued to scan the line of the convoy and the terraces that they had passed farther down the valley.

A soldier tossed another empty bottle from the truck ahead. Because the truck was higher and the road had reversed direction at the switchback, the brown-glazed ceramic shattered on the turret directly below Des Grieux. A line of heads turned from the truck's rail, shouting apologies and amused warnings to the soldier farther within the vehicle who'd thrown the bottle without looking first.

Des Grieux squeezed his tribarrel's grips, overriding its present Automatic Air-Defense setting. He slid the holographic sight picture across the startled Han faces which disappeared as the men flung themselves flat onto the truck bed.

Pesco shifted his four rear nacelles and pivoted the tank around its bow, following the switchback. They swung in behind the truck again. Des Grieux released the grips and let the tribarrel shift back to its normal search attitude: muzzles forward, at a forty-five degree elevation.

Des Grieux had only been joking. Had he been serious, he'd have put the first round into the fuel tank beneath the truck's cab. Only then would he rake his bolts along the men screaming as they tried to jump from the inferno of blazing kerosene. He'd done that often enough before.

The artificial intelligence rotated three-dimensional images of Hindi armor onto the left side of the visor in obedience to Des Grieux's command. The schematic of a tank as flat as a floor tile lifted to display the balloon tires, four per axle, which supported its weight. In particularly marshy spots—and the rice paddies on both sides of the border area were muddy ponds for most of the year—the tires could be covered with one-piece tracks to lower the ground pressure still further.

The tank did not have a rotating turret. Its long, slim gun was mounted along the vehicle's centerline. The weapon used combustion-augmented plasma to drive armor-piercing shots at velocities of several thousand meters per second.

Comparable Han vehicles mounted lasers in small turrets. Neither technology was quite as effective as the powerguns of the Slammers—and Baffin's Legion; but they would serve lethally, even against armor as thick as that of Des Grieux's tank.

The AI began to display a Hindi armored personnel carrier, also running on large tires behind a thin shield of armor. Des Grieux switched his helmet to direct vision. The images continued to flicker unwatched on the left-hand screen below in the fighting compartment. Adrenaline from the bottle incident left the mercenary too restless to pretend interest in mere holograms.

There were hundreds of vehicles behind Des Grieux's tank. The convoy snaked down and across the valley floor for as far as he could see without increasing his visor's magnification. Most of the column was of Han manufacture: laser vehicles, troop transports, maintenance vans. Huge articulated supply trucks with powerplants at both ends of the load; *they'd* be bitches to get up these ridges separating the fertile valleys.

Des Grieux didn't care about the logistics vehicles, whether indigenous or the Slammers' own. His business was with things that shot, things that fought. If he had a weapon, the form it took didn't matter. A tank like the one he commanded now was best; but if Des Grieux had been an infantryman with nothing but a semiautomatic powergun, he'd have faced a tank and not worried about the disparity in equipment. So long as he had a chance to fight. . . .

The convoy contained a Han mechanized brigade, the Black Banner Guards: the main indig striking force on the Western Wing. The tanks of Hammer's H Company were spread at intervals along the order of march to provide air and artillery defense.

Out of sight of the convoy, two companies of combat

cars and another of infantry screened the force's front and
flanks. Hammer's air cushion vehicles were much more
nimble on the boggy lowlands than the wheeled and track-
laying equivalents with which the indigs made do.

No doubt the locals would rather have built their own
ACVs, but the technology of miniaturized fusion powerplants
was beyond the manufacturing capacity of any but the most
sophisticated handful of human worlds. Without individual
fusion bottles, air-cushion vehicles lacked the range and
weight of weapons and armor necessary for frontline combat units.

So they hired specialists, the Han and Hindis both. If
one side in a conflict mortgaged its future to hire off-planet
talent, the other side either matched the ante—or forfeited
that future.

The rice on the terraces had a bluish tinge that Des
Grieux didn't remember having seen before, though he'd
fought on half a dozen rice-growing worlds over the
years. . . .

His eyes narrowed. An air-cushion jeep sped up the road
from the back of the column. It passed trucks every time
the graded surface widened and gunned directly up-slope
at switchbacks to cut corners. Des Grieux thought he
recognized the squat figure in the passenger seat.

He looked deliberately away.

Des Grieux's tank was nearing the last switchback before
the crest. The vehicle ahead began to blat through open
exhaust pipes again, though its engine note didn't change.
Han trucks used hydraulic torque converters instead of
geared transmissions, so their diesels always stayed within
the powerband. Lousy troops, but good equipment. . . .

Des Grieux imagined the jeep passing his tank—spinning a little in the high-pressure air vented beneath the
tank's skirts—sliding under the wheels of the Han truck
and then, as *Captain* Broglie screamed, being reduced to
a millimeters' thick streak as the tank overran the wreckage despite all Pesco did to avoid the obstacle.

Des Grieux caught himself. He was shaking. He didn't
know what his face looked like, but he suddenly realized

that the soldiers in the truck ahead had ducked for cover again.

The truck turned hard left and dropped down the other side of the ridge. Brakelights glowed. The disadvantage of a torque coverter was that it didn't permit compression braking. . . .

From the crest, Des Grieux could see three more ridgelines furrowing the horizon to the west. The last was in Hindi territory. Three centuries ago, this planet had been named Friendship and colonized by the Pan-Asian Cooperative Settlement Authority. The organizers' plans had worked out about as well as most notions that depended on the Brotherhood of Man.

More business for Hammer's Slammers. More chances for Slick Des Grieux to do what he did better than anybody else. . . .

Pesco pivoted the tank, changing its attitude to follow the road before sliding off the crest. As the huge vehicle paused, the jeep came up along the port side. Des Grieux expected the jeep to pass them. Instead, the passenger—Broglie, as Des Grieux had known from the first glimpse—gripped the mounting handholds welded to the tank's skirts and pulled himself aboard.

The jeep dropped back. For a moment, Des Grieux could see nothing of his new company commander except shoulders and the top of his head as Broglie found the steps behind their spring-loaded coverplates. If he slipped now—

Broglie lifted himself onto the tank's deck. Unless Pesco was using a panoramic display—which he shouldn't be, not when the road ahead was more than enough to occupy anybody driving a vehicle of the tank's bulk—he didn't know what was going on behind him. The driver would have kittens when he learned, since at least half the blame would land on him if something went wrong.

Des Grieux would have taken his share of the trouble willingly, just to see the red smear where *that* human being had been ground into the gravel.

Broglie braced one foot on a turret foothold and leaned toward the cupola. "Hello, Slick," he said. He shouted to be heard over the rush of air into the fan intakes. "Since we're going to be working together again, I figured I'd come and chat with you. Without going through the commo net and whoever might be listening in."

Des Grieux looked at his new company commander. The skin of Broglie's face was red. Des Grieux remembered that the other man never seemed to tan, just weathered. He looked older, too; but Via, they all did.

"I didn't know you were going to be here when I took the transfer to Hotel," Des Grieux blurted. He hadn't planned to say that; hadn't *planned* to say anything, but the words came out when he looked into Broglie's eyes and remembered how much he hated the man.

"Figured that," said Broglie, nodding. He looked toward the horizon, then added, "You belong in tanks, Slick. They're the greatest force multiplier there is. A man who can use weapons like you ought to have the best weapons."

It wasn't flattery; just cold truth, the way Des Grieux had admitted that Broglie was a dead shot. It occurred to Des Grieux that his personal feelings about Broglie were mutual and always had been.

He said nothing aloud. If the company commander had come to talk, the company commander could talk.

"What's your tank's name, Slick?" Broglie asked.

Des Grieux shrugged. "I didn't name her," he said. "The guy I replaced did. I don't care cop about her name."

"That's not what I asked," Broglie said. "Sergeant."

"Right," said Des Grieux. His eyes were straight ahead, toward the horizon in which the far wall of the valley rose. "The name's *Gangbuster*. *Gangbuster II*, since you care so much. Sir."

"Glad to be back in tanks?" Broglie asked. His voice was neutral, but it left no doubt that he expected answers, whether or not Des Grieux saw any point in giving them.

"Any place is fine," Des Grieux said, turning abruptly toward Broglie again. "Just so long as they let me do my job."

The anger in Des Grieux's tone surprised even him. He added more mildly, "Yeah, sure, I like tanks. And if you mean it's been five years—don't worry about it. I haven't forgotten where the controls are."

"I don't worry about you knowing how to handle any bloody weapon there is, Slick," Broglie said. They stared into one another's eyes, guarded but under control. "I might worry about the way you took orders, though."

Des Grieux swallowed. A billow of dust rose around *Gangbuster's* bow skirts and drifted back as Pesco slowed to avoid running over the truck ahead.

Des Grieux let the grit settle behind them before he said, "Nobody has to worry about *me* doing my job, Captain."

"A soldier's job is to obey orders, Slick," Broglie said flatly. "The time when heroes put on their armor and went off to single combat, that ended four thousand years ago. D'ye understand me?"

Des Grieux fumbled within the hatch and brought up his water bottle. The refrigerated liquid washed dust from his mouth but left the sour taste of bile. He stared at the horizon. It rotated sideways as Pesco negotiated a switchback.

"Do you understand me, Slick?" Captain Broglie repeated.

"I understand," Des Grieux said.

"I'm glad to hear it," Broglie said.

Des Grieux felt the company commander step away from the turret and signal to the driver of his jeep. All Des Grieux could see was the red throb of the veins behind his own eyes.

Ten kilometers to the west, the Han and Hindi outpost lines slashed at one another in a crackling barely audible through the darkness.

"These are the calculated enemy positions," said Captain Broglie. The portable projector spread a holographic panorama in red for Broglie and the three tank commanders of H Company, 2nd Platoon.

Ghosts of the coherent light glowed on the walls of the tent. The polarizing fabric gave the Slammers within privacy but allowed them to see and hear the world outside.

"And here's Baffin's Legion," Broglie continued.

A set of orange symbols appeared to the left, map West, of the red images. The Legion, a combined-arms force of battalion strength, made a relatively minor showing on the map, but none of the Slammers were deceived. Almost any mercenary unit was better than almost any local force; and Baffin's Legion was better than almost any other mercenaries. Almost.

"Remember," Broglie warned, "Baffin can move just as fast as we can. In fifteen minutes, he could be driving straight through the friendly lines."

A battery of the Slammers' rocket howitzers was attached to the Strike Force. The hogs chose this moment to send a single round apiece into the night. The white glare of their simultaneous muzzle flashes vanished as suddenly as it occurred, but afterimages from the shells' sustainer motors flickered purple and yellow across the retinas of anyone without eye protection who had been looking in the direction of those brilliant streaks.

"Are they shelling Morobad?" asked Platoon Sergeant Peres. Peres had been in command of 2nd Platoon ever since the former platoon leader vanished in an explosion on New Aberdeen that left a fifty-foot crater where his tank had been. She gestured toward the built-up area just west of the major canal that the map displayed. Morobad was the only community in the region that was more than mud houses and a central street.

Hundreds of Han soldiers started shooting as though the artillery signalled a major attack. Small arms, crew-served weapons, and even the soul-searing throb of heavy lasers ripped out from the perimeter. Flashes and the dull glow of self-sustaining brushfires marked the innocent targets downrange.

"Stupid bastards," Des Grieux muttered, his tone too flat to be sneering. "If they're shooting at anything, it's their own people."

"You got that right, Slick," Broglie agreed as he stared for a moment through the pervious walls of the tent. His face was bleak; not angry, but as determined as a storm cloud.

Han officers sped toward the sources of gunfire on three-wheeled scooters, crying orders and blowing oddly-tuned whistles. Some of the shooting came from well within the camp.

A rifle bullet zinged through the air close enough to the Slammers' tent that the fabric echoed the ballistic crack. Medrassi, the veteran commander of *Dar es Salaam*—House of Peace—swore and hunched his head lower on his narrow shoulders.

"What we oughta do," Des Grieux said coldly, "is leave these dumb clucks here and handle the job ourself. That way there's only half the people around likely t' shoot us."

Cyan streaks quivered over the horizon to the west. The light wasn't impressive until you remembered it came from ten kilometers away. Shells burst in puffs of distant orange.

Broglie lifted his thumb toward the western horizon. "I think that's what they were after, Perry," he said to Sergeant Peres. "Just checking on how far forward Baffin's artillery defenses were."

"Calliopes?" Medrassi asked.

Firing from the Han positions slackened. In the relative silence, Des Grieux heard the *pop-pop-pop* of shells, half a minute after powergun bolts had detonated them.

"Baffin uses twin-barrel three-CM rigs," Broglie explained. "They're really light anti-tank guns converted to artillery defense. He's got about eight of them. They're slow firing, but they pack enough punch that a single bolt can do the job."

He smiled starkly. "And they still retain their anti-tank function, of course."

Des Grieux spit on the ground.

"The reason that we're not going to leave our brave allies parked here out of the way, Slick," Broglie continued, "is that we're going to need all the help we can get. Indigenous forces may include an entire armored brigade. The Hindis are tough opponents in their own right—don't judge them by the Han we're saddled with. And Baffin's Legion by itself would be a pretty respectable opponent—even for a Slammers' battalion combat team."

"Great," Peres said, kneading savagely at the scar on the back of her left hand. "Let's do it the other way, then. We keep the hell outa the way while our indig buddies mix it with Baffin and get all this wild shooting outa their system."

"What we're going to do," Broglie said, taking charge of the discussion again, "is turn a sow's ear into a . . . nice synthetic purse, let's say. Second Platoon is going to do that."

He looked at his subordinates. "And I am, because I'm going to be with you tomorrow.

The holographic display responded to Broglie's gestures. Blue arrows labeled as units of the Black Banner Guards wedged their way across the map toward the Hindi lines. Four gray dots, individual Slammers' tanks, advanced beyond the arrows like pearls on a velvet tray.

"The terrain is pretty much what we've seen in each of the valleys we crossed on the Han side of the boundary," Broglie said. "Dikes between one and two meters high. Some of them broad enough to carry a tank but *don't* count on it. Mostly the dikes are planted with hedges that give good cover, and Hindi troops are dug into the mud of the banks. At least Hindi troops—Baffin may be stiffening them."

"Morobad's not the same," Medrassi said through the hedge of his dark, gnarled fingers. "Fighting in a city's not the same as nothing. 'Cept maybe fighting in Hell."

"Don't worry," said Broglie dismissively. "Nobody's going anywhere near that far."

He looked at his tank commanders. "What the Strike Force is going to do, guys," he said. "You, me, and the Black Banner Guards . . . is move up—" blue arrows came in contact with the red symbols "—hit 'em—" the arrows flattened "—and retreat in good order, Lord willing and we all do our jobs."

"We'll do *our* jobs," Sergeant Peres grunted, "but where the hell's the rest of H Company?"

She raised her eyes from the horrid fascination of the holographic display, where blue symbols retreated eastward across terrain markers and red bars formed into arrows to pursue. "Where the *hell* is the rest of the battalion, Echo, Foxtrot, and Golf?"

The blue arrows on the display had attacked ahead of the gray tank symbols. As the Han forces began to pull back, the tanks provided the bearing surface on which the advancing Hindis ground in an increasingly desperate attempt to reach their planetary enemies.

"Fair question," Broglie said, but he didn't cue the holographic display. Symbolic events proceeded at their own pace.

Outside the Slammers' shelter, a multi-barreled machine gun broke the near silence by firing skyward. Loops of mauve tracers rose until the marking mixture burned out two thousand meters above the camp. Han officers went off again in their furious charade of authority.

Des Grieux sneered at the lethal fireworks on the other side of the one-way fabric. The bullets would be invisible when they fell; but they were going to fall, in or bloody close to the Han lines. Broglie was a fool if he thought *this* lot was going to do the Slammers' fighting for them.

Red arrows forced their way forward over holographic rice paddies. The counterattack spread sideways as Han symbols accelerated their retreat. The gray pearls of the four tanks shifted back more quickly under threat of being overrun on both flanks. Orange arrows joined the red when the computer model estimated that Baffin would commit his far-more-mobile forces to exploit the Hindi victory.

"The rest of our people are here," Broglie said as lines and bars of gray light sprang into place to the north, south, and east of the enemy salient. "Waiting in low-observables mode until Baffin's got too much on his plate to worry about fine tuning his sensor data. Waiting to slam the door."

On either flank of the red-and-orange thrust was a four-tank platoon from H Company and a full company of combat cars. Gray arrows curving eastward indicated combat cars racing across rice paddies in columns of muddy froth, moving to rake the choke point just east of Morobad where enemy vehicles bunched as reinforcements collided with units attempting a panicked retreat.

The dug-in infantry of the Slammers' Echo Company blocked the Hindi eastward advance. On the holographic display, blue Han symbols halted their retreat, then moved again to attack their trapped opponents in concert with Hammer's infantry and the tanks of 2nd Platoon.

The display still showed Second to have four vehicles. Everybody in the shelter knew that rearguard actions always meant casualties—and didn't always mean survivors.

Medrassi grunted into his hands.

"The hogs'll provide maximum effort when the time comes," Broglie said. "The locals have about thirty self-propelled guns also, but their fire direction may leave something to be desired."

"It's not," Peres said, "going t' be a lot of fun. Until the rest of our people come in."

"The battle depends on 2nd Platoon," Broglie said flatly. "You're all highly experienced, and mostly your drivers are as well. Slick, how do you feel about your driver, Pesco? He's the new man."

Des Grieux shrugged. "He'll do," he said. Des Grieux was looking at nothing in particular through the side of the tent.

Broglie stared at Des Grieux for a moment without expression. Then he resumed, "Colonel Hammer put Major Chesney in command of this operation, but it's not going to work unless Second does its job. That's why I'm here with you. We've got to convince the Hindis—and particularly Baffin—that the attack is real and being heavily supported by the Slammers. After the locals pull back—"

He looked grimly at the display, though its image—enemy forces trapped in a pocket while artillery hammered them into surrender—was cheerful enough for Pollyanna.

"After the Han pull back," the captain continued softly, "it's up to us to keep the planned withdrawal from turning into a genuine rout. Echo can't hold by itself if Baffin's Legion slams into them full tilt . . . and if that happens—"

Broglie smiled the hard, accepting smile of a professional describing events which would occur literally over his own dead body.

"—then Baffin can choose which of our separated flanking forces he swallows up first, can't he?"

A Han laser slashed the empty darkness from the perimeter.

"Bloody marvelous," Peres murmured. "But I suppose if they knew what they was doing, they wouldn't need us t' do it for them."

Medrassi laughed. "Dream on," he said.

"Do you all understand our mission, then?" Broglie asked. "Sergeant Peres?"

"Yessir," Peres said with a nod.

"Sergeant Medrassi?"

"Yeah, sure. I been in worse."

"Slick?"

Des Grieux stared at the wall of the shelter. His mind was bright with the rich, soul-devouring glare of a tank's main gun.

"Sergeant Des Grieux," Broglie said. His voice was no louder than it had been a moment before, but it cut like an edge of glass. "Do you understand the operation we will carry out tomorrow?"

Des Grieux looked at his commanding officer. "Chesney never came up with anything this cute," he said mildly. "This one was your baby? Sir."

"I had some input in the planning, that's right," Broglie said tonelessly. "Do you understand the operation, Slick?"

"I understand that it makes a real pretty picture, Cap'n Broglie," Des Grieux replied. "Tomorrow we'll see how it looks on the ground, won't we?"

Outside the shelter, machine gun fire etched the sky in pointless response.

The Han armored personnel carrier was supposed to be amphibious, but it paused for almost thirty seconds on the first dike. The wheels of the front two axles spun in the air; those of the rear pair churned in a suspension of mud and water with the lubricating properties of motor oil.

A Hindi anti-tank gun ripped the APC with a fifty-MM osmium penetrator. Half of the carrier's rear-mounted engine blew through the roof of the tilted vehicle with a *crash* much louder than the Mach 4 ballistic crack of the shot.

The driver hopped out of the forward hatch and fell down on the dike. His legs continued to piston as though he were running instead of thrashing in mud. Sidehatches opened a fraction of a second later and a handful of unhurt infantrymen flopped clear as well.

Inertia kept the APC's front wheels rotating for some seconds. A rainbow slick of diesel fuel covered the rice paddy behind the vehicle. It did not ignite.

Des Grieux smiled like a shark from his overwatch position on the first terrace east of the floodplain. He traversed his main gun a half degree. The Hindi anti-tank gun was a towed piece with optical sights. It had no electronic signature to give it away, and *Gangbuster II*'s magnetic anomaly detector was far too coarse a tool to provide targeting information at a range of nearly a kilometer.

When the weapon fired, though—

Des Grieux stroked his foot trip and converted the anti-tank gun into a ball of saturated cyan light.

Han vehicles hosed the landscape with their weapons. Bullets from APC turrets and the secondary armament of laser-vehicles flashed as bright explosions among the foliage growing on dikes and made the mud bubble.

High-powered lasers raised clouds of steam wherever their pale beams struck, but they were not very effective. The lasers were line of sight weapons like the Slammers' powerguns. The gunners could hit nothing but the next hedge over while the firing vehicles sheltered behind dikes themselves.

The entire Han advance stopped when the Hindis fired their first gun.

Des Grieux had a standard two-cm Slammers' carbine clipped to the side of his seat. Over his head, *Gangbuster's* tribarrel pumped short bursts into the heavens in automatic air-defense mode. The sky, still a pale violet color in the west, was decorated with an applique of shell tracks and the bolts of powerguns which detonated the incoming.

Both sides' artillery fired furiously. Neither party had any success in breaking through the webs of opposing defenses, but there was no question of taking *Gangbuster II* out of AAD. The infantry carbine and the tank's main gun were the only means of slaughter under Des Grieux's personal control.

"Blue Two," Captain Broglie's voice ordered. "On command, advance one dike. Remaining elements look sharp."

Blue Two, *Dar es Salaam*, was on the southern edge of the advance, half a kilometer from *Gangbuster II*. Broglie's command tank, *Honey Girl*, was a similar distance to starboard of Des Grieux; and Blue One, Peres, backstopped the Han right flank a full kilometer north of *Gangbuster II*. The causeway carrying the main road to Morobad was the axis of the Strike Force advance.

The dikes turned the floodplain into a series of ribbons, each about a hundred meters wide. By advancing one at a time from their overwatch positions behind the Black Banner Guards, maybe the Slammers' tanks could get the Han force moving again. . . .

Though if instead the four tanks burst straight ahead in a hell-for-leather dash, they'd open up the Hindi lines like so many bullets through a can of beans.

"Blue Two, *go*."

Medrassi's tank lurched forward at maximum acceleration. The driver—Des Grieux didn't know his name; *her* name, maybe—had backed thirty meters in the terraced paddy to give himself a run before they hit the dike.

Water and bright green rice shoots, hand planted only days before, spewed to either side as the fans compressed a cushion of air dense enough to float 170 tonnes. For a moment, *Dar es Salaam's* track through the field was a barren expanse of wet clay; then muddy water slopped back to cover the sudden waste.

The tank didn't lift quite high enough to clear the dike, but the driver didn't intend to. The belly plates were the vehicle's thinnest armor. Hindi gunners, much less the Legion mercenaries, could penetrate even a Slammers' tank if it waved too much of its underside in the direction of the enemy.

Dar es Salaam's bow skirts rammed the top layer of the bank ahead of the tank. Fleshy-branched native osiers flailed desperately as they fell with the dike in which they had grown.

Honey Girl fired its main gun. Des Grieux didn't see Broglie's target but there *was* a target, because the bolt detonated an anti-tank gun's 400-liter bottle of liquid propellant in a huge yellow flash. The barrel of the Hindi weapon flew toward the Han lines. The bodies of the gun crew shed parts all around the hemispherical blast.

Des Grieux didn't have a target. That bastard Broglie was good, Lord knew.

A pair of Han laser-vehicles resumed the planned advance; or tried to, they'd bogged in the muck when they stopped. Spinning wheels threw brown undulations to either side but contributed nothing to the forward effort. The Han vehicles were supposed to be all-terrain, but they lacked the supplementary treads the Hindi tanks used. The paddies might have been too much for the balloon tires even if the heavy vehicles had kept moving.

Four APCs grunted into motion—drawn by *Dar es Salaam* and encouraged by the deadly 20-CM powerguns on the mercenary tanks. The carriers found the going difficult also, but their lower ground pressure made them more mobile than the laser-vehicles were.

Thirty or more of the APCs joined the initial quartet. The advance, one or two vehicles revving into motion at a time, looked like individual drivers and officers making their own decisions irrespective of orders from above—but it had the effect of a planned leapfrog assault.

"Blue One," Broglie ordered. "On command, advance

one dike. Remaining elements look sharp." Only buzzbombs and a few light crew-served weapons replied to the empty storm of Han fire. The Hindis kept their heads down and picked their targets.

Bullet impacts glittered on the glacis plate of an APC driving parallel to the causeway. The commander had been conning his vehicle with his head out of the cupola hatch. He ducked down immediately. The driver must have ducked also, even though he was using his periscopes. The APC ran halfway up the side of the causeway and overturned.

"Blue One, *go!*"

As Peres' driver kicked *Dixie Dyke* forward, Des Grieux's gunnery screen marked a target with a white carat. The barrel of a Hindi gun was rotating to bear when Peres' tank exposed its belly. Excellent camouflage concealed the motion from even the Slammers' high-resolution optics, but the magnetic anomaly detector noticed the shift against the previous electromagnetic background.

Gangbuster II's turret traversed four degrees to starboard on its magnetic gimbals. The cupola tribarrel snarled up at incoming artillery fire, but the only sound within the fighting compartments was the whine of the turret drive motors and the whistling intake of Des Grieux's breath as he prepared to kill a. . . .

The target vanished in the blue-white glare of *Honey Girl's* bolt. Broglie had beaten Des Grieux to the shot again, and *fuck* that the target was in *Honey Girl's* primary fire zone.

"Blue Three," Broglie ordered with his usual insouciant calm. "On command, advance two, I repeat two, dikes. Remaining elements, look sharp."

"Driver," Des Grieux ordered, "you heard the bastard."

Medrassi fired, but he didn't have a bloody target for a main-gun bolt, there *wasn't* one. A section of dike flash-baked and blew outward as ceramic shards, but Via! what did a couple Hindi infantry matter?

Des Grieux ordered, "Booster, echo main screen, left side of visor, out," and pulled up hard on the seat-control lever. The seat rose. Des Grieux's head slid out of the hatch just as the cupola rotated around him and the tribarrel spat three rounds into the western sky with an acrid stench from the ejected empties.

"Blue Three, *go!*"

"Goose it, driver!" Des Grieux said as he unclipped the shoulder weapon from his seat and felt *Gangbuster II* rise beneath him on the thrust of its eight drive fans to mount the dike.

The Han advance was proceeding in reasonable fashion, though at least a score of APCs hung back at the start point. Several laser-vehicles were moving also. The inaction of the rest was more likely the bog than cowardice, though cowardice was never an unreasonable guess when unblooded troops ran into their first firefight.

One laser-vehicle balanced on top of a dike. The fore and aft axles spun their tires in the air, while the grip of the central wheels was too poor to move them off the slick surface. Hindi skirmishers lobbed their buzzbombs at long range toward the teetering vehicle, but the anti-tank guns contemptuously ignored it to wait for a real threat.

To wait for the Slammers' tanks.

Des Grieux's eyes were four meters above the ground surface, higher than the tank's own sensors, when *Gangbuster II* humped itself over the dike. Through the clear half of his visor Des Grieux saw the movement, the glint of the plasma generator trunnion-mounted to an anti-tank gun, as it swung beneath its overhead protection.

The little joystick in the cupola was meant as a manual control for the defense array, but it was multi-function at need—and Des Grieux needed it. He rotated and depressed the main gun with his left hand as *Gangbuster II* started her fierce rush down the reverse side of the dike and the Hindi weapon traversed for the kill.

The pipper on the left side of Des Grieux's visor merged in a stereo image with the view of his right eye. He thumbed the firing tit with a fierce joy, knowing that *nobody* else was that good.

But Slick Des Grieux was. As the tank bellied down into the spray of her fans, a yellow fireball lifted across the distant fields. A direct hit, snap-shooting and on the move, but Des Grieux was the best!

Broglie fired also, from the other side of the empty road to Morobad. He must've got something also, because a secondary explosion followed the bolt, but the Hindis—strictly locals, no sign at all of the Legion— weren't done yet. A hypervelocity shot *spanged* from *Gangbuster*'s turret. Kinetic energy became heat with a flash almost as bright as that of a plasma bolt, rocking Des Grieux backward.

He turned toward the shot, pointing his short-barreled shoulder weapon as though it were a heavy pistol. The tank bottomed on the paddy, then bounced upward nearly a meter as water rushed in to fill the cavity, sealing the plenum chamber to maximum efficiency.

The Hindi weapon was dug in low; it had fired through a carefully-cut aisle. Now the gunners waited to shoot again, hoping for more of a target than Des Grieux's helmeted head bobbing over the planted dikes between them. None of the three Slammers' tanks providing the base of fire could bear on the anti-tank gun even now that it had exposed itself by firing. *Gangbuster II*'s main gun was masked by the vegetation also, but Des Grieux's personal weapon spat three times on successive bounces as the tank porpoised forward. The gun's frontal camouflage flashed and burned when a two-CM bolt flicked it. Han officers, guided by the powergun, sent a dozen ropes of tracer arcing toward the Hindi weapon from the cupolas of their APCs. Hindi gunners splashed away from the beaten zone, hampered by the mud and raked by the hail of explosive bullets.

The *peepeepeep* in Des Grieux's earphones warned him to attend to the miniature carat on his visor: Threat Level I, a laser rangefinder painting *Gangbuster II* from the hedge bordering the causeway. No way to tell what weapon the rangefinder served, but somebody thought it could kill a Slammers' tank. . . .

Des Grieux rotated the turret with the joystick, thrusting hard as though his muscles rather than the geartrain were turning the massive weight of iridium. "Driver, hard right!"

he screamed, because the traversing mechanism wasn't going to slew the main gun fast enough by itself.

And maybe nothing was going to slew the main gun fast enough.

Des Grieux shot twice with the carbine in his right hand. His bolts splashed near the bottom of the hedge. One round blew glassy fragments of mud in the air; the other carbonized a gap the size of a pie plate at the edge of the interwoven stems of native shrub.

The laser emitter itself was two meters high in the foliage, but that was only a bead connected to the observer's hiding place by a coaxial optical fiber. The observer was probably *close* to the emitter, though; and if the weapon itself was close to the observer, it would simply pop up and make parallax corrections.

Soldiers liked things simple.

Pesco was trying to obey Des Grieux's order, but *Gangbuster II* had enormous forward momentum and there was the dike they were approaching to consider also. A sheet of spray lifted to the tank's port side as the driver dumped air beneath the left skirt. The edge of the right skirt dipped and cut yellow bottom clay to stain the roostertail sluicing back on that side.

Gangbuster II started to lift for the dike. That was almost certainly the Hindi aiming point, but Des Grieux had the sight picture he wanted, he *needed*—

Des Grieux tripped the main gun. Five meters of mud and vegetation exploded as the twenty-CM bolt slanted across the base of the hedge.

The jolt of sun-hot plasma certainly blinded the laser pickup. It probably incinerated the observer as well: no mud burrow could withstand the impact of a tank's main gun.

The causeway was gouged as if a giant shark had taken a bite out of it. The soil steamed. Fragments of hedge blazed and volleyed orange sparks for twenty meters from where the bolt hit.

The weapon the observer controlled, a rack of four hypervelocity rockets dug into the edge of the causeway ten meters west of the rangefinder, was not damaged by the bolt. The observer's dying reflex must have closed the firing circuit.

A section of causeway collapsed from the rockets' backblast. *Gangbuster II*'s automatic defense system fired too late to matter. The sleet of steel pellets disrupted the razor-sharp smoke trails, but the projectiles themselves were already past.

The exhaust tracks fanned out slightly from the launcher. One of the four rockets missed *Gangbuster*'s turret by little more than the patina on the iridium surface. The sound of their passage was a single brittle *c-c-crack!*

Because *Gangbuster II* was turning in the last instant before the missiles fired—and because the main gun had blasted the observer into stripped atoms and steam before he could correct for the course change—the tank was undamaged, and Des Grieux was still alive to do what he did best.

It was time to do that now, whatever Broglie's orders said.

"Driver, steer for the road!" Des Grieux ordered. "Highball! We're gonna gut 'em like fish, all the way t' the town!"

"Via, we can't do that!" Pesco blurted. *Gangbuster II* dropped off the dike in a flurry of dirt, water, and vegetation diced by the fans. "Cap'n Broglie said—"

Des Grieux craned his body forward and aimed his carbine. He fired, dazzling the direct vision sensors built into the driver's hatch coaming. The bolt vaporized a tubful of water ahead of *Gangbuster II* and sent cyan quivers through a semicircle of the paddy.

"Drive, you son of a bitch!" Des Grieux shouted.

Pesco resumed steering to starboard, increasing the slant *Gangbuster II* had taken to bring the twenty-CM gun to bear. The gap that bolt had blown in the causeway's border steadied across the tank's bow slope.

A dozen Hindi machine guns in the dikes and causeway rang bullets off *Gangbuster II*'s armor. One round snapped the air close enough to Des Grieux's face to fluff his moustache. It reminded him that he was still head and shoulders out of the cupola.

He shoved down the crash bar and dumped himself back

into the fighting compartment. The hatch clanged above him, shutting out the sound of bullets and *Gangbuster II's* own tribarrel plucking incoming artillery from the air.

Des Grieux slapped the AAD plate to put the tribarrel under his personal control again.

All three of the tanks in overwatch fired within split seconds of one another. A column of flame and smoke mounted far to the north, suggesting fuel tanks rather than munitions were burning.

Of course, the victim might have been one of the Han vehicles.

The topographic display on *Gangbuster II's* left-hand screen showed friendly units against a pattern of fields and hedges. The entire Han line was in motion, spurred by the mercenaries' leapfrog advance and the Han's own amateur enthusiasm for war.

They'd learn. At least, the survivors would learn.

"General push," Des Grieux said, directing the tank's artificial intelligence to route the following message so that everyone in the Strike Force—locals as well as mercenaries—could receive it. "All units, follow me to Morobad!"

His hand reached into the breaker box and disconnected *Gangbuster II* from incoming communications.

The flooded rice paddies slowed the tank considerably. One hundred seventy tonnes were too much for even the eight powerful drive fans to lift directly. The vehicle floated on a cushion of air, but that high-pressure air required solid support also.

The water and thin mud of the paddies spewed from the plenum chamber. *Gangbuster II* rode on the clay undersurface—but the liquid still created drag on the outside of the skirts as the tank drove through it. To make the speed Des Grieux knew it needed to survive, *Gangbuster II* had to have a smooth, hard surface beneath her skirts.

The causeway was such an obvious deathtrap that none of the Han vehicles had even attempted it—but the locals didn't have vehicles with the speed and armor of a Slammers' tank.

And anyway, they didn't have Des Grieux's awareness

of how important it was to keep the enemy off balance by punching fast as well as often.

Des Grieux latched the two-CM carbine back against his seat. The barrel, glowing from the half magazine the veteran had fired through it, softened the patch of cushion it touched. The stench intertwined with that oozing from the main gun empties on the floor of the turret basket.

Gangbuster II was now leading the Han advance instead of supporting it. Three Hindi soldiers got up and ran, left to right, across a dike two hundred meters west of the tank. All were bent over, their bodies tiger-striped by foliage. The trailing pair carried a long object between them, a machine gun or rocket launcher.

Maybe the Hindis thought they were getting into a better position from which to fire at *Gangbuster II*. Des Grieux's tribarrel, *his* tribarrel again, sawed the men down in a tangle of flailing limbs and blue-white flashes.

Des Grieux didn't need to worry about indirect fire anymore, because the Hindi artillery wouldn't fire into friendly lines . . . and besides, *Gangbuster II* was moving too fast to be threatened by any but the most sophisticated terminally-guided munitions. The locals didn't have anything of that quality in their arsenals.

Baffin's Legion *did* have tank-killing rounds that were up to the job. Still, the cargo shells which held two or three self-forging fragments—shaped by the very blasts that hurled them against the most vulnerable spots in a tank's armor— were expensive, even for mercenary units commanding Baffin's payscale, or Hammer's. For the moment, the guns on both sides were flinging cheap rounds of HE Common at one another, knowing that counterfire would detonate the shells harmlessly in the air no matter what they were.

It'd take minutes—tens of seconds, at least—for Legion gunners to get terminally-guided munitions up the spout. That would be plenty of time for the charge Des Grieux led to blast out the core of enemy resistance.

"Hang on!" Pesco cried as though Des Grieux couldn't see for himself that *Gangbuster II* was about to surge up onto the causeway.

A Hindi soldier stood transfixed, halfway out of a spider hole in the hedge on the other side of the road. His rifle was pointed forward, but he was too terrified to sight down it toward the tank's huge, terrible bow. Des Grieux cranked the tribarrel with his right joystick.

Gangbuster II rose in a slurp of mud as dark and fluid as chocolate cake dough. The Hindi disappeared, not into his hole but by jumping toward the paddies north of the causeway. A Han gunner, lucky or exceptionally skillful, caught the Hindi in mid-leap. A splotch of blood hung in the air for some seconds after the corpse hit the water.

An anti-tank shot struck the rear of *Gangbuster II*'s turret. The bustle rack tore away in a scatter of the tankers' personal belongings, many of them afire. Impact of the dense penetrator on comparably dense armor heated both incandescent, enveloping the clothes and paraphernalia in a haze of gaseous osmium and iridium.

The projectile had only a minuscule direct effect on the inertia of *Gangbuster*'s 170 tonnes, but the shock made Pesco's hand twitch on the control column. The tank lurched sideways. The lights in the fighting compartment darkened and stayed out, but the screens only flickered as the AI routed power through pathways undamaged when the jolting impact severed a number of conduits.

The second shot blew through the northern hedge a half-second later. Pesco was fighting for control. The projectile hit, but only a glancing blow this time. The shot ricocheted from high on the rear hull, leaving a crease a half-meter long glowing in the back deck.

Des Grieux spun the tribarrel because the cupola responded more quickly than the massive turret forging, but he didn't have a clear target—and the anti-tank gunner didn't need one.

Powergun bolts would dump all their energy on the first solid object they touched. It was pointless trying to shoot at a target well to the other side of dense vegetation. Heavy osmium shot, driven by a jolt of plasma generated in a chamber filled with liquid propellant, carried through the hedge with no significant degradation of its speed or stability.

Gangbuster II hesitated while Pesco swung the bow to port, following the causeway, and coarsened the fan pitch to regain the speed lost in climbing the embankment. The tank was almost stationary for the moment.

Hindi soldiers rose from spiderholes in the hedge and raised buzzbomb launchers. One of the rocketeers was a hundred meters ahead of *Gangbuster II*; the other was an equal distance behind, his position already enveloped by the Han advance.

Des Grieux's tribarrel was aimed directly to starboard, and even the main gun was twenty degrees wide of the man in front. The tanker's right hand strained against the joystick anyway. The Hindis fired simultaneously.

The third shot from the anti-tank gun punched in the starboard side of the tank's plenum chamber and exited to port in a white blaze of burning steel. Each hole was approximately the size of a human fist. Air roared out while *Gangbuster II* rang like a struck gong. The fan nacelles were undamaged, and the designers had overbuilt pressurization capacity enough to accept a certain amount of damage without losing speed or maneuverability.

The rocket from the man in the rear hit the hedge midway between launcher and the huge intended target. The buzzbomb's pop-out fins caught in the interlaced branches; the warhead did not go off.

The other buzzbomb was aimed well enough as to line, but the Hindi soldier flinched upward as he squeezed the ignition trigger. The rocket sailed over *Gangbuster II* in a flat arc and exploded in the dirt at the feet of the other Hindi. The body turned legless somersaults before flopping onto the causeway again.

Des Grieux and Broglie fired their twenty-CM guns together. The Hindi rocketeer and thirty meters of hedge behind him blazed as *Gangbuster II*'s bolt raked along it. Through the sudden gap, Des Grieux saw the cyan-hearted fireball into which Broglie's perfect shot converted the Hindi gun that had targeted the tank on the causeway.

"Go, driver!" Des Grieux shouted hoarsely, but Pesco didn't need the order. Either he understood that their survival lay in speed, or blind panic so possessed him that he had no mind for anything but accelerating down the hedged three-kilometer aisle.

The Black Banner Guards were charging at brigade strength. It was a bloody shambles. The Hindis might have run when they saw the snouts of hundreds of armored personnel carriers bellowing toward them—

But they hadn't. More than a score of anti-tank guns unmasked and began firing, now that the contest was clearly a slugging match and not a game of cat-and-mouse. It took less than a second to purge the chamber of a Hindi gun, inject another projectile and ten liters of liquid propellant, and convert a tungsten wire into plasma in the center of the fluid.

Each shot was sufficiently powerful to lance through four APCs together if they chanced to be lined up the wrong way. Broglie, Peres, and Medrassi ripped away at the luxuriance of targets as fast as they could, but the paddies were already littered with torn and blazing Han vehicles.

The heavy anti-tank weapons were only part of the problem. Hindi teams of three to six men crouched in holes dug into the sides of the dikes, then rose to volley buzzbombs into the oncoming vehicles at point-blank range. Some of the rockets missed, but the hollow *whoomp!* of a single warhead was enough to disable any but the luckiest APC.

For those targets which the first volley missed, additional buzzbombs followed within seconds.

The jet of fire from a shaped charge would rupture fuel cells behind an APC's thin armor. Diesel fuel atomized an instant before it burst into flame. Hindi machine gunners then shot the Han crews to dog-meat as they tried to abandon their burning vehicles.

Des Grieux *knew* that green locals always broke if you charged them. His mind hadn't fully metabolized the fact that these Hindis might not be particularly accurate with their weapons, but they sure as *blood* weren't running anywhere.

As for the Han, who'd already lost at least a quarter of their strength in an unanswered turkey shoot . . . well, Des Grieux had problems of his own. "Booster!" he said. "Clear vision!"

The images echoed onto the left side of his visor from *Gangbuster II*'s central screen vanished, leaving the screen itself sharp and at full size. Normally Des Grieux would have touched a finger to his helmet's mechanical controls, but this wasn't normal and both his hands were on the gunnery joysticks.

Gangbuster II was so broad that the tank's side skirts *brushed* one, then the other, hedge bordering the causeway. Morobad was a distant haze at the end of an aisle as straight as peasants with stakes and string could draw it. Des Grieux's right hand stroked the main gun counterclockwise to center its hollow pipper on the community. He didn't need or dare to increase the display's magnification to give him actual images.

A Hindi soldier aimed a buzzbomb out of the left-hand hedge. The man's mottled green uniform was so new that the creases were still sharp. His dark face was as fixed and calm as a wooden idol's.

Gangbuster II's sensors noted a human within five meters. They tripped the automatic defense system attached to a groove encircling the tank just above the skirts. A 50x 150-mm strip of high explosive fired, blowing its covering of steel polygons into the Hindi like the blast of a huge shotgun.

The Hindi and his rocket launcher, both riddled by shrapnel, hurtled backward. Leaves and branches stripped from the hedge danced in the air, hiding the carnage.

A second rocketeer leaned out of the hedge three steps beyond the first. The ADS didn't fire because the cell that bore on the new target had just been expended on his comrade. The Hindi launched his buzzbomb from so close that the stand-off probe almost touched the tank's hull.

The distance was too short for the buzzbomb's fuze to arm. The missile struck *Gangbuster II*'s gun mantle and ricocheted upward instead of exploding. A bent fin made the buzzbomb twist in crazy corkscrews.

Now another explosive/shrapnel cell aligned. The automatic defense system went off, shredding the rocketeer's torso. Useless, except as revenge for the way the Hindi had made Des Grieux's heart skip a beat in terror—

But revenge had its uses.

Des Grieux put one, then another twenty-CM bolt into Morobad without bothering to choose specific targets—if there were any. All he was trying to do for the moment was shake up the town. Some of the Legion's anti-artillery weapons were emplaced in Morobad. If the other side kept its collective head, *Gangbuster II* was going to get a hot reception.

Deafening, dazzling bolts from a tank's main gun pretty well guaranteed that nobody in the impact zone would be thinking coolly.

That was all right, and Des Grieux's tank was all right so far, seventy KPH and accelerating. *Gangbuster II* pressed a broad hollow down the causeway. The surface of dirt and rice-straw matting rippled up to either side under the tank's 170 tonnes, even though the weight was distributed as widely as possible by the air cushion.

The Han brigade that Des Grieux had led to attack was well and truly fucked.

Smoke bubbled from burning vehicles, veiling and clearing the paddies like successive sweeps of a bullfighter's cape. Some APCs had been abandoned undamaged. Their crews cowered behind dikes while Hindi buzzbomb teams launched missile after missile at the vehicles.

The rocketeers weren't particularly skillful: buzzbombs were reasonably accurate to a kilometer, but hits were a toss-up for most of the Hindis at anything over 100 meters. Determination and plenty of reloads made up for deficiencies in skill.

Han gunfire was totally ineffective. The officer manning the cupola machine gun also had his vehicle itself to command. As the extent of the disaster became clear, finding a way to safety overwhelmed any desire to place fire on the Hindis concealed by earth and foliage.

The infantry in the APC cargo compartments had individual gunports, but the Lord himself couldn't have hit a target while looking through a viewslit and shooting from the port beneath it. The APCs bucked and slipped on the slimy terrain. In the compartments, men jostled one another and breathed the hot, poisonous reek of powdersmoke and fear. Their bullets and laser beams either vanished into the landscape or glanced from the sideplates of friendly vehicles.

Des Grieux hadn't a prayer of a target either. He was trapped within the strait confines of the hedges for the two minutes it would take *Gangbuster II* to travel the length of the causeway.

His tribarrel raked the margins of the road, bursts to the right and left a hundred meters ahead of the tank's bluff bow. Stems popped like gunfire as they burned. That might keep a few heads down, but it wasn't a sufficient use for the most powerful unit on the battlefield.

Des Grieux could order his driver into the paddies again, but off the road the tank would wallow like a pig. This time there would be Hindi rocketeers launching buzzbombs from all four sides. Des Grieux no longer thought the local enemy would panic because it was a shark they had in the barrel to shoot at.

By contrast, the remaining Slammers' tanks were having a field day with the targets Des Grieux and the Han had flushed for them. Tribarrels stabbed across a kilometer of paddies to splash cyan death across Hindis focused on nearby APCs. Straw-wrapped packets of buzzbombs exploded, three and four at a time, to blow gaps in the dikes.

The left-hand situation display in *Gangbuster*'s fighting compartment suddenly lighted with over a hundred red carats. The tanks of a Hindi armored brigade, lying hidden on the east side of the canal which formed the eastern boundary of Morobad, had been given the order to advance. When the drivers lighted their gas turbine powerplants, *Gangbuster*'s sensors noted the electronic activity and located the targets crawling up onto prepared firing steps.

Morobad was less than a kilometer away. Hindi tanks maneuvered on both sides of the causeway to bring the guns fixed along the centerline of their hulls in line with *Gangbuster II*. The Hindi vehicles mounted combustion-augmented plasma weapons, like the anti-tank guns but more powerful because a tank chassis permitted a larger plasma generator than that practical on a piece of towed artillery.

Des Grieux's situation display showed the condition clearly. The visuals on his gunnery screen were the same as they'd been for the past minute and a half: unbroken hedgerows which would stop bolts from his powerguns as surely as thirty centimeters of iridium could.

A Hindi shot *cracked* left-to-right across the road a tank's length behind *Gangbuster II*. Somebody'd gotten a little previous with his gunswitch, but the tank that had fired was still backing one track to slew its weapon across the Slammers' vehicle.

Des Grieux traversed his main gun, panning the target, and rocked the foot-trip twice. Instinct and the situation display at the corner of his eye guided him: the orange circle on the gunnery screen showed only foliage.

The first bolt flash-fired the wall of hedge. The second jet of cyan plasma crashed through the gap and made a direct hit on the Hindi tank.

The roiling orange fireball rose a hundred meters. The column of smoke an instant later mounted ten times as high before flattening into an anvil shape which dribbled trash back onto the paddies. The compression wave of the explosion flattened an expanding circle of new-planted rice. Rarefaction following the initial shock jerked the seedlings upright again.

A tank on the north side of the causeway slammed a shot into *Gangbuster II*'s bow. A hundred kilos of iridium armor and #2 fan nacelle turned into white-hot vapor which seared leaves on which it cooled.

Pesco shouted and briefly lost control of his vehicle. The tank's enormous inertia resisted turning and kept the skirts on the road despite a nasty shimmy because of the drop in fan pressure forward.

Des Grieux tried to traverse his main gun to bear on the new danger, but the turret had seventy-five degrees to swing clockwise after its systems braked the momentum of the opposite rotation. He wasn't going to make it in the half-second before the next Hindi shot transfixed *Gangbuster II*'s relatively thin side armor—

But he didn't have to, because Captain Broglie's command tank nailed the Hindi vehicle. Plates of massive steel armor flew in all directions even though the bolt failed to detonate the target's munitions.

Score one for Broglie, *the bastard*; and if he'd brought the rest of the platoon along with Des Grieux, maybe *Gangbuster II* wouldn't be swinging in the breeze right now.

Hindi tanks were firing all along the line. They ignored *Gangbuster II* because the tanks destroyed to the immediate north and south of the causeway blocked the aim of their fellows.

The Hindi CAP guns were useless except against armored vehicles—their solid projectiles had no area effect whatever. Against armor, they were neither quite as effective shot for shot, nor quite as quick-firing as the Slammers' twenty-CM guns.

They were effective enough, though, and there was a bloody swarm of them.

Broglie and his two overwatching companions hit half a dozen of the Hindi vehicles, destroying them instantly even though most of the cyan bolts struck the thickest part of the targets' frontal armor. Then the surviving Hindis got the range and volleyed their replies.

A shot hit the cupola above Broglie. Ammo burned in the feed tube of *Honey Girl*'s tribarrel. A blue-white finger poked skyward, momentarily dimming the rising sun. Des Grieux's display cross-hatched *Dixie Dyke* as well, indicating the north-flank tank had been damaged as Peres raked Hindi lines with both main gun and tribarrel. All three units jerked backward to turret-down positions as quickly as their drivers could cant their fans.

"Driver!" Des Grieux said as *Gangbuster II*, its front skirts dragging sparks from the stone road surface, crossed the canal bridge. "Turn us and we'll hit the bastards from behind. Booster, gimme a fucking city map!"

The cheap buildings of Morobad's canal district were ablaze. Some of the walls were plastered wattle-and-daub; other builders had hung painted sheetiron on scantlings of flimsy wood. Neither method could resist the two main-gun rounds Des Grieux snapped toward the town when *Gangbuster II* started its rush. The bolts had the effect of flares dropped into a tinder box.

The tank drove into a curtain of flame at ninety KPH. There was something in the way, a wrecked vehicle or the corner of a building. *Gangbuster's* skirts shunted it aside with no more commotion than the clang the automatic defense system made when it went off.

The tank's AI obediently replaced the topographic display on the left screen with a map of Morobad from *Gangbuster II's* data banks. The streets were narrow and twisting, even the thoroughfare leading west from the causeway.

Two hundred meters from the canal was a market square bordered by religious and governmental buildings. That would give Pesco room to turn. When *Gangbuster II* roared out of the city again and took the turretless Hindi tanks in the rear, it'd be all she wrote.

The air cleared at street level. *Gangbuster II* scraped the brick facade of a three-story tenement which started to collapse on them. At least a score of Hindi soldiers opened fire with automatic weapons. Bullets ricocheted from the sloped iridium armor, scything down the shooters and their fellows. Cells of the automatic defense system fired, louder and more lethal still.

Haze closed in momentarily, but a telltale in the fighting compartment informed Des Grieux that Pesco had already switched to sonic imaging instead of using the electro-optical spectrum to drive. *Gangbuster II* swept into the market square, pulling whorls of smoke into the clear, sunlit air.

A six-tube battery of 170-MM howitzers was set up in the square. Empty obturator disks and unneeded booster charges in white silk littered the cobblestones behind the weapons. The crews were desperately cranking their muzzles down to fire point-blank at *Gangbuster II*. Hindi infantry cut loose with small arms from all windows facing the square and from the triple tile overhangs of the large temple behind the walled courtyard to the south.

As Des Grieux squeezed both firing tits, a hundred-kilogram shell hit the turret. The round was a thin-cased HE, what the crew happened to have up the spout when they got warning of the tank's approach. The red flash destroyed thirty percent of *Gangbuster II*'s forward sensors and rocked the tank severely, but the hatches were sealed and the massive turret armor was never even threatened.

"Driv—" Des Grieux started to say as his hazy screens showed him Hindi gunners doubling up, flying apart, burning in puffs of vaporized steel as the powergun sights slid across the battery.

A legless Hindi battery captain jerked the lanyard of his last howitzer. The shell was a capped armor-piercing round. Even so, the round would not have penetrated *Gangbuster II*'s frontal armor if it had struck squarely. Instead, it hit Pesco's closed hatch edge-on and spalled the backing plate down through the driver's helmet and skull.

Pesco convulsed at the controls of *Gangbuster II*. The tank skidded across the square, swapping ends several times. The courtyard wall braked but did not stop the careening vehicle. Des Grieux shouted curses, but words had no effect on the tank or its dead driver.

Gangbuster II slid bow-first into the stone-built temple. Blocks and tiles from the multiple roofs cascaded onto the tank and over the courtyard beyond.

All *Gangbuster II*'s systems crashed at the massive overload.

Des Grieux knew nothing about that. Despite his shock

harness, his head slammed sideways into the map display so that he shut down an instant before his tank did.

Existence was a pulsing red blur until Des Grieux opened his eyes. The pulsing continued every time his heart beat, but now he could see real light: the tiny yellow beads of *Gangbuster II*'s standby illumination system.

The air in the fighting compartment was hot and foul. When the power went off, so did the air conditioning. The expended twenty-CM casings on the floor continued to radiate heat and complex gases.

Des Grieux reached for the reset switch to bring *Gangbuster II*'s systems alive again. Movement brought blinding pain. The tank's shock harness had retracted when movement stopped, but the straps left tracks in the form of bruises and cracked ribs where they had gripped Des Grieux to prevent worse.

His mouth tasted of blood, and there seemed to be a layer of ground glass between his eyes and their lids.

"Blood and martyrs," Des Grieux whispered. The taste in his mouth came from his tongue, which had swollen to twice its normal size because he had bitten it.

When the world ceased throbbing and his stomach settled again, Des Grieux finished his movement to the reset switch. Pain just meant you were alive. If you were alive, you could do for the bastard who'd done *you*.

The snarl of powerguns dimly penetrated to the tank's interior. Neither of the indig forces had powerguns of their own. Either the Slammers had entered Morobad, or Baffin had committed his Legion to exploit the ratfuck the Black Banner Guards had made when they tried to follow *Gangbuster II*'s lead.

Des Grieux knew which alternative *he'd* put his money on.

Gangbuster II came to life crisply and fast. That was better than the man in her fighting compartment had managed.

"Booster," Des Grieux said. His injured tongue slurred his words. "Order of Battle on Number One."

Screen #1, the left-hand unit, came up with the map of Morobad Des Grieux had ordered onto it before the crash and shutdown. The new overlay showed Des Grieux just what he'd bloody expected, the orange symbols of Legion vehicles streaming through the town and fanning out when they crossed the canal.

This was no feint or stiffening force. Baffin was committing his entire battalion-strength command to end the war here on the Western Wing.

"Like bloody hell . . ." Des Grieux muttered. "Driver! Report!"

Nothing. "Pesco?"

Nothing. Des Grieux would have to crawl forward and see what the hell was going on; but first he checked the condition of his tank.

Gangbuster II was fully operable. The tank was down one fan and had five fist-sized holes in her skirts. Des Grieux had no recollection of several of those hits. Both guns were all right, and sixty percent of the massively-redundant sensor suite checked out as well.

The only problem was that, according to the echo-ranging apparatus, the tank was covered by several meters of variegated rubble: bricks, tiles, wooden beams, and the bodies of Hindi soldiers who'd been shooting from the temple roofs up to the moment *Gangbuster II* brought the building's facade down on itself. All the visual displays were blank because the pickups were buried.

Of course, if the Slammers' vehicle hadn't been so completely concealed, Baffin's troops would have finished Des Grieux off by reflex. Veteran mercenaries were generally men who'd survived by never trusting a corpse until they'd put in a bayonet of their own.

A four-ship platoon of Baffin's tank destroyers slid eastward across the map of Morobad. They were air-cushion vehicles mounting fifteen-CM powerguns behind frontal armor almost as thick as that of the Slammers' tanks. The main guns were in centerline mountings like those of the Hindi tanks—turrets were relatively heavy, and an air-cushion vehicle could rotate easily in comparison to wheeled or track-laying armor.

Companies of infantry preceded and followed the tank destroyers in four air-cushion carriers apiece. Baffin carried his infantry in large, lightly-armored vehicles; Hammer mounted his men on one-man skimmers with their heavy weapons on air-cushion jeeps. Either method worked well with good troops; and both *these* units were very good indeed.

Gangbuster II shone brightly on Des Grieux's display as a cross-hatched blue symbol, but the Legion troops advancing through Morobad showed no sign of awareness. Their screens would be tuned to the Han/Slammers defenses kilometers to the east . . . , if there were any Han troops left to thicken the line of cursing Slammers infantry and the survivors of 2nd Platoon.

Not all the Legion equipment in the square outside the collapsed temple was moving. Des Grieux's #1 display marked four of Baffin's three-CM twin guns, half the Legion's anti-artillery defenses, with neat orange symbols. The weapons were emplaced to either side of the thoroughfare. Support troops had hastily bulldozed the wreckage of the Hindi battery out of the way.

Ideally, artillery-defense guns should have a clear view to the horizon on all sides. In practice, crews preferred to set up in defilade where they were safe from hostile direct-fire weapons. Even so, the buildings surrounding the market square reduced the defended area to what seemed at first an unusually narrow cone.

Three command vehicles, armored air-cushion vans filled with communications gear, were parked back-to-back in a trefoil at the northwest corner of the square. *That* was what the three-CM guns were protecting: Baffin in his advanced command post.

Des Grieux's muscles began to tremble with reaction. He no longer felt the pain in his ribs; fresh adrenaline smoothed the knotted veins flowing to his brain. Baffin himself, a hundred and fifty meters from *Gangbuster II's* main gun. . . .

"Pesco, you lazy bastard!" Des Grieux snarled, but he'd already given up on raising a response from his driver. He climbed out of his seat and slid between the hull and the frame of the turret basket.

Thick twenty-CM disks littered the deck, the empty matrixes that had aligned the copper atoms which the powerguns released as plasma. One disk blocked the small hatch separating the fighting compartment from the driver's compartment. Des Grieux tossed the empty angrily behind him. The polyurethane was hot and still tacky; it clung to his fingertips.

As soon as he opened the hatch, the smell told Des Grieux that his driver was dead. Pesco had voided his bowels when the fragment sliced off the upper half of his skull. The liters of blood his heart pumped before the autonomic nervous system shut down had already begun to rot in the warm compartment.

Des Grieux swore. The hatch—the part of it that hadn't decapitated Pesco—was jammed beyond opening by anything short of rear-echelon maintenance. He didn't know what the *bloody* hell he was going to do with the driver's body.

He released the seat latch so that the back flopped down. The remaining contents of Pesco's cranial cavity slopped over Des Grieux's hands. He rotated the seat forty-five degrees to its stop, then tilted the corpse sideways out onto the forward deck of the compartment. There it blocked the foot pedals, but Des Grieux wouldn't be able to use those anyway.

Des Grieux leaned over the bloody seat, set the blade angles at zero incidence, and switched on the drive fans. All the necessary controls were on the column; the duplicate nacelle-attitude controls on the foot pedals permitted a driver to do four things simultaneously in an emergency—

But *Gangbuster II* didn't have a driver any more.

Seven green lights and a red one marked the fan status screen beneath the main driving display, but that was only half the story. Des Grieux knew the intake ducts were blocked as surely as *Gangbuster II*'s hatches. That didn't matter at the moment, but it would as soon as he rotated the pitch control and the fans started to suck wind.

No choice. Des Grieux could only hope that vibration as the nacelles drew against the rubble above them would help to clear the vehicle. Because that was what he needed to do first.

Des Grieux breathed deeply. He didn't really notice the smell; other things could get in his way, but not that. He adjusted the nacelle angle to a balance between lift and thrust. He hoped he had the mixture right, but whatever he came up with would have to do.

Des Grieux had been a lousy driver; he was far too heavy handed, forcing the controls the way he forced himself.

For this particular job, a heavy hand was the only choice.

The fans hummed, running at full speed though the throttles were at their idle setting. With the pitch at zero, the leading edges of the blades knifed the air with minimal resistance. *Gangbuster II* began to resonate with a bell-note deeper than usual because the hull didn't hang free in the air.

Des Grieux sucked in another breath. His right hand drew the linked throttles full on, while his left thumb adjusted the pitch to sixty degrees. The tank wheezed and bucked like a choking lion. Des Grieux scrambled backward out of the hatch.

The empties jounced on the floor with the violence of *Gangbuster II's* attempts to draw air through choked intakes. Des Grieux threw himself into his seat and grasped the gunnery joysticks. The orange pippers glowed against a background of uniform gray because the visual pickups were shrouded.

Des Grieux twisted the left joystick. Metal screeched as the turret began to swing clockwise against its weight of rubble. Hot insulation tinged the atmosphere of the fighting compartment as the turret drive motors overloaded.

Des Grieux twisted the control in the opposite direction. The turret reversed a few centimeters. There was a squawling crash as the mass of overburden shifted and slid away from *Gangbuster II*'s turret and deck. The tank bobbed like a diver surfacing through a sea of rubble.

The fan blades bit the air for which they had been starving. Uncontrolled, *Gangbuster II* lurched backward at an accelerating pace.

Des Grieux shouted with glee as he rotated his turret and cupola controls again. Now he had a sight picture and targets.

Gangbuster II had hit the temple facade nose on. Now it backed through the hole it had torn in the wall, bucking over and plowing through tiles and masonry from the building's upper stories.

The Hindis were using the temple's forecourt as a field hospital for casualties from Des Grieux's initial attack. Medics and the wounded who could move under their own power ran or crawled from *Gangbuster II*'s bellowing reappearance.

Des Grieux ignored them. The gap his tank had smashed in the courtyard wall showed at one edge of his gunnery screen, and a pair of Legion three-CM carriages were visible through it. The Legion guns were firing upward at a forty degree angle, snapping incoming shells from the air as soon as they notched the horizon.

The tribarrel's solid sight indicator covered the Legion weapons an instant before the main gun swung on target. Brilliant cyan bolts raked the Legion crews and the receivers of their guns. A pannier of ammunition exploded with a flash like that of a miniature nova. It destroyed everything within a five-meter sphere, pavement included.

Gangbuster II slewed across the courtyard in a scraping, sparking curve. The tank wasn't going to follow the track by which it had plunged in from the market square. The gap in the courtyard wall foreshortened into solidity as the damaged skirts slid the tank toward a point twenty meters west of its initial entry. The screams of wounded men in the vehicle's path were lost in the howl of steel on stone.

Des Grieux took his right hand from the joystick long enough to close the commo breaker. "Blue Three to Big Dog One-Niner!" he shouted hoarsely to battalion fire control. "Get some arty on top of us! Get us—"

Gangbuster II struck the courtyard wall for the second time. The shock threw Des Grieux forward into his harness. Redoubled pain shrank objects momentarily to pinhead size in his vision, but he did not black out.

The tank's iridium hull armor smashed through the brickwork, but the impact stripped off the already-damaged skirts. Momentum drove *Gangbuster II* partway into the market square. The vehicle halted there because half the plenum chamber was gone.

"—some firecracker rounds!" Des Grieux gasped to artillery control, demanding anti-personnel shells as his hands worked his joysticks.

Two of the three-CM pieces were undamaged. The crew of the gun nearest the ammunition blast was dead or writhing shriveled on the pavement, but the gunners of the fourth piece were cranking down their twin muzzles to bear on the unexpected threat.

A bolt from *Gangbuster II*'s main gun struck the shield just below the stubby barrels of the artillery-defense weapon. The gun seemed to suck in, then flash outward as a ball of sunbright vapor.

A loader had turned to run when she saw death pointing down *Gangbuster II*'s twenty-CM bore. Gaseous metal enveloped all of the Legion soldier but her outflung hand. When the glowing ball condensed and vanished, the hand remained like a wax dummy on a framework of carbonized sticks.

Des Grieux's tribarrel raked the Legion command group. The plating of the vehicles' boxy sides was thick enough to turn about half the two-CM bolts—but at this short range, *only* half.

Gangbuster II's main gun continued to rotate on target. One of the three vans already sparkled with electrical shorts, while another puffed black smoke from the holes the powergun had blown across its flank.

"Blue Leader to Blue Three," Captain Broglie cried across the crackling, all-band static of powergun discharges. "Abandon your vehicle immediately! Anti-tank rounds are incoming on your location!"

"Screw you, Broglie!" Des Grieux screamed as his main gun slammed a bolt into the central command track, the one that was bow-on with its thicker frontal armor toward *Gangbuster II*'s tribarrel. The twenty-CM bolt blew out the vehicle's back and sides with a piston of vaporized metal which had been the glacis plate a micro-second earlier.

The Legion tank destroyer entering the square from the west snapped a bolt from its fifteen-CM powergun into *Gangbuster II*'s turret. The tank rocked backward under the impact.

Des Grieux slammed into the seat. The screens and regular lighting went out, but the inner face of the turret armor glowed a sulphurous yellow.

Heat clawed at the skin of Des Grieux's face and hands. He started to draw in a breath. The air was fire, but he had to breathe anyway.

Gangbuster II's nacelles stopped bucking in the stripped plenum chamber when the power shut off. Now the tank shuddered with heat stresses.

Des Grieux punched the reset switch. A conduit across the turret burst with a green flash. The holographic displays quivered to life, then went blank.

A salvo of shells landed near enough to rock the tank with their *crumpcrumpcrump*-CRUMP! They were HE Common, not anti-tank. The rounds had been in flight before the battery commander knew there was a hole blasted in the Legion's artillery defenses.

The seat controls were electrical; nothing happened when Des Grieux tugged the bar. He reached up—his ribs hurt almost as much as his lungs did—and slid the cupola hatch open manually.

Buildings around the market square were burning. Smoke mingled with ozone from the powerguns, organic residues from propellants and explosive, and the varied stench of bodies ripped open as they died.

It was like a bath in cool water compared to the interior of the tank.

The iridium barrel of *Gangbuster II*'s main gun was shorter by eighty centimeters. That was what saved Des

Grieux's life. At this range, the tank destroyer's bolt would have penetrated if it had struck the turret face directly.

The stick of shells that just landed had closed the boulevard entering the square from the west. The tank destroyer that hit *Gangbuster II* wriggled free of collapsed masonry fifty meters away. The vehicle was essentially undamaged, though shrapnel had pecked highlights from its light-absorbent camouflage paint, and the cupola machinegun hung askew.

Bodies, and the wreckage of equipment too twisted for its original shape to be discerned, littered the pavement of the square.

Des Grieux set the tribarrel's control to thermal self-powered operation. It wouldn't function well, but it was better than nothing.

The manual traverse wheel refused to turn; the fifteen-CM bolt had welded the cupola ring to the turret. The elevating wheel spun, though, lowering the triple muzzles as the tank destroyer's own forward motion slid it into Des Grieux's sight picture.

Cargo shells popped open high in the heavens. Des Grieux ignored the warning. He squeezed the butterfly triggers to rip the tank destroyer's skirts. Bolts which might not have penetrated the vehicle's heavy iridium hull armor tore fist-sized holes in the steel.

Des Grieux got off a dozen rounds before his tribarrel jammed. They were enough for the job. The tank destroyer vented its air cushion through the gaps in the plenum chamber and grounded with a squealing crash.

Des Grieux bailed out of *Gangbuster II*, carrying his carbine. He slid down the turret and hit the pavement on his feet, but his legs were too weak to support him. He sprawled on his face.

The anti-tank submunition, one of three drifting down from the cargo shell by parachute, went off a hundred meters in the air. The *whack!* of the blast knocked Des Grieux flat as he started to get up. The supersonic penetrator which the explosion forged from a billet of

depleted uranium had already punched through the thin
upper hull of *Gangbuster II*.

Ammunition and everything else flammable within the
tank *whuffed* out in a glare that seemed to shine through
the armor. The fusion bottle did not fail. The turret settled
again with a clang, askew on its ring.

Secondary explosions to the east and further west within
Morobad marked other effects of the salvo, but none of
the submunitions had targeted the disabled tank destroyer.
Des Grieux sat up and crossed his legs to provide a stable
firing position. He wasn't ready to stand, not quite yet. Heat
from his tank's glowing hull washed across his back.

What sounded like screaming was probably steam
escaping from a ruptured boiler. Humans couldn't scream
that loud. Des Grieux knew.

He pointed his carbine.

The tank destroyer's forward hatch opened. The driver
started to get out. Des Grieux shot him in the face. The
body fell backward. Its feet were still within the hatch, but
the arms flailed for a time.

The hull side hatch—the tank destroyer had no turret—
opened a crack. Des Grieux covered the movement.
Cloth—it wasn't white, just a gray uniform jacket, but the
meaning was clear—fluttered from the opening.

"We've surrendered!" a woman called from inside. "Don't
shoot!"

"Come on out, then," Des Grieux ordered. His voice
was a croak. He wasn't sure the vehicle crew could hear
him, but a woman wearing lieutenant's insignia extended
her head and shoulders from the hatch.

Her face was expressionless. When she saw that Des
Grieux did not fire, she climbed clear of the tank destroyer.
A male commo tech followed her. If they had sidearms,
they'd left them within the vehicle.

"We've all surrendered," she repeated.

"Baffin's surrendered?" Des Grieux asked. He had
trouble hearing. He wanted to order his prisoners closer,
but he couldn't stand up and he didn't want them looking down at him.

"Via, Colonel Baffin was *there*," the lieutenant said, gesturing toward the three command vehicles.

The center unit that Des Grieux hit with his main gun was little more than bulged sidewalls above the running gear.

She shook her head to clear it of memories. "The Legion's surrendered, that's what I mean," she said.

"We must've lost ten percent of our equipment from that one salvo of artillery. No point in just getting wasted by shells. There'll be other battles. . . ."

The lieutenant's voice trailed off as she considered the implications of her own words. The commo tech stared at her in cow-eyed incomprehension.

Des Grieux leaned against a slope of shattered brick. The corners were sharp.

That was good. Perhaps their jagged touch would prevent him from passing out before friendly troops arrived to collect his prisoners.

Regimental HQ was three command cars backed against a previously-undamaged two-story school building. Flat cables snaked out of the vehicles, through windows and along corridors.

The combination wasn't perfect. Still, it provided Hammer's staff with their own data banks and secure commo, while permitting them some elbow room in the inevitable chaos at the end of a war—and a contract.

"Yeah, what is it?" demanded the orderly sergeant. The lobby was marked off by a low bamboo barrier. Three Han clerks sat at desks in the bullpen area, while the orderly sergeant relaxed at the rear in the splendor of his computer console. Behind the staff was a closed door marked HEADMASTER in Hindi script and ADJUTANT/HAMMER'S REGIMENT in stenciled red.

Des Grieux withdrew the hand which he'd stretched toward the throat of the Han clerk. "I'm looking for my bloody unit," he said, "and this bloody wog—"

"C'mon, c'mon back," the orderly sergeant demanded with a wave of his hand. "Been partying pretty hard?"

Des Grieux brushed a bamboo post and knocked it down as he stepped into the bullpen. The local clerks jabbered and righted the barrier.

"Wasn't a party," Des Grieux muttered. "I been in a POW camp the past week."

The orderly sergeant blinked. "A *Han* POW camp," Des Grieux amplified. "Our good wog buddies here—" he kicked out at the chair of the nearest clerk; the boot missed, and Des Grieux almost overbalanced "—picked me up when they swept Morohad. Baffin's troops got paroled out within twenty-four hours, but *I* got stuck with the Hindi prisoners 'cause nobody knew I was there."

The orderly sergeant's name tag read Hechinger. His nose wrinkled as Des Grieux approached. The Han diet of the POW camp differed enough from what the Hindi prisoners were used to that it gave most of them the runs. Latrine facilities within the camp were wherever you wanted to squat.

"Well, why didn't you tell them you were a friendly?" Hechinger asked in puzzlement.

Des Grieux's hands trembled with anger. "Have you ever tried to tell a wog *anything*?" he whispered. "Without a gun stuck down their throat when you say it?"

He got a grip on himself and added, more calmly, "And don't ask me for my ID bracelet. One of the guards lifted that first thing. Thought the computer key was an emerald, I guess."

Hechinger sighed. "Mary, key data," he ordered the artificial intelligence in his console. "Name?"

"Des Grieux, Samuel, Sergeant-Commander," the tanker said. "H Company, 2nd Platoon, Platoon Sergeant Peres commanding. She *was* commanding, anyhow. She may've bought it last week."

The console hummed and projected data. Des Grieux, standing at the back of the unit, could see the holograms only as refractions in the air.

"One of our trucks was going by and I shouted to the driver," Des Grieux muttered, glaring at the clerks. The three of them hunched over their desks, pretending to be busy. "He didn't know me, but he knew I wasn't a wog. I could've been there forever."

"Well," said the orderly sergeant, "three days longer and you'd sure've been finding your own transport back to the Regiment. We're pulling out. Got a contract on Plessy. Seems the off-planet workers there're getting uppity and think they oughta have a share in the shipyard profits."

"Anyplace," Des Grieux said. "Just so long as I've got a gun and a target."

"Well, we got a bit of a problem here, trooper," Hechinger said as he frowned at his display. "Des Grieux, Sergeant-Commander, is listed as dead."

"I'm not bloody *dead*," Des Grieux snarled. "Blood'n Martyrs, ask Sergeant Peres."

"Lieutenant Peres, as she'll be when she comes off medical leave," the orderly sergeant said, "isn't a lotta help right now either. And if you're going to ask about—" he squinted at the characters on his display "—Sergeant-Commander Medrassi, he bought the farm."

Hechinger smirked. "Like you did, y'see? Look, don't worry, we'll—"

"Look, I just want to get back to my unit," Des Grieux said, hearing his voice rise and letting it. "Is Broglie around? *He* bloody knows me. I just saved his ass—again!"

The orderly sergeant glanced over his shoulder. "Captain Broglie we might be able to round up for you, trooper," he said carefully. He nodded back toward the Adjutant's office.

"Anyhow," Hechinger continued, "he was captain when he went in there. Don't be real surprised if he comes out with major's pips on his collar, though."

"That *bastard* . . ." Des Grieux whispered.

"Captain Broglie's very much the fair-haired boy just now, you know, buddy," Hechinger continued in his careful voice. "He stopped near a brigade of Hindi armor with one tank platoon. It was kitty-bar-the-door, all the way back to Xingha, if it hadn't been for him."

The office door opened. Sergeant Hechinger straightened at his console, face forward.

Des Grieux looked up expecting to see either the Adjutant or Broglie—

And met the eyes of Major Joachim Steuben, as cold and hard as beads of chert. Hammer's bodyguard looked as stiffly furious as Des Grieux had ever seen a man who was still under control.

Des Grieux didn't think that Steuben would recognize him. It had been years since the last time they were face to face. There was crinkled skin around the corners of the major's eyes, though his was still a pretty-boy's face if you didn't look closely; and Des Grieux just now looked like a scarecrow. . . .

Joachim was more than just a sociopathic killer, though the Lord knew he was *that*. He looked at the tanker and said, "Well, well, Des Grieux. Seeking our own level, are we?"

The way Joachim shot his hip could have been an affectation . . . , but it also shifted the butt of his pistol a further centimeter clear of the tailored blouse of his uniform. Des Grieux met his eyes. Anyway, there was no place to run.

"Well, I understand your decision, Luke," said Colonel Hammer as he came out of the Adjutant's office with his hand on the arm of the much larger Broglie. The moon-faced Adjutant followed them, nodding to everything Hammer said. "But believe me, I regret it. Remember you've always got a bunk here if you change your mind."

Broglie wore no rank insignia at all.

Hechinger had to say *something* to avoid becoming part of the interchange between Steuben and Des Grieux. Nobody in his right mind—except maybe the Colonel—wanted to be part of Joachim's interchanges, even as a spectator.

"Okay, Des Grieux," he said in a voice just above a whisper. "I'll cut you some temporary orders so's you can get chow and some kit."

Broglie heard the name. He glanced at Des Grieux. His face blanked and he said, in precisely neutral tones, "Hello, Slick. I didn't think you'd make it back from that one."

"Oh, you ought to show more warmth than *that*, Mister

Broglie," Joachim drawled. He didn't look at Broglie and Hammer behind him. "After all, without Sergeant Des Grieux here to create that monumental screw-up, you wouldn't have been such a hero for straightening things out. Would you, now?"

"What d'ye mean screw-up?" Des Grieux said, *knowing* that Steuben was looking for an excuse to kill something. "*I'm* the one who blew the guts outa Baffin's Legion!"

"That's the man?" Hammer said, speaking to Broglie.

The Colonel's eyes were gray. They had none of the undifferentiated hatred for the world that glared from Major Steuben's, but they were just as hard as the bodyguard's when they flicked over Des Grieux.

"Yessir," Broglie murmured. "Joachim—Major Steuben? I'm not taking the job the Legion offered me out of any disrespect for the colonel. If you like, I'll promise that the Legion won't take any contracts against the Slammers so long as I'm in charge."

Joachim turned as delicately as a marionette whose feet dangle above the ground. "Oh, my . . ." he said, letting his left hand dangle on a theatrically limp wrist. "And a traitor's promise is *so* valuable!"

"I'm not—" said Broglie.

"Joachim!" said the Colonel, stepping in front of Steuben—and between Steuben and Broglie, though that might have been an accident, if you believed Colonel Alois Hammer did things by accident. "Go to the club and have a drink. I'll join you there in half an hour."

Steuben grimaced as though he'd been kicked in the stomach. "Sir," he said. "I'm . . ."

"Go on," Hammer said gently, putting his hand on the shoulder of the dapper killer. "I'll meet you soonest. No problem, all right?"

"Sir," Steuben said, nodding agreement. He straightened and strode out of the headquarters building. He looked like a perfect band-box soldier, except for his eyes. . . .

"And as for you, Luke," Hammer said as he faced around to Broglie again, "I won't have you talking nonsense. Your first duty is to your own troops. You'll take any bloody contract that meets your unit's terms and conditions . . . and I assure you, I'll do the same."

"Look, sir," Broglie said. He wouldn't meet Colonel Hammer's eyes. "I wouldn't feel right—"

"I said," Hammer snapped, "put a sock in it! Or stay with me—the Lord knows I'm going to have to replace Chesney anyway, after the lash-up he made when the wheels came off at Morobad."

Des Grieux was dizzy. The world had disconnected itself from him. He was surrounded by glassy surfaces which only seemed to speak and move in the semblance of people he had once known. "Major Chesney—" Broglie began.

"Major Chesney had to be told twice," Hammer said, "first by you and then by *me*, a thousand kays away with 3d Operational Battalion, to set his flanking tank platoons to cover artillery defense for the center. You shouldn't have had to hold Chesney's hand while you were organizing Han troops into a real defense."

Broglie smiled. "Their laser-vehicles were mostly bogged," he said, "so they couldn't run. I just made sure they knew I'd shoot 'em faster than the Hindis could if they *tried* to run."

"Whatever works," said Hammer with an expression as cold as the hatred in Joachim's eyes a moment before.

The expression softened. "Listen to me, Luke," Hammer went on. "People are going to hire mercenaries so long as they're convinced mercenaries are a good investment. Having the Legion in first-rate hands like yours is good for all of us in this business. I'll miss you, but I gain from this, too."

Broglie stiffened. "Thank you, sir," he said.

"Listen!" Des Grieux shouted. "I'm the one who broke them for you! *I* killed Baffin."

"Oh, you killed a lot of people, Des Grieux," Colonel Hammer said in a deceptively mild voice. "And way too many of them were mine."

"Sir," said Broglie. "The disorganization in the Legion's rear really was Slick's doing. We pieced it together in post-battle analysis, and—"

"Saved about ten minutes, didn't it, Broglie?" the Colonel said. "Before the flanking units closed on Morobad?"

Broglie smiled again, thinly. "That was ten minutes I was real glad to have, sir," he said.

Hammer stared up and down at Des Grieux. The Colonel's expression did not change. "So, you think he's a good soldier, do you?" he asked softly.

"I think," said Broglie, "that . . . if he'd learn to obey orders, he'd be the best soldier I've ever seen."

"Fine, Mister Broglie," Hammer said. "I'll tell you what. . . ."

He continued to look at Des Grieux as if daring the tanker to move or speak again. Major Steuben was gone, but the White Mice at the outer doorway watched the discussion with their hands on the grips of their sub-machine guns.

"I'll let you have him, then," Hammer continued. "For Broglie's Legion."

Broglie grimaced and turned away. "No," he muttered. "Sorry, that wouldn't work out."

Hammer nodded crisply. "Hareway," he said to the Adjutant, "have Des Grieux here put in the lockup until we lift. Then demote him to Trooper and put him to driving trucks for a while. *If* he cares to stay in the Slammers, as I rather hope he will not."

The lobby had a terrazzo floor. Hammer's boot-heels clacked on it as he strode off, arm and arm with Broglie. Their figures shrank in Des Grieux's eyesight, and he barely heard the orderly sergeant shout, "Watch it! He's fainting!"

PART III

The Slammers' lockup was a sixty-meter shipping container. The paired outer leaves were open, and the single inner door had been replaced by a grate. The facility was baking hot when the white sun of Meridienne cast its harsh shadows across the landscape. At night, when the clear air cooled enough to condense out the dew on which most of the local vegetation depended, the lockup became a shivering misery.

If the conditions in the lockup hadn't been naturally so wretched, Colonel Hammer would have used technology to make them worse. A comfortable detention facility would be counterproductive.

"Rise'n shine, trooper," called the jailor, a veteran of twenty-five named Daniels. "They want you there yesterday, like always."

Daniels' two prosthetic feet worked perfectly well—so long as they were daily retuned to match his neural outputs. He had the choice of moving to a high-technology world where the necessary electronics were available, or staying with the Slammers in a menial capacity. Since Daniels' only saleable skill—firing a tribarrel from a moving jeep—had no civilian application, he became one of the Regiment's jailors.

"Nobody's waiting for me," said Slick Des Grieux, lying on his back with his knees raised. He didn't open his eyes. "Nobody cares if I'm alive or dead. Not even me."

"C'mon," Daniels insisted as he inserted his microchip key in the lock. "Get moving or they'll be on *my* back."

He clashed the grate as best he could. It was formed of beryllium alloy, while the container itself had been extruded from high-density polymers. The combination made a tinny/dull rattle, not particularly arousing.

Des Grieux got to his feet with a smooth grace which belied his previous inertia. There was a three-CM pressure cut above his right temple, covered now with SpraySeal. His pale hair was cut so short that there had been no need to shave the injured portion before repairing it.

"What's going on, then?" Des Grieux asked. His tongue quivered against his lips as the first wisps of adrenaline began to dry his mouth. *There was going to be action.* . . .

"Sounds like it really dropped in the pot," said Daniels as he swung the grate outward. "Dunno how. *I* thought it was gonna be a walkover this time."

He nodded Des Grieux toward the climate-controlled container that he used for an office. "I wonder," Daniels added wistfully, "if it's bad enough they're gonna put support staff in the line . . . ?"

Des Grieux couldn't figure why he was getting out of the lockup five days early. The Hashemite Brotherhood controlled the northern half of Meridienne's single continent and claimed the whole of it. They'd been raiding into territory of the Sincanmo Federation to the south—pinpricks, but destructive ones. Unchecked vandalism had destabilized governments and economic systems more firmly based than anything the Sincanmos could claim.

In order to prevent the Sincanmos from carrying the fighting north, the Hashemites had hired off-planet mercenaries, the Thunderbolt Division, to guard their territory and deter the Sincanmos from escalating to all-out war with local forces. The situation had gone on for one and a half standard years, with the Hashemites chuckling over their cleverness.

The Thunderbolt Division was a good choice for the Hashemite purposes. It was a large organization which could be distributed in battalion-sized packets to stiffen local forces of enthusiastic irregulars; and the Thunderbolt Division was cheap, an absolute necessity. Meridienne was not a wealthy planet, and the Hashemites expected their "confrontation" to continue for five or more years before the Sincanmo Federation collapsed.

The Thunderbolt Division was cheap because it wasn't much good. Its equipment was low-tech, little better than what Meridienne's indigenous forces had bought for themselves. The mercenaries' main benefit to their employers was their experience. They *were* full-time, professional soldiers, not amateurs getting on-the-job training in their first war.

Then the Sincanmos met the threat head on: they hired Hammer's Slammers and prepared to smash every sign of organization in the northern half of the continent in a matter of weeks.

Des Grieux didn't see any reason the Sincanmo plan wouldn't work. Neither did Captain Garnaud, the commanding officer of Delta Company.

Normally line troops expected to serve disciplinary sentences after the fighting was over. In this case, Garnaud had decreed immediate active time for Des Grieux. D Company didn't need the veteran against the present threat, and Garnaud correctly believed that missing the possibility of seven days' action was a more effective punishment for Slick Des Grieux than a year's down-time restriction.

But now he was getting out early. . . .

Des Grieux followed Daniels into the close quarters of the jailor's office. The communications display was live with the angry holographic image of a senior lieutenant in battledress.

The face was a surprise. The officer was Katrina Grimsrud, the executive officer of H Company, rather than one of D Company's personnel. "Where the bloody hell have you been?" she snarled as soon as the jailor moved into pickup range of the display's cameras.

Daniels sat down at the desk crammed into the half of the container which didn't hold his bed and living quarters. His artificial feet splayed awkwardly at the sudden movement; they needed tuning or perhaps replacement.

"Sorry, sir," he muttered as he manipulated switches. His equipment was old and ill-mated, cast-offs from several different departments. Junk gravitated to this use on its way to the scrap pile. "Had to get the prisoner."

He adjusted the retinal camera. "Okay, Des Grieux," he said. "Look into this."

Des Grieux leaned his forehead against the padded frame. "What's going on?" he demanded.

Light flashed as the unit recorded his retinal pattern and matched it with the file in Central Records. Daniels' printer whined, rolling out hard copy. Des Grieux straightened, blinking as much from confusion as from the brief glare.

"Listen, Des Grieux," Lieutenant Grimsrud said. "We don't want any of your cop in this company. If you get cute, you're out. D'ye understand? Not busted, not in lockup: out!"

"I'm not *in* Hotel Company," Des Grieux snapped. He was confused. Besides, the adrenaline sparked by a chance of action had made him ready—as usual to fight anybody or anything, including a circle saw.

"You are now, Sarge," Daniels said as he handed Des Grieux the hard copy.

"Get over to the depot soonest," Grimsrud ordered as Des Grieux stared at his orders. "Jailor, you've got transport, don't you? Carry him. We've got a replacement tank there with a newbie crew. Des Grieux's to take over as commander; the assigned commander'll drive."

Des Grieux frowned. He was transferred from Delta to Hotel, all right. It didn't matter a curse one way or the other; they were both tank companies.

Only . . . transfers didn't occur at finger-snap speed—but they did this time, with the facsimile signature of Colonel Hammer himself releasing Sergeant-Commander Samuel Des Grieux (retinal prints attached) from detention and transferring him to H Company.

"Look, sir," Daniels said, "it's not my job to dr—"

"It's bloody well your job if you *don't* get him to the depot ASAP, buddy!" Lieutenant Grimsrud said. "I can't spare the time or the man to send a driver back. D'ye understand?"

Des Grieux folded the orders into the right cargo pocket of his uniform. "*I* don't understand," he said to the holographic image. "Why such a flap over the Thunderbolt Division? We could put truck drivers in line and walk all over them."

"Too right," Grimsrud said forcefully. "Seems the towelheads figured that out for themselves in time to hire Broglie's Legion. Colonel Hammer wants all the veterans he's got in line—and with you, that gives my 3d Platoon one, I say again *one*, trooper with more than two years in the Regiment. Get your ass over to our deployment area *soonest*."

Lieutenant Grimsrud cut the connection. Des Grieux stared in the direction of blank air no longer excited by coherent light. His whole body was trembling.

"Don't sound like she's lookin' for excuses," Daniels

grumbled as he got to his feet. "C'mon, Sarge, it's ten keys to the depot from here."

Des Grieux whistled tunelessly as he followed the jailor to an air-cushion jeep as battered as the equipment in Daniels' office. His kit was still in D Company. He didn't care. He didn't care about anything at all, except for the chance fate offered him.

Daniels started the jeep. At least one drive fan badly needed balancing. "Hey, Sarge?" he said. "I never asked you—what was the fight about? The one that landed you here?"

"Some bastard called me a name," Des Grieux said. He braced himself against the tubular seat frame worn through the upholstery. The jeep lurched into motion.

Des Grieux's eyes were closed. His face looked like the blade of a hatchet. "He called me 'Pops,'" Des Grieux said. Memory of the incident pitched his voice an octave higher than normal. "So I hit him."

Daniels looked at the tanker, then frowned and looked away.

"Thirty-two standard years don't make me an old man," Slick Des Grieux added in an icy whisper.

A starship tested its maneuvering jets on the landing pad beside the depot's perimeter defenses. The high screech was so loud that the air seemed to ripple. Though the lips of Warrant Leader Farrell, the depot superintendent, continued to move for several seconds, Des Grieux hadn't the faintest notion of what the man was saying.

Des Grieux didn't much care, either. There was only one tank among the depot's lesser vehicles and stacked shipping containers. He stepped past Farrell and tested the spring-loaded cover of a step with his fingertip. It gave stiffly.

"Right," said Farrell. He held Des Grieux's transfer orders and, on a separate flimsy, the instructions which Central had down-loaded directly to the depot. "Ah, here's the, ah, the previous crew."

Two troopers stood beside the depot superintendent.

Both were young, but the taller, dark-haired one had a wary look in his eyes. The other man was blond, pale, and soft-seeming despite the obvious muscle bulging his khaki uniform.

Des Grieux gave them a cursory glance, then returned his attention to the important item: the vehicle he was about to command.

The tank was straight out of the factory in Hamburg on Terra. Farrell's crew would have—should have done the initial checks, but the bearings would be stiff and the electronics weren't burned in yet.

The tank didn't have a name, just a skirt number in red paint: H271.

"Trooper Wartburg will move to driver," Farrell said. The dark-haired man acknowledged the statement by raising his chin a centimeter. "Trooper Flowers here was going to drive, but he'll go back to Logistics till we get another vehicle in."

Des Grieux climbed deliberately onto the deck of H271. The bustle rack behind the turret held personal gear in a pair of reused ammunition containers.

"You got any experience, Wartburg?" Des Grieux asked without looking back toward the men on the ground.

"Year and a half," the dark-haired man said. "Wing gunner on a combat car, then I drove for a while. This was going to be my first command."

Wartburg's tone was carefully precise. If he was disappointed to be kicked back to driver at the last instant, he kept the fact out of his voice.

Des Grieux slid the cupola hatch closed and open, ignoring the others again.

"One question, Sarge," Wartburg called. The irritation he had hidden before was now obvious. "Grimsrud told us a veteran'd be taking over the tank, but she didn't say who. You got a name?"

"Des Grieux," the veteran said. The tribarrel rotated on its ring, even with the power off. That was good, and a little surprising in a tank that hadn't yet been broken in. "Slick Des Grieux. You just do what I tell you and we'll get along fine."

Wartburg laughed brittlely. "The bloody hell I will," he said as he hopped up to the tank's deck himself.

Des Grieux turned in surprise. His eyes were flat and wide open. All he was sure of was that he'd need to pay more attention than he wanted to his new driver.

Wartburg said nothing further. He reached into the bustle rack and pulled out one of the cases, then tossed it to the ground.

The container crashed down and bounced before it fell flat. Flowers jumped to avoid it. The dense plastic was designed to protect 3,000 disks of two-CM ammunition against anything short of a direct from another powergun. It withstood the abuse, and its hinged lid remained latched.

"What d'ye think you're doing?" Des Grieux demanded.

Wartburg threw down the other container. "I think I'm not doin' *any*bloodything with you, Des Grieux," he said. He jumped to the ground.

"Wait a minute, trooper!" said the outraged depot superintendent. "You've got your orders!"

He waggled the flimsies in his hand at Wartburg, though in fact neither of the documents directly mentioned that trooper.

Trooper Flowers looked from Wartburg to Des Grieux to Farrell—and back. His mouth was slightly open.

"Look, Warrant Leader," Wartburg said to Farrell. I *heard* about this bastard. No way I'm riding with him. *No* way. You want me to resign from the Regiment, you got it. You wanna throw me in the lockup, that's your business."

He turned and glared at the man still on the deck of H271. "But I don't ride with Slick Des Grieux. If I ever get that hot to die, I'll eat my gun!"

"Screw you, buddy," Des Grieux said softly. He looked at the depot superintendent. "Okay, Mister Farrell, you get me a driver. That's your job. If you can't do that, then I'll drive and fight this mother both, if that's what it takes."

The three men on the ground began speaking to one another simultaneously in rasping, nervous voices. Des Grieux lowered himself through the cupola hatch.

H271's fighting compartment had the faintly medicinal odor of solvents still seeping from recently-extruded plastics. Des Grieux touched control buttons, checking them for feel and placement. There were always production-line variations, even when two vehicles were ostensibly of the same model.

He heard the clunk of boot toes on the steps formed into H271's armor. Somebody was boarding the vehicle.

Des Grieux threw the main power switch. Gauges and displays hummed to life. There was a line of distortion across Screen #3, but it faded after ten seconds or so. A tinge of ozone suggested arcing somewhere, probably in a microswitch. It would either clear itself or fail completely in the next hundred hours.

A hundred hours was a lifetime for a tank on the same planet as Colonel Luke Broglie. . . .

A head shadowed the light of the open hatch. Des Grieux looked up, into the face of Trooper Flowers.

"Sarge?" Flowers said. "Ah, I'm gonna drive for you. If that's all right?"

"Yeah, that's fine," said Des Grieux without expression. He turned to his displays again.

"Only, I've just drove trucks before, y'see," Flowers added.

"I don't care if you rolled hoops," Des Grieux said. "Get in and let's get moving."

"Ah—I'll get my gear," said Flowers. "I off-loaded when they said I was back in Logistics."

"Booster," said Des Grieux, keying H271's artificial intelligence. "Course data on Screen One."

He watched the left-hand screen. He wasn't sure that the depot had gotten around to loading the course information into the tank's memory, but the route and topography came up properly. Des Grieux thought there was a momentary hesitation in the AI's response, but that might have been his own impatience.

The deck clanked as Flowers jumped directly to the ground in his haste. The way things were going, the kid probably slipped 'n broke his neck. . . .

The course to Base Camp Two and H Company was a blue line curving across three hundred kilometers of arid terrain. No roads, but no problems either. Gullies cut by the rare cloudbursts could be skirted or crossed.

Des Grieux spread his hands, closed his eyes, and rested his forehead against the cool surface of the main screen. Everything about H271 was smooth and cold. The tank functioned, but it didn't have a soul.

He shivered. He could remember when he had enough hair that it wasn't bare scalp that touched the hologram display when he leaned forward like this.

Tank H271 was the right vehicle for Slick Des Grieux.

In the gully beside H271, twenty or so Sincanmo troops sang around a campfire to the music of strings and a double flute. There'd been drums, too. Lieutenant Kuykendall threatened to send a tank through the group if the drummer didn't toss his instrument into the fire *immediately*

That was one order from the commander of Task Force Kuykendall that Des Grieux would have cheerfully obeyed. Not that he had anything against this particular group of indigs.

There were thirty or forty other campfires scattered among the gullies like opals on a multistrand necklace. With luck, the force's camouflage film concealed the firelight from the hostile outpost two kilometers away on the Notch. Silencing the drums, whose low-frequency beat carried forever in the cool desert air, was as much of a compromise as Kuykendall thought she could enforce.

The Sincanmos were a militia organized by extended families. Each family owned four to six vehicles which they armed with whatever the individuals fancied and could afford. Medium-powered lasers; post-mounted missile systems, both guided and hypervelocity; automatic weapons; even a few mortars, each of a different caliber. . . .

Logistics would have been a nightmare—if the Sincanmo Federation had *had* a formal logistics system. On the credit side, each band was highly motivated, extremely mobile, and packed a tremendous amount of firepower for its size.

The families made decisions by conclave. They took orders from their own Federation rather more often than they ignored those orders; but as for an off-planet mercenary—and a *female*—Kuykendall's authority depended on her own platoon of combat cars and the four H Company tanks attached to her for this operation.

Des Grieux chewed a ration bar in the cupola of his tank. The Sincanmos made their fire by soaking a bucket of sand in motor fuel and lighting it. The flames were low and red and quivered with frustrated anger, much like Des Grieux's thoughts. There was going to be a battle very soon. In days, maybe hours.

But not here. If Colonel Hammer had expected significant enemy forces to cross the Knifeblade Escarpment through the Notch, he wouldn't have sent Hotel Company's 3d Platoon with the blocking force. The platoon had been virtually reconstituted after a tough time on Mainstream during the previous contract. In a few years, some of these bloody newbies would be halfway decent soldiers. The ones who survived that long.

"Booster," Des Grieux muttered. "Ninety degree pan, half visor."

H271's artificial intelligence obediently threw a high-angle view of the terrain which Task Force Kuykendall guarded onto the left side of Des Grieux's visor. The nameless sandstone butte behind the blocking force was useless as a defensive position in itself, because the only way for military equipment to get up or down its sheer faces was by crane. The mass of rock would confuse the enemy's passive sensors—at least the sensors of the Thunderbolt Division; Broglie's hardware certainly had the discrimination to pick out tanks, combat cars, and the Sincanmo 4x4s, even though the vehicles were defiladed and backed by a 500-meter curtain of stone.

The butte also provided a useful pole on which to hang the Slammers' remote sensors, transmitting their multispectral information down jam-free, undetectable fiber optics cables. Des Grieux at ground level had as good a vantage point as that of the Hashemite outpost in the Notch; and because the image fed to the tanker's helmet was light enhanced and computer sharpened, Des Grieux *saw* infinitely more.

Not that there was any bloody thing to see. Gullies cut by the infrequent downpours meandered across the plain. They were shallow as well as directionless, because the land didn't really drain. Rain sluiced from the buttes and the Escarpment, flooded the whole landscaper—and evaporated.

Winds had scoured away the topsoils to redeposit them thousands of kilometers away as loess. The clay substrates which remained were virtually impervious to water.

Seen from Des Grieux's high angle, the gullies were dark smears of gray-green vegetation against the lighter yellow-gray soil. Low shrubs with hard, waxy leaves grew every few meters along the gully floors, where they were protected from wind and sustained by the memory of moisture. The plants were scarcely noticeable at ground level, but they were the plain's only feature.

The butte was a dark mass at Des Grieux's back. In front of him, two kilometers to the south, was the Knifeblade Escarpment: a sheer wall of sandstone for a hundred kays east and west, except for the Notch carved by meltwater from a retreating glacier thirty millions of years in the past. A one in five slope led from the Notch to the plain below. It was barely negotiable by vehicles; but it *was* negotiable.

South of the escarpment, the Hashemites and their mercenaries faced the Sincanmo main force—and Hammer's Slammers. Task Force Kuykendall was emplaced to prevent the enemy from skirting the Knifeblade to the north and falling on the Slammers' flank and rear.

The Hashemites themselves would never think of that maneuver; the Thunderbolt Division could not possibly carry out such a plan in the time available. But Broglie was smart enough, and his troops were good enough . . . if he were willing to split his already outgunned force.

Alois Hammer wasn't willing to bet that Broglie wouldn't do what Hammer himself would do if the situation were desperate enough.

But neither did Hammer *expect* a real fight north of

the escarpment. All odds were that Task Force Kuykendall, two platoons of armor and 600-800 Sincanmo irregulars, would wait in bored silence while their fellows chewed on Hashemites until the Brotherhood surrendered unconditionally.

Thunder rumbled far beyond the distant horizon. In this climate, a storm was less likely than the Lord coming down to appoint Slick Des Grieux as master of the universe.

No, it was artillery promising imminent action. For other people.

The most recent bite of ration bar was a leaden mass in Des Grieux's mouth. He spat it into the darkness, then tossed the remainder of the bar away also.

"Booster," he said. "Close-up of the Notch."

A view of flamelit rock replaced the panorama before the last syllable was out of the tanker's mouth. The Hashemites were as feckless and unconcerned as their planetary enemies; and unlike the Sincanmos, the Hashemites didn't have the Slammers' logistics personnel to dispense an acre of camouflage film which would conceal equipment, personnel, and campfires from—hostile eyes.

Of course, the Hashemites didn't think there were any hostile eyes. They had stationed an outpost here to prevent the Sincanmos from using the Notch as a back door for attack, but the force was a nominal one of a few hundred indig troops with no leavening of mercenaries. The real defenses were the centrally-controlled mines placed in an arc as much as a kilometer north of the Notch.

The outpost hadn't seen Task Force Kuykendall move into position in the dark hours this morning. In a few hours or days, when the main battle ground to a conclusion, they would *still* be ignorant of the enemy watching them from the north.

The troops of the outpost probably thanked their Lord that they were safely out of the action . . . and they were.

Des Grieux swore softly.

The outpost had a pair of heavy weapons, truck-mounted railguns capable of pecking a hole in tank armor in twenty seconds or so. Des Grieux wouldn't *give* them twenty seconds, of course, but while he dealt with the railguns, the remainder of the Hashemites would loose a barrage of missiles at H271. And then there were the mines to cross. . . .

If the platoon's other three tanks were good for anything—if one of the crews was good for anything—it'd be possible to pick through the minefields with clearance charges, sonics, and ground-penetrating radar. Trusting *this* lot of newbies to provide covering fire would be like trusting another trooper with your girl and your bottle for the evening.

Kuykendall's platoon was of veterans, but she had orders to keep a low profile unless the enemy sallied out. Kuykendall took orders real good. She'd do fine with Colonel Bloody Broglie. . . .

Hashemites drank and played a game with dice and markers around fuel-oil campfires on the Notch. The sensor pack high on the mesa gave Des Grieux a beautiful view of the enemy, but they were beyond the line-of-sight range of his guns.

A salvo of artillery ricocheting from the sandstone walls would grind the towelheads to hamburger, but the shells would first have to get through the artillery defenses south of the Escarpment. Des Grieux remembered being told the first thing Broglie had done after taking command was to fit every armored vehicle in the Legion with a tribarrel capable of automatic artillery defense.

Guns muttered far to the south. When Des Grieux listened very carefully, he could distinguish the hiss-*crack* reports of big-bore powerguns. Tanks and tank destroyers were beginning to mix it—twenty kilometers away.

Des Grieux shivered and cursed; and after a time, he began to pray to a personal God of Battles. . . .

"Sir?" said Trooper Flowers from the narrow duct joining his station to H271's fighting compartment. The driver's shoulders were a tight fit in the passage. "I'm ready to take my watch, sir. Do you want me in the cupola, or . . . ?"

Des Grieux adjusted a vernier control on Screen #1,

dimming the topographic display fractionally. "I'm not 'sir,' "
he said. He didn't bother to look toward Flowers through
the cut-out sides of the turret basket. "And *I'll* worry about
keeping watch till I tell you different."

He returned his attention to Screen #3 on the right side
of the fighting compartment. It was live but blank in pearly
lustrousness; Des Grieux was missing a necessary link in
the feed he wanted to arrange.

"Ah, S-sergeant?" the driver said. The only light in the
fighting compartment was scatter from the holographic
screens. Flowers' face appeared to be slightly flushed.
"Sergeant Des Grieux? What do you want me to do?"

On the right—astern—edge of the topo screen, a company of Slammers' infantry supported by combat cars moved
up the range of broken hills held by the Thunderbolt
Division. The advance seemed slow, particularly because
the map scale was shrunk to encompass a ten-kilometer
battle area; but it was as certain and regular as a gear train.

If navigational data passed to the map display, then there
had to be a route for—

"Sir?" said Flowers.

"Go play with yourself!" Des Grieux snarled. He glared
angrily at his driver.

As Des Grieux's mind refocused to deal with the interruption, the answer to the main problem flashed before
him. *The information he wanted wasn't passing on the
command channels he'd been tapping out of the Regiment's
rear echelon back in Sanga: it was in the machine-to-
machine data links, untouched by human consciousness. . . .*

"Right," Des Grieux said mildly. "Look, just stick close
to the tank, okay, kid? Do anything you please."

Flowers ducked away, surprised at the tank commander's
sudden change of temper. His boots scuffled hollowly as
he backed through the internal hatch to the driver's compartment.

"Booster," Des Grieux ordered the tank's artificial intelligence, "switch to Utility Feed One and synthesize on
Screen Three."

The opalescent ready status on the right-hand screen

dissolved into multicolored garbage. Whatever data was coming through UF1 didn't lend itself to visual presentation.

"Via!" Des Grieux snarled. "Utility Feed Two." He heard boots on H271's hull, but he ignored them because Screen #3 was abruptly live with what appeared to be a live-action view through the gunnery screen of another tank. The orange circle of the main-gun pipper steadied on a slab of rock kilometers away. There was no visible target—

Until the point of aim disintegrated in a gout of white-hot glass under the impact of the twenty-CM powergun of another tank. The ledge cracked from heat shock. Half of it slid away to the left in a single piece, while the remainder crumbled into gravel.

Iridium armor gleamed beneath the pipper. Des Grieux's boot trod reflexively on his foot trip, but the safety interlock still disengaged his guns.

The real gunner, kilometers away, was only a fraction of a second slower. The image blurred with the recoil of the sending tank's main gun, and the target—a Legion tank destroyer—erupted at the heart of the cyan bolt.

"Sergeant Des Grieux?" said a voice from the open cupola hatch. "I'm just checking how all my people are—good Lord!"

Des Grieux looked up. Lieutenant Carbury, 3d Platoon's commanding officer and almost as new to the business of war as Des Grieux's driver was, stared at the images of Screen #3.

"What on earth is that?" Carbury begged/demanded as he turned to scramble backward into the fighting compartment of H271. "Is it happening now?"

"More or less," the veteran replied, deliberately vague. He pretended to ignore the lieutenant's intrusion by concentrating on the screen. His AI had switched the image feed to that from a gun camera on a combat car. Mortar rounds flashed in a series of white pulses from behind the hillcrest a hundred meters away.

The images were not full-spectrum transmissions. Each vehicle's artificial intelligence broadcast its positional and sensory data to the command vehicle of the unit to which it was attached. Part of the command vehicle's communications suite was responsible for routing necessary information—including sensory data stripped to digital shorthand to the central data banks at the Slammers' rear-area logistical headquarters.

The route was likely to be long and poor, because communications satellites were the first casualties of war. Here on Meridienne, the Regiment depended on a chain of laser transponders strung butte to butte along the line of march. When sandstorms disrupted the chain of coherent light, commo techs made do with signals bounced from whichever of Meridienne's moons were in a suitable location.

The signals did get through to the rear, though.

Des Grieux had set his tank's artificial intelligence to enter Central through Task Force Kuykendall's own long data link. The AI sorted out gunnery feeds, then synthesized the minimal squibs of information into three-dimensional holograms.

On Screen #3, fuel blazed from a vehicle struck by the probing mortar shells. A moment later a light truck accelerated up the forward slope of the next hill beyond. A dozen Hashemite irregulars clung to the truck. Their long robes flapped with the speed of their flight.

Des Grieux expected the camera through which he watched to record a stream of cyan bolts ripping the vehicle. Nothing happened. The Hashemite truck ducked over the crest to more distant cover again.

Three half-tracked APCs of the Thunderbolt Division grunted up the forward slope, following the Hashemite vehicle. Their steel-cleated treads sparked wildly on the stony surface.

The tribarrel through which Des Grieux watched and those of the combat car's two wing gunners poured a converging fire into the center APC. It exploded, flinging out the fiery bodies of Thunderbolt infantrymen. The rest of the combat car platoon concentrated on the other two carriers. Their thin armor collapsed with similar results.

Slammers infantry on one-man skimmers slid forward to consolidate the new position just as Des Grieux's AI cut to a new viewpoint.

"How do you *do* that?" asked Lieutenant Carbury as he stared at the vivid scenes.

The platoon leader was as slim as Des Grieux and considerably shorter, but the fighting compartment of a line tank had not been designed for two-person occupancy. Des Grieux could have provided a little more room by folding his seat against the bulkhead, but he pointedly failed to do so.

"Prob'ly the same way they showed you at the Academy," Des Grieux said. *They didn't teach cadets how to use a tank's artificial intelligence to break into Central, but Via! they were fully compatible systems.* "Sir."

The sound of real gunfire whispered through the night.

"Wow," said Carbury. He was sucking in his belly so that he could lean toward Screen #3 without pressing the veteran's shoulder. "Exactly what is it that's happening, Sergeant? They, ah, they aren't updating me very regularly."

Des Grieux rotated his chair counterclockwise. The back squeezed Carbury against the turret basket until the lieutenant managed to slip aside.

"It's all right there," Des Grieux said, pointing toward the map display on Screen #1. "He's got Broglie held on the left—" orange symbols toward the western edge of the display "—but that's just sniping, no *way* they're gonna push Broglie out of ground that rugged."

He gathered spit in his mouth, then swallowed it. "The bastard's good," the veteran muttered to himself. "I give him that."

"Right," said Carbury firmly in a conscious attempt to assert himself. Strategy *was* a major part of the syllabus of the Frisian Military Academy. "So instead he's putting pressure on the right flank where the terrain's easier—"

Not a lot easier, but at least the hills didn't channel tanks and combat cars into a handful of choke points.

"—and there's only the Thunderbolt Division to worry

about." Carbury frowned. "Besides the Hashemites themselves, of course."

"*You* worry about the towelheads," Des Grieux said acidly. He glared at the long arc of yellow symbols marking elements of the Thunderbolt Division.

Though the enemy's eastern flank was anchored on hills rising to join the Knifeblade Escarpment well beyond the limits of the display, the center of the long line stretched across terrain similar to that in which Task Force Kuykendall waited. Gullies; scattered shrubs; hard, windswept ground that rolled more gently than a calm sea.

Perfect country for a headlong armored assault.

"*That's* what he ought to do," Des Grieux said, more to himself than to the intruding officer. He formed three fingers of his left hand into a pitchfork and stabbed them upward past the line of yellow symbols.

On Screen #3 at the corner of his eye, an image flashed into a cyan dazzle as another main-gun bolt struck home.

"Umm," said Carbury judiciously. "It's not really that simple, Sergeant." His manicured index finger bobbed toward the left, then the right edge of the display. "They'd be enfiladed by fire from the Legion, and even the Thunderbolts have anti-tank weapons. You wouldn't want to do that."

Des Grieux turned and stared up at the lieutenant. "Try me," he said. The tone was unemotional, but Carbury's head jerked back from the impact of the veteran's eyes.

Screen #3 showed a distant landscape through the sights of a combat-car tribarrel. The image expanded suddenly as the gunner dialed up times forty magnification. The target was a—

Des Grieux's attention clicked instantly to the display. Freed from the veteran's glare, Carbury blinked and focused on the distant scene also.

The target was a Thunderbolt calliope, shooting upward from a pit that protected the eight-barreled weapon while it knocked incoming artillery shells from the air. The high ground which the combat car had gained gave its tribarrels a slanting view down at the calliope four kilometers away.

The line-straight bolts from a powergun cared nothing for distance, so long as no solid object intervened. A five-round burst from the viewpoint tribarrel raked the gun pit, reducing half the joined barrels and the crew to ions.

That would have been enough, but the calliope was in action when the bolts struck it. One of the weapon's own high-intensity three CM rounds discharged in a barrel which the Slammers' fire had already welded shut.

A blue-white explosion blew open the multiple breeches. That was only the momentary prelude to the simultaneous detonation of the contents of an ammunition drum. Plasma scooped out the sides of the gun pit and reflected pitilessly from rockfaces several kilometers away.

As if an echo, three more of the Thunderbolt Division's protective calliopes exploded with equal fury.

The Slammers' toehold on the eastern hills wasn't the overture to further slogging advances on the same flank: it was a vantage point from which to destroy at long range the artillery defenses of the entire hostile center.

"Good *Lord*," Lieutenant Carbury gasped. He leaned forward in amazement for a closer view. Des Grieux shoved Carbury back with as little conscious volition.

H271's artificial intelligence switched its viewpoint to that of a jeep-mounted infantry tribarrel. Six red streaks fanned through the sky above the narrow wedge of vision, a full salvo from a battery of the Slammers' rocket artillery.

Powerguns fired from the hills to the west. Some of Broglie's defensive weapons had retargeted abruptly to help close the sudden gap in the center of the line. That was dangerous, though, since Hammer's other two batteries continued to pound the flanks of the enemy position.

Broglie's powerguns detonated two of the incoming shells into bright flashes and smears of ugly smoke. The help was too little, too late: the other four firecracker rounds popped open at preset altitudes and strewed their deadly cargo widely over the Thunderbolt lines.

For the moments that the anti-personnel bomblets took to fall, nothing seemed to happen. Then white light like burning magnesium erupted over four square kilometers. Hair-fine lengths of glass shrapnel sawed in all directions. The coverage was thin, but the blasts carved apart anyone within a meter of an individual bomblet.

Lieutenant Carbury jumped for the hatch, aiming his right boot at the back of the tank commander's seat but using Des Grieux's shoulder as a step instead. "Remote that feed to my tank *now*, Sergeant!" the lieutenant shouted as he pulled himself out of H271's cupola.

Des Grieux ignored Carbury and keyed his intercom. *Flowers had better be wearing his commo helmet.* "Driver!" the veteran snarled. "Get your ass aboard!"

On Screen #3, another salvo of anti-personnel shells howled down onto the Thunderbolt Division's reeling battalions.

Powerguns snapped and blasted at a succession of targets on H271's right-hand screen. For the past several minutes, the real excitement, even for Des Grieux, was on the map display on the other side of the fighting compartment.

The Hashemites and their mercenary allies were getting their clocks cleaned.

The AI's interpretation of data from the battle area cross-hatched all the units of the Thunderbolt Division which were still on the plain. A few minutes of hammering with firecracker rounds had reduced the units by twenty percent of their strength from casualties—

And to something closer to zero combat efficiency because of their total collapse of morale. The battle wasn't over yet, but it was over for *those* men and women. They retreated northward in disorder, some of them on foot without even their personal weapons. Their only thought was to escape the killing zone of artillery and long-range sniping from the Slammers' powerguns.

Half of the Thunderbolt Division remained as an effective fighting force on the high ground to the east—the original left-flank battalions and the troops which had retreated to their protection under fire. Even those units were demoralized, but they would hold against anything except an all-out attack from the Slammers.

If the mercenary commander surrendered now, while his position was tenable and his employers were still fighting, the Thunderbolt Division would forfeit the performance bond it had posted with the Bonding Authority on Terra. That would end the division as an employable force—and shoot the career of its commander in the nape of the neck.

H271 quivered as its fans spun at idle. The tank was ready to go at a touch on the throttle and pitch controls. "Sarge?" Flowers asked over the intercom channel. "Are we gonna move out soon?"

"Kid," Des Grieux said as he watched holographic dots crawling across holographic terrain, "when I want to hear your voice, I'll tell you."

If he hadn't been so concentrated on the display, he would have snarled the words.

The Thunderbolt Division's employers weren't exactly fighting, but neither had they surrendered. The Hashemite Brotherhood was no more of a monolith than were their Sincanmo enemies; and Hashemite troops were concentrated on the plains, where their mobility seemed an advantage. Des Grieux suspected that the Hashemites *would* have surrendered by now if they'd had enough organization left to manage it.

Broglie's armored elements on what had been the Hashemite right flank, now cut off from friendly forces by the collapse of the center, formed a defensive hedgehog among the sandstone boulders. The terrain gave them an advantage that would translate into prohibitive casualties for anybody trying to drive them out—even the panzers of Colonel Hammer's tank companies. Broglie's Legion wasn't going anywhere.

But Broglie himself had.

Within thirty seconds of the time artillery defense had collapsed in the center of the Hashemite line, four tank destroyers sped from the Legion's strong point to reinforce the Thunderbolt infantry. There was no time to redeploy vehicles already in the line, and Broglie had no proper reserve. These tank destroyers were the Legion's Headquarters/Headquarters Platoon.

The move was as desperate as the situation itself. Des Grieux wasn't surprised to learn Broglie had figured the only possible way out of Colonel Hammer's trap, but it was amazing to see that Broglie had the balls to put himself on the line that way. Des Grieux figured that Broglie obeyed orders because he was too chicken not to. . . .

By using gullies and the rolling terrain, three of the low-slung vehicles managed to get into position. The single loss was a tank destroyer that paused to spike a combat car five kilometers away on the Slammers' right flank. A moment later, the Legion vehicle vanished under the impact of five nearly-simultaneous twenty-CM bolts from Slammers' tanks.

Tribarrels on the roofs of the three surviving tank destroyers ripped effectively at incoming artillery, detonating the cargo shells before they strewed their bomblets over the landscape. The tank destroyers' fifteen-CM main guns were a threat nothing, not even a bow-on tank, could afford to ignore. The leap-frog advance of Slammers' units toward the gap in the enemy center slowed to a lethal game of hide-and-seek.

But it was still too little, too late. The Hashemite and Thunderbolt Division troops were broken and streaming northward. All the tank destroyers could do was act as a rear guard, like Horatius and his two companions.

There was no bridge on their line of retreat, but the only practical route down from the Knifeblade Escarpment was through the Notch. Task Force Kuykendall and tank H271 had that passage sealed, as clever-ass *Colonel* Luke Broglie would learn within the next half hour.

Des Grieux began to chuckle hoarsely as he watched beads ooze across a background of coherent light. The sound that came from his throat blended well with the increasingly loud mutter of gunfire from south of the escarpment.

"Shellfish Six to all Oyster and Clam elements," Des Grieux's helmet said.

Des Grieux had ignored the chatter which broke out among the Slammers' vehicles—the combat cars were code named Oyster; the tanks were Clam—as soon as Carbury gave the alarm. He couldn't ignore this summons, because it was the commander of Shellfish—Task Force Kuykendall—speaking over a unit priority channel.

"All blower captains to me at Golf Six-five ASAP. Acknowledge. Over."

This was no bloody time to have all the senior people standing around in a gully, listening to some bitch with lieutenant's pips on her collar!

There were blips of static on Des Grieux's headset. Several commanders used the automatic response set on their consoles instead of replying—protesting—in person.

"Clam Six to Shellfish Six . . ." said Lieutenant Carbury nervously. The tank-platoon commander was not only beneath Kuykendall in the chain of command, he was well aware that she was a ten-year veteran of the Slammers while he had yet to see action. "Suggest we link our vehicles for a virtual council, sir. Over."

"Negative," Kuykendall snapped. "I need to make a point to our employers and allies, here, Clam Six, and they're not in the holographic environment."

She paused, then added in a coldly neutral voice. "Break. This means you, too, Slick. Don't push your luck. Shellfish Six out."

Des Grieux cursed under his breath. After a moment, he slid his seat upward and climbed out of the tank. He'd grabbed a grenade launcher and a bandolier of ammunition at the depot; he carried them in his left hand.

He didn't acknowledge the summons.

Occasional flashes to the south threw the Knifeblade Escarpment into hazy relief, like a cloudbank lighted by a distant storm. Sometimes the wind sounded like human cries.

The gullies at the base of the butte twisted Task Force Kuykendall's position like the guts of a worm. Two combat cars and a tank were placed between H271 and Kuykendall's vehicle, *Firewalker*, in the rough center of the line. The gaps between the Slammers' units were filled by indigs in family battlegroups.

The restive Sincanmos had let their campfires burn down. The way through the gullies was marked by metal buckets glowing from residual heat. Men in bright, loose garments fingered their personal weapons and watched Des Grieux as he trudged past.

There was a group of fifty or more armed troops—all men except for Kuykendall and one of the tank commanders, and overwhelmingly indigs—gathered at *Firewalker* when Des Grieux arrived. Kuykendall had switched on the car's running lights with deep yellow filters in place to preserve the night vision of those illuminated.

"Glad you could make it, Slick," Kuykendall said. She perched on cargo slung to the side of her combat car. It was hard to make out Kuykendall's words over the burble of Sincanmo conversation because she spoke without electronic amplification. "I want all of you to hear what I just informed Chief Diabate."

The name of the senior Sincanmo leader in the task force brought a partial hush. Men turned to look at Diabate, white-bearded and more hawk-faced than most of his fellows. He wore a robe printed in an intricate pattern of black/russet/white, over which were slung a two-CM powergun and three silver-mounted knives in a sash.

"Colonel Hammer has ordered us back ten kays," Kuykendall continued. Two crewmen stood at *Firewalker*'s wing tribarrels, but the weapons were aimed toward the Notch. The air of the gathering was amazement, not violence. "So we're moving out in half an hour."

"Don't be bloody crazy!" Des Grieux shouted over the indig babble. "*You* saw what's happening south of the wall."

He pointed the barrel of his grenade launcher toward the Escarpment. The bandolier swung heavily in the same hand. "Inside an hour, there'll be ten thousand people trying t' get through the Notch, and *we're* here t' shut the door in their face?

Sincanmo elders shook their guns in the air and cried approval.

Kuykendall's sharp features pinched tighter. She muttered an order to *Firewalker*'s AI, then—regardless of the Hashemites in the Notch—blared through the combat car's external speakers, "*Listen* to me, gentlemen!"

Her voice echoed like angry thunder from the face of the butte. Shouting men blinked and looked at her.

"The Colonel *wants* them to run away instead of fighting like cornered rats," Kuykendall went on, speaking normally but continuing to use amplification. "He wants a surrender, not a bloodbath."

"But—" Chief Diabate protested.

"What the Colonel orders," Kuykendall said firmly, "I carry out. And I'm in charge of this task force, by order of your own council."

"We know the Hashemites!" Diabate said. This time, Kuykendall let him speak. "If they throw away their guns and flee now, they will find more guns later. Only if we kill them all can we be sure of peace. This is the time to kill them!"

"I've got my orders," Kuykendall said curtly, "and you've got yours. Slammers elements, saddle up. We move out in twenty . . . seven minutes."

Khaki-uniformed mercenaries turned away, shrugging at the slings and holsters of their personal weapons. Des Grieux did not move for a moment.

"I wanted you to see," Kuykendall continued to the shocked Sincanmo elders. "This isn't a tribal council, this is war and I'm in charge. If you refuse to obey my orders, *you're* in breach of the contract, not me and Colonel Hammer."

Sincanmos shouted in anger and surprise. Des Grieux strode away from the crowd, muttering commands through his commo helmet to the artificial intelligence in H271. The AI obediently projected a view of the terrain still closer to the base of the mesa onto the left side of Des Grieux's visor.

Flowers waited with his torso out of the driver's hatch. "What's the word, Sarge?" he called as Des Grieux stepped around the back of a Sincanmo truck mounted with a cage launcher and a quartet of forty-kilo bombardment rockets.

"We're moving," Des Grieux said. He lifted himself to the deck of his tank. "There's a low spot twenty meters from the base of the butte. I'll give directions on your screen. Park us there."

He clambered up the turret side and thrust his legs through the hatch.

"Ah, Sarge?" Flowers called worriedly. The curved armor hid him from Des Grieux. "Should I take down the cammie film?"

Des Grieux switched to intercom. Screen #1 now showed the terrain in the immediate vicinity of H271. The site Des Grieux had picked was within two hundred meters of the tank's present location.

"It'll bloody come down when you bloody drive through it, won't it?" Des Grieux snarled. He slashed his finger across the topo map, marking the intended route with a glowing line that echoed on the driver's display. "Do it!"

The microns-thick camouflage film was strung, then jolted with high-frequency electricity which caused it to take an optical set in the pattern and colors of the ground underneath it. The film was polarized to pass light impinging on the upper surfaces but to block it from below. The covering was permeable to air as well, though it did impede ventilation somewhat.

H271's fans snorted at increased power, sucking the thin membrane against its stretchers. Sincanmo troops moved closer to their own vehicles, eyeing the 170-tonne tank with concern.

Flowers rotated H271 carefully in its own length, then drove slowly up the back slope of the gully. The nearest twenty-meter length of camouflage film bowed, then flew apart when the stresses exceeded its limits. Gritty soil puffed from beneath the tank's skirts.

"Clam Four, this is Clam Six," said Lieutenant Carbury over the 3rd Platoon push. "What's going on there? Over."

Des Grieux closed the cupola hatch above him. This was

going to be very tricky. Not placing the shot—he could do that at ten kays—but determining where the shot had to *be* placed.

H271 lurched as Flowers drove it down into a wash-out directly at the base of the mesa. Des Grieux let the tank settle as he searched the sandstone face through his gunnery screen.

"This where you want us, Sarge?" Flowers asked.

"Clam Four, this is Shellfish Six. Report! Over."

"Right," said Des Grieux over the intercom. "Shut her down. Is your hatch closed?"

The intake howl dimmed into the sighing note of fans winding down. Iridium clanged forward as Flowers slammed his hatch.

"Yessir," he said.

Des Grieux fired his main gun. Cyan light filled the world.

The rockface cracked with a sound like the planetary mantle splitting. The shattered cliff slumped forward in chunks ranging in size from several tons to microscopic beads of glass. H271 rang and shuddered as the wave of rubble swept across it, sliding up against the turret.

"Clam Four to Clam Six," Des Grieux said. He didn't try to keep his voice free of the satisfaction he felt at the perfect execution of his plan. "I've had an accidental discharge of my main gun. No injuries, but I'm afraid my tank can't be moved without mebbe a day's work by heavy equipment. Over."

"Slick," said Lieutenant Kuykendall, "you stupid son of a bitch."

She must have expected something like this, because she didn't bother raising her voice.

Kuykendall's right wing gunner worked over the Notch with his tribarrel as *Firewalker* idled at the base of the butte.

When H271 lighted the night with its main gun, the Hashemites guarding the Notch came to panicked alertness. During the ten minutes since, combat cars fired short bursts to keep enemy heads down while the Slammers pulled out.

This thirty-second slashing was different. The gunner's needless expenditure of ammunition was a way to let out his frustration—at what Des Grieux had done, or at the fact that the rest of the Slammers were running while Des Grieux and the indigs stayed to fight.

The troopers of Task Force Kuykendall were professional soldiers. If they'd been afraid of a fight, they would have found some other line of work.

Kuykendall squeezed the gunner's biceps, just beneath the shoulder flare of his body armor. The trooper's thumbs came off the butterfly trigger. The weapon's barrel-set continued to rotate for several seconds to aid in cooling. The white-hot iridium muzzles glowed a circle around their common axis.

Trooper Flowers lifted himself into *Firewalker*'s fighting compartment. His personal gear—in a dufflebag; Flowers was too junior to have snagged large-capacity ammo cans to hold his belongings—was slung to the vehicle's side. Combat cars made room for extra personnel more easily than Carbury's remaining tanks could.

Des Grieux braced his feet against the cupola coaming and used his leg muscles to shove at a block of sandstone the size of his torso. Thrust overcame friction. The slab slid across a layer of gravel, then toppled onto H271's back deck.

The upper surfaces were clear enough now that Des Grieux could rotate the turret.

Lieutenant Carbury's *Paper Doll* was an old tank, frequently repaired. An earlier commander had painted kill rings on the stubby barrel of the main gun. Holographic screens within the fighting compartment illuminated Carbury from below. His fresh, youthful face was out of place peering from the veteran vehicle.

"Sergeant Des Grieux," the lieutenant said. His voice was pitched too high for the tone of command he wished to project. "You're acting like a fool by staying here, and you're disobeying my direct orders."

Carbury spoke directly across the twenty meters between himself and tank H271 instead of using his commo helmet. The *hoosh* of lift fans idling almost washed his voice away. In another few seconds, minutes at most, Des Grieux would be alone with fate.

The veteran brushed his palms against the front of his jumpsuit. He had to be careful not to rub his hands raw while moving rocks. He'd need delicate control soon, with the opening range at two kays.

"Sorry, sir," he called. "I figure the accident's my fault. It's my duty to stay with the tank since I'm the one who disabled it."

A combat car spat at the Notch. The Sincanmos, still under their camouflage film, were keeping as quiet as cats in ambush while the two platoons of armored vehicles maneuvered out of the gullies.

The Sincanmos didn't take orders real well, but they were willing to do whatever was required for a chance to kill. Des Grieux felt a momentary sympathy for the indigs, knowing what was about to happen.

But Via! if they hadn't been a bunch of stupid wogs, they'd have known, too. They weren't his problem.

"Clam Six," said Lieutenant Kuykendall remotely, "this is Shellfish Six." She used radio, a frequency limited to the Slammers within the task force. "Are all your elements ready to move? Over."

Carbury stiffened and touched the frequency key on the side of his commo helmet. "Clam Six to Six," he said. "Yessir, all ready. Over."

Instead of giving the order, Kuykendall turned to look at Des Grieux. She raised the polarized shield of her visor. "Goodbye, Slick," she called across the curtain of disturbed air. "I don't guess I'll be seeing you again."

Des Grieux stared at the woman who had been his driver a decade before. They were twenty meters apart, but she still flinched minutely at his expression.

Des Grieux smiled. "Don't count on that, Lieutenant-sir," he said.

Kuykendall slapped her visor down and spoke a curt

order. Fan notes changed, the more lightly-loaded rotors of the combat cars rising in pitch faster than those of the tanks.

Moving in unison with a tank in the lead, the Slammers of Task Force Kuykendall howled off into the night. Their powerguns, main guns as well as tribarrels, lashed the Notch in an unmistakable farewell gesture. The sharp *crack* of the bolts and the dazzling actinics reflected back and forth between the Escarpment and the sheer face of the mesa.

For Des Grieux, the huge vehicles had a beauty like that of nothing else in existence. They skated lightly over the soil, gathering speed in imperceptible increments. Occasionally a skirt touched down and sparked, steel against shards of quartz. Then they were gone around the mesa, leaving the sharpness of ozone and the ghost-track of ionized air dissipating where a main gun had fired at the Hashemites.

Des Grieux felt a sudden emptiness; but it was too late now to change, and anyway, it didn't matter. He slid down into H271 and tried his gunnery controls again. Added weight resisted the turret motors briefly, but this time it was only gravel and smaller particles which could rearrange themselves easily.

The sight picture on H271's main screen rotated: off the blank wall of the butte and across open desert, to the Notch that marred the otherwise smooth profile of the Knifeblade Escarpment. Des Grieux raised the magnification. Plus twenty; plus forty, and he could see movement as Hashemites crawled forward, over rocks split and glazed by blue-white bolts, to see why the punishing fire had ceased; plus eighty—

A Hashemite wearing a turban and a dark blue jellaba swept the night with the image-intensifying sight of his back-pack missile.

He found nothing. Des Grieux stared at the Hashemite's bearded face until the man put down his sight and called his fellows forward. His optics were crude compared to those of H271, and the Hashemite didn't know where to look.

Des Grieux smiled grimly and shut down all his tank's

systems. From now until he slammed home the main switch again, Des Grieux would wait in a silent iridium coffin.

It wasn't his turn. Yet. He raised his head through the cupola hatch and watched.

Because of the patient silence the Sincanmos had maintained, Des Grieux expected the next stage to occur in about half an hour. In fact, it was less than five minutes after the Slammers' armored vehicles had noisily departed the scene before one of the outposts switched the minefield controls to Self Destruct. Nearly a thousand charges went off simultaneously, any one of them able to destroy a 4x4 or cripple a tank.

An all-wheel drive truck laden with towelheads lurched over the lip of the Notch and started for the plains below.

The locals on both sides were irregulars, but the Sincanmos in ambush had something concrete to await. All the Hashemite guards knew was that a disaster had occurred south of the Escarpment, and that they had themselves been released from a danger unguessed until the Slammers drove off through the night. *They* saw no reason to hold position, whatever their orders might be.

Three more trucks followed the first—a family battlegroup, organized like those of the Sincanmos. One of the vehicles towed a railgun on a four-wheeled carriage. The slope was a steep twenty percent. The railgun threatened to swing ahead every time the towing vehicle braked, but the last truck in the group held the weapon's barrel with a drag line to prevent upset.

The Sincanmos did not react.

A dozen more trucks grunted into sight. H271's sensors could have placed and identified the vehicles while they were still hidden behind the lip of rock, but it didn't matter one way or the other to Des Grieux. Better to keep still, concealed even from sensors far more sophisticated than those available to the indigs.

More trucks. They poured out of the Notch, three and four abreast, as many as the narrow opening would accept.

Forty, sixty—still more. The entire outpost was fleeing at its best speed.

The Hashemites must have argued violently. Should they go or stay? Was the blocking force really gone, or did it lurk on the other side of the butte, waiting to swing back into sight spewing blue fire?

But somebody was bound to run; and when that group seemed on the verge of successful escape, the others would follow as surely as day follows night.

There would be no day for most of this group of Hashemites. When their leading vehicles reached the bottom of the slope, the Sincanmos opened up with a devastating volley.

The two-kilometer range was too great for sidearms to be generally effective, though Des Grieux saw a bolt from a semi-automatic powergun—perhaps Chief Diabate's personal weapon—light up a truck cab. The vehicle went out of control and rolled sideways. Upholstery and the driver's garments were afire even before ammunition and fuel caught.

Mostly the ambush was work for the crew-served weapons. For the Sincanmo gunners, it was practice with live pop-up targets. Dozens of automatic cannon punched tracers into and through soft-skinned vehicles, leaving flames and torn flesh behind them. Mortars fired, mixing high explosive and incendiary bombs. Truck-mounted lasers cycled with low-frequency growls, igniting paint, tires, and cloth before sliding across the rock to new targets.

A pair of perfectly-aimed bombardment rockets landed within the Notch itself, causing fires and secondary explosions among the tail end of the line of would-be escapees. The smooth, inclined surface of the Escarpment provided no concealment, no hope. Hashemites stood or ran, but they died in either case.

Des Grieux smiled like a sickle blade and pulled the hatch closed above him. He continued to watch through the vision blocks of the cupola.

Truckloads of Sincanmo troops drove up out of their concealment, heading for the loot and the writhing wounded scattered helplessly on the slope.

Have fun while you can, wogs, Des Grieux thought. *Because you won't see the morning either.*

Thirty-seven minutes after Chief Diabate sprang his ambush, Sincanmo troops in the Notch began firing southward. The shooters were the bands who'd penetrated farthest in their quest for loot and throats to cut. Other bright-robed irregulars were picking over the bodies and vehicles scattered along the slope. When the guns sounded, they looked up and began to jabber among themselves in search of a consensus.

Des Grieux watched through his vision blocks and waited. H271's fighting compartment was warm and muggy with the environmental system shut down, but a cold sweat of anticipation beaded the tanker's upper lip.

Half—apparently the junior half—of each Sincanmo battlegroup waited under camouflage film in the gullies to provide a base of fire for the looters. The Sincanmos were not so much undisciplined as self-willed, and they had a great deal of experience in hit-and-run guerrilla warfare.

The appearance of a well-prepared defense was deceptive, though. The heavy weapons that were effective at a two-kilometer range had expended much of their ammunition in the first engagement; and besides, the irregulars were about to find themselves out of their depth.

They were facing the first of the retreating Thunderbolt Division troops. The Thunderbolts weren't much; but they were professionals, and this lot had Luke Broglie with them. . . .

At first the Sincanmos in the Notch fired small arms at their unseen targets; automatic rifles pecked the night with short bursts. Then somebody got an abandoned Hashemite railgun working. The Notch lighted in quick pulses, the corona discharge from the weapon's generator. The *crackcrackcrack* of hypervelocity slugs echoed viciously.

A blue-white dazzle outlined the rock surfaces of the Notch. A Legion tank destroyer kilometers away had put a fifteen-CM bolt into the center of the captured outpost. Two seconds later the sound reached Des Grieux's ears, the glass-breaking *crash* as rock shattered under unendurable heat stresses.

Three Sincanmo survivors scampered down the Escarpment. One man's robe smoldered and left a fine trail of smoke behind him. The men were on foot, because their trucks fed the orange-red flames lighting the Notch behind them.

The Sincanmo irregulars had gotten their first lesson. A siren on Chief Diabate's 8x8 armored car, halfway up the slope, wound slowly from a groan to a wail. Exhaust blatted through open pipes as the indigs leaped aboard their vehicles and started the engines.

The first salvo howled from the Thunderbolt Division's makeshift redoubt to the southeast. The shells burst with bright orange flashes in the empty plains, causing no casualties. The Sincanmos were either in the gullies well north of the impact area or still on the slope, where the height of the Knifeblade Escarpment provided a wall against shells on simple ballistic trajectories.

Indig vehicles grunted downslope as members of their crews threw themselves aboard. Another four-tube salvo of high explosive struck near where the previous rounds had landed. One shell simply dug itself into the hard soil without going off. Casing fragments rang against the side of a truck, but none of the vehicles slowed or swerved.

The camouflage film fluttered as indigs in the gullies packed their belongings. The trucks were both cargo haulers and weapons platforms for the battle groups. When the Sincanmos expected action, they cached non-essentials— food, water, tents and bedding—beside the vehicles, then tossed them aboard again when it was time to leave.

Another round streaked across the Escarpment from the south*west*. The Sincanmos ignored the shell because it didn't come within a kilometer of the ground at any point in its trajectory.

Broglie's Legion had a single six-gun battery, very well equipped as to weapons (self-propelled 210-mm rocket howitzers) and the selection of shells those hogs launched. The battery's first response to the new threat was a reconnaissance round which provided real-time images through a laser link to Battery Fire Control.

Had Des Grieux powered up H271, his tribarrel in Automatic Artillery Defense mode could have slapped the spy shell down as soon as it sailed over the Escarpment. It was no part of the veteran's plan to give the tank's presence away so soon, however.

At least thirty guns from the Thunderbolt Division opened fire according to target data passed them by the Legion's fire control. Spurts of black smoke with orange hearts leaped like poplars among the Sincanmo positions, shredding camouflage film that had not deceived the Legion's recce package.

A truck blew up. Men were screaming. Vehicles racing back from the slope to load cached necessities skidded uncertainly as their crews wondered whether or not to drive into the shellbursts ahead of them.

The Legion's howitzers ripped out a perfect Battery Three, three shells per gun launched within a total of ten seconds. They were firecracker rounds. The casings popped high in the air, loosing approximately 7,500 bomblets to drift down on the Sincanmo forces.

For the most part, the Sincanmo looters under Chief Diabate didn't know what hit them. A blanket of white fire fell over the vehicles which milled across the plain for fear of Thunderbolt shells. Thousands of bomblets exploded with a ripping sound that seemed to go on forever.

For those in the broad impact zone, it *was* forever. Smoke and dust lifted over the soil when the explosive light ceased. A dozen Sincanmo vehicles were ablaze; more crashed and ignited in the following seconds. Only a handful of trucks were under conscious control, though run-while-flat tires let many of the vehicles careen across the landscape with their crews flayed to the bone by glass-filament shrapnel.

Fuel and munitions exploded as the Thunderbolt Division continued to pound the gully positions. A pair of heavy caliber shells landed near H271, but they were overs—no cause for concern. The indigs dying all across the plain provided a perfect stalking horse for the tank in ambush.

Chief Diabate's armored car—the only vehicle in the Sincanmo force with real armor—had come through the barrage unscathed. It wallowed toward the eastern flank of the butte with its siren summoning survivors from the gullies to follow it to safety. Sincanmo 4x4s lurched through the remnants of the camouflage film, abandoning their cached supplies to the needs of the moment.

Sparks and rock fragments sprang up before and beside the armored car. Diabate's driver swerved, but not far enough: a second three-round burst punched through the car's thin armor. A yellow flash lifted the turret, but the vehicle continued to roll on inertia until a larger explosion blew the remainder of the car and crew into pieces no larger than a man's hand.

Leading elements of the Thunderbolt Division had reached the Notch. One of them was a fire support vehicle, a burst-capable ninety-MM gun on a half-tracked chassis. The gun continued to fire, switching from solid shot to high explosive as it picked its targets among the fleeing Sincanmo trucks. Other mercenary vehicles, primarily armored personnel carriers with additional troops riding on their roofs, crawled through the Notch and descended the slope littered by the bodies of indigs locked in the embrace of death.

It was getting to be time. Des Grieux closed his main power switch.

H271's screens came alive and bathed the fighting compartment with their light. Des Grieux lifted his commo helmet, ran his fingers through his close-cropped hair, and lowered the helmet again. He took the twin joysticks of the gunnery controls in his hands.

"Booster," Des Grieux said to the tank's artificial intelligence. "On Screen One, gimme vehicles on a four-kay by one strip aligned with the main gun."

The topographic map of the main battle area flicked out and returned as a narrow holographic slice centered on the Notch. The APCs and other vehicles already north of the

Knifeblade Escarpment were sharp symbols that crawled down the holographic slope toward—unbeknownst to themselves—H271 waiting at the bottom of the display.

The symbols of vehicles on the other side of the sandstone wall were hollow, indicating the AI had to extrapolate from untrustworthy data. The electronics, pumps, and even ignition systems of Thunderbolt and Hashemite trucks had individual radio-frequency spectrum signatures which H271's sensor suite could read. Precise location and assignment was impossible at a four-kilometer range beyond an intervening mass of sandstone, however.

One vehicle was marked with orange precision: the Legion tank destroyer which had huffed itself to within five hundred meters of the Notch. The tank destroyer's tribarrel licked skyward frequently to keep shells from decimating the retreating forces. The lines of cyan fire, transposed onto the terrain map in the tank's data base, provided H271 with a precise location for the oncoming vehicle. The other two tank destroyers were at the very top of the display, where they acted as rear guard against the Slammers.

They would come in good time. As for the closest of the three—it would have been nice to take out the tank destroyer with the first bolt, the round that unmasked H271, but that wasn't necessary. Waiting for the Legion vehicle to rise into range would mean sparing some of the half-tracks that drove off the slope and disappeared into swales concealed from the tank.

Des Grieux didn't intend to spare anything that moved this night.

The gunnery screen shrank in scale as it incorporated both orange pippers, the solid dot that marked the tribarrel's target—the leading APC, covered by the flowing robes of a score of Hashemites riding on top of it—and the main-gun's hollow circle, centered at the turret/hill junction on the fire support vehicle which still, from its vantage point in the Notch, covered the retreat.

Des Grieux fired both weapons together.

It took a dozen rounds from the tribarrel before the

carrier blew up. By then, the screaming Hashemite riders were torches flopping over the rocks.

The main-gun's twenty-CM bolt vaporized several square meters of the fire support vehicle's armor. Ammunition the Thunderbolts hadn't expended on Sincanmo targets were sufficient to blow a passing APC against the far wall of the Notch; the crumpled wreckage then slid forward, down the slope, shedding parts and flames.

Nothing remained of the fire support vehicle except its axles and wheels, stripped of their tires.

Des Grieux left his main gun pointed as it was. He worked the tribarrel up the line of easy targets against the slanted rock, giving each half-track the number of cyan bolts required to detonate its fuel, its on-board ammunition, or both. Secondary explosions leaped onto the slope like the footprints of a fire giant.

Nothing more came through the Notch after the twenty-CM bolt ripped it, but Screen #1 showed the Legion tank destroyer accelerating at its best speed to reach a firing position.

Des Grieux's face was terrible in its joy.

So long as H271 was shut down and covered by broken rock, it was virtually indetectable. When Des Grieux opened fire, anybody but a blind man could call artillery in on the tank's position. A number of Thunderbolt Division personnel survived long enough to do just that.

Four HE shells landed between ten and fifty meters of H271 as Des Grieux walked two-CM bolts across an open-topped supply truck with armored sides. His sight picture vanished for a moment in the spouting explosions. A fifth round struck in a scatter of gravel well up the side of the mesa. It brought down a minor rockslide, but no significant chunks landed near the tank.

Des Grieux ignored the artillery because he didn't have any choice. He'd ignited all eight of the supply truck's lowside tires with the initial burst. When the debris of the shellbursts cleared, the vehicle was toppling sideways. Its cargo compartment was full of wounded troops who screamed as they went over.

Twenty or thirty shells landed within a dozen seconds. A few of the Thunderbolt gun crews had switched to armor piercing, but none of those rounds scored a direct hit on the tank. A heavy shell burst on H271's rock-covered back deck. The shock made all the displays quiver. The air of the fighting compartment filled with dust shaken from every minute crevice.

Screen #1 showed the Legion tank destroyer's orange symbol entering the Notch from the south side. The heavy vehicle had collided with several Thunderbolt Division APCs in its haste to reach a position from which it could fire at the Slammers' tank.

Des Grieux slapped the plate that set his tribarrel on Automatic Artillery Defense. He said in a sharp, clear voice, "Booster, sort incoming from the southeast first," as his foot poised on the firing pedal for the main gun.

The twenty-CM weapon was already aligned. The eighty-times magnified tube of the tank destroyer's gun slid into the hollow circle on Screen #2. More shells burst near H271, but not very near, and the tribarrel was already snarling skyward at the anti-tank rounds which the Legion battery hurled.

The tank destroyer's glacis plate filled Des Grieux's display. He rocked forward on the foot trip. The saturated blue streak punched through the mantle of the fifteen-CM weapon before the Legion gunner could find his target.

The tank destroyer's ready magazine painted the Notch cyan. Then the reserve ammunition storage went off and lifted the vehicle's armored carapace a meter in the air before dropping it back to the ground.

The iridium shell glowed white. Nothing else remained of the tank destroyer or its crew.

Des Grieux laughed with mad glee. "Have to do better 'n that, Broglie!" he shouted as he slid his aiming point down the slope. He fired every time the hollow pipper covered an undamaged vehicle.

There were seventeen twenty-CM rounds remaining in H271's ready magazine. Each bolt turned a lightly-armored truck or APC into a fireball that bulged steel plates like the skin of a balloon. The last two half-tracks Des Grieux hit had already been abandoned by their crews.

Artillery fire slackened, though Des Grieux's tribarrel snarled uninterruptedly skyward. A delay-fused armor-piercing shell struck short of H271 and punched five meters through the hard soil before going off. The explosion lifted the tank a hand's breadth despite the mass of rock overburden, but the vehicle sustained no damage.

Screen #1 showed a killing zone south of the Escarpment, where fleeing troops bunched and the Slammers maneuvered to cut them apart. Because the powerguns were deadly at any range so long as they had a sight line, every knob of ground Hammer's troops took cut a further swath through far-distant enemy positions.

When the Legion and Thunderbolt artillery directed its fire toward Des Grieux, the cupola guns of the tanks were freed to kill. The process of collapse accelerated as tanks and combat cars took the howitzer batteries themselves under direct fire.

Des Grieux waited. H271's fighting compartment was a stinking furnace. Empties from the rapidly-fired main gun loosed a gray haze into the atmosphere faster than the air conditioning could absorb it. The tank chuckled mechanically as it replenished the ready magazine from storage compartments deep in its armored core.

Fuel fires lighted the slope all the way to the Notch. Hashemite, Sincanmo, and Thunderbolt vehicles—all wrecked and burning. Flames wove a dance of victory over a landscape in which nothing else moved.

Hundreds of terrified soldiers were still alive in the wasteland. The survivors remained motionless. Incoming artillery fire had ceased, giving Des Grieux back the use of his tribarrel. He used it and H271's night vision equipment to probe at whim wherever a head raised.

Des Grieux waited as he watched Broglie's two tank destroyers.

They were no longer the rear guard for the Central Sector refugees. The tank destroyers moved up to the Notch at a deliberate pace which never exposed them to the guns of the panzers south of the Knifeblade Escarpment. Always a cunning bastard, Broglie. . . .

Ammunition in a supply truck near the bottom of the slope cooked off. The blast raised a mushroom-shaped cloud as high as the top of the Escarpment. Two kilometers away, H271 shook.

The battle was going to be over very soon. The Thunderbolt Division's horrendous butcher's bill gave its commander a legitimate excuse for surrendering whether his Hashemite employers did so or not. The bodies heaped on both sides of the Notch would ransom the lives of their fellows.

It occurred to Des Grieux that he could probably drive H271 away, now. Incoming shells had done a day's work for excavating equipment in freeing the tank from his deliberate rockfall.

There wasn't anyplace else in the universe that Des Grieux wanted to be.

Screen #1 showed the tank destroyers pausing just south of the Notch. A fifteen-CM bolt stabbed across the intervening kilometers and vaporized a portion of the mesa's rim. Sonic echoes of the plasma discharge rumbled across the plain below.

Des Grieux blinked, then understood. When the Slammers in Task Force Kuykendall moved out, they'd abandoned the sensor pack they'd placed on the butte. H271 wasn't connected to the pack, but Broglie didn't know that.

And trust that clever bastard not to miss a point before he made his move!

Des Grieux chuckled through a throat burned dry by ozone and the other poisons he breathed. His hands rested lightly on the two joysticks. The pippers were already locked together, solid in circle, where they needed to be.

The left-hand tank destroyer backed, then began to accelerate toward the Notch at high speed. The other Legion vehicle moved forward also, but at a relative crawl.

The right-hand tank destroyer had made the one-shot kill on the tiny sensor pack two kilometers away.

It happened the way Des Grieux knew it would happen.

The tank destroyer rushing through the left side of the Notch braked so abruptly that its skirts rubbed off a shower of sparks against the smooth rock. The other tank destroyer, Broglie's own vehicle, continued to accelerate. It burst into clear sight while H271's gunner was supposed to be concentrating on the target ten meters to the side.

But it was Des Grieux below, and Des Grieux's pippers filled with the mass of iridium that slid into the sight picture. His tribarrel and main gun fired in unison at the massive target.

The interior of H271 turned cyan, then white, and finally red with heat like a hammer. The shockwave was not a sound but a blow that slammed Des Grieux down in his seat.

The cupola was gone. Warning lights glowed across Des Grieux's console. Screen #3 switched automatically to a damage-assessment schematic. The tribarrel had vaporized, but the main gun was undamaged and the turret rotated normally the few mills required to bring the hollow pipper onto its remaining target.

Luke Broglie was very good. He'd fired a fraction of a second early, but he must have known that he wouldn't get the additional instant he needed to center his sight squarely on the tank turret.

He must have known that he was meeting Slick Des Grieux for the last time.

Broglie's vehicle was a white glow at the edge of the Notch. The other crew should have bailed out of their tank destroyer and waited for the Hashemite surrender, but they tried to finish the job at which their Colonel had failed.

Three fifteen-CM bolts cut the night, two shots before the tank destroyer *had* a sight picture and the last round thirty meters wide of H271. Des Grieux penetrated the tank destroyer's thick glacis plate with his first bolt, then sent a second round through the hole to vaporize the wreckage in a pyre of its own munitions.

They should have known it was impossible to do what Luke Broglie couldn't manage. Nobody was as good as Broglie . . . except Slick Des Grieux.

❖   ❖   ❖

Des Grieux could see both north and south of the Knifeblade Escarpment from where he sat on top of the burned-out tank destroyer. Smudgy fires still burned over the sloping plain where the Slammers' artillery and sharpshooting powerguns had slashed the Hashemite center into retreat, then chaos.

Clots of surrendered enemies waited to be interned. Thunderbolt Division personnel rested under tarpaulins attached to their vehicles and a stake or two driven into the soil. The defeated mercenaries were not exactly lounging: there were many wounded among them, and every survivor from the punished battalions knew at least one friend who hadn't been so lucky.

But they would be exchanged back to their own command within hours or days. A mercenary's war ended when the fighting stopped.

The Hashemite survivors were another matter. They huddled in separate groups. Many of their trucks had been disabled by the rain of anti-personnel bomblets which the armor of the mercenary half-tracks had shrugged off. The Hashemites' personal weapons were piled ostentatiously at a slight distance from each gathering.

That wasn't necessarily going to help. Sincanmo irregulars were doing the heavy work of interning prisoners: searching, sorting, and gathering them into coffles of two hundred or so to be transferred to holding camps. The Slammers overseeing the process wouldn't permit the Sincanmos to shoot their indig prisoners here in public.

What happened when converted cargo vans filled with Hashemites were driven ten kays or so into the desert was anybody's guess.

A gun jeep whined its way up the south face of the Escarpment. Victorious troops and prisoners watched the vehicle's progress. The jeep's driver regarded them only as obstacles, and the passenger seated on the other side of the pintle-mounted tribarrel paid them no attention at all.

Des Grieux rolled bits of ivory between the ball of this thumb and his left hand. He turned his face toward the north, where H271 sat in the far distance with a combat car and a heavy-lift vehicle from the Slammers' maintenance battalion in attendance.

Des Grieux wasn't interested in the attempts to dig out H271, but he was unwilling to watch the jeep. Funny about it being a jeep. He'd expected at least a combat car; and Joachim Steuben present, not some faceless driver who wasn't even one of the White Mice.

The slope looked much steeper going down than it had when Des Grieux was on the plain two kilometers away. By contrast, the tilted strata on the south side of the Escarpment rose very gently, though they were as sure a barrier as the north edge that provided the name Knifeblade. There wasn't any way down from the Escarpment, except through the Notch.

And no way down at all, when Slick Des Grieux waited below with a tank and the unshakeable determination to kill everyone who faced him.

They'd rigged a bucket on the maintenance vehicle's shearlegs. A dozen Hashemite prisoners shoveled rock from H271's back deck into the bucket.

Des Grieux snorted. *He* could have broken the tank free in minutes. If he'd had to, if there were someplace he needed to be with a tank. While there was fighting going on, nothing mattered except a weapon; and the Regiment's panzers were the greatest weapons that had ever existed.

When the fighting was over, nothing mattered at all.

The sun had risen high enough to punish, and the tank destroyer's armor was a massive heat sink, retaining some of the fury which had devoured the vehicle. Nothing remained within the iridium shell except the fusion bottle, which hadn't ruptured when the tank destroyer's ammunition gang-fired.

The jeep was getting close. The angry sound of its fans changed every time the light vehicle had to jump or circle a large piece of debris. H271's main gun had seen to it that vehicle parts covered much of the surface of the Notch.

The heavy-lift vehicle had arrived at dawn with several hundred Sincanmos and a platoon of F Company combat cars—not Kuykendall, Des Grieux didn't know where Kuykendall had gone. Des Grieux turned H271 over to the maintenance crew and, for want of anything better to do, wandered into the gully where the blocking force had waited.

A 4x4 with two bombardment rockets in their launching cage was still parked beside H271's initial location. The Sincanmo crew sprawled nearby, riddled by shrapnel too fine to be visible under normal lighting. One of them lay across a lute with a hemispherical sound chamber.

Des Grieux lifted the driver out of his seat and laid him on the ground with the blood-speckled side of his face down. The truck was operable. Des Grieux drove it up the steep slope to the Notch, shifting to compound low every time he had to skirt another burned-out vehicle or windrow of bodies.

Troopers in the combat cars watched the tanker, but they didn't interfere.

The gun jeep stopped. Its fans whirred at a deepening note as they lost power. Des Grieux heard boots hit the soil. He turned, but Colonel Hammer had already gripped a handrail to haul himself up onto the tank destroyer.

"Feeling proud of yourself, Des Grieux?" the Colonel asked grimly.

Hammer wore a cap instead of a commo helmet. There was a line of SpraySeal across his forehead, just above the pepper-and-salt eyebrows, where a helmet would have cut him if it were struck hard. His eyes were bloodshot and very cold.

"Not particularly," Des Grieux said. He wasn't feeling anything at all.

The driver was just a driver, a Charlie Company infantryman. He'd unclipped his carbine from the dash and pointed it vaguely in Des Grieux's direction, but he wasn't one of Joachim Steuben's field police.

Des Grieux had left his grenade launcher behind in H271. He was unarmed.

"They're trying to find Colonel Broglie," Hammer said. "The Legion command council is, and I am."

"Then you're in luck," Des Grieux said.

He opened his left hand. Bones had burned to lime in the glare of the tank destroyer's ammunition, but teeth were more refractory. Des Grieux had found three of them when he sifted the ashes within the tank destroyer's hull through his fingers.

Hammer pursed his lips and stared at the tanker. "You're sure?" he said. Then, "Yeah, you would be."

"Nobody else was that good, Colonel," Des Grieux said softly. His eyes were focused somewhere out beyond the moons' orbits.

Hammer refused to look down into Des Grieux's palm after the first brief glance. "You're out of here, you know," he snapped. "Out of the Slammers for good, and off-planet *fast* if you know what's good for you. I told Joachim I'd handle this my own way, but that's not the kind of instruction you can count on him obeying."

"Right," Des Grieux said without emotion. He closed his hand again and resumed rubbing the teeth against his palm. "I'll do that."

"I ought to let Joachim finish you, you know?" Hammer said. There was an edge in his voice, but also wonder at the tanker's flat affect. "You're too dangerous to leave alive, but I guess I owe something to a twelve-year veteran."

"I won't be joining another outfit, Colonel," Des Grieux said; a statement, not a plea for the mercy Hammer had already granted. "Not much point in it now."

Alois Hammer touched his tongue to his lips in order to have time to process what he had just heard. "You know, Des Grieux?" he said mildly. "I really don't know why I don't have you shot."

Des Grieux looked directly at his commanding officer again. "Because we're the same, Colonel," he said. "You and me. Because there's nothing but war for either of us."

Hammer's face went white, then flushed except for the pink splotch of SpraySeal on his forehead. "You're a bloody fool, Des Grieux," he rasped, "and a bloody *liar*. I wanted to end this—" he gestured at the blackened wreckage of vehicles staggering all the way to the bottom of the slope, "—by a quiet capitulation, not a bloodbath. Not like this!"

"You've got your way, Colonel," Des Grieux said. "I've got mine. Had mine. But it's all the same in the end."

He smiled, but there was only the memory of emotion behind his straight, yellowed teeth. "You haven't learned that yet. Have fun. Because when it's over, there isn't anything left."

Colonel Hammer pressed the SpraySeal with the back of his left hand, not quite rubbing it. He slid from the iridium carapace of the tank destroyer. "Come on, Des Grieux," he said. "I'll see that you get aboard a ship alive. You'll have your pension and discharge bonus."

Des Grieux followed the shorter man. The tanker walked stiffly, as though he were an infant still learning gross motor skills.

At the jeep, Hammer turned and said savagely, "And Via! Will you please throw those curst teeth away?"

Des Grieux slipped the calcined fragments into his breast pocket. "I need them," he said. "To remind me that I was the best.

"Some day," he added, "you'll know just what I mean, Colonel."

His smile was terrible to behold.

Caught in the Crossfire

Margritte grappled with the nearest soldier in the instant
her husband broke for the woods. The man in field-gray
cursed and tried to jerk his weapon away from her, but
Margritte's muscles were young and taut from shifting bales.
Even when the mercenary kicked her ankles from under
her, Margritte's clamped hands kept the gun barrel down
and harmless.

Neither of the other two soldiers paid any attention to
the scuffle. They clicked off the safety catches of their
weapons as they swung them to their shoulders. Georg was
running hard, fresh blood from his retorn calf muscles
staining his bandages. The double slap of automatic fire
caught him in mid-stride and whipsawed his slender body.
His head and heels scissored to the ground together. They
were covered by the mist of blood that settled more slowly.

Sobbing, Margritte loosed her grip and fell back on the
ground. The man above her cradled his flechette gun again
and looked around the village. "Well, aren't you going to
shoot me too?" she cried.

"Not unless we have to," the mercenary replied quietly.
He was sweating despite the stiff breeze, and he wiped
his black face with his sleeve. "Helmuth," he ordered, "start
setting up in the building. Landschein, you stay out with

me, make sure none of these women try the same damned thing." He glanced out to where Georg lay, a bright smear on the stubbled, golden earth. "Best get that out of sight too," he added. "The convoy's due in an hour."

Old Leida had frozen to a statue in ankle-length muslin at the first scream. Now she nodded her head of close ringlets. "Myrie, Della," she called, gesturing to her daughters, "bring brush hooks and come along." She had not lost her dignity even during the shooting.

"Hold it," said Landschein, the shortest of the three soldiers. He was a sharp-featured man who had grinned in satisfaction as he fired. "You two got kids in there?" he asked the younger women. The muzzle of his flechette gun indicated the locked door to the dugout which normally stored the crop out of sun and heat; today it imprisoned the village's twenty-six children. Della and Myrie nodded, too dry with fear to speak.

"Then you go drag him into the woods," Landschein said, grinning again. "Just remember—you might manage to get away, but you won't much like what you'll find when you come back. I'm sure some true friend'll point your brats out to us quick enough to save her own."

Leida nodded a command, but Landschein's freckled hand clamped her elbow as she turned to follow her daughters. "Not you, old lady. No need for you to get that near to cover."

"Do you think *I* would run and risk—everyone?" Leida demanded.

"Curst if I know what you'd risk," the soldier said. "But we're risking plenty already to ambush one of Hammer's convoys. If anybody gets loose ahead of time to warn them, we can kiss our butts good-bye."

Margritte wiped the tears from her eyes, using her palms because of the gritty dust her thrashings had pounded into her knuckles. The third soldier, the broad-shouldered blond named Helmuth, had leaned his weapon beside the door of the hall and was lifting bulky loads from the nearby air cushion vehicle. The settlement had become used to whining gray columns of military vehicles, cruising the road at random. This truck, however, had eased over the second canopy of the forest itself. It was a flimsy cargo-hauler like the one in which Krauder picked up the cotton at season's end, harmless enough to look at. Only Georg, left behind for his sickle-ripped leg when a government van had carried off the other males the week before as "recruits," had realized what it meant that the newcomers wore field-gray instead of khaki.

"Why did you come here?" Margritte asked in a near-normal voice.

The black mercenary glanced at her as she rose, glanced back at the other women obeying orders by continuing to pick the iridescent boles of Terran cotton grown in Pohweil's soil. "We had the capital under siege," he said, "until Hammer's tanks punched a corridor through. We can't close the corridor, so we got to cut your boys off from supplies some other way. Otherwise the Cartel'll wish it had paid its taxes instead of trying to take over. You grubbers may have been pruning their wallets, but Lord! they'll be flayed alive if your counter-attack works."

He spat a thin, angry stream into the dust. "The traders hired us and four other regiments, and you grubbers sank the whole treasury into bringing in Hammer's armor. Maybe we can prove today those cocky bastards aren't all they're billed as. . . ."

"We didn't care," Margritte said. "We're no more the Farm Bloc than Krauder and his truck is the Trade Cartel. Whatever they did in the capital—*we* had no choice. I hadn't even seen the capital . . . oh dear Lord, Georg would have taken me there for our honeymoon except that there was fighting all over. . . ."

"How long we got, Sarge?" the blond man demanded from the stark shade of the hall.

"Little enough. Get those bloody sheets set up or we'll have to pop the cork bare-ass naked; and we got enough problems." The big noncom shifted his glance about the narrow clearing, wavering rows of cotton marching to the edge of the forest's dusky green. The road, an unsurfaced track whose ruts were not a serious hindrance to air cushion traffic, was the long axis. Beside it stood the hall, twenty meters by five and the only above-ground structure in the settlement. The battle with the native vegetation made dug-outs beneath the cotton preferable to cleared land wasted for dwellings. The hall became more than a social center and common refectory: it was the gaudiest of luxuries and a proud slap to the face of the forest.

Until that morning, the forest had been the village's only enemy.

"Georg only wanted—"

"God *damn* it" the sergeant snarled. "Will you shut it off? Every man but your precious husband gone off to the siege—no, shut it off till I finish!—and him running to warn the convoy. If you'd wanted to save his life, you should've grabbed him, not me. Sure, all you grubbers, you don't care about the war—not much! It's all one to you whether you kill us yourselves or your tankers do it, those bastards so high and mighty for the money they've got and the equipment. I tell you, girl, I don't take it personal that people shoot at me, it's just the way we both earn our livings. But it's fair, it's even . . . and Hammer thinks he's the Way made Flesh because nobody can bust his tanks."

The sergeant paused and his lips sucked in and out. His thick, gentle fingers rechecked the weapon he held. "We'll just see," he whispered.

"Georg said we'd all be killed in the crossfire if we were out in the fields when you shot at the tanks."

"If Georg had kept his face shut and his ass in bed, he'd have lived longer than he did. Just shut it off!" the non-com ordered. He turned to his blond underling, fighting a section of sponge plating through the door. "Via, Bornzyk!" he shouted angrily. "Move it!"

Helmuth flung his load down with a hollow clang. "Via, then lend a hand! The wind catches these and—"

"I'll help him," Margritte offered abruptly. Her eyes blinked away from the young soldier's weapon where he had forgotten it against the wall. Standing, she far lacked the bulk of the sergeant beside her, but her frame gave

no suggestion of weakness. Golden dust soiled the back
and sides of her dress with butterfly scales.

The sergeant gave her a sharp glance, his left hand
spreading and closing where it rested on the black barrel-
shroud of his weapon. "All right," he said, "you give him
a hand and we'll see you under cover with us when the
shooting starts. You're smarter than I gave you credit."

They had forgotten Leida was still standing beside them.
Her hand struck like a spading fork. Margritte ducked away
from the blow, but Leida caught her on the shoulder and
gripped. When the mercenary's reversed gun-butt cracked
the older woman loose, a long strip of Margritte's blue dress
tore away with her. "Bitch," Leida mumbled through
bruised lips. "You'd help these beasts after they killed your
own man?"

Margritte stepped back, tossing her head. For a moment
she fumbled at the tear in her dress; then, defiantly, she
let it fall open. Landschein turned in time to catch the look
in Leida's eyes. "Hey, you'll give your friends more trouble,"
he stated cheerfully, waggling his gun to indicate Della and
Myrie as they returned gray-faced from the forest fringe.
"Go on, get out and pick some cotton."

When Margritte moved, the white of her loose shift
caught the sun and the small killer's stare. "Landschein!"
the black ordered sharply, and Margritte stepped very
quickly toward the truck and the third man struggling there.

Helmuth turned and blinked at the girl as he felt her
capable muscles take the windstrain off the panel he was
shifting. His eyes were blue and set wide in a face too
large-boned to be handsome, too frank to be other than
attractive. He accepted the help without question, leading the way into the hall.

The dining tables were hoisted against the rafters. The
windows, unshuttered in the warm autumn and unglazed,
lined all four walls at chest height. The long wall nearest
the road was otherwise unbroken; the one opposite it was
pierced in the middle by the single door. In the center of
what should have been an empty room squatted the
mercenaries' construct. The metal-ceramic panels had been

locked into three sides of a square, a pocket of armor open only toward the door. It was hidden beneath the lower sills of the windows; nothing would catch the eye of an oncoming tanker.

"We've got to nest three layers together," the soldier explained as he swung the load, easily managed within the building, "or they'll cut us apart if they get off a burst this direction."

Margritte steadied a panel already in place as Helmuth mortised his into it. Each sheet was about five centimeters in thickness, a thin plate of gray metal on either side of a white porcelain sponge. The girl tapped it dubiously with a blunt finger. "This can stop bullets?"

The soldier—he was younger than his size suggested, no more than eighteen. Younger even than Georg, and he had a smile like Georg's as he raised his eyes with a blush and said, "P-powerguns, yeah; three layers of it ought to . . . It's light, we could carry it in the truck where iridium would have bogged us down. But look, there's another panel and the rockets we still got to bring in."

"You must be very brave to fight tanks with just—this," Margritte prompted as she took one end of the remaining armor sheet.

"Oh, well, Sergeant Counsel says it'll work," the boy said enthusiastically. "They'll come by, two combat cars, then three big trucks, and another combat car. Sarge and Landschein buzzbomb the lead cars before they know what's happening. I reload them and they hit the third car when it swings wide to get a shot. Any shooting the blower jocks get off, they'll spread because they won't know—oh, cop I said it. . . ."

"They'll think the women in the fields may be firing, so they'll kill us first," Margritte reasoned aloud. The boy's neck beneath his helmet turned brick red as he trudged into the building.

"Look," he said, but he would not meet her eyes, "we got to do it. It'll be fast—nobody much can get hurt. And your . . . the children, they're all safe. Sarge said that with all the men gone, we wouldn't have any trouble with the women if we kept the kids safe and under our thumbs."

"We didn't have time to have children," Margritte said. Her eyes were briefly unfocused. "You didn't give Georg enough time before you killed him."

"He was . . ." Helmuth began. They were outside again and his hand flicked briefly toward the slight notch Della and Myrie had chopped in the forest wall. "I'm sorry."

"Oh, don't be sorry," she said. "He knew what he was doing."

"He was—I suppose you'd call him a patriot?" Helmuth suggested, jumping easily to the truck's deck to gather up an armload of cylindrical bundles. "He was really against the Cartel?"

"There was never a soul in this village who cared who won the war," Margritte said. "We have our own war with the forest."

"They joined the siege!" the boy retorted. "They cared that m-much, to fight us!"

"They got in the vans when men with guns told them to get in," the girl said. She took the gear Helmuth was forgetting to hand to her and shook a lock of hair out of her eyes. "Should they have run? Like Georg? No, they went off to be soldiers; praying like we did that the war might end before the forest had eaten up the village again. Maybe if we were really lucky, it'd end before this crop had spoiled in the fields because there weren't enough hands left here to pick it in time."

Helmuth cleared the back of the truck with his own load and stepped down. "Well, just the same your, your husband tried to hide and warn the convoy," he argued. "Otherwise why did he run?"

"Oh, he loved me—you know?" said Margritte. "Your sergeant said all of us should be out picking as usual. Georg knew, he *told* you, that the crossfire would kill everybody in the fields as sure as if you shot us deliberately. And when you wouldn't change your plan . . . well, if he'd gotten away you would have had to give up your ambush, wouldn't you?

You'd have known it was suicide if the tanks learned that you were waiting for them. So Georg ran."

The dark-haired woman stared out at the forest for a moment. "He didn't have a prayer, did he? You could have killed him a hundred times before he got to cover."

"Here, give me those," the soldier said, taking the bundles from her instead of replying. He began to unwrap the cylinders one by one on the wooden floor. "We couldn't let him get away," he said at last. He added, his eyes still down on his work, "Flechettes when they hit . . . I mean, sh-shooting at his legs wouldn't, wouldn't have been a kindness, you see?"

Margritte laughed again. "Oh, I saw what they dragged into the forest, yes." She paused, sucking at her lower lip. "That's how we always deal with our dead, give them to the forest. Oh, we have a service; but we wouldn't have buried Georg in the dirt, if . . . if he'd died. But you didn't care, did you? A corpse looks bad, maybe your precious ambush, your own lives. Get it out of the way, toss it in the woods."

"We'd have buried him afterwards," the soldier mumbled as he laid a fourth thigh-thick projectile beside those he had already unwrapped.

"Oh, of *course*," Margritte said. "And me, and all the rest of us murdered out there in the cotton. Oh, you're gentlemen, you are."

"Via!" Helmuth shouted, his flush mottling as at last he lifted his gaze to the girl's. "We'd have b-buried him. I'd have buried him. You'll be safe in here with us until it's all over, and by the Lord, then you can come back with us too! You don't have to stay here with these hard-faced bitches."

A bitter smile tweaked the left edge of the girl's mouth. "Sure, you're a good boy."

The young mercenary blinked between protest and pleasure, settled on the latter. He had readied all six of the tinned, gray missiles; now he lifted one of the pair of launchers. "It'll be really quick," he said shyly, changing the subject. The launcher was an arm-length tube with double handgrips and an optical sight. Helmuth's big hands easily inserted one of the buzzbombs to lock with a faint snick.

"Very simple," Margritte murmured.

"Cheap and easy," the boy agreed with a smile. "You can buy a thousand of these for what a combat car runs— Hell, maybe more than a thousand. And it's one for one today, one bomb to one car. Landschein says the crews are just a little extra, like weevils in your biscuit."

He saw her grimace, the angry tensing of a woman who had just seen her husband blasted into a spray of offal. Helmuth grunted with his own pain, his mouth dropping open as his hand stretched to touch her bare shoulder. "Oh, Lord—didn't mean to say. . . ."

She gently detached his fingers. His breath caught and he turned away. Unseen, her look of hatred seared his back. His hand was still stretched toward her and hers toward him, when the door scraped to admit Landschein behind them.

"Cute, oh bloody cute," the little mercenary said. He carried his helmet by its strap. Uncovered, his cropped gray hair made him an older man. "Well, get on with it, boy— don't keep me 'n Sarge waiting. He'll be mad enough about getting sloppy thirds."

Helmuth jumped to his feet. Landschein ignored him, clicking across to a window in three quick strides. "Sarge," he called, "we're all set. Come on, we can watch the women from here."

"I'll run the truck into the woods," Counsel's voice burred in reply. "Anyhow, I can hear better from out here."

That was true. Despite the open windows, the wails of the children were inaudible in the hall. Outside, they formed a thin backdrop to every other sound.

Landschein set down his helmet. He snapped the safety on his gun's sideplate and leaned the weapon carefully against the nest of armor. Then he took up the loaded launcher and ran his hands over its tube and grips. Without changing expression, he reached out to caress Margritte through the tear in her dress.

Margritte screamed and clawed her left hand as she tried to rise. The launcher slipped into Landschein's lap and his arm, far swifter, locked hers and drew her down against him. Then the little mercenary himself was jerked upward. Helmuth's hand on his collar first broke Landschein's grip on Margritte, then flung him against the closed door.

Landschein rolled despite the shock and his glance flicked toward his weapon, but between gun and gunman crouched Helmuth, no longer a red-faced boy but the strongest man in the room. Grinning, Helmuth spread fingers that had crushed ribs in past rough and tumbles. "Try it, little man," he said. "Try it and I'll rip your head off your shoulders."

"You'll do wonders!" Landschein spat, but his eyes lost their glaze and his muscles relaxed. He bent his mouth into a smile. "Hey, kid, there's plenty of slots around. We'll work out something afterwards, no need to fight."

Helmuth rocked his head back in a nod of acceptance with nothing of friendship in it. "You lay another hand on her," he said in a normal voice, "and you'd best have killed me first." He turned his back deliberately on the older man and the nearby weapons. Landschein clenched his left fist once, twice, but then he began to load the remaining launcher.

Margritte slipped the patching kit from her belt pouch. Her hands trembled, but the steel needle was already threaded. Her whip-stitches tacked the torn piece top and sides to the remaining material, close enough for decency. Pins were a luxury that a cotton settlement could well do without. Landschein glanced back at her once, but at the same time the floor creaked as Helmuth's weight shifted to his other leg. Neither man spoke.

Sergeant Counsel opened the door. His right arm cradled a pair of flechette guns and he handed one to Helmuth. "Best not to leave it in the dust," he said. "You'll be needing it soon."

"They coming, Sarge?" Landschein asked. He touched his tongue to thin, pale lips.

"Not yet." Counsel looked from one man to the other. "You boys get things sorted out?"

"All green here," Landschein muttered, smiling again but lowering his eyes.

"That's good," the big black said, "because we got a job to do and we're not going to let anything stop us. Anything."

Margritte was putting away her needle. The sergeant looked at her hard. "You keep your head down, hear?"

"It won't matter," the girl said calmly, tucking the kit away. "The tanks, they won't be surprised to see a woman in here."

"Sure, but they'll shoot your bleeding head off," Landschein snorted.

"Do you think I care?" she blazed back. Helmuth winced at the tone; Sergeant Counsel's eyes took on an undesirable shade of interest.

"But you're helping us," the big noncom mused. He tapped his fingertips on the gun in the crook of his arm. "Because you like us so much?" There was no amusement in his words, only a careful mind picking over the idea, all ideas.

She stood and walked to the door, her face as composed as a priest's at the gravesite. "Have your ambush," she said. "Would it help us if the convoy came through before you were ready for it?"

"The smoother it goes, the faster. . . ." Counsel agreed quietly, "then the better for all of you."

Margritte swung the door open and stood looking out. Eight women were picking among the rows east of the hall. They would be relatively safe there, not caught between the ambushers' rockets and the raking powerguns of their quarry. Eight of them safe and fourteen sure victims on the other side. Most of them could have been out of the crossfire if they had only let themselves think, only considered the truth that Georg had died to underscore.

"I keep thinking of Georg," Margritte said aloud. "I guess my friends are just thinking about their children, they keep looking at the storage room. But the children, they'll be all right; it's just that most of them are going to be orphans in a few minutes."

"It won't be that bad," Helmuth said. He did not sound as though he believed it either.

The older children had by now ceased the screaming begun when the door shut and darkness closed in on them. The youngest still wailed and the sound drifted through the open door.

"I told her we'd take her back with us, Sarge," Helmuth said.

Landschein chortled, a flash of instinctive humor he covered with a raised palm. Counsel shook his head in amazement. "You were wrong, boy. Now, keep watching those women or we may not be going back ourselves."

The younger man reddened again in frustration. "Look, we've got women in the outfit now, and I don't mean the rec troops. Captain Denzil told me there's six in Bravo Company alone—"

"Hoo, little Helmuth wants his own girlie friend to keep his bed warm," Landschein gibed.

"Landschein, I—" Helmuth began, clenching his right hand into a ridge of knuckles.

"Shut it off!"

"But, Sarge—"

"Shut it off, boy, or you'll have me to deal with!" roared the black. Helmuth fell back and rubbed his eyes. The noncom went on more quietly, "Landschein, you keep your tongue to yourself, too."

Both big men breathed deeply, their eyes shifting in concert toward Margritte who faced them in silence. "Helmuth," the sergeant continued, "some units take women, some don't. We've got a few, damned few, because not many women have the guts for our line of work."

Margritte's smile flickered. "The hardness, you mean. The callousness."

"Sure, words don't matter," Counsel agreed mildly. He smiled back at her as one equal to another. "This one, yeah; she might just pass. Via, you don't have to look like Landschein there to be tough. But you're missing the big point, boy."

Helmuth touched his right wrist to his chin. "Well, what?" he demanded.

Counsel laughed. "She wouldn't go with us. Would you, girl?"

Margritte's eyes were flat, and her voice was dead flat. "No," she said, "I wouldn't go with you."

The noncom grinned as he walked back to a window vantage. "You see, Helmuth, you want her to give up a whole lot to gain you a bunkmate."

"It's not like that," Helmuth insisted, thumping his leg in frustration. "I just mean—"

"Oh, *Lord!*" the girl said loudly, "can't you just get on with your ambush?"

"Well, not till Hammer's boys come through," chuckled the sergeant. "They're so good, they can't run a convoy to schedule."

"S-sergeant," the young soldier said, "she doesn't understand." He turned to Margritte and gestured with both hands, forgetting the weapon in his left. "They won't take you back, those witches out there. The. . . the rec girls at Base Denzil don't go home, they can't. And you know damned well that s-some-body's going to catch it out there when it drops in the pot. They'll crucify you for helping us set up, the ones that're left."

"It doesn't matter what they do," she said. "It doesn't matter at all."

"Your life matters!" the boy insisted.

Her laughter hooted through the room. "My life?" Margritte repeated. "You splashed all that across the field an hour ago. You didn't give a damn when you did it, and I don't give one now—but I'd only follow you to Hell and hope your road was short."

Helmuth bit his knuckle and turned, pinched over as though he had been kicked. Sergeant Counsel grinned his tight, equals grin. "You're wasted here, you know," he said. "And we could use you. Maybe if—"

"Sarge!" Landschein called from his window. "Here they come."

Counsel scooped up a rocket launcher, probing its breech with his fingers to make finally sure of its load. "Now you keep down," he repeated to Margritte. "Backblast'll take your head off if their shooting don't." He crouched below the sill and the rim of the armor shielding him, peering through a periscope whose button of optical fibers was unnoticeable in the shadow. Faced inward toward the girl, Landschein hunched over the other launcher in the right corner of the protected area. His flechette gun rested beside him and one hand curved toward it momentarily, anticipating the instant he would raise it to spray the shattered convoy. Between them Helmuth knelt as stiffly as a statue of gray-green jade. He drew a buzzbomb closer to his right knee where it clinked against the barrel of his own weapon. Cursing nervously, he slid the flechette gun back out of the way. Both his hands gripped reloads, waiting.

The cars' shrill whine trembled in the air. Margritte stood up by the door, staring out through the windows across the hall. Dust plumed where the long, straight roadway cut the horizon into two blocks of forest. The women in the fields had paused, straightening to watch the oncoming vehicles. But that was normal, nothing to alarm the khaki men in the bellies of their war cars; and if any woman thought of falling to hug the earth, the fans' wailing too nearly approximated that of the imprisoned children.

"Three hundred meters," Counsel reported softly as the blunt bow of the lead car gleamed through the dust. "Two-fifty." Landschein's teeth bared as he faced around, poised to spring.

Margritte swept up Helmuth's flechette gun and leveled it at waist height. The safety clicked off. Counsel had dropped his periscope and his mouth was open to cry an order. The deafening muzzle blast lifted him out of his crouch and pasted him briefly, voiceless, against the pocked inner face of the armor. Margritte swung her weapon like a flail into a triple splash of red. Helmuth died with only a reflexive jerk, but Landschein's speed came near to bringing his launcher to bear on Margritte. The stream of flechettes sawed across his throat. His torso dropped, headless but still clutching the weapon.

Margritte's gun silenced when the last needle slapped out of the muzzle. The aluminum barrel shroud had softened and warped during the long burst. Eddies in the fog of blood and propellant smoke danced away from it. Margritte turned as if in icy composure, but she bumped the door jamb and staggered as she stepped outside. The racket of the gun had drawn the sallow faces of every woman in the fields.

"It's over!" Margritte called. Her voice sounded thin in the fresh silence. Three of the nearer mothers ran toward the storage room.

Down the road, dust was spraying as the convoy skidded into a herringbone for defense. Gun muzzles searched; the running women; Margritte armed and motionless; the sudden eruption of children from the dugout. The men in the cars waited, their trigger fingers partly tensed.

Bergen, Delia's six-year-old, pounded past Margritte to throw herself into her mother's arms. They clung together, each crooning to the other through their tears. "Oh, we were so afraid!" Bergen said, drawing away from her mother. "But now it's all right." She rotated her head and her eyes widened as they took in Margritte's tattered figure. "Oh, Margi," she gasped, "whatever happened to *you*?"

Delia gasped and snatched her daughter back against her bosom. Over the child's loose curls, Della glared at Margritte with eyes like a hedge of pikes. Margritte's hand stopped half way to the child. She stood—gaunt, misted with blood as though sunburned. A woman who had blasted life away instead of suckling it. Della, a frightened mother, snarled at the killer who had been her friend.

Margritte began to laugh. She trailed the gun three steps before letting it drop unnoticed. The captain of the lead car watched her approach over his gunsights. His short, black beard fluffed out from under his helmet, twitching as he asked, "Would you like to tell us what's going on, honey, or do we got to comb it out ourselves?"

"I killed three soldiers," she answered simply. "Now there's nothing going on. Except that wherever you're headed, I'm going along. You can use my sort, soldier."

Her laughter was a crackling shadow in the sunlight.

The Immovable Object

Hoodoo, the only one of the Slammers' gigantic tanks remaining on Ambiorix, hulked in the starlight beyond the barred window of the maintenance shed where the party was going on. Lamartiere looked at the gray bulk again, then tossed down the last of the drink he'd been nursing for an hour.

It wasn't quite time for him to act. Since Franciscus, the commander of the Company of Death, had sent the orders three days ago, Lamartiere had been worried sick over what he had to do. Now he just wished it was over, one way or the other.

Sergeant Heth tried to stand but toppled back onto a couch improvised from rolls of insulating foam. He was *Hoodoo*'s commander and the ranking mercenary on Ambiorix since the remainder of Hammer's Regiment had lifted during the past three weeks. Even though the stubby, dark-skinned mercenary had drunk himself legless, his gaze was sharp as he searched the crowd of Local Service Personnel to focus on Lamartiere.

"Hey Curly!" he called. It was a joke: Lamartiere's straight blond hair was so fine that he looked bald in a strong light. "I want you to know that you were a good

167

LSP, and I'd say that even if you hadn't just fed me the best whiskey I ever had in my life!"

"Yeah, Denis," said L'Abbaye, another of the LSPs. "I didn't know your folks had money. What're you doing in a job like this, anyhow?"

"Because of my faith," Lamartiere said simply. His mouth was dry, but oddly enough the question steadied him. "I thought the best way I could serve God was by serving the mercenaries who came here to fight the Mosite rebels. These refreshments are also a way of serving God."

That was quite true. The Company of Death, the special operations commando of the Mosite rebellion, had recruited Lamartiere from the ranks of ordinary guerrillas and ordered him to take this job.

He came from the planetary capital, Carcassone, rather than the western mountains where the Mosite faith—Mosite *heresy*, the Synod of the Established Church would have it—was centered. Lamartiere had his father's fair complexion. Perhaps in compensation his sister Celine was darker than most pure-blood Westerners, but they both had their mother's faith. Lamartiere's technical education from the Carcassone Lyceum made im an ideal recruit to the Local Service Personnel whom the mercenaries hired for cleaning and fetch-and-carry during depot maintenance of their great war machines.

Heth prodded *Hoodoo*'s driver, Trooper Stegner, with a boot toe. "Here that, Steg?" the sergeant said. "We're the Sword of God again. How many gods d'ye suppose we been the swords for, hey?"

"We ain't nobody's sword now," Stegner said, lying on his back on the floor with a block of wood for his pillow. His eyes were closed and the straw of an emergency water bottle projected into the corner of his mouth. "We been fired, cast into the outer darkness of space just because we want to be paid."

Before Stegner lay down on the concrete, he'd filled the water bottle with the whiskey Lamartiere brought to this farewell party for the two mercenaries. Though the trooper had seemed to be asleep, his Adam's apple moved at intervals as he sucked on the straw.

"You weren't fired, sir," said another of the LSPs. "You've won and can go home now."

Everyone in the shed except Lamartiere was drunk or almost drunk. For this operation, Franciscus had provided enough liquor to fill *Hoodoo*'s heat exchanger. The money to buy it had come from folk on whom the yoke of war and the Synod lay heavy; but they paid the tax, just as they paid in blood—for their Mosite faith.

"Home?" muttered Stegner. "Where's that?"

"We won the battles we fought, son," Sgt Heth said, turning to the LSP who'd spoken. "The Slammers generally do. That's why people hire us. But don't kid yourself that the war's over. That's not going to happen until either you give your rebels a piece of the government or you kill everybody in the Western District."

"But they're heretics!" Fourche blurted. "We aren't going to allow Ambiorix to be ruled by heretics!"

Heth belched loudly. He stared at his empty glass. Lamartiere filled it from the bottle he held.

"Well, that leaves the second way, don't it?" Heth said. "I don't think we'd be able to handle the job, not kill *all* of them, even if you had the money to pay us. And not to be unkind son, but your National Army *sure* can't do it, which is why you hired us in the first place."

"Cast into the darkness . . ." Stegner mumbled. He started to laugh, choked, and turned his head away from the bottle to vomit.

It was time. Lamartiere stood, wobbly with adrenalin rather than liquor, and said, "We're getting low on whiskey. I'll fetch more."

"I'll give you a hand," volunteered L'Abbaye. He was a friendly youth but all thumbs on any kind of mechanical task. Lamartiere thought with grim humor that if the secret police came looking for Mosites among the LSPs, L'Abbaye's clumsiness could easily be mistaken for systematic sabotage.

Lamartiere handed him the present bottle. There was just enough liquor to slosh in the bottom. "You hold this," he said. "I'll be right back."

Lamartiere stepped outside, feeling the night air bite like a plunge into cold water. He was shivering. He closed the shed's sturdy door, then threw the strap over the hasp and locked it down with the heavy padlock he'd brought for the purpose.

He trotted to the sloped gray bow of *Hoodoo*, a vast boulder ropping out of the spaceport's flat expanse. Lamartiere had the feeling that the tank was watching him, even now when it was completely shut down.

The mercenaries had used the spaceport of Brione, the major city of Ambiorix' Western District, as their planetary logistics base during operations against the Mosites in the surrounding mountains. The seventeen tanks of H Company provided base security during the Slammers' withdrawal at the end of their contract.

The withdrawal had gone so smoothly that the government in Carcassone was probably congratulating itself on the savings it had made by ceasing to pay the enormously high wages of the foreign mercenaries. Over a period of three weeks starship after starship had lifted, carrying the Slammers' equipment and personnel to Beresford, 300 lightyears distant, where the dictator of a continental state didn't choose to become part of the planetary democracy.

The last transport was supposed to carry H Company. As the tanks headed for the hold, *Hoodoo*'s aft and starboard pairs of drive fans failed because of an electrical fault. This wasn't a serious problem or an uncommon one—vibration and grit meant wiring harnesses were almost as regular an item of resupply as ammunition. With the Regiment's tank transporters and dedicated maintenance personnel already off-planet, though, Major Harding—the logistics officer overseeing the withdrawal—had a problem.

Hoodoo's crew could repair the tank themselves as they'd done many times in the field, but the job might take anything up to a week. Harding had to decide whether to delay sixteen tanks whose punch was potentially crucial on Beresford, or to risk leaving *Hoodoo* behind alone to rejoin when Heth and Stegner got her running again.

For the moment Ambiorix seemed as quiet as if Bishop

Moses had never had his revelation. Harding had chosen the second option and lifted with the remainder of H Company.

Hoodoo's crew spent the next thirteen hours tracing the fault through the on-board diagnostics, then six more hours pulling the damaged harness and reeving a new one through channels in armor thick enough to deflect all but the most powerful weapons known to man. Then and only then, they had slept.

It was four more days before the tramp freighter hired to carry *Hoodoo* to Beresford would be ready to lift, but Heth and Stegner could relax once they had the tank running again. *Hoodoo*'s speed, armor and weaponry meant there was nothing within twenty light years of Ambiorix to equal her.

And she was about to enter the service of the Mosite Rebellion.

A boarding ladder pivoted from *Hoodoo*'s hull, but Lamartiere walked up the smooth iridium bow slope instead like a real tanker. Local Service Personnel were taught to drive the Slammers' vehicles so that they could ferry them between maintenance and supply stations, freeing the troops for more specialized tasks.

Personal travel on Ambiorix, where roads were bad and often steep, was generally by air-cushion vehicle. A 170-tonne tank didn't handle like a 2-tonne van, but the principle was the same. Most of the LSPs were competent tank drivers, and Lamartiere flattered himself that he was pretty good—at least within the flat confines of the spaceport.

Lamartiere didn't need his stolen electronic key because the driver's hatch wasn't locked. He gripped the handle and slid the curved plate forward, feeling the counterweights move in greasy balance with the massive iridium forging.

He lowered himself into the compartment. The seat was raised for the driver to look out over the hatch coaming instead of viewing the world through the multi-function flat-plate displays that ringed his position.

Lamartiere took a deep breath and switched on *Hoodoo*'s drive fans.

The whine of the powerful impellers coming up to speed told everyone within a kilometer that the tank was in operation, but only the crew and the LSPs with them realized something was wrong. Lamartiere had cut the landlines into the building when he'd gone out earlier 'to fetch another bottle'.

The maintenance building had barred windows and heavy doors to safeguard the equipment within. Even if those partying inside had been sober, they wouldn't have been able to break out in time to affect the result. No one on base could hear their shouts over the sound of the adjacent tank. They were the least of Lamartiere's problems.

None of *Hoodoo*'s electronics were live, and that *was* a problem. Lamartiere realized what had happened as soon as he switched on: Heth and Stegner had disabled the systems while they were working on the wiring. They hadn't bothered to reconnect anything but the drive train to test it when they were done. There was probably a panel of circuit breakers in some easily accessible location, but Lamartiere didn't know where it was and he didn't have time to find it now in the dark.

He increased the bite of the fans so that instead of merely spinning they began to pump air into *Hoodoo*'s plenum chamber. The skirts enclosing the chamber were steel, not a flexible material like that used for lighter air-cushion vehicles. These had to support the tank's enormous mass while at rest. They couldn't deform to seal the chamber against irregularities in the ground, but the output of the eight powerful fans driven by a fusion generator made up for the leakage.

Hoodoo shivered as the bubble of air in the plenum chamber reached the pressure required to lift 170 tonnes. The tank hopped twice, spilling air beneath the skirts, then steadied as the flow through the fans increased to match the leakage. She was now floating a finger's breadth above the ground.

Lamartiere moved the control yoke forward. The fan nacelles tilted within the plenum chamber to direct their thrust rearward instead of simply down. *Hoodoo* moved at a sedate pace, scarcely more than a fast walk, through the shops area toward the spaceport's main gate.

Lamartiere shook violently in relief. He released the control yoke for the moment: the tank's AI would hold their speed and heading, which was all that was required now.

Using both hands, Lamartiere fumbled in a bellows pocket of his coveralls and brought out a hand-held radio stolen from government stores. He keyed it on the set frequency and said, "Star, on the way. Out."

He switched off without waiting for a response. He couldn't hear anything over the intake howl, and it really didn't matter. Whether or not Franciscus and the rest of the outside team were in position, Denis Lamartiere couldn't back out now.

The spaceport perimeter was defended, but the mines, fences and guard towers were no danger to a supertank. At the main gate, however, was a five-story citadel containing the tactical control center and a pair of 25-CM powerguns on dual-purpose mountings. Those weapons could rend a starship in orbit and when raised could bear on every route out of the port. A bolt from one of them would vaporize even *Hoodoo*'s thick iridium armor.

A spur from the four-lane Brione-Carcassone highway fed the spaceport. As Lamartiere drove slowly toward the gate, an air cushion van and a fourteen-wheel semi, turned onto the approach road from the other direction.

There was regular truck traffic to the port: a similar vehicle had just passed the checkpoint and was headed toward the warehouses. Guards at the gate waited for the oncoming semi, chatting and chewing wads of the harsh tobacco grown in Carcassone District.

Hoodoo's drive fans drew a fierce breeze past Lamartiere's face despite the tank's slow forward progress. He backed off the throttle even more. Without the tank's electronics Lamartiere had to keep his head out of the hatch to drive, so he couldn't afford to be too close when the semi reached the gate.

The small van pulled into the ditch beside the road and

stopped. The semi accelerated past with the ponderous deliberation its weight made necessary.

Lamartiere watched as *Hoodoo* crawled forward, waiting for the driver to bail out. The truck continued to accelerate, but no one jumped from the cab. Had Franciscus decided to sacrifice himself, despite Lamartiere's loud refusal to be a part of a suicide mission?

It was too late to back out. If he met Franciscus in Hell, he could object then.

A machine gun on top of the citadel opened fire before any of the guards at the checkpoint appeared to understand what was happening. The gunner deserved full marks for reacting promptly, but his sparkling projectiles were aimed several meters high. A round flashed red when it cut one of the steel hoops supporting the trailer's canvas top, but none hit the cab. It was protected against small-arms anyway.

The driver was definitely going to stay with his vehicle. Lamartiere's stomach turned. Risk was one thing. No God Lamartiere worshipped demanded suicide of Her followers.

A siren called from the Port Operations Center in the center of the base. Half a dozen automatic rifles were firing from the roof and entranceway of the citadel. One of the guards at the checkpoint raked the truck from front to back as it swept past him. Most of his fellows had flung themselves down, though one stood in the guard kiosk and gabbled excitedly into the handset of the landline phone there.

The semi bounced over the shallow ditch—it was for drainage rather than protection—and wobbled across rough grass toward the citadel. The machine gun stopped firing because the target was too close for the gun to bear.

A guard leaned over the roof coping to aim a shoulder-launched anti-tank rocket but lost his balance in his haste. He bounced against the side of the building halfway down. From there to the ground he and the rocket launcher fell separately.

The semi hit the sloped glacis at the citadel's base.

Lamartiere lowered his seat, even though that meant he was driving blind.

The disk of sky above Lamartiere flashed white. The pavement rippled, hitting the base of *Hoodoo*'s skirts an instant before an airborne shockwave twisted the tank sideways. It pounded Lamartiere brutally despite his protected location.

Hoodoo straightened under the control of its AI. Lamartiere raised his seat and rocked the control yoke forward with the fans spinning at maximum power. The tank accelerated with the slow certainty of a boulder falling from a cliff.

A pillar of smoke and debris was still rising when Lamartiere lifted his head above the hatch coaming. It was nearly a kilometer high before it topped out into a mushroom and began to rain back on the surroundings. The citadel was a faded dream within the column, a hint of vertical lines within the black corkscrew of destruction.

The semi had vanished utterly. The Mosite Rebellion had never lacked explosives and people to use them expertly. The mines of the Western District had provided most of Ambiorix' off-planet exports in the form of hard coal with trace elements that made it the perfect culture medium for anti-aging drugs produced in the Semiramis Cluster. Ten-year-olds in the mountain villages could set a charge of slurry that would bring down a cliff face—or a two-meter section of it, if that was their intent.

The 25-cm guns were housed in pits surrounded by a berm and protective dome, invulnerable until they came into action, but the control system was in the citadel. Eight tonnes of slurry exploding against the glacis wouldn't destroy the structure, but neither the gunnery computers nor their operators would be in working order for at least the next several minutes.

Nothing remained of the checkpoint or the troops who'd been firing from the top of the building. One of the objects spinning out of the mushroom might have been a torso from which the blast had plucked head and limbs.

Hoodoo hit a steel pole with a clang, one of the uprights from the perimeter fencing. The blast had thrown it onto the roadway. Lamartiere ducked without thinking. The reflex saved him from decapitation when a coil of razor wire writhed up the bow slope and hooked under *Hoodoo*'s main gun. A moment later the wire parted with a vicious twang at the end of its stretch, leaving a bright scar on the iridium.

The van that had guided the truck to its destruction now pulled out of the sheltering ditch. A figure hopped from the passenger side of the cab and ran into *Hoodoo*'s path, arms windmilling. *What fool was—*

Crossed bandoliers flopped as the figure gestured; he carried a slung rifle in addition to the sub-machine gun in his right had. Colonel Franciscus was identifiable even at night because of his paraphernalia.

If Franciscus was here, who had been driving the truck of explosives? Though that didn't matter, not really, except to the driver's widow or mother.

When Lamartiere realized Franciscus wasn't going to get out of his way, he swore and sank the control yoke in his belly, switching the nacelles' alignment from full rearward to full forward. Even so he was going to overrun the man. Halting the inertia of a 170-tonne mass with thrust alone was no sudden business.

"Idiot!" Lamartiere screamed as he spilled pressure from the vents on top of the plenum chamber. "Idiot!"

Hoodoo skidded ten meters in a dazzle of red sparks ground from the skirts by the concrete roadway. The bow halted just short of Franciscus. The shriek of metal was as painful as the blast a moment before and seemed equally loud.

Franciscus, his clothes smoldering in a dozen places from sparks—perhaps a just God had care of events after all—climbed aboard clumsily, grabbing a headlight bracket with his free hand. He waved the other until Lamartiere grabbed his wrist to keep from being slapped in the face with the sub-machine gun.

"I'll man the guns!" Franciscus shouted over the roar

of the fans. He started climbing upward, this time grasping the muzzle of the stubby 20-CM main gun.

"They don't work!" Lamartiere said. The vents slapped closed. He raised the yoke to vertical for a moment, building pressure before he started accelerating again. The air was harsh and dry with lime burned from the concrete by friction. "You should have stayed with the van!"

Franciscus couldn't hear him. He would have ignored the comment anyway, as he seemed to ignore everything but his own will and direct orders from Father Renaud, the spiritual head of the Company of Death.

Lamartiere needed to concentrate on his driving.

The van sprinted off now that Franciscus had boarded the tank. It had been supposed to pick up the semi's driver; there was no longer any reason for its presence.

The van's relatively high power-to-weight ratio allowed it to accelerate faster than *Hoodoo*, but air resistance limited the lighter vehicle's top speed to under a hundred kph. With the correct surface and time to accelerate, *Hoodoo* could easily double that rate.

Neither vehicle outsped gunshots, but the tank could shrug them off. If the government forces were even half awake, for the van to wait while Franciscus played games had been a very bad idea.

Franciscus was shouting something about the hatch. It might be locked, but Lamartiere suspected the colonel was just trying to open it in the wrong direction, pushing it back instead of pulling it open. There was nothing the driver could do until—

Shells rang off *Hoodoo*'s rear hull. Rounds that missed sailed past, the tracers golden in the night air, and exploded in red pulses on the westbound lanes of the highway ahead.

If the tank's screens had been live, Lamartiere could have seen what was happening behind him without even turning his head. Now his choice was to ignore the pursuit or to swing the tank sideways so that he could see past the turret.

He twisted the yoke. The pursuers might have anti-tank missiles as well as automatic cannon, and even cannon could riddle the skirts and ground *Hoodoo* as surely as if they'd shot out her fan nacelles.

Two of the air-cushion vehicles that patrolled the perimeter fence had followed *Hoodoo* out of the spaceport. They had no armor to speak of, but they were fast and the guns in their small turrets had a range of several kilometers.

Because *Hoodoo* turned the next burst missed her, but red flashes ate across the back of the van. It flipped on edge and cartwheeled twice before the fuel cell ruptured. Lamartiere ducked as he drove through the fireball. He smelled flesh burning, but at least he couldn't hear the screams.

Franciscus must have opened the turret hatch because the flow past Lamartiere's chest and legs increased violently. The cross-draft cut off a moment later as Franciscus closed the cupola behind him.

Now that the colonel was clear, Lamartiere braked the tank at the end of the access road. Cannon shells crossed in front of him, then slapped both sides of the turret at the gunners adjusted. *Hoodoo* roared across the highway's eastbound lanes on inertia.

Lamartiere dumped pressure on the median, grounding in a gulp of yellow-gray soil far less spectacular than the sparks on the concrete. The tank pitched violently. Franciscus screamed in fury as he bounced around the fighting compartment, but Lamartiere had strapped in by habit.

He closed the vents and rotated *Hoodoo* clockwise. One of the patrol cars was trying to swing around their right side. It brushed the tank's bow and disintegrated as though it had hit a granite cliff. Building speed again, Lamartiere brought *Hoodoo* in line after the remaining government vehicle.

The minuscule bump might have been dirt, part of the patrol car, or the corpse of a government soldier. It made no difference after it passed beneath the tank's skirts.

They crossed the northern lanes of the highway, driving into the brush that grew on arid soil. If the car's driver had been thinking clearly, he'd have doubled back immediately and used his agility to escape. He'd panicked when he changed from hunter to hunted, though, and he tried to outrun the tank.

The gunner rotated his turret halfway, then gave it up as a bad job. A side door opened. The gunner jumped out, hit a thorn tree, and hung there impaled before *Hoodoo's* skirts ran him under.

The tank was pitching because of irregularities in the surface, but brush thick enough to slow the patrol car had no effect on 170 tonnes. The driver looked back over his shoulder an instant before *Hoodoo* crushed car and driver both. Lamartiere had only a glimpse of staring eyes and the teeth that framed the screaming mouth.

There were no more immediate enemies. Lamartiere angled *Hoodoo's* bow to the northwest. He should hit a road after a kilometer or so of brush busting. The mountains were within a hundred kilometers on this heading; Pamiers, his destination, was only another eighty kilometers beyond. He'd have *Hoodoo* under cover before government troops could mount a pursuit.

They'd won. He'd won.

In the fighting compartment behind Lamartiere, Franciscus swore in darkness. He was unable even to reopen the cupola hatch.

Pamiers had been shelled repeatedly since the start of the rebellion, and once a government column had taken out its frustration at recent sniping by burning every building in the village. Besides, a city resident like Lamartiere wouldn't have been impressed by the place on its best day.

The locals seemed happy, though. Children played shrilly on the steep hillside. They'd wanted to stay beside the tank, but that would have given away *Hoodoo's* location. Women chatted as they hung laundry or cooked on outdoor stoves. The flapping clothes made bright primary contrasts with the general coal-dust black of the landscape.

Hoodoo stood at the north side of a tailings pile, covered by a camouflage tarpaulin with the same thermal signature as bare ground. Lamartiere had heard reconnaissance aircraft twice this morning. If the government learned where *Hoodoo* was, they would come for her; but government troops only entered the mountains when they were in overwhelming force, and even that had a way of being risky.

"I'm not an engineer," Dr Clargue muttered from the driver's compartment. "I'm a medical man. I should not be here!"

"You and I are what the rebellion has for a technical staff in Pamiers," Lamartiere said. He was in the turret and couldn't see the doctor. A narrow passage connected the two portions of the tank, but that was for emergency use only. "And we've *got* to figure out where the switches are. Without the guns and sensors, this is just scrap metal."

It was a good thing that Lamartiere needed to encourage Clargue: otherwise he'd have been screaming in frustration himself. Lamartiere had been in intimate contact with the mercenaries' armored vehicles for three months, learning every detail he could about them. It hadn't occurred to him that he'd need to know where the cut-off switches were, but without that information he might as well have waited to wave goodbye when the freighter lifted with *Hoodoo* tomorrow. At least that way Lamartiere would have his final pay packet to donate to the rebellion.

The fighting compartment darkened as Captain Befayt stuck her head in the cupola hatch. "How are you coming?" she asked. "Say, there really isn't much room in there, is there?"

"No," Lamartiere said, trying not to snarl. "And we don't even have the interior lights working, so while you're standing there I can't see anything inside."

Befayt commanded the company of guerrillas who provided security for Pamiers. She had a right to be concerned since the tank was a risk to the community for as long as it remained here.

Besides that, Lamartiere liked Befayt. Too often in rebel communities the fighters ate and drank well while the civilians, even the children, starved. In Pamiers all shared, and anybody who thought his gun made him special found he had the captain to answer to.

Having said that, Lamartiere *really* didn't need to have the heavy-set woman looking over his shoulder while everything was a frustrating mess.

"Here, I'll come down with you," Befayt said. She lowered her legs through the hatch, then paused for a moment. Her boots dribbled dirt and cinders down on Lamartiere. After laying her equipment belt on top of the turret to give her ample waist more clearance, she dropped the rest of the way into the compartment.

Maybe Lamartiere *should* have snarled, though people pretty much heard what they wanted to hear. Befayt wanted a look at this wonderful, war-winning piece of equipment.

Twelve hours earlier, Lamartiere too had believed the tank was all those things. Now he wasn't sure.

The trouble was that there were so many marvelous devices packed into *Hoodoo's* vast bulk that the breaker box Lamartiere was looking for was concealed like a grain of sand in the desert. If the electronics had been live, Dr Clargue could have called up a schematic that would tell them where the switches were. . . .

Befayt stood on the seat which Lamartiere had lowered to give him more light within the fighting compartment. He and Clargue had handlights as well, but the focused beams distorted appearances by shutting off the ambiance beyond their edges.

Befayt peered around the turret in wonder. "Boy," she said with unintended irony, "I'm glad it's you guys figuring this stuff out instead of me. This the big gun?"

She patted what was indeed the breech of the main gun. Lamartiere had seen a 2-CM weapon tested after armorers had replaced the tube. The target was a range of hills ten kilometers south of the firing point. The cyan bolt had blasted a cavity a dozen meters wide in solid rock.

"Yes," Lamartiere said shortly. "The round comes from the ready magazine in the turret ring, shifts to the transfer chamber—"

He slid back a spring-loaded door beside the breech. The interior was empty.

"—and then into the gun when the previous round's ejected. That way all but the one round's under heavy armor at all times."

"Amazing," Befayt said with a gratified smile. "Guess we'll be giving the Synod's dogs back some of what they been feeding us, right?"

"If we're given a chance to get the tank in working order, yes we will!" Lamartiere said. To cover his outburst he immediately went on, "Say, captain, I'd been meaning to ask you: do you know where my sister Celine's gone? I thought she might be here to, you know, say hello when I arrived."

"She was until about a week ago," Befayt said, relaxing deliberately. The captian didn't want a pointless confrontation either. "Then she got a message and went back with the supply trucks to Goncourt. You might check with Franciscus when he comes back from there tonight."

"Yes, I'll do that," Lamartiere said. The only good thing about the past hours of failure were that Colonel Franciscus had gone on to Goncourt to confer with Father Renaud instead of staying to watch Lamartiere.

"Guess I'll get out of your way," Befayt said with a tight control that showed she knew she'd been unwelcome. She wasn't the sort to let that affect her unduly, but it wasn't something that anybody liked to feel. "Celine seemed chirpy as a cricket when I last saw her, though."

She braced her hands on the edges of the hatch.

"Here, let me raise the seat," said Lamartiere. He touched the button on the side of the cushion. It was hydraulic, not electrical, and worked off an accumulator driven directly by Number Four fan. "I know I shouldn't worry about her, but we're all each other has since—"

As the seat whined upward, Lamartiere saw the flat box attached to the base plate. It had a hinged cover.

"Clargue!" he shouted. "I found it! There's a breaker box on the bottom of the seat!"

He flipped the cover open. The seat had halted at

midcolumn when Lamartiere took his finger off the control. Befayt, excited though uncertain about what was going on, squatted on the cushion and tried to look underneath without getting in the way.

Lamartiere aimed his handlight at the interior of the box. There was a triple row of circuit breakers. All of them were in the On position.

"Turn them one at a time!" Dr Clargue said. "We don't want a surge to damage the equipment."

"They're already on, doctor," Lamartiere said. He felt sandbagged. Were the electronics dead because of a fault, one the crew hadn't bothered to fix once they had *Hoodoo* mobile again? But Heth and Stegner wouldn't have relaxed until they had the tank's guns working, surely!

"Doctor!" Lamartiere said. "Check under your seat. Both crew members would have the cut-offs so they—"

"Yes, it's here!" said Clargue. "I've got it open. . . ."

Lamartiere heard ventilation motors hum. The interior lights, flat and a deep yellow that didn't affect night vision, came on; then the thirty-centimeter gunnery screen above the breech of the main gun glowed.

Hoodoo rang with a violent explosion against the turret. Choking smoke swirled through the open hatch. The ventilation system switched to high speed.

Befayt jumped out of the hatch, moving quickly and without the awkwardness with which she'd entered. "What is happening?" Clargue shouted. The doctor's voice faded as he climbed out of the driver's compartment. "Are we attacked?"

Lamartiere tried to rotate the turret. It didn't move: that breaker was still off. He pulled himself into the open air. He couldn't do anything inside and he didn't choose to wait in the turret to be killed if that was what was going to happen.

The smoke was dissipating. The tarpaulin had been hurled up the tailings pile, but Lamartiere saw no other sign of damage. Dr Clargue was coming around the front of the tank. Befayt stood on the back deck, staring in consternation at fresh scars on the side of the turret.

"My belt blew up," Befayt said. "May God cast me from Her if that's not what happened. My *belt* blew up."

The women and children who made up most of Pamiers' population were disappearing into the mouths of the mines that had sheltered them through previous attacks. The traverses weren't comfortable homes, but they were proof against anything the government could throw against them. Guerrillas had dived into fighting positions as quickly. Those in sight of their leader were looking toward her for direction.

"What?" said Clargue. "Did you have electrically-primed explosives on your belt, captain?"

"Well," said Befayt. "Sure, I—Oh, Mother God. You turned the radios on, didn't you?"

"Of course a tank like this has radios, you idiot!" the doctor screamed. His goatee wobbled. Clargue was a little man in his late sixties, unfailingly pleasant in all the encounters Lamartiere had had with him to this moment. "What did you mean bringing blasting caps here!"

"I . . . ," Befayt said. She looked completely stupefied. Everyone in the district knew that a powerful radio signal generated enough current in the wires of an electrical blasting cap to detonate the primer. On reflection it was obvious that a tank would have radios; but Lamartiere hadn't thought of that, and neither had the guerrilla commander.

Clargue had scrambled back into the driver's compartment. "Doctor, I'm sorry!" Befayt called after him. "I'll warn the men. And I'll get the tarpaulin over you again."

She trotted toward the entrance of the mine which served as the village's command post. Her hand-held radio had been on the equipment belt.

Clargue reappeared. Lamartiere looked at him in dismay and said, "It was my fault. I should have warned her."

"No," said Clargue. "It was my fault for turning on the power without thinking of the radios. It's not only the blasting caps. We—I—sent out a signal that the government listening posts almost certainly picked up. They know where we are now. They'll be coming."

He shook his head with an expression of miserable frustration. Lamartiere remembered Clargue looking the same way six months before, when a child who'd stepped on a bomblet died despite anything the doctor could do.

"I'll apologize to Captain Befayt," Clargue said. "I was angry with myself, but I blamed her."

"First we need to get *Hoodoo* working," Lamartiere said. Befayt was leading a group of guerrillas toward them to re-erect the camouflage cover. "So that when the government troops arrive, we're ready for them."

The villagers came out in the evening when they heard the truck approaching from Goncourt. They bowed low in the honor due a holy man on seeing that Father Renaud rode beside Franciscus in the cab. There wasn't, Lamartiere thought, much warmth in their greetings.

Father Renaud was a slim, deeply ascetic man with a fringe of white hair and a placid expression. He was personally very gentle, a man who would let an insect drink its fill of his blood rather than needlessly crush one of God's creatures.

But there was no compromise in the father's attitude as to what was owed God. He had blessed a young mother before she walked into a government checkpoint with six kilos of explosive hidden beneath the infant in her backpack.

Most people in the mountains respected Father Renaud and his faith. A man who spent so much of his time with God wasn't entirely safe for ordinary folk to be around, however.

The driver pulled up beside *Hoodoo* to let out Renaud and the colonel, then circled back to the center of the village to distribute the few crates of supplies which the Council in Goncourt could spare to Pamiers. The gardens planted in the rubble of burned-out buildings here couldn't support the population. Without some supplement the refugees would move to Goncourt, adding to the health and safety problems of what remained of the Mosites' alternative seat of government.

Befayt and several of her aides had started for *Hoodoo* when they heard the fans of the oncoming truck. The captain knelt and accepted the blessing from Father Renaud, but she and Franciscus exchanged only the briefest nods of greeting. There was no love lost between the Company of Death and local guerrilla units. As for rank— an officer could call himself anything he pleased, but in the field it came down to who accepted his orders.

In Pamiers, only Lamartiere took orders from Colonel Franciscus. Little as Lamartiere liked the man, he knew that local groups like Befayt's could never defeat the central government, though they might keep the mountains ungovernable indefinitely now that the mercenaries had left. In Lamartiere's opinion, decades of hungry squalor like this would be worse even than haughty repression by the government and Synod.

Franciscus waited impatiently for Lamartiere to take the blessing, then snapped, "Have you fixed the tank yet? I've told the Council that we can move on Brione as soon as they've concentrated our forces, but that I have to be in charge. The tank is crucial, and *I* command it."

"We have all the electronic systems working," Dr Clargue said in a voice as thin as a scalpel. "The guns are not in operation yet because the magazines seem to be empty."

Clargue wasn't a member of any military body, but he was a Mosite believer and had been an expert on Ambiorix' most advanced medical computer systems before he left Carcassone Central Hospital for hands-on care of the folk of his home village. His presence was the reason the Council had picked Pamiers as an initial destination for the stolen tank.

"What do you mean?" Franciscus said. He turned on Lamartiere with all the fury of a terrier facing a rat. "Didn't you bring ammunition? Did you think we were going to stand on the turret and throw *rocks*?"

Lamartiere was taller than Franciscus, but the colonel was an athlete who went through a long exercise regimen every morning and who gloried in hand-to-hand combat. He didn't need his trappings of guns, bombs and knives to be dangerous. He was physically capable of beating Lamartiere to death at this moment, and he was very possibly willing to do so as well.

"*Hoodoo* has a full load of ammunition, both two-centimeter and twenty-centimeter," Lamartiere said quietly, forcing himself not to flinch back as Franciscus stepped toe to toe with him. "I drove the ammo trailer to her myself and watched Sergeant Heth load her. But the rounds are in storage magazines in the floor of the hull. The ready magazines in the turret are empty."

"You must understand," Clargue said, breaking in with an expression that implied he didn't care whether Franciscus understood how to breathe, "that this tank is a very complex system. As yet I haven't found the command that will transfer ammunition between locations or even the command set it belongs to. It doesn't seem to be part of the gunnery complex, as I would have expected."

He shrugged. His frustration was as great as Lamartiere's, but the doctor was better at hiding it. "We're working through the range of possibilities. It will take time."

Clargue knew, as Lamartiere did, that there might be very little time because of the RF spike when *Hoodoo*'s radios came on.

"Well look," said Befayt. She wore a new equipment belt, but this one didn't contain any of the electrically-primed bombs that were a staple of the guerrillas' ambush techniques. "Why don't you move the disks by hand? I can supply the people if the weight's a problem."

"The storage magazines are sealed and locked," Lamartiere explained. *This* was something he knew about. "It takes a special fitting on the end of the ammo trailer to get into the tube. If there's dust on the rounds, they might explode when they're fired."

"We don't have time to be picky!" Franciscus said. He was a little off-balance around Clargue, perhaps because the doctor was so completely Franciscus' opposite in personality. "Blow open the magazines and load the turret by hand."

"No!" said Lamartiere and Clargue together.

"Like bloody Hell!" Befayt said, speaking directly to the colonel for the first time since he'd arrived. "I've looked at those fittings. Enough charge to blow one open and the best thing you're going to do is crush all the disks so they don't work. There's a better chance that you'll set one off and the whole lot gang fires. How does that help us, will you tell me, Mister Colonel?"

Franciscus looked as though he was going to hit her. Befayt's aides must have thought so too, because they backed slightly and leveled their weapons at the colonel: a pair of Ambiorix-made electromotive slug-throwers, and a 2-cm powergun stolen or captured from the Slammers' stocks.

"Children," Father Renaud said with none of the sarcasm the word might have carried had it come from another mouth. "If we squabble among ourselves then we fail the Lord in Her time of need. There is no greater sin."

"Sorry, father," Befayt muttered. Franciscus gave her a sour look, then dipped his head to Renaud in a sign of contrition.

Renaud returned his attention to Clargue and Lamartiere. "Go on with your work," he said calmly. "Remember, have faith and She will provide."

Lamartiere bowed and turned to board the tank again. He mostly kept silent while Dr Clargue methodically went over the software, but there was always the possibility that he would recognize something that the doctor had missed.

It hadn't happened yet, though. Working on the mercenaries' vehicles in depot didn't teach him anything about the way they operated in combat, and to ask questions on the subject would have compromised Lamartiere as surely waving a sign saying, I AM A MOSITE SPY!

The radio on Befayt's belt buzzed. She unhooked it and held it to her cheek, shielding the mouthpiece by reflex even in this company. When she lowered the unit, her face looked as though it had been hacked from stone.

"The government outposts at Twill, Lascade, and on Marcelline Ridge have just been reinforced," she said. "That's an anvil all around Pamiers. There's a mechanized battalion heading south out of the Ariege cantonment to be the hammer."

"It's because of my mistake," Dr Clargue said in a stricken voice. "I shouldn't be involved in this. I'm not a man of war."

"Well, there's no problem," Franciscus said. "Just get the tank working and we'll wipe out this whole Synod battalion. The first battle will be in Pamiers instead of us having to go to them."

"I don't know how long I will need," Clargue said. "Finding the right command is like—"

He pointed to the sky. The sun had set and the first stars were appearing in the twilight.

"Like finding one star at random in all the heavens. How long is it before the enemy will attack?"

"It's forty klicks from Ariege," Befayt said uncomfortably. "I won't say they're going to have clear going, but after the way the villages on the route got ground up over the past five months I wouldn't expect a whole lot of resistance. Even though it's just government troops and not the mercenaries this time."

"Two hours," Lamartiere translated. "Less if they're willing to push very hard and abandon vehicles that break down."

"I can't guarantee success," Dr Clargue said. His face wrinkled in misery. "I can't even expect success. There's no sign that I will ever find the right command."

"Well, then we have to move our tank to a new location," Franciscus said. He looked at Father Renaud, less for counsel than to indicate he wasn't attempting to give the priest orders. "Boukasset, I think? Even if they find us again, it'll take them days to mount an attack there. And even reinforced, none of those patrol posts can stop *us*."

He patted *Hoodoo*'s iridium flank with a proprietary gesture that made Lamartiere momentarily furious. He knew it was stupid to give in to personal dislike in a crisis like this, but he also knew human beings were much more than cold intellects in a body.

Aloud Lamartiere said, "We can break through, I'm pretty

sure. But the villagers can't escape, and the government troops won't leave without doing all the damage they can. I'm afraid they'll blow up the mine entrances this time."

Befayt grimaced. "Yeah," she said. "I figure that too."

She nodded toward *Hoodoo*. "They're scared of this thing. If they don't have it to fight after all, well, they'll find some other way to work off their energy."

"I'll get back to work," Clargue said simply. He put his hand on the boarding ladder.

"And I'll put my people in place at the crossing," Befayt said. "I don't know that we can slow them up much, not a battalion, but they'll know they been in a fight before they get across the Lystra."

"Wait," said Lamartiere. He pointed to the guerrilla carrying the powergun. "Captain, you've got several soldiers with two-centimeter guns, don't you? Give me all their ammunition. I can hand-feed it into the tribarrel's ready magazine and use the tank's gunnery system to aim and fire."

The guerrilla looked shocked at the thought he should surrender the weapon that gave him status in any gathering of fighters. Befayt nodded to him and said, "Yeah, do what he says, Aghulan. You can keep the gun. Just give him the ammo."

She smiled bitterly and added, "I'd say you could have it for your tombstone, but I don't guess there'll be enough of any of us left to bury in a couple hours."

The aide was a man in his sixties. He looked at the hills and said, "Well, I said I never wanted to leave this valley. Guess I'll get my wish."

He spat on the coal-blackened ground.

"Right," said Franciscus. "I'll man the tank's gun."

"No," said Lamartiere before Clargue could step away from the ladder. "I need the doctor with me. He understands the parts of the systems that I'll need but don't know anything about."

Clargue looked at Lamartiere in surprise. Both of them knew that was a lie.

Franciscus glared at Lamartiere and rang the edge of

his fist angrily on *Hoodoo*'s skirt. "I should have infiltrated the base myself," he snarled, accepting the statement at face value. "Then we'd have somebody who knew what he was doing!"

Father Renaud looked at the colonel sharply. "Emmanuel," he said. "Glory will come to those who strive for the Lord, but neither glory nor martyrdom is an end in itself. Sometimes I fear that you forget that."

"Sorry, father," Franciscus muttered.

"And captain?" Lamartiere added as another idea struck him. The sky over the western hills was fully dark now. "Can your men make me up flash charges with about three meters of wire leads on each? As many as you can. And I'll need a clacker to set them off."

"Why?" Franciscus demanded. "What do you think you're going to do with them?"

If Franciscus hadn't spoken first, Befayt might have asked the same question. As it was, she gave the colonel a flat glare and said, "Yeah, I'll put a couple of the boys on it while the rest of us go wait at the crossing."

She looked at Renaud and added, "Father? I'd appreciate it if you'd bless us all before we go. It don't look like there'll be another chance."

There was a reconnaissance drone overhead. Darkness and altitude hid it, but the hum of its turbofan occasionally reached the ground.

"I'm going to button up," Lamartiere said over *Hoodoo*'s intercom. He grimaced to hear himself deliberately using jargon to prove he was a real tanker. "I'm going to close the hatches, I mean," he added. "Make sure you're clear of yours."

He touched the switch on the compartment's sidepanel; both hatches slid closed with cushioned thumps. One thing Lamartiere had proved he *wasn't* was a tanker. The damage *Hoodoo*'s skirts had taken on the run from Brione suggested he wasn't much of a tank driver either, though he supposed he'd call himself adequate given haste and the condition of roads through the mountains.

"Denis, you know that I can't operate these weapons, don't you?" Dr Clargue said. When the tank was sealed, the vehicle intercom was good enough for parties to hear one another even over the roar of the fans, though for greater flexibility on operations the mercenaries always wore commo helmets. Lamartiere had a momentary daydream of what he could do if he had all the equipment of Hammer's Regiment under his control.

He might not be able to do anything. Hardware was wonderful, but the training to use it was more wonderful still. He should have asked a few more questions when he worked for the mercenaries. He might have been exposed and shot, but at least the civilians of Pamiers would face less risk.

"I know that," Lamartiere said aloud. "We'll change places when we get to the crossing and I'll take over the gun. I just couldn't afford to have Franciscus in the turret. He doesn't know any more about the equipment than you do, and _he_ wouldn't trade with me."

He started the fans, bringing the blades up to speed at a flat angle so that they didn't bite the air. The driver's compartment had two displays, one above the other. On default the lower screen was a 360° panorama with a keyboard overlay, while the upper one showed the view forward with system readouts overlying the right and left edges. By touching any gauge, Lamartiere could expand it to half the screen.

The fans and power system were within parameters. They shouldn't give any trouble on the three kilometers between here and the Lystra River.

The truck that had brought supplies was ferrying the last of the guerrillas to the defensive positions at the crossing. Befayt had allowed Franciscus to go with the first group. Tonight she wasn't about to turn away anyone with a gun and a willingness to die.

"You don't have to change places, you know," Clargue said. "Unless you want to, of course. You can control the weapons from your compartment by touching Star-Gee."

"What?" said Lamartiere, taking his hands off the control yoke. "I didn't know. . . ."

He pressed °-G on the keyboard. The display had no more give than the bulkhead, but the orange symbols of a gunnery screen replaced the center of the panorama. The crossed circle to the right of the display was a trigger.

"Oh . . . ," Lamartiere whispered. For the first time he thought that the bluff he planned might actually work.

He checked the command bar on the left side of the display, chose SEEK, and raised the search area to 10° above the horizon. The tarpaulin covered the region selected, so for the moment neither the pipper on the screen nor the tribarrel in the cupola reacted.

"Hang on," he called to the doctor. "We're going to just move out a little ways."

Leaving the gunnery display set, Lamartiere adjusted fan angle with the right grip and slid *Hoodoo* onto clear ground. Dust and pebbles spun outward in the spray of air escaping beneath the edge of the plenum chamber.

Lamartiere let *Hoodoo* settle. The gunnery display appeared to scroll down past the pipper until vague motion quivered in the center of the crosshairs. In the turret Clargue exclaimed when the tribarrel also moved.

Lamartiere expanded his image. The target was a drone with long slender wings and a small engine mounted on a pylon above the fuselage. The default option was AUTO; Lamartiere switched to MANUAL because he simply didn't have the ammunition to spare the burst a computer might think was necessary to make sure of the target. He tapped the trigger once.

In the closed-up tank, the 2-CM weapon merely *whacked* as it sent a bolt of ionized copper skyward at light speed. The main display compensated automatically for the burst of intense light; unless set otherwise, the AI used enhancement and thermal imaging to keep the apparent illumination at 100% of local daylight.

There was a cyan flash on the gunnery display, though. The lightly-built drone broke apart in a flurry of wing panels and a mist of vaporized fuel. There was no fireball. The drone operating at too high an altitude for atmospheric pressure to sustain combustion.

"It worked!" Clargue shouted. "You made it work!"

"Mother God!" Lamartiere said as fumbled to modify the screen. He was shaking. After a moment's confusion he realized that *of course* Clargue had been able to echo the gunnery display on his own screens. "You understand this so much better than I do, doctor."

"No," said Clargue. "And even if I did, you are a man of war, Denis. As I will never be."

Lamartiere reduced the image and switched from SEEK to PROTECT. When the map display came up, he expanded the region from the default—a ten meter fringe surrounding *Hoodoo*—to include the whole area of Pamiers.

He touched AUTO. The civilians were under cover, deep in the mines, but an incoming round might shatter rock and bring down a traverse on huddled forms. One of them might have been his sister Celine.

Taking the yoke in both hands again, Lamartiere drove toward the eastern exit from the valley at a sedate pace. He didn't need to rush to get into position, and high speed on this terrain would waste precious ammunition when the AI responded to incoming artillery.

Because he concentrated on his driving, Lamartiere heard the whine of the cupola before he noticed motion on the gunnery screen. The tribarrel fired: three rounds, two, three more. Cyan and the dull red light of high explosive quivered on the gunnery screen.

Hoodoo's sensors and AI permitted her to sweep shells from the sky when they were still so far away that the explosions couldn't be seen by the naked eye. Given a vantage point and enough 2-CM ammunition, this tank could defend the whole area from horizon to horizon.

The sticking point now was the ammunition.

The second salvo came over just before *Hoodoo* reached the mouth of the valley. The shells were fired out of the northwest, probably from guns in the government base at Ariege. The tribarrel hummed and crackled, rotating barrels between rounds so that the polished iridium bores had a chance to cool. The powergun bolts detonated the shells when they were barely over the horizon.

Driving with one hand, Lamartiere adjusted the gunnery screen. He hoped the gunners wouldn't waste any
more of their expensive terminally-guided rounds. They
didn't have direct observation of the results since the drone
had been knocked down, but observers with the mechanized battalion would tell them their fire was fruitless.

"I'm setting the gun only to respond to shells aimed at
us from now on, doctor," he explained to Clargue. He
supposed he was trying to pass on the burden of the choice
he'd just made. "We're down to seventy-seven rounds. If
I keep covering the village, we'll use up all the ammunition and then we lose everything."

"Yes," Clargue said. He sounded cool; certainly not
judgmental. "Rather like triage."

"Pardon?" Lamartiere said. "Triage?"

Driving *Hoodoo* with the electronics working was infinitely less wearing than the trip Lamartiere had made in
the early hours of the morning, trying to pick his way over
narrow, half-familiar roads in the dark. The screens showed
the path as though in daylight, and the tank's microwave
imaging ignored dust and the mist beginning to rise in low
points where aquifers bled through the rocks.

"When there are many injured and limited medical facilities," Clargue explained, "you divide the casualties into three
groups. You ignore the ones who aren't in immediate danger so you can concentrate on helping those who will survive only if they get immediate help. And you also ignore
those who will probably die even if you try to help them."

He coughed to clear his throat. "It's a technique of
setting priorities that was developed during wartime."

Hoodoo crested a rise and entered the floodplain of the
Lystra River. Except in springtime, the Lystra ran in a
narrow channel only a few hundred meters wide—though
deep and fast-flowing. There was only one ford on the
upper river, and the bridges that spanned it during peace
had been blown early in the rebellion.

The ford was a dike of basalt intruding into the surrounding limestone, raising the channel and spreading it
to nearly a kilometer in width. One of the bridges had been

here. The abutments and two pillars still stood, but the tangle of dynamited girders had tumbled out of sight downstream last year when the snow melted.

Befayt's troops were hidden in fighting holes, covered with insulating blankets that dispersed their thermal signatures. They'd learned to be careful eight months before, when elements of the Slammers began accompanying government units who entered the mountains.

The guerrillas had been wary of the mercenaries' firepower. They'd quickly learned that the sensor suites of the vast iridium behemoths were even more of a threat.

Given a little time, Dr Clargue could put those sensors in the hands of the rebels. Clargue—and *Hoodoo*—just had to survive this night.

Lamartiere found the spot he'd noticed on previous visits to Pamiers, a shallow draw that carried overflow from the channel during the spate. He took *Hoodoo* over the edge; gently, he thought, but bank broke away and the tank rushed to the bottom of gravel and coarse vegetation with a roar. A geyser of dust rose.

Hoodoo's skirts dug into the ground, sealing the plenum chamber for an instant before the pressure rose enough to pop the tank up like a cork from a champagne bottle. The plume of debris followed the breeze upstream, settling and dissipating while the echoes of Lamartiere's ineptitude slowly faded.

"Befayt's people must think I'm an incompetent fool," Lamartiere muttered. "And they're right."

"What they think," Dr Clargue replied with his usual dispassion, "is that the most powerful machine on Ambiorix is on their side. And they are indeed right."

Lamartiere revved his fans. He took *Hoodoo* slowly back up the slope until the cupola and its sensors peeked over crest to view the ford. Then he shut down again and studied the display.

"Doctor?" he said, wishing he could see Clargue's face as he spoke. "I'm going to try to bluff the Synod troops into thinking *Hoodoo* has her full armament. A two-centimeter round doesn't have anything like the power of the main gun, but it's no joke. I'm hoping if there's a big flash here, they'll think whatever hits them is from the twenty-centimeter gun."

"Ah," said Clargue, quick on the uptake as always. "So these little bombs Lieutenant Aghulan put in the compartment with me are to make the flashes. You want me to throw them out one at a time for you to detonate when you fire the tribarrel."

"That's right," said Lamartiere, "but you'll have to detonate them yourself when I call, 'Shoot'. Do you know how to use a clacker?"

"Of course I know how to use a clacker," Clargue said with frigid disdain. "I was born in Pamiers, was I not? But have you forgotten how to turn on the radios, Denis? The timing will be more accurate if you do both things yourself; and as for the remaining blasting caps, the transfer chamber for the big gun will provide a Faraday cage to shield them."

"Mother God," said Lamartiere in embarrassment. "Yes, doctor, that's a much better idea. I'm very sorry."

He heard the cupola hatch open. "I've placed the first bomb," Clargue said mildly. "You have a great deal to think about, Denis. You are doing well."

I wish I were a million light years away, Lamartiere thought as he concentrated on his displays. But he wasn't, and the rebellion would have to make do with him for want of better.

Hoodoo's sensors indicated the government battalion had halted on the reverse slope of the ridge north of the Lystra River. Their commander had the same problem as a hunter who thinks he's trapped a dangerous animal in a deep cave: the only way to be sure is to go straight in.

If the rebels were going to defend Pamiers, the ford was the obvious location. On the other hand they might well have drifted higher in the mountains, leaving behind boobytraps and snipers instead of trying to stop a force they knew was unstoppable. That had generally been the case in the past when the government focused its strength.

Besides, months of battering by government units supported
by mercenaries had virtually eliminated the Mosites' ability
to mass large forces of their own.

But now there was a tank, a devouring superweapon,
which the rebels *might* have in operating condition. All the
battalion from Ariege knew for sure was that they had been
ordered to assault Pamiers and eliminate the stolen tank
at all cost.

Lamartiere grinned despite himself as he considered his
enemy's options. The government troops knew one other
thing: they, and not the brass in Carcassone, would being
paying that cost.

He could have felt sorry for them if he hadn't remembered the villages Synod troops had 'cleansed' after an
nearby ambush. Of course, there'd been the garrisons of
overrun government bases left with their genitals sewn into
their mouths. In the name of God. . . .

An 8-wheeled 'tank' accelerated over the crest and
bounced down the road to the crossing at too high a speed.
The driver was afraid of a rebel ambush, but nothing the
Mosites could do would be worse than flipping the 30-tonne
vehicle to tumble sideways into the river.

The hidden rebels didn't respond.

The tank slowed, spraying gravel from its locked wheels.
It pulled off the road at the end of a switchback and settled
into a hull-down position from which its long 10-CM coil
gun could cover the crossing.

Three more tanks came into sight one after another, following the first without the initial panicked haste. They all
took overwatch positions on the forward slope. They weren't
well shielded—one of them was in a clump of spiny shrubs
that wouldn't stop smallarms, let alone a 20-CM bolt—but
at least there was psychological benefit for the crews.

The government tanks had good frontal protection and
powerful electromotive guns that could throw either HE
or long-rod tungsten armor-piercers. Local technology
couldn't carry the gun, the armor, and the banks of
capacitors which powered the weapon, on an air-cushion
chassis of reasonable size, though.

The Slammers' 30-tonne combat cars, like their tanks, had miniaturized fusion powerplants. The Government of Ambiorix would have had to import fusion units at many times the cost of the gun vehicles as completed with locally-manufactured diesels. The 8-wheeled chassis was probably the best compromise between economics and the terrain.

With the tanks in position, the remainder of the battalion came over the hill and headed for the river. Thirty-odd air-cushion armored personnel carriers made up the bulk of the unit. Each APC mounted an automatic cannon in a small turret and could carry up to sixteen troops in addition to its own crew.

To Lamartiere's surprise there was an air-cushion jeep in the middle of the column. It pulled out of line almost at once and vanished behind an outcrop too slight to hide a vehicle of any size.

A lightly-loaded air-cushion vehicle can sail across water because its weight is spread evenly over the whole surface beneath the plenum chamber. Government APCs carried too high a density of armor and payload for that. They sank, but where the bottom was as shallow and firm as it was here they could pogo across without flooding their fans.

Even so, the Lystra was dangerously high. Only a crisis could induce a battalion to force the crossing now instead of waiting for the load of melting snow to recede for another week.

Rather than driving straight into the water as Lamartiere expected, the APCs formed three lines abreast well short of the bank. Their turret guns nervously searched the hills across the river, and troops pointed personal weapons from the open hatches in the vehicles' top decks.

Four more tanks closed the battalion's line of march. They drove past their fellows in overwatch positions to halt at the river's edge. A pair of crewmen got out of each vehicle and erected a breathing tube over the engine vents. While they worked, the third crew member closed the coil gun's muzzle with a tompion.

The crews got back in their waterproofed tanks and

drove slowly into the river. The initial drop-off brought water foaming over the tops of the big wheels, but the slope lessened. The vehicles were nearly at the Lystra's midpoint before their turrets went completely under, leaving only the snorkel tubes and occasionally the raised muzzle of a coil gun to mark their progress.

The first rank of APCs bounded into the river with a roar and wall of spray like that at the base of a waterfall. They had waited so that their boisterous passage didn't swamp the tanks while the latter were still in deep water.

"Here we go," Lamartiere warned Clargue. He fed power to the fans and lifted *Hoodoo* several meters higher up the swale, exposing her turret and main gun to view of the government forces.

The tanks across the river fired before *Hoodoo* came to rest. Two shells landed ringing hammerblows against the turret and a third exploded just short, flinging half a tonne of dirt over the bow slope. If Lamartiere had been looking out of his hatch, the blasts would have decapitated him.

The government vehicles had fired HE, not armor-piercing shot. That meant they hadn't really expected to meet the Slammers' tank here. They must be terrified already. . . .

Lamartiere laid the pipper on the gun mantle of the tank on the left. *He* was too busy to be frightened now.

Befayt's guerrillas and the APCs were firing wildly. Government automatic weapons stitched the night together with golden tracers. Rebel coil guns showed only puffs of fluorescent mist, the ionized vestiges of the projectiles' driving bands.

Lamartiere tapped his trigger while his left index finger clicked the radios on and off. Light more brilliant than the shellbursts lit *Hoodoo*'s turret. Remnants of the copper leads bled blue-green across the flash of aluminized slurry. Simultaneously the tribarrel's bolt struck at the base of the target's electromotive gun, cratering the armor and stripping insulation from the tube's windings.

"Another charge!" Lamartiere screamed.

The guerrillas were concentrating on tank snorkels and the APCs which had entered the stream. A line of bullets tore out the side of an APC's skirts. The vehicle rolled over on its back, spilling soldiers through the open hatches. The weight of their gear sucked them down.

The government tanks fired again. The tank Lamartiere had damaged dissolved in a sizzling short circuit. The current meant to accelerate a kilo of tungsten to 4000 kph instead ate metal. Everything flammable in the interior ignited, including the flesh of the crew.

The other three rounds missed *Hoodoo*. The gunners had switched to AP, but in their haste they'd forgotten to correct for the much flatter trajectory of the high velocity shot.

"Ready!" Clargue called. Lamartiere hit the second tank exactly where he'd nailed the first. A 2-CM bolt couldn't penetrate the government tanks' frontal armor, but accurately used it put paid to their armament. This time, the hatches flew open and the crew bailed out as soon as the bolt hit as soon as the bolt hit.

The government command vehicles carried hoop antennas that set them apart from the ordinary APCs. A guerrilla hit one with a shoulder-launched buzz bomb. The shaped-charge warhead sent a line of white fire through the interior and triggered a secondary explosion that blew the turret off.

In his triumph the rebel forgot the obvious. He reloaded and rose again from the same location. At least a dozen automatic cannon chewed him to a fiery memory.

Lamartiere laid his pipper on the third target. He didn't have time to shoot: the crew was already abandoning their untouched vehicle.

The APCs of the first wave were mostly bogged in the Lystra, though one had managed to wallow back to dry land with riddled skirts. An air-cushion vehicle could move with a leaking plenum chamber, but the fans shed their blades if they tried to push water.

Three of the fording tanks were only ripples on the surface of the river. The fourth had started to climb the south bank. Its bow and turret were clear, but the engine compartment was still under water when rebels had shot the breathing tube away. The bodies of the three crewmen lay halfway out of their hatches.

Lamartiere settled his pipper on the last of the overwatching tanks. The government driver backed and turned sharply, trying to retreat the way he had come. Lamartiere hit the vehicle in the middle of the flank, blowing the thin armor into the capacitor compartment. This time the short circuit was progressive rather than instantaneous as with the first victim, but the tank's ultimate destruction was no less complete.

The surviving APCs roared up the north slope of the valley, going back the way they'd come. Some of them had reversed their turrets and were spraying cannonshells southward, but they no longer made a pretense of aiming. Several vehicles stood empty, though without magnification Lamartiere couldn't see any signs of damage.

There were a dozen brush fires on the south side of the river, and almost that many burning vehicles on the north. It had been a massacre.

Guerrillas sniped at soldiers who were still moving, but some of Befayt's people were already splashing into the water to gather loot from the nearest tank. There was a cable bridge slung underwater a kilometer upstream. Organized parties of guerrillas would cross to sweep the northern bank in a few hours.

The jeep Lamartiere had forgotten suddenly accelerated out of cover, heading uphill. Lamartiere slapped his pipper on it for magnification rather than in a real attempt to shoot.

The vehicle jinked left and vanished before he *could* have shot. He was almost sure from the brief glimpse that the two figures aboard were wearing Slammers' uniforms.

Lamartiere heard the tribarrel whine under the AI's guidance. It began firing short bursts: the artillery in Ariege was shelling again. The gunners hadn't had enough warning to support the crossing with the concentrations they must have prepared in case of rebel resistance.

"They could have crushed us, doctor," Lamartiere said

in wonder. "They could have gone right through except they panicked. We won because we frightened them, not because we beat them."

"In my proper profession," Clargue said, "a cure is a cure. I don't see a distinction between the psychological effect of a placebo and the biological effect of a real drug— so long as the beneficial effect occurs."

He paused before adding, "I find it difficult to view this destruction as beneficial, but I suppose it's better than the same thing happening to Pamiers."

The last of the surviving APCs had crossed the ridge to safety, leaving behind a pall of dust and the wreckage of their fellows. The tribarrel continued to fire. The gunners no longer had the site under observation, but they were making noise for much the same reason as savages beat drums when the sun vanishes in eclipse.

"I'm going back to Pamiers," Lamartiere said. He was extraordinarily tired. "There's some damage to the skirts—" rips from fragments of the shells that hit the turret in the first salvo "—that needs to be repaired. Then we have to get out of here."

Franciscus jumped onto the bow slope. Lamartiere hadn't seen him approaching; there'd been more on his mind than his immediate surroundings.

"We won!" the colonel shouted. "By God, the Council'll know who to give charge of the war to now! We won't stop in Brione, we'll take Carcassone!"

The cupola hatch was open because Dr Clargue had been throwing the flash charges out of it. Franciscus climbed up and said, "I'll ride inside on the way back."

Lamartiere heard the hatch thump closed. Franciscus shouted in anger.

Lamartiere drove *Hoodoo* up and onto the road. Neither he nor the doctor spoke on the way back to Pamiers.

Lamartiere shut off the fans in the center of Pamiers. He opened his hatch.

Franciscus looked down at him. He wasn't wearing a

shirt so the bomb-heavy bandoliers wobbled across the curly hair of his chest. He hadn't been around when Befayt provided the reminder about blasting caps and radios. Lamartiere didn't comment.

Despite the consciously heroic pose, the colonel looked vaguely unsure of himself. Being closed out of *Hoodoo* on the drive back had caused him to consider Lamartiere as something more than a pawn for the colonel to play. He asked, "Why didn't you put us under cover?"

"Because all it covers now," Lamartiere said as he got out, "is our sensors' ability to see any shells the Synod sends over. They know from the drone where we were hiding, so it's a fixed target for them. This way *Hoodoo* protects herself."

Of course there were only thirty-seven rounds left in the tribarrel's loading tube. Maybe Dr Clargue would be able to find the transfer command in the respite he and *Hoodoo*—and Denis Lamartiere, for all Lamartiere felt a failure—had won. But the first order of business was to repair the tank and get *out* of here.

Lamartiere slid down the bow and walked toward the pit where Pelissier had his workshop. Civilians ran to the tank, some of them carrying lanterns. They cheered and waved yellow Mosite flags. Lamartiere tried to smile as he brushed his way through them.

A child handed him a garland of red windflowers. Lamartiere took it, but the streaming blooms made him think of blood in water. The Lystra's current would have carried the carnage kilometers downstream by now. . . .

Franciscus stood, using the tank as a podium. He began to tell the story of the battle in a loud, triumphant voice. Lamartiere didn't look back.

Pelissier had been only a teenager when he lost both legs in a mine accident. Since that time he'd served as Pamiers' machinist, living in an increasingly ornate house during peacetime and at the entrance of a disused mine since rebellion had destroyed the village.

Pelissier had a chair mounted on a four-wheeled tray.

The seat raised and lowered, and there was an electric motor to drive him if required. For the most part, the cripple trundled himself around his immediate vicinity by hand. He never went far from his dwelling.

Pelissier and his old mother doffed their caps as Lamartiere approached. "So," the machinist said. "I congratulate you. But you have learned that no matter how powerful a machine may seem to be, it still can break. That is so?"

"I worked in the depot at Brione, Pelissier," Lamartiere said. "I never doubted that tanks break. Now I need you to weld patches over holes in the skirts so that I can get *Hoodoo* away from here. Otherwise she'll draw worse down on you."

Madame Pelissier spat. Her son looked past Lamartiere toward the ruined houses and said, "Worse? But no matter. Can I get within the chamber? The patches should be made from inside. That way pressure will hold them tighter."

"There's access ports in the skirts," Lamartiere said. He knew better than to suggest the cripple would be unable to use an opening made for a man with legs.

Pelissier nodded. "Bring your great machine up here, then, so that we don't have to move the welder through this wasteland."

He spun his tray back toward the entrance and his equipment. Over his shoulder he said, "I cannot fight them myself, Lamartiere. But to help you, that I can do."

Lamartiere walked back toward *Hoodoo*. He'd have to move the crowd away before he started the fans: pebbles slung under the skirts could put a child's eye out.

He still held the garland. He was staring at the flowers, wondering how he could decently rid himself of an object that made him feel queasy, when he realized that Father Renaud was standing in his path.

Lamartiere stopped and bowed. "I'm sorry, Father," he said. "I wasn't looking where I was going."

"You have much on your mind," Renaud said. "I wouldn't bother you merely to offer praise."

The priest's lips quirked in a tiny smile. "Glory is in God's hands, not mine, but I have no doubt that She will mete out a full measure to you, Denis."

Renaud's face sobered into its usual wax-like placidity. "I know I'm thought to be hard," he continued. "Perhaps I am. But I feel the loss of every member of my flock, even those I know are seated with God in heaven. You have my sincere sympathy for the loss of your sister."

"Loss?" said Lamartiere. He wasn't sure what he'd just heard. "Celine is . . . ?"

Father Renaud blinked. He looked honestly shocked for the first time in the year Lamartiere had known him. "You didn't know?" he said. "Oh, my poor child. Celine drove the truck into the gate so that you could escape from Brione. I think she did it as much for your sake as for God's, but God will receive her in Her arms nonetheless."

Lamartiere hung the garland around his neck. Some child had picked the flowers as the only gift she could offer the man she thought had saved her. It would please that child to see him wearing them.

"I see," Lamartiere said. He heard his voice catch, but his mind was detached, dispassionate. "Celine wasn't the sort to refuse when called to duty, Father. She would have sacrificed herself as quickly for faith alone as for me. As I would very willingly have sacrificed myself for her."

He bowed and stepped past Renaud.

"Denis?" Renaud called. "If there is anything I can offer . . . ?"

"Your faith needs *Hoodoo* in working order, Father," Lamartiere said without looking around. "I'm going to go take care of that now."

Hundreds of civilians crowded around the tank; the vast metal bulk dwarfed them. The superweapon, the machine that would win the war. . . .

"Let me through!" Lamartiere said. People stepped aside when they saw who was speaking. "I have to get the tank repaired immediately. Everyone get back to the tunnels!"

Franciscus stood on *Hoodoo*'s turret. He called something; Lamartiere couldn't hear him over the crowd noise. The colonel was everything a military hero needed to be: trim, armed to the teeth, and willing to sacrifice anything to achieve his ends.

Dr Clargue sat nearby on a man-sized lump of tailings, rubbing his temples. He looked as tired as Lamartiere felt.

Lamartiere climbed up *Hoodoo*'s bow slope. "Doctor," he called. "Get everyone out of here. It's very dangerous to be here!"

"Lamartiere!" Franciscus said. "I want you to teach me how to operate the guns. We can start right now, while the repairs are being done."

"Yes, all right," said Lamartiere, slipping into the driver's compartment. He threw the switch closing the cupola hatch before Franciscus could get in.

"Sorry, wrong button," he called over the colonel's angry shout. "Just a moment. Let me start the fans and I'll open it."

He didn't want Franciscus inside *Hoodoo*'s turret. Lamartiere still owed something to the rebellion; and Celine had, after all, sacrificed herself for the purpose of stealing the tank.

The civilians were drifting away, but some were still too close. Lamartiere revved the fans with the blades flat. They made a piercing whine as unpleasant as fingernails on a blackboard.

Children shrieked, holding their hands over their ears. They and their mothers scampered away. Clargue chivied them with a fierceness that suggested he guessed what was about to happen.

Franciscus shouted, "You idiot, what are you trying to do?"

Lamartiere looked up at the man on the turret. "Goodbye, colonel," he said. "Give my love to Celine if you meet her."

He closed the driver's hatch over himself. He wasn't doing this for Celine, because Celine was already dead; but perhaps he was doing it so that Colonel Franciscus wouldn't create any more Celines.

Lamartiere switched on *Hoodoo*'s radios. The simultaneous blast of the six bombs on Franciscus' bandoliers barely made the tank shudder.

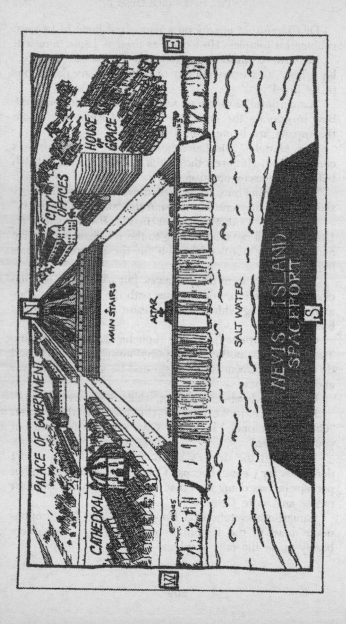

Counting The Cost

To Sergeant Ronnie Hembree
Who did good work.

CHAPTER ONE

They'd told Tyl Koopman that Bamberg City's starport was on an island across the channel from the city proper, so he hadn't expected much of a skyline when the freighter's hatches opened. Neither had he expected a curtain of steam boiling up so furiously that the sun was only a bright patch in mid-sky. Tyl stepped back with a yelp. The crewman at the controls of the giant cargo doors laughed and said, "Well, you were in such a *hurry*, soldier"

The Slammers issue-pack Tyl carried was all the luggage he'd brought from six month's furlough on Miesel. Strapped to the bottom of the pack was a case of homemade jalapeno jelly that his aunt was sure—correctly—was better than any he could get elsewhere in the galaxy.

But altogether, the weight of Tyl's gear was much less than he was used to carrying in weapons, rations, and armor when he led a company of Alois Hammer's infantry. He turned easily and looked at the crewman with mild sadness—the visage of a dog that's been unexpectedly kicked . . . and maybe just enough else beneath the sadness to be disquieting.

The crewman looked down at his controls, then again to the mercenary waiting to disembark. The squealing stopped when the triple hatches locked open. "Ah," called the crewman, "it'll clear up in a minute er two. It's always like this on Bamberg the first couple ships down after a high tide. The port floods, y'see, and it always looks like half the bloody ocean's waiting in the hollows t' burn off."

The steam—the hot mist; it'd never been dangerous, Tyl realized now—was thinning quickly. From the hatchway he could see the concrete pad and, in the near distance the bulk of the freighter that must have landed just before theirs. The flecks beyond the concrete were the inevitable froth speckling moving water, the channel or the ocean itself—and the water looked cursed close to somebody who'd just spent six months on a place as dry as Miesel.

"Where do they put the warehouses?" Tyl asked. "Don't they flood?"

"Every three months or so they would," the crewman agreed. "That's why they're on the mainland, in Bamberg City, where there's ten meters of cliff and seawall t' keep 'em dry. But out here's flat, and I guess they figured they'd sooner the landing point be on the island in case somebody, you know, landed a mite hard."

The crewman grinned tightly. Tyl grinned back. They were both professionals in fields that involved risks. People who couldn't joke about the risks of the jobs they'd chosen tended to find other lines of work in a hurry.

The ones who survived.

"Well, I guess it's clear," Tyl said with enough question in his tone to expect a warning if he were wrong. "There'll be ground transport coming?"

"Yeah, hovercraft from Bamberg real soon," the crewman agreed. "But look, there's a shelter on the other side a' that bucket there. You might want to get over to it right quick. There's some others in orbit after us, and it can be pretty interesting t' be out on the field when it's this wet and there's more ships landing."

Tyl nodded to the man and strode down the ramp that had been the lower third of the hatch door. He was nervous, but it'd all be fine soon. He'd be back with his unit and not alone, the way he'd been on the ship—

And for the whole six months he'd spent with his family and a planet full of civilians who understood his words but not his language.

The mainland shore, a kilometer across Nevis Channel, was a corniche. The harsh cliffs were notched by the mouth of the wide river which was responsible for Bamberg City's location and the fact it was the only real city on the planet. Tyl hadn't gotten the normal briefing because the regiment shifted employers while he was on furlough, but, the civilian sources available on Miesel when he got his movement orders were about all he needed anyway.

Captain Tyl Koopman wasn't coming to the planet Bamberia; he was returning to Hammer's Slammers. After five years in the regiment and six months back with his family, he had to agree with the veterans who'd warned him before he went on furlough that he wasn't going home.

He had left home, because the Slammers were the only home he'd got.

The shelter was a low archway, translucent green from the outside and so unobtrusive that Tyl might have overlooked it if there had been any other structure on the island. He circled to one end, apprehensive of the rumbling he heard in the sky—and more than a little nervous about the pair of star freighters already grounded in the port.

The ships were quiescent. They steamed and gave off pings of differential cooling, but for the next few days they weren't going to move any more than would buildings of the same size. Nevertheless, learned reflex told Tyl that big metal objects were tanks . . . and no infantryman lived very long around tanks without developing a healthy respect for them.

The door opened automatically as Tyl reached for it, wondering where the latch was. Dim shadows swirled inside the shelter, behind a second panel that rotated aside only when the outside door had closed again.

There were a dozen figures spaced within a shelter that had room for hundreds. All those waiting were human; all were male; and all but one were in civilian garb.

Tyl walked toward the man in uniform—almost toward him, while almost meeting the other man's eyes so that he could stop and find a clear spot at the long window if the fellow glared or turned his head as the Slammers officer approached.

No problem, though. The fellow's quirking grin suggested that he was as glad of the company as Tyl was.

It was real easy to embarrass yourself when you didn't know the rules—and when nobody wore the rank tabs that helped you figure out what those rules might be.

From within the shelter, the windows had an extreme clarity that proved they were nothing as simple as glass or thermoplastic. The shelter was unfurnished, without even benches, but its construction proved that Bamberia was a wealthy, high technology world.

There was a chance for real profit on this one. Colonel Hammer must have been delighted.

"Hammer's Regiment?" the waiting soldier asked, spreading his grin into a look of welcome.

"Captain Tyl Koopman," Tyl agreed, shaking the other man's hand. "I'd just gotten E Company when I went on furlough. But I don't know what may've happened since, you know, since we've shifted contracts."

He'd just blurted the thing that'd been bothering him ever since Command Central had sent the new location for him to report off furlough. He'd sweated blood to get that company command—sweated blood and spilled it . . . and the revised transit orders made him fear that he'd have to earn it all over again because he'd been gone on furlough when the Colonel needed somebody in the slot.

Tyl hadn't bothered to discuss it with the folks who'd been his friends and relatives when he was a civilian; they already looked at him funny from the time one of them asked about the scrimshaw he'd given her and he was drunk enough to tell the real story of the house-to-house on Cachalot. But this guy would understand, even though Tyl didn't know him and didn't even recognize the uniform.

"Charles Desoix," the man said, "United Defense Batteries." He flicked a collar tab with his finger. "Lieutenant and XO of Battery D, if you don't care what you say. It amounts to gopher, mainly. I just broke our Number Five gun out of Customs on Merrinet."

"Right, air defense," Tyl said with the enthusiasm of being able to place the man in a structured universe. "Calliopes?"

"Yeah," agreed Desoix with another broad grin, "and the inspectors seemed to think somebody in the crew had stuffed all eight barrels with drugs they were going to sell at our transfer stop on Merrinet. Might just've been right, too—but we needed the gun here more than they needed the evidence."

The ship that had been a rumble in the sky when Tyl ducked into the shelter was now within ten meters of the pad. The shelter's windows did an amazing job of damping vibration, but the concrete itself resonated like a drum to the freighter's engine note. The two soldiers fell silent. Tyl shifted his pack and studied Desoix.

The UDB uniform was black with silver piping that muted to non-reflective gray in service conditions. It was a little fancier than the Slammers' khaki—but Desoix's unit wasn't parade-ground pansies.

The Slammers provided their own defense against hostile artillery. Most outfits didn't have the luxury that Fire Central and the vehicle-mounted powerguns gave Hammer. Specialists like United Defense Batteries provided multi-barreled weapons—calliopes—to sweep the sky clear over defended positions and to accompany attacking columns which would otherwise be wrecked by shellfire.

It wasn't a job Tyl Koopman could imagine himself being comfortable doing; but Via! he didn't see himself leading a tank company either. A one-man skimmer and a 2-CM powergun were about all the hardware Tyl wanted to handle. Anything bigger cost him too much thought that would have been better spent on the human portion of his command.

"Your first time here?" Desoix asked diffidently. The third freighter was down. Though steam hissed away from the vessel with a high-pitched roar, it was possible to talk again.

Tyl nodded. Either the tide was falling rapidly or the first two ships had pretty well dried the pad for later comers. The billows of white mist were sparse enough that he could still see the city across the channel: or at any rate, he could see a twenty-story tower of metal highlights and transparent walls on one side of the river, and a domed structure across from it that gleamed gold—except for the ornate cross on the pinnacle whose core was living ruby.

"Not a bad place," Desoix said judiciously. He looked a few years older than the Slammers officer, but perhaps it was just that, looks, dark hair and thin features contrasting with Tyl's broad pale face and hair so blond that you could hardly see it when it was cropped as short as it was now.

"The city, I mean," Desoix said, modifying his earlier comment. "The sticks over on Continent Two where it looks like the fighting's going to be, well—they're the sticks."

He met Tyl's eyes. "I won't apologize for getting a quiet billet this time 'round."

"No need to," Tyl said . . . and they were both lying, because nobody who knows the difference brags to a combat soldier about a cushy assignment; and no combat soldier but wishes, somewhere in his heart of hearts, that he'd gotten the absolutely necessary assignment of protecting the capital while somebody else led troops into sniper-filled woodlands and endured the fluorescent drum-beat of hostile artillery.

But Via! *Somebody* had to do the job.

Both of them.

"Hey, maybe the next time," Tyl said with a false smile and a playful tap on the shoulder of the man who wasn't a stranger any more.

Several boats—hovercraft too small to haul more than a dozen men and their luggage—were putting out from Bamberg City, spraying their way toward the island with an enthusiasm that suggested they were racing.

Tyl's view of them was unexpectedly cut off when a huge surface-effect freighter slid in front of the shelter and settled. The freighter looked like a normal sub-sonic aircraft, but its airfoils were canted to double their lift by skimming over water or smooth ground. The bird couldn't really fly, but it could carry a thousand tonnes of cargo at 200 kph—a useful trade-off between true ships and true aircraft.

"Traders from Two," Desoix explained as men began scuttling from the freighter before its hydraulic outriggers had time to lock it firmly onto the pad. "They circle at a safe distance from the island while the starships are landing. Then, if they're lucky, they beat the Bamberg factors to the pad with the first shot at a deal."

He shrugged. "And if their luck's *really* out, there's another starship on its way in about the time they tie up. Doesn't take much of a shock wave to make things real interesting aboard one of those."

Tyl squinted at the men scuttling from the surface-effect vehicle. Several of those waiting in the shelter were joining them, babbling and waving documents. "Say, those guys 're—"

"Yeah, rag-heads," Desoix agreed. "I mean, I'm sure they're in church every day, kissing crosses and all the proper things, but . . . yeah, they're looking at some problems if President Delcorio gets his crusade going."

"Well, that's what we're here for," Tyl said, looking around horizons that were hemmed by starships to the back and side and the surface-effect vehicle before him.

"Now," he added, controlling his grimace, "how do we get to the mainland if we're not cargo?"

"Ah, but we are," Desoix noted as he raised the briefcase that seemed to be all the luggage he carried. "Just not very valuable cargo, my friend. But I think it's about time to—"

As he started toward the door, one of the hovercars they'd watched put out from the city drove through the mingled cluster of men from the starships and the surface freighter. Water from the channel surrounded the car in a fine mist that cleared its path better than the threat of its rubber skirts. While the driver in his open cab exchanged curses with men from the surface freighter, the rear of his vehicle opened to disgorge half a dozen civilians in bright garments.

"Our transportation," Desoix said, nodding to the hovercar as he headed out of the shelter. "Now that it's dropped off the Bamberg factors to fight for their piece of the market. Everybody's got tobacco, and everybody wants a share of what may be the last cargoes onto the planet for a while."

"Before the shooting starts," Tyl amplified as he strode along with the UDB officer. They hadn't sent a briefing cube to Miesel for him . . . but it didn't take that or genius to figure out what was going to happen shortly after a world started hiring mercenary regiments.

"That's the betting," Desoix agreed. He opened the back of the car with his universal credit key, a computer chip encased in noble metal and banded to his wrist.

"Oh," said Tyl, staring at the keyed door. "Yeah, everything's up to date here in Bamberg," said the other officer, stepping out of the doorway and waving Tyl through. "Hey!" he called to the driver. "My friend here's on me!"

"I can—" Tyl said.

"—delay us another ten minutes," Desoix broke in, "trying to charge this one to the Hammer account or pass the driver scrip from Lord knows where."

He keyed the door a second time and swung into the car, both men moving with the trained grace of soldiers who knew how to get on and off air cushion vehicles smoothly—because getting hung up was a good way to catch a round.

"Goes to the UDB account anyway," Desoix added. "Via, maybe we'll need a favor from you one of these days."

"I'm just not set up for this place, coming off furlough,"

Tyl explained. "It's not like, you know, Colonel Hammer isn't on top of things."

The driver fluffed his fans and the car began to cruise in cautious arcs around the starships, looking for other passengers. All the men they saw were busy with merchants or with the vessels themselves, preparing the rails and gantries that would load the vacuum-sealed one-tonne bales of Bamberg tobacco when the factors had struck their deals.

No one looked at the car with more than idle interest. The driver spun his vehicle back into the channel with a lurch and building acceleration.

CHAPTER TWO

"One thing," Desoix said, looking out the window even though the initial spray cloaked the view. "Money's no problem here. Any banking booth can access Hammer's account and probably your account back home if it's got a respondent on one of the big worlds. Perfectly up to date. But, ah, don't talk to anybody here about religion, all right?"

He met Tyl's calm eyes. "No matter how well you know them, you don't know them that well. Here. And don't go out except wearing your uniform. They don't bother soldiers, especially mercs; but somebody might make a mistake if you were in civilian clothes."

Their vehicle was headed for the notch in the sea cliffs. It was a river mouth as Tyl had assumed from the spaceport, but human engineering had overwhelmed everything natural about the site.

The river was covered and framed into a triangular plaza by concrete seawalls as high as those reinforcing the corniche.

Salt water from the tide-choked sea even now gleamed on the plaza, just as it was streaming from the spaceport. Figures—women as well as men, Tyl thought, though it was hard to be sure between the spray and the loose costumes they wore here—were pouring into the plaza as fast as the water had left it.

For the most part the walls were sheer and ten meters high, but there were broad stairs at each apex of the plaza—two along the seaside east and west and a third, defended by massive flood works, that must have been built over the channel of the river itself.

"What's the problem?" Tyl asked calmly. From what he'd read, the battle lines on Bamberia were pretty clearly drawn. The planetary government was centered on Continent One— wealthy and very centralized, because the Pink River drained most of the arable land on the continent. All the uniquely-flavorful Bamberg tobacco could be barged at minimal cost to Bamberg City and loaded in bulk onto starships.

There hadn't been much official interest in Continent Two for over a century after the main settlement. There was good land on Two, but it was patchy and not nearly as easy to develop profitably as One proved.

That didn't deter other groups who saw a chance that looked good by their standards. Small starships touched down in little market centers. Everything was on a lesser scale: prices, quantities, and profit margins. . . .

But in time, the estimated total grew large enough for the central government to get interested. Official trading ports were set up on the coast of Two. Local tobacco was to be sent from them to Bamberg City, to be assessed and trans-shipped.

Some was; but the interloping traders continued to land in the back country, and central government officials gnashed their teeth over tax revenues that were all the larger for being illusory.

It didn't help that One had been settled by Catholic Fundamentalists from Germany and Latin America, and that the squatters on Two were almost entirely Levantine Muslims.

The traders didn't care. They had done their business in holographic entertainment centers and solar-powered freezers, but there was just as much profit in powerguns and grenades.

As for mercenaries like Alois Hammer—and Tyl Koopman. . . . They couldn't be said not to care; because if there wasn't trouble, they didn't have work.

Not that Tyl figured there was much risk of galactic peace being declared.

Desoix laughed without even attempting to make the sound humorous. "Well," he said, "do you know when Easter is?"

"Huh?" said Tyl. "My family wasn't, you know, real religious . . . and anyway, do you mean on Earth or here or where?"

"That's the question, isn't it?" Desoix answered, glancing around the empty cabin just to be *sure* there couldn't be a local listening to him.

"Some folks here," he continued, "figure Easter according to Earth-standard days. You can tell them because they've always got something red in their clothing, a cap or a ribbon around their sleeve if nothing else. And the folks that say, 'We're on Bamberia so God meant us to use Bamberg days to figure his calendar . . . ,' well, they wear black."

"And the people who wear cloaks, black or red," Desoix concluded. "Make sure they know you're a soldier. Because they'd just as soon knock your head in as that of any policeman or citizen—but they won't, because they know that killing soldiers gets expensive fast."

Tyl shook his head. "I'd say I didn't believe it," he said with the comfortable superiority of somebody commenting on foolishness to which he doesn't subscribe. "But sure, it's no screwier than a lot of places. People don't need a reason to have problems, they make their own."

"And they hire us," agreed Desoix.

"Well, they hire us to give 'em more control over the markets on Two," Tyl said, not quite arguing. "This time around."

Their vehicle was approaching the plaza. It stood two meters above the channel, barely eye-height to the men in the back of the hovercar. A pontoon-mounted landing stage slid with the tides in a vertical slot in the center of the dam blocking the river beneath the plaza; the car slowed as they approached the stage.

"If they dam the river—" Tyl started to say, because he wouldn't have commanded a company of the Slammers had he not assessed the terrain about him as a matter of course.

Before Desoix could answer, slotted spillways opened at either end of the dam and whipped the channel into froth with gouts of fresh water under enough pressure to fling it twenty meters from the concrete. The hovercar, settling as it made its final approach to the stage, bobbed in the ripples; the driver must have been cursing the operator who started to drain the impoundment now instead of a minute later.

"Hydraulics they know about," Desoix commented as their vehicle grounded on the stage with a blip of its fans and the pontoons rocked beneath them. "They can't move the city—it's here because of the river, floods or no. But for twenty kilometers upstream, they've built concrete levees. When the tides peak every three months or so— as they just did—they close the gates here and divert the river around Bamberg City."

He pointed up the coast. "When the tide goes down a little, they vent water through the main channel again until everything's normal. In about two days, they can let barges across to the spaceport."

The hovercar's door opened, filling the back with the roar of the water jetting from a quarter kilometer to either side. "Welcome to Bamberg City," Desoix shouted over the background as he motioned Tyl ahead of him.

The Slammers officer paused outside the vehicle to slip on his pack again. Steel-mesh stairs extended through the landing stage, up to the plaza—but down into the water as well: they did not move with the stage or the tides, and they were dripping and as slick as wet, polished metal could be.

"No gear?" he asked his companion curiously. Desoix waved his briefcase. "Some, but I'm leaving it to be off-loaded with the gun. Remember, I'm travelling with a whole curst calliope."

"Well, you must be glad to have it back," said Tyl

as he gripped the slick railing before he attempted the
steps.

"Not as glad as my battery commander, Major Borodin,"
Desoix said with a chuckle. "It was his ass, not mine, if
the Merrinet authorities had decided to keep it till it grew
whiskers."

"But—" he added over the clang of his boots and Tyl's
as they mounted the stairs, "—he's not a bad old bird, the
Major, and he cuts me slack that not every CO might be
willing to do."

The stairs ended on a meter-wide walkway that was part
of the plaza but separated from it by a low concrete building,
five meters on the side parallel to the dam beneath it and
narrower in the other dimension. On top, facing inward to
the plaza, was an ornate, larger than life, crucifix.

Tyl hesitated, uncertain as to which way to walk around
the building. He'd expected somebody from his unit to be
waiting here on the mainland if not at the spaceport itself.
He was feeling alone again. The raucous babble of locals
setting up sales kiosks on the plaza increased his sense of
isolation.

"Either way," Desoix said, putting a hand on the other
man's shoulder—in comradeship as well as direction. "This
is just the mechanical room for the locks except—"

Desoix leaned over so that his lips were almost touching Tyl's ear and said, "Except that it's the altar of Christ
the Redeemer, if you ask anybody here. I *really* put my
foot in it when I tried to get permission to site one of my
guns on it. Would've been a perfect place to cover the sea
approaches, but it seems that they'd rather die here than
have their cross moved."

"Of course," the UDB officer added, a professional who
didn't want another professional to think that he'd done
a bad job of placing his guns, "I found an all-right spot
on a demolition site just east of here."

Desoix nodded toward the thronged steps at the eastern end of the plaza. "Not quite the arc of fire, but nothing
we can't cover from the other guns. Especially now we've
got Number Five back."

In the time it had taken the hovercar to navigate from the spaceport to the mainland, a city of small shops had sprung up in the plaza. Tyl couldn't imagine the development could be orderly—but it was, at least to the extent that a field of clover has order, because the individual plants respond to general stimuli that force them into patterns.

There were city police present, obvious from their peaked caps, green uniforms, and needle stunners worn on white cross-belts . . . but they were not organizing the ranks of kiosks. Men and women in capes were doing that; and after a glance at their faces, Tyl didn't need Desoix to tell him how tough they thought they were.

They just might be right, too; but things have a way of getting a lot worse than anybody expected, and it was then that you got a good look at what you and the rest of your crew were really made of.

Traffic in the plaza was entirely pedestrian. Vehicles were blocked from attempting the staircases at either sea-front corner by massive steel bollards, and the stairs at the remaining apex were closed by what seemed to be lockworks as massive as those venting the river beneath the plaza. They'd *have* to be, Tyl realized, because there needed to be some way of releasing water from the top of its levee-channeled course in event of an emergency.

But that wasn't a problem for Captain Tyl Koopman just now. What *he* needed was somebody wearing the uniform of Hammer's Slammers, and he sure as blazes didn't see such in all this throng.

"Ah," he said, "Lieutenant . . . do you—"

The transceiver implanted in his mastoid bone beeped, and an unfamiliar voice began to answer Tyl's question before he had fully formed it.

"Transit Base to Captain Tyl Koopman," said the implant, scratchy with static and the frustration of the man at the other end of the radio link. "Captain Koopman, are you reading me? Over."

Tyl felt a rush of relief as he willed his left little finger to crook. The finger didn't move, but the redirected nerve impulse triggered the transmitter half of his implant. "Koopman to Transit," he said harshly. "Where in *blazes* are you, anyway? Over."

"Sir," said the voice, "this is Sergeant Major Scratchard, and you don't need to hear that I'm sorry about the cock-up. There's an unscheduled procession, and I can't get into the main stairs until it's over. If you'll tell me where you are, I swear I'll get t' you as soon as the little boys put away their crosses and let the men get back to work."

"I'm—" Tyl began. Desoix was turned half aside to indicate that he knew of the conversation going on and knew it wasn't any of this business. That gave the Slammers officer the mental base he needed for a reasoned decision rather than nervously agreeing to wait in place.

"All, sir," Scratchard continued; he'd paused but not broken the transmission. "There's a load of stuff for you here from Central. The Colonel wants you to lead the draft over when you report to Two. And, ah, the President, ah, Delcorio, wants to see you ASAP because you're the ranking officer now. Over."

"The main stairs," Tyl said, aloud rather than sub-vocalizing the way he had done thus far through the implant. Desoix could hear him. To underscore that he *wanted* the UDB officer to listen, Tyl pointed toward the empty stairs at the third apex. "That's at the end farthest from the sea, then?"

Desoix nodded. Scratchard's voice said, "Ah, yessir," through the static.

"Fine, I'll meet you there when you can get through," Tyl said flatly. "I'm in uniform and I have one pack is all. Koopman out."

He smiled to Desoix. "It'll give me a chance to look around," he explained. Now that his unit had contacted him he felt confident—whole, for the first time in . . . Via, in six months, just about.

Desoix smiled back. "Well, you shouldn't have any real problems here," he said. "But" his head tilted, just notice-ably, in the direction of three red-cloaked toughs "—don't forget what I told you. Myself, I'm going to check Number

Three gun so long as I'm down on the corniche anyway. See you around, soldier."

"See you around," Tyl agreed confidently. He grinned at his surroundings with a tourist's vague interest. Captain Tyl Koopman was home again, or he would be in a few minutes.

CHAPTER THREE

Charles Desoix thought about the House of Grace as he mounted the eastern stairs from the plaza. The huge hospital building, Bishop Trimer's latest but not necessarily last attempt to impose his presence on Bamberg City, was about all a man could see as he left the plaza in this direction. For that matter, the twenty glittering stories of the House of Grace were the only portions of the city visible from the floor of the plaza, over the sea walls.

It was like looking at a block of blue ice; and it was the only thing about being stationed in Bamberg City that Desoix could really have done without. But the Bishop certainly wasn't enough of a problem that Desoix intended to transfer to one of the batteries out in the boonies on Two, rumbling through valleys you could be *sure* the ragheads had mined and staked for snipers.

Thousands of people, shoppers as well as shopkeepers, were still pouring into the plaza; Desoix was almost alone in wanting to go in the opposite direction. He wasn't in a big hurry, so he kept his temper in check. An unscheduled inspection of Gun Three was a good excuse for the battery XO to be there, not just sneaking around. . . .

He had some business back at the Palace of Government, too; but he wasn't so horny from the trip to Merrinet that he was willing to make that his first priority. Quite.

Three prostitutes, each of them carried by a pair of servants to save their sandals and gossamer tights, were on their way to cribs in the plaza below. Desoix made way

with a courteous bow; but uniform or not, he was going
to make way. The phalanx of red-cloaked guards surrounding the girls would have made sure of that.

One of the girls smiled at Desoix as she rocked past.
He smiled back at her, thinking of Anne McGill . . . but
Blood and *Martyrs*! he could last another half hour. He'd
get his job done first.

There was an unusual amount of congestion here, but
that was because the main stairs were blocked. Another
procession, no doubt; Bishop Trimer playing his games
while President Delcorio and his wife tried to distract the
populace with a crusade on Two.

As for the populace, its members knocked in each other's
heads depending on what each was wearing that day.

Just normal politics, was all. Normal for places that hired
the United Defense Batteries and other mercenary regiments, at any rate.

At dawn, the shadow of the House of Grace lay across
the Cathedral on the other side of the plaza, so that the
gilded dome no longer gleamed. Desoix wrinkled his nose
and thought about dust-choked roads on Two with a sniper
every hundred meters of the wooded ridges overlooking
them.

To blazes with all of them.

There was even more of a crush at the head of the
stairs. Vehicles slid up to the bollards to drop their cargo
and passengers—and then found themselves blocked by
later-comers, furious at being stopped a distance from
where they wanted to be. A squad of city police made
desultory efforts to clear the jam, but they leaped aside
faster than the bystanders did when the real fighting started.

Two drivers, one with a load of produce and the other
carrying handbags, were snarling. Three black-cloaked
toughs jumped the driver with the red headband, knocked
him down, and linked arms in a circle about the victim
so that they could all three put the boot in.

At least a dozen thugs in red coalesced from nowhere
around the fight. It grew like a crystal in a supersaturated
solution of hate.

The police had their stunners out and were radioing for help, but they kept their distance. The toughs wore body armor beneath their cloaks, and Desoix heard the slam of at least one slug-throwing pistol from the ruck.

He willed his body to stay upright and to stride with swift dignity between vehicles and out of the potential line of fire. It would have griped his soul to run from this scum; but more important, anyone who ducked and scurried was a worthy victim, while a recognized mercenary was safe except by accident.

Anyway, that was what Desoix told himself.

But by the Lord! it felt good to get out of the shouted violence and see Gun Three, its six-man crew alert and watching the trouble at the stairhead with their personal weapons ready.

The calliope's eight stubby barrels were mounted on the back of a large air-cushion truck. Instead of rotating through a single loading station as did the 2 CM tri-barrels on the Slammers' combat cars, each of the calliope's tubes was a separate gun. The array gimballed together to fire on individual targets which the defenders couldn't afford to miss.

Any aircraft, missile, or artillery shell that came over the sector of the horizon which Gun Three scanned—when the weapon was live—would be met by a pulse of high-intensity 3 CM bolts from the calliope's eight barrels. Nothing light enough to fly through the air could survive that raking.

A skillful enemy could saturate the gun's defensive screen by launching simultaneous attacks from several directions, but even then the interlocking fire of a full, properly-sited six-calliope battery should be able to hold out and keep the target it defended safe.

Of course, proper siting was an ideal rather than a reality, since every irregularity of terrain—or a building like the House of Grace—kept guns from supporting one another as they could do on a perfectly flat surface. Bamberg City wasn't likely to be surrounded by hostile artillery batteries, though, and Charles Desoix was proud of the single-layer coverage he had arranged for the whole populated area.

He did hope his gunners had sense enough not to talk about saturating coverage when they were around civilians. Especially civilians who looked like they'd been born to squatter families on Two.

"Good to see you back, sir," said Blaney, the sergeant in command of Gun Three on this watch.

He was a plump man and soft looking, but he'd reacted well in an emergency on Hager's World, taking manual control of his calliope and using it in direct fire on a party of sappers that had made it through the perimeter Federal forces were trying to hold.

"Say," asked a blond private Desoix couldn't call by name until his eye caught stenciling on the fellow's helmet: Karsov. "Is there any chance we're going to move, sir? Farther away from all this? It gets worse every day."

"What's . . ." Desoix began with a frown, but he turned to view the riot again before he finished the question—and then he didn't have to finish it.

The riot that Desoix had put out of his mind by steely control had expanded like mold on bread while he walked the three hundred meters to the shelter of his gun and its crew. There must have been nearly a thousand people involved—many of them lay-folk with the misfortune of being caught in the middle, but at least half were the cloaked shock troops of the two Easter factions.

Knives and metal bars flashed in the air. A shotgun thumped five times rapidly into a chorus of screams.

"Via," Desoix muttered.

A firebomb went off, spraying white trails of burning magnesium through the curtain of petroleum flames. Police air cars were hovering above the crowd on the thrust of their ducted fans while uniformed men hosed the brawlers indiscriminately with their needle stunners.

"This is what we're defending?" Blaney asked with heavy irony.

Desoix squatted, motioning the gun crew down with him. No point in having a stray round hit somebody. The men

were wearing their body armor, but Desoix himself wasn't.
He didn't need it on shipboard or during negotiations on
Merrinet, and it hadn't struck him how badly the situation in Bamberg City could deteriorate in the two weeks
he was gone.

"Well," he said, more or less in answer. "They're the
people paying us until we hear different. Internal politics,
that's not our business. And anyhow, it looks like the police
have it pretty well under control."

"For now," muttered Karsov.

The fighting had melted away, as much in reaction to
the firebomb as to the efforts of the civil authorities. Thugs
were carrying away injured members of their own parties.
The police tossed the disabled battlers whom they picked
up into air cars with angry callousness.

"It'd be kinda nice, sir," said Blaney, turning his eyes
toward the House of Grace towering above them, "if we
could maybe set up on top of there. Get a nice view all
around, you know, good for defense; and, ah, we wouldn't
need worry about getting hit with the odd brick or the like
if the trouble comes this way next time."

The chorus of assent from the whole crew indicated that
they'd been discussing the point at length among themselves.

Desoix smiled. He couldn't blame the men, but wishing something strongly didn't make it a practical solution.

"Look," he said, letting his eyes climb the sculptured
flank of the hospital building as he spoke. The narrower
sides of the House of Grace, the north and south faces,
were of carven stone rather than chrome and transparent
panels.

The south face, toward Gun Three and the sea front,
was decorated with the miracles of Christ: the sick rising
from their beds; the lame tossing away their crutches; loaves
and fishes multiplying miraculously to feed the throng
stretching back in low relief.

On the opposite side were works of human mercy: the
poor being fed and lodged in church kitchens; orphans
being raised to adulthood; medical personnel with crosses

on their uniforms healing the sick as surely as Christ did on the south face.

But over the works of human mercy, the ascetic visage of Bishop Trimer presided in a coruscance of sun-rays like that which haloed Christ on the opposite face. A determined man, Bishop Trimer. And very sure of himself.

"Look," Desoix repeated as he reined in his wandering mind. "In the first place, it's a bad location because the gun can only depress three degrees and that'd leave us open to missiles skimming the surface."

Karsov opened his mouth as if to argue, but a snarled order from Sergeant Blaney shut him up. Lieutenant Desoix was easy-going under normal circumstances; but he was an officer and the Battery XO . . . and he was also hard as nails when he chose to be, as Blaney knew by longer experience than the private had.

"But more important . . ." Desoix went on with a nod of approval to Blaney. "Never site a gun in a spot where you can't drive away if things really get bad. Do you expect to ride down in the elevators if a mob decides what they really ought to do tomorrow is burn the hospital?"

"Well, they wouldn't . . ." Karsov began.

He looked at the wreckage and smoke near the plaza stairs and thought the better of saying what a mob would or wouldn't do.

"Were you on Shinano, Sergeant?" Desoix asked Blaney.

"Yessir," the non-com said. "But I wasn't in the city during the riots, if that's what you mean."

"I was a gun captain then," Desoix said with a smile and a lilting voice, because it was always nice to remember the ones you survived. "The Battery Commander—this was Gilt, and they sacked him for it—sited us on top of the Admin Building. Ten stories in a central park."

"So we had a *really* good view of the mob, because parts of it were coming down all five radial streets with torches. And they'd blown up the transformer station providing power to the whole center of town."

He coughed and rubbed his face. "There were air cars flying every which way, carrying businessmen who knew they weren't going to get out at ground level. ., but we didn't have a car, and we couldn't even get the blazes off the roof. It didn't have a staircase, just the elevator—and that quit when the power went off."

Blaney was nodding with grim agreement; so were two of the other veterans in the gun crew.

"How—how'd you get out, sir?" Karsov asked in a suitably chastened tone.

Desoix grinned again. It wasn't a pleasant expression. "Called to one of those businessmen on a loud-hailer," he said. "Asked him to come pick us up. When he saw where we had the calliope pointed, he decided that was a good idea."

The slim officer paused and looked up at the House of Grace again. "Getting lucky once doesn't mean I'm going to put any of my men in that particular bucket again, though," he said. "Down here—" he smiled brightly, but there was more than pure humor in this expression too "—at the worst, you've got the gun to keep anybody at a distance."

"Think it's going to be that bad, sir?" one of the crewmen asked.

Desoix shrugged. "I need to report to the Palace," he said. "I guess it's clear enough to do that now."

As he turned to walk away from the gun position, he heard Sergeant Blaney saying, "Not for us and the other mercs, maybe. But yeah, it's going to get that bad here. You wait and see."

CHAPTER FOUR

Tyl Koopman strolled through a series of the short aisles into which the plaza was marked by freshly-erected kiosks. In most cases the shop proprietors were still setting out their goods, but they were willing to call Tyl over to look at their merchandise. He smiled and walked on—the smile becoming fixed in short order.

He'd learned Spanish when the Slammers were stationed on Cartagena three years before, so he could have followed the local language without difficulty. It was interesting that most of the shopkeepers recognized Tyl's uniform and spoke to him in Dutch, fluent at least for a few words of enticement.

It was interesting also that many of those keeping shops in the plaza were of Levantine extraction, like the merchants who had disembarked from the surface-effect freighter. They were noticeable not only for their darker complexions but also because their booths and clothing were so bedecked with crosses that sometimes the color of the underlying fabric was doubtful.

Not, as Lieutenant Desoix had suggested, that their desperate attempts to belong to the majority would matter a hoot in Hell when the Crusade really got moving. Tyl wasn't a cynic. Like most line mercenaries, he wasn't enough of an intellectual to have abstract positions about men and politics.

But he had a good mind and plenty of data about the way things went when politicians hired men to kill for them.

The section Tyl was walking through was given over to tobacco and smoking products—shops for visitors rather than staples for the domestic market which seemed to fill most of the plaza.

Tobacco from Bamberia had a smooth melding of flavors that remained after the raw leaf was processed into the cold inhalers in which most of the galaxy used imported tobacco. Those who couldn't afford imports smoked what they grew in local plots on a thousand worlds . . . but those who could afford the best and wanted the creosote removed before they put the remainder of the taste into their bodies, bought from Bamberia.

Most of the processing was done off-planet, frequently on the user world where additional flavorings were added to the inhalers to meet local tastes. There were a few inhaler factories on the outskirts of Bamberg City, almost the only manufacturing in a metropolis whose wealth was based on transport and government. Their creations were displayed on the tables in the plaza, brightly colored plastic tubes whose shapes counterfeited everything from cigarillos to cigars big enough to pass for riot batons.

But the local populace tended to follow traditional methods of using the herb that made them rich. Products for the local market posed here as exotica for the tourists and spacers who wanted something to show the folks back home where they'd been.

Tourists and spacers and mercenaries. The number of kiosks serving outsiders must have increased radically since President Delcorio started hiring mercenaries for his Crusade.

Tyl passed by displays of smoking tobacco and hand-rolled cigars—some of the boxes worth a week's pay to him, even now that he had his captaincy. There were cigar cutters and pipe cleaners, cigarette holders and pipes carved from microporous meerschaum mined on the coasts of Two.

Almost all the decoration was religious: crosses, crucifixes, and other symbols of luxuriant Christianity. That theme was almost as noticeable to Tyl as the fact that almost everyone in the plaza—and every kiosk—was decorated with either black or red, and never both.

Each staggering aisle was of uniform background. To underscore the situation, cloaked toughs faced off at every angle where the two colors met, glowering threats that did not quite—while Tyl saw them—come to open violence.

Great place to live, Bamberg City. Tyl was glad of his khaki uniform. He wondered how often the silver and black of the United Defense Batteries was mistaken for black by somebody with a red cloak and a brick in his hand.

Grimacing to himself, the Slammers officer strode more swiftly toward his goal, the empty stairs at the north end of the plaza. The scene around him was colorful, all right, and this was probably one of the few chances he'd have to see it.

You served on a lot of worlds in a mercenary regiment, but what you mostly *saw* there were other soldiers and the wrack of war . . . which was universal, a smoky gray ambiance that you scanned and maybe shot at before you moved on.

Even so, Tyl didn't want to spend any longer than he had to in this plaza. He could feel the edge of conflict which overlay it like the cloaks that covered the weapons and armor of the omnipresent bullies, waiting for an opportunity to strike out. He'd seen plenty of fighting during his years with the Slammers, but he didn't want it hovering around him when he was supposed to be in a peaceful rear area.

The stairs were slimy with water pooling in low spots, but Nevis Island and its spaceport shielded the plaza from most of the sea-weed and marine life that the high tides would otherwise have washed up. Tyl picked his way carefully, since he seemed to be the first person to climb them since the tide dropped.

A procession, Scratchard had said, blocking normal traffic. Maybe that would be a little easier to take than the human bomb waiting to go off below in the plaza.

At the top of the stairs were ten pairs of steel-and-concrete doors. Each side-hung panel was five meters across and at least three meters high. The doors—lock-gates— were fully open now. They rotated out toward the plaza on trunnions in slotted rails set into the concrete. As Tyl neared them on his lonely climb, he heard the sound of chanted music echoing from beyond the doors.

Tyl had expected to see gaily-bedecked vehicles when he reached the top of the stairs and could look into the covered mall beyond. Instead there were people on foot, and most of *them* were standing rather than marching from left to right.

The mall was at least a hundred meters wide; its pavement was marked to pass heavy ground traffic from one side of the river to the other. At the moment, a sparse line of priests in full regalia was walking slowly down the center of the expanse, interspersed with lay-folk wearing robes of ceremonially-drab coarseness.

Some carried objects on display. Ornate crucifixes were the most common, but there were banners and a reliquary borne by four women which, if *pure* gold, must have cost as much as a starship.

Every few paces, the marchers paused and chanted something in Latin. When they began to move again, a refrain boomed back from the line of solid-looking men in white robes on either side of the procession route. The guards—they could be nothing else—wore gold crosses on the left shoulders of their garments, but they also bore meter-long staffs.

There was no need for the procession to be blocking the whole width of the mall; but when Tyl stepped through the door, the nearest men in white gave him a look that made it real clear what would happen to anybody who tried to carry out secular business in an area the Church had marked for its own.

Tyl stopped. He stood in a formal posture instead of lounging against a column while he waited. No point in offending the fellows who watched him with hard eyes even when they bellowed verses in a language he knew only well enough to recognize.

No wonder Scratchard hadn't been able to make it to the plaza as he'd intended. The other two staircases were open and in use, but the procession route certainly extended some distance to either side of the river; and Scratchard, with business of his own to take care of, would have waited till the last minute before setting out to collect an officer returning from furlough.

No problem. But it calmed Tyl to remember that there *were* other Slammers nearby, in event of a real emergency.

The gorgeous reliquary was the end of the procession proper. When that reached the heavy doors at the west end of the mall, a barked order passed down the lines of guards, repeated by every tenth man.

The men in white turned and began to doubletime in the direction the procession was headed, closing up as they moved. They carried their staffs vertically before them, and their voices boomed a chant beginning, *"Fortis iuventus, virtus audax bellica . . ."* as they strode away.

They marched in better order than any mercenary unit

Tyl could remember having seen—not that close order drill was what folks hired the Slammers for.

And there were a lot of them, for the double lines continued to shift past and contract for several minutes, more and more quick-stepping staff-wielders appearing from farther back along the procession route to the east. They must have timed their withdrawal so that the whole route would be cleared the instant the procession reached its destination, presumably the cathedral.

At least *something* in this place was organized. It just didn't appear to be what called itself the government.

CHAPTER FIVE

Tyl didn't follow the procession when the route cleared, nor did he try to raise Sergeant-Major Scratchard on his implant again. He'd told Scratchard where he'd be; and if the non-com couldn't find him, then that was important information for Captain Tyl Koopman to know.

There was a surge of civilians—into the mall and through it down the stairs to the plaza—as soon as the procession was clear. Normal folk, so far as Tyl could tell from the loose-fitting fashions current here. Most of them wore a red ribbon or a black one, but there was no contingent of cloaked thugs.

Which meant that the bullies, the enforcers, had gotten word that the main stairs would be blocked when the tide cleared the plaza—although Scratchard and apparently a lot of civilians had been caught unaware. That could mean a lot of things: none of them particularly good, and none of them, thank the Lord, the business of Tyl Koopman or Hammer's Slammers.

He caught sight of a uniform of the right color. Sergeant Major Scratchard muscled his way through the crowd, his rank in his eyes and his grizzled hair. His khaki coveralls were neat and clean, but there were shiny patches over the shoulders where body armor had rubbed the big man's uniform against his collarbone.

Tyl hadn't recognized the name, but sight of the man rang a bell in his mind. He swung away from the pillar and, gripping the hand the non-com extended to him, said, "Sergeant Major Scratchard? Would that be Ripper Jack?"

Scratchard's professional smile broadened into something as real and firm as his handshake. "Cap'n Koopman, then? Yeah, when I was younger, sir. . . . Maybe when I was younger."

He shifted his right leg and the hand holding Tyl's, just enough to point without apprising the civilians around of the gesture.

Scratchard wore a knife along his right calf. Most of the sheathed blade was hidden within his boot but the hand-filling grip was strapped to mid-calf. "Pistols jam on you, happen," the big man half bragged, half explained. "This'n never did."

His face hardened. "Though they got me pretty much retired to Admin now with my bum knees."

"Didn't look that quiet a billet just now," Tyl said, pitching his voice lower than the civilians, scurrying on their own errands, could have overheard. "Down in the plaza just now, the enforcers in cloaks . . . And I was talking to a UDB lieutenant landed the same time I did."

"Yeah, you could maybe figure that," Scratchard said in a voice too quietly controlled to be really neutral. "Open your leg pocket, sir, and stand real close."

Tyl, his face still, ran a finger across the seal of the bellows pocket on the right leg of his cover-alls. He and the non-com pressed against one of the door pillars, their backs momentarily to the crowd moving past them. He felt the weight of what Scratchard had slipped into his pocket.

Tyl didn't need to finger the object to know that he'd been given a service pistol, a 1 CM powergun. In the right hands, it could do as much damage as a shotgun loaded with buck.

Tyl's were the right hands. He wouldn't have been in the Slammers if they weren't. But the implications. . . .

"We're issuing sidearms in Bamberg City, then?" he asked without any emotional loading.

Scratchard, an enlisted man reporting to an officer, said stiffly, "Sir, while I was in charge of the Transit Detachment, I gave orders that none of the troopers on port leave were to leave barracks in groups of less than three. And no, sidearms aren't officially approved. But I won't have men under my charge disarmed when I sure as blazes wouldn't be disarmed myself. You can change the procedures if you like."

"Yes, Sergeant Major, I can," Tyl said with just enough iron to emphasize that he was well aware of their respective ranks. "And if I see any reason to do so, I will."

He smiled, returning the conversation to the footing where he wanted to keep it. "For now, let's get me to the barracks and see just what it is the Colonel has on line."

Pray to the Lord that there'd be orders to take over E Company again.

Scratchard hesitated, looking first toward the east, then the western lock doors. "Ah, sir," he said. "We're billeted in the City Offices—" he pointed toward the eastern end of the mall, the side toward the huge House of Grace. "Central's cut orders for you to carry the Transit Detachment over to Two for further assignment . . . but you know, nothing that can't wait another couple days. We've still got half a dozen other troopers due back from furlough."

"All right," Tyl said, to show that he wasn't going to insist on making a decision before he'd heard Scratchard's appraisal of the situation. "What else?"

"Well, sir," said the non-com. "President Delcorio really wants to see the ranking Slammers officer in the city. Didn't call the message over, his nephew brought it this morning. I told him you were in orbit, due down as soon as the port cleared—'cause I'm bloody not the guy to handle that sort of thing. I checked with Central, see if they'd courier somebody over from Two, but they didn't want. . . ."

Tyl understood why Colonel Hammer would have turned down Scratchard's request. It was obvious what President

Delcorio wanted to discuss . . . and it wasn't something that Hammer wanted to make a matter of official regimental policy by sending over a staff officer.

The Slammers hadn't been hired to keep public order in Bamberg City, and Colonel Hammer wanted all the time he could get before he had to officially make a decision that might involve the Bonding Authority either way.

"Central said you should handle it for now," Scratchard concluded. "And I sure think *somebody* ought to report to the President ASAP."

"Via," muttered Tyl Koopman.

Well, he couldn't say that he hadn't been given a responsible job when he returned from furlough.

He shrugged his shoulders, settling the pack more comfortably. "Right," he said. "Let's do it then, Sergeant Major."

"Palace of Government," Scratchard said in evident relief, pointing west in the direction the procession had been headed. He stepped off with a stiff-legged stride that reminded Tyl that the non-com had complained about his knees.

The crowd had thinned enough that the Slammers officer could trust other pedestrians to avoid him even if he glanced away from his direction of movement. "You go by Jack when you're with friends?" he asked, looking at the bigger man.

"Yessir, I do," Scratchard replied.

He grinned, and though the expression wasn't quite natural, the non-com was working on it.

Mercenary units were always outnumbered by the indigenous populations that hired them—or they were hired to put down. Mercenaries depended on better equipment, better training—and on each other, because everything else in the world could be right and you were still dead if the man who should have covered your back let you down.

Tyl and Scratchard both wanted—needed—there to be a good relationship between them. It didn't look like they'd be together long . . . but life itself was temporary, and that wasn't a reason not to make things work as well as they could while it lasted.

"This way," said Scratchard as the two soldiers emerged from the mall crossing the river. "Give you a bit of a view, and we don't fight with trucks."

There was a ramp from the mall down to interlocking vehicular streets—one of them paralleling the river, the plaza, and then sweeping west along the corniche. The other was a park-like boulevard which tied into the first after separating the gold-domed cathedral from a large, three story building whose wings enclosed a central courtyard open in the direction of the river.

"That's the . . . ?" Tyl said, trying to remember the name.

"Palace of Government, yeah," Scratchard replied easily. He was taking them along the pedestrian walk atop the levee.

Glancing over the railing to his right, Tyl was shocked to see the water was within two meters of the top of the levee. He could climb directly aboard the scores of barges moored there, silently awaiting for the locks to open. All he'd have to do was swing his legs over the guard rail.

"Vial" he said, looking from the river to the street and the buildings beyond it. "What happens if it comes up another couple meters? All that down there floods, right?"

"They've got flood shutters on all the lower floors," Scratchard explained/agreed. "They say it happened seventy-odd years ago when everything came together—tides and a storm that backed up the outlet channels up-coast. But they know what they're doing, their engineers."

He paused, then added in a tone of disgust, "Their politicians, now . . . But I don't suppose they know their asses from a hole in the ground, any of 'em anywhere."

He didn't expect an argument from an officer of Hammer's Slammers; and Tyl Koopman wasn't about to give him one.

Bamberg City was clean, prosperous. The odor of toasted tobacco lead permeated it, despite the fact that the ranks of hogsheads on the waiting barges were all vacuum-sealed;

but that was a sweet smell very different from the reeks that were the normal concomitant of bulk agriculture.

Nothing wrong here but the human beings.

A flagpole stood in the courtyard of the Palace of Government. Its twelve-man honor guard wore uniforms of the same blue and gold as the fabric of the drooping banner.

In front of the cathedral were more than a thousand of the men in cross-marked white robes. They were still chanting and blocking vehicles, though the gaps in the ranks of staff-armed choristers permitted pedestrians to enter the cathedral building. The dome towered above this side of the river, though it in turn was dwarfed by the House of Grace opposite.

There was a pedestrian bridge from the embankment to the courtyard of the Palace of Government, crossing the vehicular road. As they joined the traffic on it, heavy because of the way vehicles were being backed up by the tail end of the procession, Tyl asked, "Who wears white here? The ones who hold Easter on Christmas?"

"Umm," said the sergeant major. The non-com's tone reminded Tyl of the pistol that weighted his pocket—and the reason it was there.

In a barely audible voice, Scratchard went on, "Those are orderlies from the House of Grace. They, ah, usually turn out for major religious events."

Neither of the mercenaries spoke again until they had reached the nearly empty courtyard of the government building. Then, while the honor guard was still out of earshot, Tyl said, "Jack, they don't look to me like they empty bedpans."

"Them?" responded the big sergeant major. "They do whatever Bishop Trimer tells them to do, sir."

He glanced over his shoulder in the direction of the massed orderlies. His eyes held only flat appraisal, as if he were estimating range and the length of the burst he was about to fire.

"Anything at all," he concluded.

Tyl Koopman didn't pursue the matter as he and

Scratchard—the latter limping noticeably—walked across the courtyard toward the entrance of the Palace of Government.

He could feel the eyes of the honor guard following them with contempt. It didn't bother him much, any more.

Five years in the Slammers had taught him that parade-ground soldiers always felt that way about killers in uniform.

CHAPTER SIX

The flood shutters of the Palace of Government were closed, and Charles Desoix wasn't naive enough to think that the thick steel plates had been set against the chance of a storm surge. Bamberg City had really come apart in the two weeks he was gone.

Or just maybe it was starting to come together, but President John Delcorio wasn't going to be part of the new order.

Desoix threw a sharp salute to the head of the honor guard. The Bamberg officer returned it while the men of his section presented arms.

Striding with his shoulders back, Desoix proceeded toward the front entrance—the only opening on the first two stories of the palace that wasn't shuttered.

As Desoix looked at it, the saluting was protective coloration. It was purely common sense to want the respect of the people around you . . . and when you've wangled billets for yourself and your men in the comfort of the Palace of Government, that meant getting along with the Executive Guards.

By thumbing an epaulet loop, Desoix brightened the gray-spattered markings of his uniform to metallic silver—and it was easy to learn to salute, as easy as learning to hold the sight picture that would send a bolt of cyan death down-range at a trigger's squeeze. There was no point in not making it easy on yourself.

He thought of making a suggestion to the Slammers officer who'd just arrived, but . . . Tyl Koopman seemed a good sort and as able as one of Colonel Hammer's company commanders could be expected to be.

But Koopman also seemed the sort of man who might be happier with his troops in the police barracks beneath the City Offices than he would be in the ambiance of the Palace.

The captain in command of the guards at the entrance was named Sanchez; he roomed next door to Desoix in the officers' quarters in the West Wing. Instead of saluting again, Desoix took the man's hand and said, "Well, Rene, I'm glad to be back on a civilized planet again . . . but what on *earth* has been going on in the city since I left?"

The Guards captain made a sour face and looked around at the sergeant and ten men of his section. Everyone in the Executive Guard was at least sponsored by one of the top families on the planet. Not a few of them were members of those families, asserting a tradition of service without the potential rigors of being stationed on Two if the Crusade got under way.

"Well, you know the people," Sanchez said, a gentleman speaking among gentlemen. "The recent taxes haven't been popular, since there are rumors that they have more to do with Lady Eunice's wardrobe than with propagation of Christ's message. Nothing that we need worry about."

Desoix raised an eyebrow. The Executive Guards carried assault rifles whose gilding made them as ornamental as the gold brocade on the men's azure uniforms . . . but there were magazines in the rifles today. That was as unusual as the flood shutters being in place.

"Ah, you can't really stay neutral if things get · · · out of hand, can you?" the UDB officer asked. He didn't like to suggest that he and Sanchez were on different standards; but that was better than using "we" when the word might seem to commit the United Defense Batteries.

The guardsman's face chilled. "We'll follow orders, of course," he said. "But it isn't the business of the army to get involved in the squabbles of the mob: or to attempt to change the will of the people."

"Exactly," said Desoix, nodding enthusiastic agreement. "*Exactly.*"

He was still nodding as he strode into the entrance rotunda. He hoped he'd covered his slip with Sanchez well enough.

But he certainly *had* learned where the army—or at least the Executive Guard stood on the subject of the riots in the streets.

There was a small, separately guarded, elevator off the rotunda which opened directly onto the Consistory Room on the third floor. Desoix hesitated. The pager inset into his left cuff had lighted red with Major Borodin's anxiety, and Desoix knew what his commander wanted without admitting his presence by answering.

It would be a *very* good idea to take the elevator. Borodin was awkward in the company of President Delcorio and his noble advisors; the major, the battery, and the situation would all benefit from the presence of Lieutenant Charles Desoix.

But Desoix had some personal priorities as well, and. . . .

There was traffic up and down the central staircase—servants and minor functionaries, but not as many of them as usual. They had an air of nervousness rather than their normal haughty superiority.

When the door of the small meeting room near the elevator moved, Desoix saw Anne McGill through the opening.

Desoix strode toward her, smiling outwardly and more relieved than he could admit within. He wasn't the type who could ever admit being afraid that a woman wouldn't want to see him again—or that he cared enough about her that it would matter.

The panel, dark wood placed between heavy engaged columns of pink and gray marble, closed again when he moved toward it. She'd kept it ajar, watching for his arrival, and had flashed a sight of herself to signal Desoix closer.

But Lady Anne McGill, companion and confidante of

the President's wife, had no wish to advertise her presence here in the rotunda.

Desoix tapped on the door. He heard the lock click before the panel opened, hiding Anne behind it from anyone outside. Maybe her ambivalence was part of the attraction, he thought as he stepped into a conference room. There was a small, massively-built table, chairs for six, and space for that many more people to stand if they knew one another well.

All the room held at the moment was the odor of heavy tobaccos, so omnipresent on Bamberia that Desoix noticed it only because he'd been off-planet for two weeks . . . and Anne McGill in layers of silk chiffon which covered her like mist, hiding everything while everything remained suggested.

Desoix put his arms around her.

"Charles, it's very dangerous," she said, turning so that his lips met her cheek.

He nuzzled her ear and, when she caught his right hand, he reached for her breast with his left.

"Ah . . ." he said as a different level of risk occurred to him. "Your husband's still stationed on Two, isn't he?"

"Of course," Anne muttered scornfully.

She was no longer fighting off his hands, but she was relaxing only slightly and that at a subconscious level. "You don't think Bertrand would be *here* when things are like this, do you? There's a Consistory Meeting every morning now, but things are getting worse. *Anyone* can see that. Eunice says that they're all cowards, all the men, even her husband."

She let her lips meet his. Her body gave a shudder and she gripped Desoix to her as fiercely as her tension a moment before had attempted to repel him. "You should be upstairs now," she whispered as she turned her head again. "They need you and your Major, he's very upset."

"My call unit would have told me that if I'd asked it," the UDB officer said as he shifted the grip of his hands. Anne was a big woman, large boned and with a tendency toward fat that she repressed fiercely with exercise and various diets. She wore nothing beneath the bottom layer of chiffon except the smooth skin which Desoix caressed. His hand ran up her thigh to squeeze the fat of her buttock against the firm muscle beneath.

"Then don't be long . . ." Anne whispered as she reached for the fly of his trousers.

Desoix didn't know quite what she meant by that.

But he knew that it didn't matter as he backed his mistress against the table, lifting the chiffon dress to spill over the wood where there would be no risk of staining the fabric.

CHAPTER SEVEN

"Captain Tyl Koopman, representing Hammer's Regiment," boomed the greeter, holding the door of the Consistory Room ajar—and blocking Tyl away from it with her body, though without appearing to do so.

"Enter," said someone laconically from within. The greeter swept the panel open with a flourish, bowing to Tyl.

Machines could have done all the same things, Tyl thought with amusement; but they wouldn't have been able to do them with such pomp. Even so, the greeter, a plump woman in an orange and silver gown, was only a hint of the peacock-bright gathering within the Consistory Room.

There were twenty or thirty people, mostly men, within the domed room above the rotunda. Natural lighting through the circumference of arched windows made the Slammers officer blink. It differed in quality (if not necessarily intensity) from the glowstrips in the corridors through which he had been guided to reach the room.

The only men whose garments did not glitter with metallic threads were those whose clothing glowed with internal lambency from powerpacks woven into the seams. President

John Delcorio, in black velvet over which a sheen trembled from silver to ultra-violet, was the most striking of the lot.

"Good to see you at last, Captain," Delcorio boomed as if in assurance that Tyl would recognize him—as he did from the holograms set in niches in the hallways of the Palace of Government. "Maybe your veterans can put some backbone into our own forces, don't you think? So that we can all get down to the real business of cleansing Two for Christ."

He glowered at a middle-aged man whose uniform was probably that of a serving officer, because its dark green was so much less brilliant than what anyone else in the room seemed to be wearing.

John Delcorio was shorter than Tyl had assumed, but he had the chest and physical presence of a big man indeed. His hair, moustache, and short beard were black with gray speckles that were probably works of art: the President was only thirty-two standard years old. He had parlayed his position as Head of Security into the presidency when the previous incumbent, his uncle, died three years before.

Delcorio's eyes sparkled, and the flush on his cheeks was as much ruddy good health as a vestige of his present anger. Tyl could understand how a man with eyes that sharp could cut his way to leadership of a wealthy planet.

But he could also see how such a man's pushing would bring others to push back, push hard. . . .

Maybe too hard.

"Sir," Tyl replied, wondering what you were *supposed* to call the President of Bamberia when you met him. "I haven't been fully briefed yet on the situation. But Hammer's Slammers carry out their contracts."

He hoped that was neutral enough; and he hoped to the *Lord* that Delcorio would let him drop into the background now.

"Yes, well," said Delcorio. The quick spin of his hand was more or less the dismissal Tyl had hoped for. "Introduce Major Koopman to the others, Thomas. Have something to drink—" There was a well-stocked sideboard beneath one of the windows, and most of those present had glasses in their hands. "We're waiting for Bishop Trimer, you see."

"How *long* are you going to wait before you send for him, John?" asked the woman in the red dress that shimmered like a gasoline flame. She wasn't any taller than the President; but like him, she flashed with authority as eye-catching as her clothes. "You *are* the President, you know."

It struck Tyl that Delcorio and this woman who could only be his wife wore the colors of the Easter factions he had seen at daggers-drawn in the plaza. That made as little sense as anything else in Bamberg City.

"Major, then, is it?" murmured a slender fellow at Tyl's elbow, younger than the mercenary had been when he joined the Slammers. "I'm Thom Chastain, don't you see, and this is my brother Richie. What would you like to drink?"

"Ah, I'm really just a captain," Tyl said, wondering whether Delcorio had misheard, was being flattering—or was incensed that Hammer had sent only a company commander in response to a summons from his employer. "Ah, I don't think. . . ."

"Eunice," the President was saying in a voice like a slap, "this is *scarcely* the time to precipitate disaster by insulting the man who can stabilize the situation."

"The *army* can stabilize—" the woman snapped.

"It isn't the business of the army—" boomed the soldier in green.

The volume of his interruption shocked him as well as the others in the wrangle. All three paused. When the discussion resumed, it was held in voices low enough to be ignored if not unheard.

"Queen Eunice," said Thom Chastain, shaking his head. There was a mixture of affection and amusement in his voice, but Tyl had been in enough tight places to recognize the flash of fear in the young man's eyes. "She's really a terror, isn't she?"

"Ah," Tyl said while his mind searched for a topic that

had nothing to do with Colonel Hammer's employers. "You gentlemen are in the army also, I gather?"

There were couches around most of the walls. Near one end was a marble conference table that matched the inlaid panels between the single-sheet vitril windows. Nobody was sitting down, and the groups of two or three talking always seemed to be glancing over their collective shoulders toward the door, waiting for the missing man.

"Oh, well, these," said the other Chastain brother, Richie—surely a twin. He flicked the collar of his blue and gold uniform, speaking with the diffidence Tyl had felt at being addressed as "Major."

"We're honorary colonels in the Guards, you know," said Thom. "But it's because of our grandfather. We're not very inter. . . ."

"Well, Grandfather Chastain was, you know," said Richie, taking up where his brother's voice trailed off. "He was president some years ago. Esteban Delcorio succeeded him, but Thom and I are something like colonels for life—"

"—and so we wear—"

They concluded, both together, "But we aren't soldiers the way you are, Major."

"Or Marshal Dowell, either," Thom Chastain added later, nodding to the man in green who had broken away from the Delcorios—leaving them to hiss at one another. "Now, what would you like to drink?"

Just about anything, thought Tyl. So long as it had enough kick to knock him on his ass . . . which, in a situation like this would get him sacked if the Colonel didn't decide he should instead be shot out of hand. Why in *blazes* hadn't somebody from the staff been couriered over on an "errand" that left him available to talk informally with the civil authorities?

"Nothing for me, thank you," Tyl said aloud. "Or, ah, water?"

Marshal Dowell had fallen in with a tall man whose clothes were civilian in cut, though they carried even more metallic brocade than trimmed the military uniforms. The temporary grouping broke apart abruptly when Dowell turned away and the tall man shouted at his back, "No, I *don't* think that's a practical solution, Marshal! Abdicating your responsibilities makes it impossible for me to carry out mine."

"Berne is the City Prefect," Thom whispered into Tyl's ear. The Chastain brothers were personable kids—but "kid" was certainly the word for them. They *seemed* even younger than their probable age—which was old enough to ride point in an assault force, in Tyl's terms of reference.

From the other side, Richie was saying, "There's been a lot of trouble in the streets recently, you know. Berne keeps saying that he doesn't have enough police to take care of it."

"It is *not* in the interests of God or the State," responded Marshal Dowell, his voice shrill and his face as red as a flag, "that we give up the Crusade on Two because of some rabble that the police would deal with if they were used with decision!"

Tyl saw a man in uniform staring morosely out over the city. The uniform was familiar; desire tricked the Slammers officer into thinking that he recognized the man as well.

"'Scuse me," he muttered to the Chastains and strode across the circular room. "Ah, Lieutenant Desoix?"

Tyl's swift motion drew all eyes in the room to him— so he felt/knew that everyone recognized his embarrassment when the figure in silhouette at the window turned: a man in his mid forties, jowls sagging, paunch sagging, . . . Twenty years older than Charles Desoix and twenty kilos softer.

"Charles?" the older man barked as his eyes quested the room for the subject of Tyl's call.

"Where have you—"

Then he realized, from the way the Slammers officer's face went from enthusiastic to stricken, what had happened. He smiled, an expression that reminded Tyl of snow slumping away from a rocky hillside in the spring, and said, "You'd be Hammer's man? I'm Borodin, got the battery of the UDB here that keeps them all—" he nodded toward nothing in particular, pursing his lips to make the gesture encompass everyone in the room "—safe in their beds."

The scowl with which Major Borodin followed the statement made a number of the richly-dressed Bamberg officials turn their interest to other parts of the room.

Tyl was too concerned with controlling his own face to worry about the reason for Borodin's anger—which was explained when the UDB officer continued, "I gather we're looking for the same man. And I must say, if *you* could get down from orbit in time to be here, I don't understand what Charles' problem can be."

"He—" said Tyl. Then he smiled brightly and replaced his intended statement with, "I'm sure Lieutenant Desoix will be here as soon as possible. It's very—difficult out there, getting around, it seems to me."

"Tell me about it, boy," Borodin grunted as he turned again to the window, not so much rude as abstracted.

They were looking out over the third-story porch which faced the front of the Palace of Government. In the courtyard below were the foreshortened honor guard and the flag, still drooping and unrecognizable. The river beyond was visible only by inference. Its water, choked between the massive levees, was covered with barges ten and twelve abreast, waiting to be passed through beneath the plaza.

On the other side of the river—

"That's the City Offices, then?" Tyl asked.

Where he and the men under his temporary charge were billeted. And where now police vehicles swarmed, disgorging patrolmen and comatose prisoners in amazing numbers.

"Claims to be," Borodin grunted. "Don't see much sign that anything's being run from there, do you?"

He glanced around. He was aware enough of his surroundings to make sure that nobody but the other mercenary officer would overhear the next comment. "Or from here, you could bloody well say."

The door opened. The scattered crowd in the Consistory Room turned toward the sound with the sudden unanimity of a school of fish changing front.

"Father Laughlin, representing the Church," called the greeter in a clear voice that left its message unmistakable.

The President's face settled as if he had just watched one wing of the building crumble away. Eunice Delcorio swore like a transportation sergeant.

"Wait out here, boys," said a huge man—soft-looking but not far short of two meters in height—in white priestly vestments. "You won't be needed."

He was speaking, Tyl saw through the open door, to a quartet of "hospital orderlies." They looked even more like shock troops than they had in the street, though these weren't carrying their staffs.

Eunice Delcorio swore again. The skin over her broad cheekbones had gone sallow with rage.

Father Laughlin appeared to be at ease and in perfect control of himself, but Tyl noticed that the priest ducked instinctively when he entered the room—though he would have had to be a full meter taller to bump his head on any of the lintels in the Palace of Government.

"Where's Trimer?" Delcorio demanded in a voice that climbed a note despite an evident attempt to control it.

"Bishop Trimer, you—" Laughlin began smoothly.

"Where's Trimer?"

"Holding a Service of Prayer for Harmony in the cathedral," the priest said, no longer trying to hide the ragged edges of emotion behind an unctuous wall.

"He was told to be here!" said Berne, the City Prefect, breaking into the conversation because he was too overwhelmed by his own concerns to leave the matter to the President. He stepped toward the priest, his green jacket fluttering—a rangy mongrel snarling at a fat mastiff which will certainly make a meal of it should the mastiff deign to try.

"Bishop Trimer appreciated the President's invitation," Laughlin said, turning and nodding courteously toward Delcorio. "He sent me in response to it. He was gracious enough to tell me that he had full confidence in my ability to report your concerns to him. But his first duty is to the Church—and to all members of his flock, rather than to the secular authorities who have their own duties."

The Chastain brothers were typical of those in the Consistory Room, men of good family gathered around the President not so much for their technical abilities but because they controlled large blocks of wealth and personnel on their estates. They watched from the edges of the room with the fascination of spectators at a bloody accident, saying nothing and looking away whenever the eyes of one of the principals glanced across them.

"All right," said Eunice Delcorio to her husband. Her eyes were as calm as the crust on a pool of lava. "Now you've got to recall troops. Tell him."

She pointed toward Marshal Dowell scorning to look at the military commander directly.

"Your will, madam—" Dowell began with evident dislike.

"My *will* is that you station two regiments in the city at once, Marshal Dowell," Eunice Delcorio said with a voice that crackled like liquid oxygen flowing through a field of glass needles. "Or that you wait in the cells across the river until some successor of my husband chooses to release you."

"With your leave, sir," Dowell huffed in the direction of the President.

The Marshal was angry now, and it wasn't the earlier flashing of someone playing dangerous political games with his peers. He was lapsing into the normal frustration of a professional faced with laymen who didn't understand why he couldn't do something they thought was reasonable.

"Madam," Dowell continued with a bow to Eunice Delcorio, "your will impresses me, but it doesn't magically make transport for three thousand men and their equipment available on Two. It doesn't provide rations and accommodations for them here. And if executed with no more consideration than I've been able to give it in this room, away from my staff, it will almost certainly precipitate the very disasters that concern you."

"You—" Dowell went on.

"You—" Eunice Delcorio snapped.

"You—" the City Prefect shouted.

"You—" Father Laughlin interrupted weightily.

"You will all be silent!" said John Delcorio, and though the President did not appear to raise his voice to an exceptional level, none of the angry people squabbling in front of him continued to speak.

The two mercenary officers exchanged glances. It had occurred to both of them that any situation was salvageable if the man in charge retained the poise that President Delcorio was showing now.

"Gentlemen, Eunice," Delcorio said, articulating the thought the mercenaries had formed. "We are the *government*, not a mob of street brawlers. So long as we conduct ourselves calmly but firmly, this minor storm will be weathered and we will return to ordinary business."

He nodded to the priest. "And to the business of God, to the Crusade on Two. Father Laughlin, I trust that Bishop Trimer will take *all* necessary precautions to prevent his name from being used by those who wish to stir up trouble?"

Delcorio's voice was calm, but nobody in the room doubted how intense the reaction might be if the priest did not respond properly.

"Of course, President Delcorio," Laughlin said, bowing low.

There was a slight motion on the western edge of the room as a door opened to pass a big woman floating in a gown of white chiffon. She wasn't announced by a greeter, and she made very little stir at this juncture in the proceedings as she slipped through the room to stand near Eunice Delcorio.

"Lord Berne," Delcorio continued to his tall prefect, "I expect your police to take prompt, firm action wherever trouble erupts." His eyes were piercing.

"Yes sir," Berne said, his willing enthusiasm pinned by his master's fierce gaze. Alone of the civilians in the room, he owed everything he had to his position in the government. The richness of his garments showed just how much he had acquired in that time.

"I've already done that," he explained. "I've canceled leaves and my men have orders that all brawling is to be met with overwhelming force and the prisoners jailed. I've suspended normal release procedures for the duration of the emergency also."

Berne hesitated as the implications of what he had just announced struck him anew. "Ah, in accordance with your previous directions, sir. And your assurance that additional support would be available from the army as required."

Nobody spoke. The President nodded as he turned slowly to his military commander and said, "Marshal, I expect you to prepare for the transfer of two regular regiments back to the vicinity of the capital."

Dowell did not protest, but his lips pursed.

"*Prepare*, Marshal," Delcorio repeated harshly. "Or do you intend to inform me that you're no longer fit to perform your duties?"

"Sir," Dowell said. "As you order, of course."

"And you will further coordinate with the City Prefect so that the Executive Guard is ready to support the police if and when I order it?"

Not a command but a question, and a fierce promise of what would happen if the wrong answer were given.

"Yes sir," Marshal Dowell repeated. "As you order." Berne was nodding and rubbing his hands together as if trying to return life to them after a severe chill.

"Then, gentlemen . . ." Delcorio said, with warmth and a smile as engaging as his visage moments before had threatened. "I believe we can dismiss this gathering. Father Laughlin, convey my regrets to the Bishop that he couldn't be present, but that I trust implicitly his judgment as to how best to return civil life to its normal calm."

The priest bowed again and turned toward the door. He was not the same man in demeanor as the one who had entered the meeting, emphasizing his importance by blatantly displaying his bodyguards.

"Praise the Lord," Tyl muttered, more to himself than to Major Borodin. "I've been a lotta places I liked better 'n this one—and some of them, people were shooting at me."

Nodding to take his leave of the UDB officer, Tyl started for the door that was already being opened from the outside.

"Lieutenant Desoix of United Defense Batteries," the greeter announced.

"You there," Eunice Delcorio called in a throaty contralto—much less shrill than her previous words had led Tyl to imagine her ordinary voice would be. "Captain Koopman. Wait a moment."

Father Laughlin was already out of the room. Borodin was bearing down on his subordinate with obvious wrath that Desoix prepared to meet with a wry smile.

Everybody else looked at Tyl Koopman.

She'd gotten his name and rank right, he thought as his skin flashed hot and his mind stumbled over itself wondering what to say, what she wanted, and why in *blazes* Colonel Hammer had put him in this bucket. He was a *line* officer and this was a job for the bloody staff.

"Yes, ma'am," he said aloud, turning toward his questioner. His eyes weren't focusing right because of the unfamiliar strain, so he was seeing the president's wife as a fiery blur beneath an imperious expression.

"How many men are there under your command, Captain?" Eunice continued. There was no hostility in her voice, only appraisal. It was the situation that was freezing Tyl's heart having to answer questions on this level, rather than the way in which the questions were being asked.

"Ma'am, ah?" he said. What had Scratchard told him as they walked along the levee? "Ma'am, there's about a hundred men here. That's twenty or so in the base establishment, and the rest the transit unit that, you know, I'll be taking to Two in a few days."

"No," the woman said, coolly but in a voice that didn't even consider the possibility of opposition. "We certainly aren't sending any troops away, now."

"Yes, that's right," Delcorio agreed.

A tic brushed the left side of the President's face. The

calm with which he had concluded the meeting was based
on everything going precisely as he had choreographed it
in his mind. Eunice was adding something to the equation,
and even something as minor as that was dangerous to his
state of mind if he hadn't foreseen it.

"Ah . . ." said Tyl. "I'll need to check with Cen—"

"Well, *do* it, then!" Delcorio blazed. "Do I need to be
bothered with details that a *corporal* ought to be able to
deal with?"

"Yes *sir!*" said the Slammers officer.

He threw the President a salute because it felt right.

And because that was a good opening to spinning on
his heel and striding rapidly toward the door, on his way
out of this room.

CHAPTER EIGHT

Headquarters and billets for the enlisted men of Battery D were in a basement room of the Palace of Government, converted to the purpose from a disused workers'
cafeteria. Desoix sighed to see it again, knowing that here
his superior would let out the anger he had bottled up
while the two of them stalked through hallways roamed
by folk from outside the unit.

Control, the artificial intelligence/communications center,
sat beside a wall that had been pierced for conduits to
antennas on the roof. It was about a cubic meter of electronics packed into thirty-two resin-black modules, some
of them redundant.

Control directed the battery in combat because no
human reactions were fast enough to deal with hypersonic
missiles—though the calliopes, pulsing with light-swift
violence, could rip even those from the sky if their tubes
were slewed in the right direction.

The disused fixtures were piled at one end of the room.
Control's waste heat made the room a little warmer, a little

drier; but the place still reminded Desoix of basements in too many bombed-out cities.

Major Borodin pulled shut the flap of the curtain which separated his office from the bunks on which the off-duty shift was relaxing or trying to sleep. In theory, the curtain's microprocessors formed adaptive ripples in the fabric and canceled sounds. In practice—

Well, it didn't work that badly. And if you're running an eighty-man unit in what now had to be considered combat conditions, you'd better figure your troops were going to learn what was going on no matter how you tried to conceal it.

"You should have called in at once!" the battery commander said, half furious, half disappointed, like a parent whose daughter has come home three hours later than expected.

"I needed you at that meeting," he added, the anger replaced by desperate memory. "I . . . you know, Charles, I never know what to say to them up there. We're supposed to be defending the air space here, not mixed up in riots."

"I got a good look at that this morning, Sergei," Desoix said quietly. He seated himself carefully on the collapsible desk and, by his example, urged Borodin into the only chair in the curtained-off corner. "I think we need to reposition Gun Three. It's too close to where—things are going on. Some of our people are going to get hurt."

Borodin shook his craggy head abruptly. "We can't do that," he said. "Coverage."

"Now that Five's back on-planet—" Desoix began.

"You were with that woman, weren't you?" Borodin said, anger hardening his face as if it were concrete setting. "That's really why you didn't come to me when I needed you. I *saw* her slip in just before you did."

Yes, Daddy, Desoix thought. But Borodin was a good man to work for—good enough to humor.

"Sergei," he said calmly, "now that we've got a full battery again, I can readjust coverage areas. We can handle the seafront from the suburbs east and west, I'm pretty—"

"Charles, you're going to get into really terrible trouble," Borodin continued, his voice now sepulchral. "Get us all into trouble."

He looked up at his subordinate and added, "Now, I was younger too, I understand . . . But believe me, boy, there's plenty of it going around on a businesslike basis. And that's a *curst* sight safer."

Desoix found himself getting angry—and that made him even angrier, at himself, because it meant that Anne mattered to him.

Who you screwed wasn't nearly as dangerous as caring about her.

"Look," he said, hiding the edge in his voice but unable to eliminate the tremble. "I just shook a calliope loose on Merrinet, and it cost the unit less than three grand plus my transportation. I *solve* pro—"

"You paid a fine?"

"Via, no! I didn't pay a fine," Desoix snapped.

Shifting into a frustrated and disappointed tone of his own—a good tactic in this conversation, but exactly the way Desoix was really feeling at the moment also—he continued, "Look, Sergei, I bribed the Customs inspectors to switch manifests. The gun was still being held in the transit warehouse, there wasn't a police locker big enough for a calliope crated for shipment. If I'd pleaded it through the courts, the gun would be on Merrinet when we were old and gray. I—"

He paused, struck by a sudden rush of empathy for the older man.

Borodin was a fine combat officer and smart enough to find someone like Charles Desoix to handle the subtleties of administration that the major himself could never manage. But though he functioned ably as battery commander, he was as lost in the job's intricacies as a man in a snowstorm. Having an executive officer to guide him made things safe—until they weren't safe, and he wouldn't know about the precipice until he plunged over it.

Desoix was just as lost in the way he felt about Lady

Anne McGill; and, unlike Borodin, he didn't even have a guide.

He gripped Borodin's hand. "Sergei," he said, "I won't ask you to trust me. But I'll ask you to trust me not to do anything that'll hurt the battery. All right?"

Their eyes met. Borodin's face worked in a moue that was as close to assent as he was constitutionally able to give to the proposition.

"Then let's get back to business," Charles Desoix said with a bright smile. "We need to get a crew to Gun Five for set-up, and then we'll have to juggle duty rosters for permanent manning—unless we can get Operations to send us half a dozen men from Two to bring us closer to strength."

Borodin was nodding happily as his subordinate outlined ordinary problems with ordinary solutions.

Desoix just wished that he could submerge his own concerns about what he was doing.

CHAPTER NINE

"Locked on," said the mechanical voice of Command Central in Tyl's ears. "Hold f—"

There was a wash of static as the adaptive optics of the satellite failed to respond quickly enough to a disturbance in the upper atmosphere.

"—or soft input," continued the voice from Colonel Hammer's headquarters, the words delayed in orbit while the antenna corrected itself.

The air on top of the City Office building was still stirred by the fans of air cars moving to and from the parking area behind. Their numbers had dropped off sharply since the last remnants of the riot were dispersed. In the twilight, it was easier to smell the saltiness from the nearby sea— or else the breezes three stories up carried scents trapped in the alleys lower down.

The bright static across Tyl's screen coalesced into a face, recognizable as a woman wearing a commo helmet like Tyl's own. Noise popped in his earphones for almost a second while her lips moved on the screen—the transmissions were at slightly different frequencies. Then her voice said, "Captain Koopman, how secure are these communications on your end?"

"Ma'am?" Tyl said, too recently back from furlough not to treat the communicator as a woman instead of an enlisted man. "I'm using a portable laser from the top of the police station. It's—I think it's pretty safe, but if the signal's a problem, I can use—".

"Hold one, Captain," the communicator said with a grin of sorts. Her visage blanked momentarily in static again.

A forest of antennas shared the roof of the building with the Slammers officer: local, regional, and satellite communications gear. Instead of borrowing a console within to call Central, Tyl squatted on gritty concrete.

His ten-kilo unit included a small screen, a 20 centimeter rectenna that did its best to align itself with Hammer's satellites above, and a laser transmitting unit which probably sent Central as fuzzy a signal as Tyl's equipment managed to receive.

But you can't borrow commo without expecting the folks who loaned it to be listening in; and if Tyl did have to stay in Bamberg City with the transit detachment, he didn't want the locals to know that he'd been begging Central to withdraw him.

The screen darkened into a man's face. "Captain Koopman?" said the voice in his helmet. "I appreciate your sense of timing. I'm glad to have an experienced officer overseeing the situation there at the moment."

"Sir!" Tyl said, throwing a salute that was probably out of the restricted field of the pick-up lens.

"Give me your appraisal of the situation, Captain," said the voice of Colonel Alois Hammer. His flat-surface image wobbled according to the vagaries of the upper atmosphere.

"At the moment . . ." Tyl said. He looked away from

the screen in an unconscious gesture to gain some time for his thoughts.

The House of Grace towered above him. At the top of the high wall was the visage of Bishop Trimer enthroned. The prelate's eyes were as hard as the stone in which they were carved.

"At the moment, sir, it's quiet," Tyl said to the screen. "The police cracked down hard, arrested about fifty people. Since then—

"Leaders?" interrupted the helmet in its crackling reproduction of the Colonel's voice. Hammer's eyes were like light-struck diamonds, never dull—never quite the same.

"Brawlers, street toughs," Tyl said contemptuously. "A lot of 'em, is all. But it's been quiet, and . . ."

He paused because he wasn't sure how far he ought to stick his neck out with no data, not really—but his commanding officer waited expectantly on the other end of the satellite link.

"Sir," Tyl said, determined to do the job he'd been set, even though this stuff scared him in a different way from a firefight. There he *knew* what he was supposed to do. "Sir, I haven't been here long enough to know what's normal, but the way it feels out there now . . ."

He looked past the corner of the hospital building and down into the plaza. Many of the booths were still set up and a few were lighted—but not nearly enough to account for the numbers of people gathering there in the twilight. It was like watching gas pool in low spots, mixing and waiting for the spark that would explode it.

"The only places I been that felt like this city does now are night positions just before somebody hits us."

"Rate the players, Captain," said Hammer's voice as his face on the screen flickered and dimmed with the lights of an air car whining past, closer to the roof than it should have been for safety.

The vehicle was headed toward the plaza. Its red and white emergency flashers were on, but the car's idling pace suggested that they were only a warning.

As if *he* knew anything about this sort of thing, Tyl

thought bitterly. But the Colonel was right, he could give the same sort of assessment that any mercenary officer learned to do of the local troops he was assigned to support. It didn't really matter that these weren't wearing uniforms.

Some of them weren't wearing uniforms.

"Delcorio's hard but he's brittle," Tyl said aloud. "He'd do all right with enough staff to take the big shocks, but what he's got . . ."

He paused, collecting his thoughts further. Hammer did not interrupt, but the fluctuation of his image on the little screen reminded Tyl that time was passing.

"All right," the Slammers captain continued. "The police, they seem to be holding up pretty well. Berne, the City Prefect, don't have any friends and I don't guess much support. On that end, it's gone about as far as it can and keep the lid on."

Hammer was nodding, but Tyl ignored that too. He had his data marshaled, now, and he needed to spit things out while they were clear to him. "The army, Dowell at least, he's afraid to move and he's not afraid not to move. He won't push anything himself, but Delcorio won't get much help from there.

"And the rest of 'em, the staffs—" Tyl couldn't think of the word the group had been called here "—they're nothing, old men and young kids, nobody that matters . . . ah, except the wife, you know, sir? Ah, Lady Eunice, Only she wants to push harder than I think they can push here with what they got and what they got against 'em."

"The mob?" prompted the Colonel. Static added a hiss to words without sibilants.

Tyl looked toward the plaza. The sky was still blue over the western horizon, behind the cathedral's dome and the Palace of Government. The sunken triangle of the plaza was as dark as a volcano's maw, lighted only by the sparks of lanterns and apparently open flames.

"Naw, not the mobs," Tyl said, letting his helmet direct his voice while his eyes gathered data instead of blinking toward his superior. "Them, they'd handle each other if it wasn't any more. But—"

He looked up. The sunset slid at an angle across the side of the House of Grace. The eyes of Bishop Trimer's carven face were as red as blood.

"Sir," Tyl blurted, "it's the Church behind it, the Bishop, and he's going to walk off with the whole thing soon unless Delcorio's luckier 'n anybody's got a right to expect. I think—"

No, say it right.

"Sir," he said, "I recommend that all regimental forces be withdrawn from Bamberg City at once, to avoid us being caught up in internal fighting. There are surface-effect freighters at the port right now. With your authorization, I'll charter one immediately and have the unit out of here in three hours."

Two hours, unless he misjudged the willingness and efficiency of the sergeant major; but he'd promise what he was sure of and surprise people later by bettering the offer if he could.

Hammer's lips moved. Tyl thought that the words were delayed by turbulence, but the Colonel was only weighing what he was about to say before he put it into audible syllables. After a moment, the voice and fuzzy screen said in unison, "Captain, I'm going to tell you what my problem is."

Tyl's lungs filled again. He'd been holding his breath unknowingly, terrified that his colonel was about to strip him of his rank for saying too much, saying the wrong thing. Anything else, that was all right. . . .

Even command problems that weren't any business of a captain in the line.

"Our contract," Hammer said carefully, "is with the government of Bamberia, not precisely with President Delcorio."

The image of the screen glared as if reading on Tyl's face the interjection his subordinate would never have spoken aloud. "The difference is the sort that only matters in formal proceedings—like a forfeiture hearing before the Bonding Authority, determining whether or not the Regiment has upheld its end of the contract."

"Yes *sir!*" Tyl said.

Hammer's face lost its hard lines. For a moment, Tyl thought that the hint of grayness was more than merely an artifact of the degraded signal.

"There's a complication," the Colonel said with a precision that erased all emotional content from the statement. "Bishop Trimer has been in contact with the Eaglewing Division regarding taking over conduct of the Crusade in event of a change of government."

He shrugged. "My sources," he added needlessly. "It's a small community, in a way."

Then, with renewed force and no hint of the fatigue of moments before, Hammer went on, "In event of Trimer taking over, as you accurately estimated was his intention, we're out of work. That's not the end of the world, and I *certainly* don't want any of my men sacrificed pointlessly—"

"No *sir*," Tyl barked in response to the fierceness in his commander's face.

"—but I need to know whether a functional company like yours might be able to give Delcorio the edge he needs."

Hammer's voice asked, but his eyes demanded. "Stiffen Dowell's spine, give Trimer enough of a wild card to keep him from making his move before the Crusade gets under way and whoever's in charge won't be able to replace units that're already engaged."

And do it, Tyl realized, without a major troop movement that could be called a contract violation by Colonel Hammer, acting against the interests of a faction of his employers.

It might make a junior captain—acting on his own initiative—guilty of mutiny, of course.

"Sir," Tyl said crisply, vibrant to know that he had orders now that he could understand and execute. "We'll do the job if it can be done. Ripper Jack's a good man, cursed good. I don't know the others yet, most of 'em, but it's three-quarters veterans back from furlough and only a few newbie recruits coming in."

"Understand me, Captain," Hammer said—again fiercely. "I *don't* want you to become engaged in fighting unless it's necessary for your own safety. There aren't enough of you to make any difference if the lid really comes off, and I *won't* throw away good men just to save a contract. But if your being in the capital keeps President Delcorio in power for another two weeks . . . ?"

"Yes *sir!*" Tyl repeated brightly, marveling that his commander seemed relieved at his reaction. Via, he was an officer of Hammer's Slammers, wasn't he? Of *course* he'd be willing to carry out orders that were perfectly clear—or as clear as combat orders ever could be.

Keep the men in battle dress and real visible; hint to Dowell that there was a company of panzers waiting just over the horizon to land and *really* kick butt as soon as he said the word. Make waves at the staff meetings. They couldn't bother him now with their manners and fancy clothes.

The Colonel had told Tyl Koopman what to do, and a few rich fops weren't going to affect the way he did it.

"Then carry on, Captain," Hammer said with a punctuation of static in the middle of the words that did not disguise the pleasure in his voice. "There's a lot—"

The sky was a lighter gray than the ground or the sea, but the sun had fully set. The cyan flash of a powergun lanced the darkness like a scream in silence.

"Hold!" Tyl shouted to his superior, rising from his crouch to get a better view past the microwave dish beside him.

A volley of bolts spat from at least half a dozen locations in the plaza. The orbiting police air car staggered and lifted away. Its plastic hull had been hit. The driver's desperate attempt to increase speed fanned the flames to sluggish life; a trail of smoke marked the vehicle's path.

A huge roar came from the crowd in the plaza. Led by a line of torches and lightwands, it crawled like a living thing up both the central and eastern stairs.

They weren't headed for the Palace of Government across the river. They were coming here.

Tyl flipped his helmet's manual switch to the company frequency. "Sar'ent Major," he snapped, "all men in combat gear and ready t' move *soonest*! Three days rations and all the ammo we can carry."

He switched back to the satellite push and began folding the screen—not essential to the transmission while the face of Colonel Alois Hammer still glowed on it with tigerish intensity.

"Sir," Tyl said without any emotion to waste on the way he was closing his report, "I'll tell you more when I know more."

Then he collapsed the transceiver antenna. Hammer didn't have anything as important to say as the mob did.

CHAPTER TEN

The mob was pulsing toward the City Offices like the two heads of a flood surge. Powergun bolts spiked out of the mass, some aimed at policemen but many were fired at random.

That was the natural reaction of people with the opportunity to destroy something—an ability which carries its own imperatives. Tyl wasn't too worried about that, not if he had his men armed and equipped before they and the mob collided.

But when he clumped down the stairs from the trap door in the roof, he threw a glance over his shoulder. The north doors of the House of Grace had opened, disgorging men who marched in ground-shaking unison as they sang a Latin hymn.

That was real bad for President Delcorio, for Colonel Hammer's chances of retaining his contract—

And possibly real bad for Tyl Koopman and the troops in his charge.

The transit detachment was billeted on the second floor, in what was normally the turn-out room. Temporary bunks, three-high, meant the troops on the top layer couldn't sit up without bumping the ceiling. What floor space the bunks didn't fill was covered by the foot-lockers holding the troops' personal gear.

Now most of the lockers had been flung open and stood in the disarray left by soldiers trying to grab one last valuable—a watch; a holo projector; a letter. They knew they might never see their gear again.

For that matter, they knew that the gear was about as likely to survive the night as they themselves were—but you had to act as if you were going to make it.

Sergeant Major Scratchard stumped among the few troopers still in the bunk room, slapping them with a hand that rang on their ceramic helmets. "Move!" he bellowed with each blow. "It's yer *butts*!"

If the soldier still hesitated with a fitting or to grab for one more bit of paraphernalia, Scratchard gripped his shoulder and spun him toward the door. As Tyl stuck his head into the room, a female soldier with a picture of her father crashed off the jamb beside him, cursing in a voice that was a weapon itself.

"All clear, sir," Scratchard said as the last pair of troopers scampered for the door ahead of him, geese waddling ahead of a keeper with a ready switch. "Kekkonan's running the arms locker, he's a good man."

Tyl used the pause to fold the dish antenna of his laser communicator. The sergeant major glanced at him. He said in a voice as firm and dismissing as the one he'd been using on his subordinates, "Dump that now. We don't have time fer it."

"I'll gather 'em up outside," Tyl said. "You send 'em down to me, Jack."

He clipped the communicator to his equipment belt. Alone of the detachment, he didn't have body armor. Couldn't worry about that now.

The arms locker, converted from an interrogation room, was next door to the bunk room. The hall was crowded with troopers waiting to be issued weapons and those pushing past, down the stairs with armloads of lethal hardware that they would organize in the street where there was more space.

Tyl joined the queue thumping its way downstairs. As he did so, he glanced over his shoulder and called, "We'll *have* time, Sar'ent Major. And by the Lord! we'll have a secure link to Central when we do."

CHAPTER ELEVEN

For a moment, the exterior of the City Offices was lighted by wall sconces as usual. A second or two after Tyl stepped from the door into bulk of his troops, crouching as they awaited orders, the sconces, the interior lights, and all the street lights visible on the east side of the river switched off.

There was an explosion louder than the occasional popping of slug throwers in the distance. A transformer installation had been blown up or shorted into self destruction.

That made the flames, already painting the low clouds pink, more visible.

A recruit turned on his hand light. The veteran beside him snarled, "Fuckhead! Use infra red on your helmet shield!"

The trooper on the recruit's other side—more direct—slapped the light away and crushed it beneath her boot.

"Sergeants to me," Tyl ordered on the unit push. He flashed momentarily the miniature lightwand that he carried clipped to a breast pocket—for reading and for situations like this, when his troops needed to know where he was.

Even at the risk of drawing fire when he showed them.

He hadn't called for non-coms, because the men here were mostly veterans with a minimum of the five-years service that qualified them for furlough. Seven sergeants crawled forward, about what Tyl had expected and enough for his purposes.

"Twelve-man squads," he ordered, using his commo helmet instead of speaking directly to the cluster of sergeants. That way all his troops would know what was happening.

As much as Tyl did himself, at any rate.

"Gather 'em fast, no screwing around. We're going to move as soon as everybody's clear." He looked at the sergeants, their faceshields down, just as his was—a collection of emotionless balls, and all of them probably as worried as he was: worried about what they knew was coming, and more nervous yet about all the things that might happen in darkness, when nobody at all knew which end was up.

"And no shooting, troopers. Unless we got to."

If they had to shoot their way out, they were well and truly screwed. Just as Colonel Hammer had said—there weren't enough of them to matter a fart in a whirlwind if it came down to that.

A pair of emergency vehicles—fire trucks swaying with the weight of the water on board them—roared south along the river toward the City Offices. A huge block of masonry hurtled from the roof of an apartment building just up the street. Tyl saw its arc silhouetted against the pink sky for a moment.

The stone hit the street with a crash and half, bounced, and half-rolled, into the path of the lead truck. The fire vehicle slewed to the side, but its wheels weren't adequate to stabilize the kiloliters of water in its ready-use tank. The truck went over and skidded, rotating on its side in sparks and the scream of tortured metal—even before its consort rammed it from behind.

Someone began to fire a slug thrower from the roof. The trucks were not burning yet, but a stray breeze brought the raw, familiar odor of petroleum fuel to the hunching Slammers.

There wasn't anything in Hell worse than street fighting in somebody else's city—

And Tyl, like most of the veterans with him, had done it often enough to be sure of that.

A clot of soldiers stumbled out the doorway. Scratchard was the last, unrecognizable for a moment because of the huge load of equipment he carried.

Looked as if he'd staggered out with everything the rest of the company had left in the arms locker, Tyl thought. A veteran like Jack Scratchard should've known to—

Reinforced windows blew out of the second floor with a cyan flash, a bang, and a deep orange *whoom!* that was simultaneously a sound and a vision. The sergeant major hadn't tried to empty the arms locker after all.

"Put this on, sir," Scratchard muttered to the captain as the fire trucks up the street ignited in the spray of burning fragments hurled from the demolition of the Slammers' excess stores. The actinics of the powergun ammunition detonating in its storage containers made exposed skin prickle, but the exploding gasoline pushed at the crouching men with a warm, stinking hand.

Roof floodlights, driven by the emergency generator in the basement, flared momentarily around the City Offices. Shadows pooled beneath the waiting troops. They cursed and ducked lower—or twisted to aim at the lights revealing them.

Volleys of shots from the mob shattered the lenses before any of the Slammers made up their minds to shoot. The twin pincers, from the plaza and from the House of Grace, were already beginning to envelope the office building.

The route north and away was awash in blazing fuel. The police air car that roared off that way, whipping the flames with its vectored thrust, pitched bow-up and stalled as an automatic weapon ranked it from the same roof as the falling masonry had come.

Scratchard had brought a suit of clamshell body armor for Tyl to wear—and a sub-machinegun to carry along with a bandolier holding five hundred rounds of ammo in loaded magazines.

"We're crossing the river," Tyl said in a voice that barely

danced on the spikes of his present consciousness. "By squad."

He hadn't gotten around to numbering the squads. There was a clacking sound as the sergeant major latched Tyl's armor for him.

Tyl pointed at one of the sergeants—he didn't know *any* bloody names!—with his lightwand. "You first. And you. Next—"

In the pause, uncertain in the backlit darkness where the other non-coms were, Scratchard broke in on the command frequency saying, "Haskins, third. Hu, Pescaro, Bogue and Hagemann. Move, you dickheads!"

Off the radio, his head close to Tyl's as the captain clipped his sling reflexively to the epaulet tab of his armor and shrugged the heavy bandoiler over the opposite shoulder, the sergeant major added, "You lead 'em, sir—I'll hustle their butts from here."

Even as Tyl opened his mouth to frame a reply, Scratchard barked at one of the men who'd appeared just ahead of him, "Kekkonan—you give 'im a hand with names if he needs it, right?"

Sergeant Kekkonan, short and built like one of the tanks he'd commanded, clapped Tyl on the shoulder hard enough that it was just as well the captain had already started in the direction of the thrust—toward the river and the squad running toward the levee wall as swiftly as their load of weapons and munitions permitted.

A column of men came around the northern corner of the building. Their white tunics rippled orange in the glare of the burning vehicles. The leaders carried staffs as they had when they guarded the procession route, but in the next rank back winked the iridium barrels of powerguns and the antennas of sophisticated communications gear.

They were no more than three steps from the nearest of the nervous Slammers. When the leading orderlies shouted and threw themselves out of the way, there were almost as many guns pointed at the troops as pointed by them.

"*Hold!*" Tyl Koopman ordered through his commo

helmet as his skin chilled and his face went stiff. Almost they'd made it, but now—

He was running toward the mob of orderlies—Via! *They* weren't a mob!—with his hands raised, palms forward.

"This isn't our fight!" he cried, hoping he was close enough to the orderlies to be understood by them as well as by the troops on his unit push. "Squads, keep moving—over the levee!"

The column of orderlies had stopped and flattened like the troops they were facing, but there were three men erect at the new head of the line. One carried a shoulder-pack radio; one a bull-horn; and the man in the middle was a priest with a crucifix large enough to be the standard that the whole column followed.

Tyl looked at the priest, wondering if he could grab the butt of his slung weapon fast enough to take some of them with him if the words the priest murmured to the man with the bull-horn brought a blast of shots from the guns aimed at the Slammers captain.

The burning trucks roared. Sealed parts ruptured with plosive sounds and an occasional sharp crack.

"Go on, get out of here," the bull-horn snarled, its crude amplification making the words even harsher than they were when they came from the orderly's throat.

Tyl spun and brandished his lightwand. "Third Squad," he ordered. "Move!"

A dozen of his troopers picked themselves up from the ground and shambled across the street behind him—toward the guns leveled on the mob from the levee's top. The first two squads were deployed there with the advantages of height and a modicum of cover if any of the locals needed a lesson about what it meant to take on Hammer's Slammers.

Tyl's timing hadn't been quite as bad as he'd thought. Hard to tell just what might have happened if the column from the House of Grace had arrived before Tyl's company had a base of fire across the street.

Two more squads were moving together. The leaders of the mob's other arm, bawling their way up the river road, had already reached the south corner of the City Offices. The cries of *"Freedom, Freedom!"* were suddenly punctuated with screams as a dozen or so of the leaders collapsed under a burst of electrostatic needles fired by one of the policemen inside.

Tyl heard the shots that answered the stunner, slug throwers as well as powerguns, but the real measure of the response was the barely audible clink of bottles shattering.

Then the gasoline bombs ignited and silhouetted the building from the south.

Tyl stood on the pedestrian way atop the levee, wondering when somebody would get around to taking a shot at him just because he *was* standing.

"Three and four," he ordered as the heavily-laden troops scrambled up the steps to join him. "Across the river, climb over the barges. Kekkonan, you lead 'em, set up a perimeter on the other side.

"And *wait!*" he added, though Kekkonan didn't look like the sort you had to tell that to.

The rest of the company was moving in a steady stream, lighted between the two fires of the trucks and the south front of the building they had abandoned.

"Take 'em across, take 'em across!" Tyl shouted as the Slammers plodded past. The non-coms would take the words as an order, and the rest of the troops would get the idea.

The first two squads squirmed as they waited, their guns now aimed toward both pincers of the mob. Fifty meters of the west frontage of the City Offices were clear of the rioters who would otherwise have lapped around it. It wasn't a formal stand-off; just the tense waiting of male dogs growling as they sidled toward each other, not quite certain what the next seconds would bring.

The last man was Sergeant Major Scratchard, falling a further step behind his troops with every step he took.

"We're releasing the prisoners!" boomed the array of loudspeakers on the building roof. Simultaneous words from a dozen locations echoed themselves by the amount of time that sound from the mechanical diaphragms lagged behind the electronic pulses feeding them.

"Second Squad, withdraw," Tyl ordered. He felt as if his load of gear had halved in weight when the eyes of the rioters, orange flecks lighted by the fires of their violence, turned away from him and his men to stare at the City Offices.

Tyl jumped back down the steps and put his left arm— the sub-machinegun was under his right armpit—around the sergeant major's chest. Scratchard weighed over a hundred kilos, only a little of it in the gut that had expanded with his desk job. Tyl's blood jumped with so much adrenalin that he noticed only Scratchard's inertia—not his weight.

"Lemme go!" Scratchard rasped in a voice tight with the ache in his knees.

"Shut the hell up!" Tyl snarled back. The laser communicator was crushed between them, biting both men's thighs. If he'd had a hand free, he'd have thrown the cursed thing against the concrete levee.

The mob's chanted, "Freedom!" gave way suddenly to a long bellow, loud and growing like a peal of thunder. Tyl's back was to the City Offices, and the rolling triumph had started on the far side anyway, where the jail entrance opened onto the parking area. He knew what was happening, though.

And he knew, even before the shouts turned to "*Kill* them! *Kill* them!" that this mob wasn't going to be satisfied with freeing their fellows.

Likely the police trapped inside the building had known that too; but they didn't have any better choices either.

"You, give us a hand!" Tyl ordered as he and Scratchard stumbled toward the railing across the walkway. He pointed to the nearest trooper with the gun that filled his right hand. She jumped to her feet and took the sergeant major's other arm while Tyl boomed over the radio, "First Squad, withdraw. Kekkonan, make sure you've got us covered."

The river here was half a kilometer wide between the levees, but with night sights and powerguns, trained men could sweep the far walkway clear if some of the rioters decided it'd be safe to pursue.

The river had fallen more than a meter since Tyl viewed it six hours before. The barges still floated a safe jump beneath the inner walkway of the levee—but not safe for Jack Scratchard with a load of gear.

"Gimme my arms free," the sergeant major ordered.

Tyl nodded and stepped away with the trooper on the other side. Scratchard gripped the railing with both hands and swung himself over. He crouched on the narrow lip, choosing his support, and lowered himself onto the hogsheads with which the barge was loaded. The troopers waiting to help the senior non-com had the sense to get out of the way.

"I'm fine now," Scratchard grunted. "Let's move!"

The barges were moored close, but there was enough necessary slack in the lines that some of them were over a meter apart while their rubber bumpers squealed against those of the vessel on the opposite flank. Tyl hadn't thought the problem through, but Kekkonan or one of the other sergeants had stationed pairs of troopers at every significant gap. They were ready to guide and help lift latercomers over the danger.

"Thank the Lord," Tyl muttered as four strong arms boosted him from the first barge to the next in line. He wasn't sure whether he meant for the help or for the realization that the men he commanded were as good as anybody could pray.

CHAPTER TWELVE

Charles Desoix wore a commo helmet to keep in touch with his unit, but he was looking out over Bamberg City with a handheld image intensifier instead of using the integral optics of the helmet's face shield. The separate unit gave him better illumination, crisper details. He held the imager steady by resting his elbows on the rail of the porch outside the Consistory Room, overlooking the courtyard and beyond—

The railing jiggled as someone else leaned against it, bouncing Desoix's forty magnification image of a window in the City Office building off his screen.

"*Lord* cur—" Desoix snarled as he spun. He wasn't the sort to slap the clumsy popinjay whom he assumed had disturbed him, but he was willing to give the contrary impression at the moment.

Anne McGill was at the rail beside him.

"They told me—" Desoix blurted.

"Yes, but I couldn't—" Anne said, both of them trying to cover the angry outburst that would disappear from reality if they pretended it hadn't occurred.

She'd closed the clear doors behind her, but Desoix could see into the Consistory Room. Enough light fell onto the porch to illuminate them for anyone looking in their direction.

He put his arms around Anne anyway, being careful not to gouge her back with a corner of the imaging unit. She didn't protest as he thought she might—but she gasped in surprise as her breasts flattened against her lover.

"Ah," Desoix said. "Yeah, I thought I'd wear my armor while I was out . . . Ah, maybe we ought to go inside."

"No," Anne said, squeezing him tighter. "Just hold me."

Desoix stroked her back with his free hand while the breeze brought screams and the smell of smoke from across the river.

His helmet hissed with the sound of a Situation Report. He'd programmed Control to call for a sitrep every fifteen minutes during the night. That was the only way you could be sure an outlying unit hadn't been wiped out before they could sound an alarm. . . .

That wasn't a way Charles Desoix liked to think. "Just a second, love," he muttered, blanking his mind of what the woman with her arms around him had started to say.

"Two to Control, all clear," a human voice said. "Over."

Gun Two was north of the city on a bluff overlooking

the river. It had a magnificent field of fire—and there was
very little development in the vicinity, which made it fairly
safe in the present circumstances.

"Control to Three," said the emotionless artificial intelligence in the palace basement. "Report, over."

The hollow sound of gasoline bombs igniting, deadened
by the pillow of intervening air, accompanied the gush of
fresh orange flames from across the river. One side of the
City Offices was covered with crawling fire.

"Three t' Control," came the voice of Sergeant Blaney.

There was a whining noise behind the words, barely
audible through the commo link. It nagged at Desoix's
consciousness, but he couldn't quite remember. . . .

"It's all right here," the human voice continued, "but
there's a lot of traffic in and out of the plaza. There's fires
north of us, and there's shots all round."

The sergeant paused. He wasn't speaking to Control but
rather in the hope that Borodin or Desoix were listening
even without an alert—and that they'd do something about
the situation.

"Nothing aimed at us, s' far as we can tell," Blaney
concluded. "Over."

The mechanical whining had stopped some seconds
before.

Men, lighted by petroleum flares in both direction, were
headed from the City Offices to the adjacent levee. Desoix
couldn't make out who they were without the imaging unit,
but he had a pretty good idea.

His left hand massaged Anne McGill's shoulders, to calm
her and calm him as well. He reached for his helmet's
commo key with his right hand, careful not to clash the
two pieces of sophisticated hardware together, and said,
"Blue to Three. Give me an azimuth on your gun, Blaney.
Over."

Major Borodin was Red. With luck, he wasn't monitoring
the channel just now.

Blaney hesitated, but he knew the XO could get the data
from Control as easily—and that if Desoix asked, he already
knew the answer even though Gun Three was far out of

direct sight of the Palace of Government. "Sir," he said at last. "It's two-five-zero degrees. Over."

Normal rest position for Gun Three was 165° pointing out over Nevis Channel in the direction from which hostile ship-launched missiles were most likely to come. The crew had just re-aimed their weapon to cover the east stairs of the plaza. That was what *they* obviously thought was the most serious threat of their own well-being.

"Blue to Three," said Charles Desoix. "Out."

He wasn't down there with them, and he wasn't about to overrule their assessment of the situation from up here.

"Eunice is so angry," Anne McGill murmured. Communicating with the man beside her was as important to her state of mind as the strength of his arm around her shoulders. "I'm afraid, mostly—" and the simplicity of the statement belied its truth "—and so's John, I think, though it's hard to tell with him. But Eunice would like to hang them all, starting with the Bishop."

"Not going to be easy to do," Desoix said calmly while he adjusted the imager one-handed and prayed that it wouldn't show what he thought he saw in the shuddering flames.

It did. Men and women in police uniforms were being thrown from the roof of the office building. They didn't fall far: just a meter or two, before they were halted jerking by the ropes around their necks.

Within the Consistory Room, voices burbled. Light brightened momentarily as someone turned up a wall sconce. It dimmed again as abruptly when common sense overcame a desire for gleaming surroundings.

The clear panels surrounding the circular room were shatterproof vitril. They were supposed to stop bricks or a slug from any weapon a man could fire from his shoulder, and the layer of gold foil within the thermoplastic might even deflect a powergun bolt.

But only a fool would insist on testing them while he was on the other side of the panel. That kind of test was a likely result of making the Consistory Room a beacon on a night like this.

Anne straightened slightly when she heard the sounds in the room behind them, but she didn't move away as Desoix had expected her to do. "There!" she said in a sharp whisper, pointing down toward the river. "They're moving. . . . They—are they coming for us?"

Desoix used both hands to steady the imager, though he kept the magnification down to ten power. The fuel fires provided quite a lot of light, and the low clouds scattered it broadly for the intensification circuits.

"Those are Hammer's men," the UDB officer said as the scene glowed saffron in the imager's field of view.

The troopers crossing the river on the barges moored there were foreshortened by the angle and flattened into two dimensions by the imaging circuitry, but there were a lot of them. Enough to be the whole unit, the Lord willing—and better the Slammers have the problems than United Defense Batteries.

Desoix's helmet said in Control's calm voice, "Captain Koopman of Hammer's Regiment has been calling the officer of the day on the general frequency. The OOD has not replied. Now Captain Koopman is calling you. Do you wish—"

"Patch him through," Desoix ordered. Anne's startled expression reminded him that she would think he was speaking to her, but there wasn't time to clear that up now.

"—warn the guards not to shoot at us?" came the voice of the Slammers captain he'd met just that morning. "I can't raise the bastards and I *don't* want any trouble."

"Desoix to Slammers, over?" the UDB officer said.

"Roger Desoix, over," Koopman responded instantly. The relief in the infantry captain's voice was as obvious as the threat in the previous phrase: if anybody started shooting at him and his men, he was planning to finish the job and worry later about the results.

"Tyl, I'm headed down to the front entrance right now," Desoix said. "It's quiet on this side, so don't let some recruit get nervous at the wrong time."

He'd lowered the imager and was stroking Anne's back fiercely with his free hand, feeling the soft cloth bunch and ripple over skin still softer. Her arm was around his hips, beneath the rim of his armor, caressing him as well. Hard to believe this was the woman who'd always refused to lie down on a bed with him, because if her hairdo was mussed, people might guess what she'd been doing.

Desoix turned and kissed her, vaguely amazed that the tension of the moment increased his sexual arousal instead of dampening it.

"Love," he said, and *meant* "love," for the first time in a life during which he'd used the word to a hundred woman on a score of planets. "I'm going downstairs for a moment. I'll be back soon, but wait inside."

Even as he kissed her warm lips again, he was moving toward the door and carrying the woman with him by the force of his arm as well as by his personality.

Desoix felt a moment's concern as he strode for the elevator across the circular room that he'd left his mistress to be spiked by the wondering eyes of the dozen or more men who stood in nervous clumps amidst the furniture. Anne was going to have to handle that herself, because he couldn't take her with him into what he was maybe getting into.

And if he didn't go, well—he didn't need what he'd heard in Tyl Koopman's voice to know how a company of Hammer's Slammers was going to respond if a bunch of parade-ground soldiers tried to bar their escape from a dangerous situation.

CHAPTER THIRTEEN

The way some of the Executive Guards in the rotunda were waving their weapons around would have bothered Desoix less if he'd believed the men involved had ever fired their guns deliberately. A couple of them might honestly not know the difference between the trigger and the safety catch, making the polished-marble room as dangerous as a foxhole at the sharp end of the front.

If Koopman's unit blew off the flood shutters and tossed in grenades, the rotunda was going to be as dangerous as an abattoir.

Captain Rene Sanchez must have been off duty by now, but there were more guards in the rotunda than the usual detachment and he was among them.

"Rene," Desoix called cheerfully as he stepped off the elevator, noticing that the Bamberg officer had unlatched the flap covering his pistol. "I've come to give you a hand. We're getting some reinforcements, Hammer's men. They're on the way now.

Sanchez turned with a wild expression. "Nobody comes in or out," he said in a voice whose high pitch increased the effect of his eyes being focused somewhere close to infinity. The Guardsman was either drugged to a razor's edge, or his nerves unaided had honed him to the same dangerous state.

"We're going to take care of this, Rene," Desoix said, putting a friendly hand on Sanchez's shoulder.

The local man was quivering and it wasn't just fear. Sanchez was ready to go, go off in *any* direction. He was in prime shape to lead a night assault with knives and grenades—and he was just about as lethal as a live grenade, too.

You could never tell about the ones who'd never in their lives done anything real. They could react any way at all when the universe forced itself to their attention. About all a professional like Charles Desoix knew to expect was that he wouldn't like the result, whatever it turned out to be.

The Guard Commandant, Colonel Drescher, was present. Arm in arm with Sanchez, the UDB officer walked toward him. Desoix had nodded to Drescher in the past, but they had never spoken.

"Colonel," he said, using Rene Sanchez and a brisk manner as his entree, "We've got some reinforcements coming in a few moments. I'm here to escort them in."

"Charles, I got a squad in the courtyard now," said

Desoix's helmet. "Let's get a door open, all right? Over."

He didn't respond to Koopman's call, because the Guards colonel was saying, "You? UDB? I'm sorry, mister mercenary, the Marshal has given orders that the shutters not be opened."

"I just came from Marshal Dowell in the Consistory Room," Desoix said, letting his voice rise as only control had kept it from doing earlier. The best way to play this was to pretend to be on the edge of blind panic. That wasn't so great a pretense as he would have wished.

"He *ordered* me down here to inform you," Desoix continued. He thought he'd glimpsed Dowell upstairs. Certainly that was possible, at any rate. "By the Lord! man. Do you realize what the Marshal will do if you endanger him by keeping out his reinforcements? He'll have you—well, it's obvious."

The Guards colonel blinked. "Jorge Dowell doesn't give *me* orders!" he snapped, family pride overwhelming whatever trace of military obedience was in Drescher's makeup.

The Executive Guard was enough a law unto itself that Desoix had been sure that Drescher's references to army orders was misdirection—though Dowell might well have given such orders if anybody had bothered to ask him.

But because they hadn't . . . Desoix's present bluff wasn't beyond the realm of Dowell's possible response either.

"Still," Colonel Drescher continued. "Since you're here, we'll make an exception for courtesy's sake."

The waxen calm of his expression lapsed into gray fear for a moment. "But be quick, Lieutenant, or I swear I'll shut you out with them and the animals across the river."

Soldiers who'd been listening to the exchange touched the undogging mechanism without orders, but they paused and drew back instead of engaging the gears to slide the shutters away.

"We'll get on with it!" cried another voice.

One of the guards pressed the switch before Desoix's hand reached it; the UDB officer glanced at the speaker instead.

There were four men together. They were wearing civilian

clothes now in place of the ornate uniforms they'd worn in the Consistory Room this morning and in days past. The considerable entourage behind them stretched beyond the rotunda: servants, very few of them real bodyguards—but most of the males were now armed with rifles and pistols which looked as though they came from government stores.

"Charles, how we holding?" came Tyl Koopman's voice through the commo helmet. "Over."

The words lacked the overtone of threat that had been in his earlier query. The Slammers could see or at least hear that a door was opening.

"Blue to Slammers," Desoix responded. He could feel a smile starting to twitch the corners of his mouth. "Just a second. There's some restructuring going on in here and we're, ah, making room for you in the guest quarters. Let these folks pass."

Desoix made sure that he was with the quartet of wealthy landholders as they forced their way through the door ahead of their servants.

"No, no," one of the men was saying to another. "My townhouse will have to take care of itself. I'm off to my estates to rally support for the President. I'll inform John of what I'm doing just as soon as I get there, but of course I couldn't waste time now with goodbyes."

Desoix thought for a moment that Captain Sanchez would step outside with him because that was the direction in which the Guards officer had last been pointed. Sanchez was lost in the turmoil, though, and Desoix stood alone beside the door as minor rats streamed out past him, following the lead of the noble rats they served.

Fires glowed against the cloud cover from at least a dozen directions in the city, not just the vicinity of the City Offices directly across the river. The smell of burning was more noticeable here than it had been on the porch six meters high.

Desoix looked up. The porch was a narrow roof above him. He couldn't tell from this angle whether Anne McGill had stayed inside as he'd ordered, or if she were out in the night again watching for him, watching for hope.

"You, sir," a soldier said with enough emphasis to make the question a demand. "You our UDB liaison?"

"Roger," Desoix said. "I'm—"

But the close-coupled soldier in Slammers battle-dress was already relaying the information on his unit frequency.

There were several dozen of Hammer's men in the courtyard already. More were arriving with every passing moment. He didn't see Captain Koopman or the sergeant major he'd met once or twice before Tyl had arrived to take command.

The troopers jogged across the open street, hunched over. When they reached the courtyard they slowed. The veterans swept the Palace's empty, shuttered walls with their eyes, waiting for the motion that would unmask gunports and turn the paved area into a killing ground unless they shot first.

The new recruits only stared, more confused than frightened but certainly frightened enough.

"They know something we don't?" asked the Slammers non-com with KEKKONAN stenciled on his helmet. He nodded in the direction of the servants, the last of whom were clearing the doorway.

"They know they're scared," Desoix said.

Kekkonan laughed. "That just shows they're breathin'," he said.

He grunted something into his commo helmet—waved left-handed to Desoix because his right hand was on the grip of his slung sub-machinegun—and trotted into the rotunda with his troopers filing along after him.

The UDB officer had intended to lead the Slammers inside himself to avoid problems with the Bamberg guards. He hadn't moved quickly enough, but that wasn't likely to matter. Nobody with good sense was going to get in the way of *those* jacked-up killers.

Ornamental lighting still brightened the exterior of the palace, though the steel-shuttered facade looked out of place in a glittering myriad of tiny spotlights. It illuminated well the stooped forms in khaki and gray ceramic armor as they arrived, jogging because their loads were too heavy for them to run faster.

There were six in the last group, four troopers carrying a fifth while Captain Tyl Koopman trotted along behind with a double load of guns and bandoliers.

Casualty, Desoix thought, but Sergeant Major Scratchard was cursing too fluently for anyone to think his wound was serious.

"Listen, you idiots," Scratchard said in a voice of sudden calm as the UDB officer ran up to help. "If you don't let me down now we're under the lights, I got no authority from here on out. Your choice, Cap'n."

"Right, we'll all walk from here," said Koopman easily. He handed one of the guns he carried to Scratchard while looking at Desoix. "Lieutenant," he added, "I'm about as glad to see you as I remember being."

Desoix looked over the other officer's shoulder toward the fires and shouts across the river. For a moment he thought it was his imagination that the sounds were coming closer.

Light flickering through the panels of the mall disabused him of his hopes. A torch-lit column was marching over the river. What the rioters had done to the City Offices suggested that they weren't headed for the cathedral now to pray for peace.

"Let's get inside," said Charles Desoix. "When this is all over, then you can thank me."

He didn't need to state the proviso: *assuming either of us is still alive.*

CHAPTER FOURTEEN

Tyl hadn't ridden in the little elevator off the back of the rotunda before. He and the UDB officer just about filled it, and neither of them was a big man.

Of course, in his armor and equipment Tyl wasn't the slim figure he would have cut in coveralls alone.

"Don't like to leave the guys before we know just what's

happening here," he said aloud, though he was speaking as much to his own conscience as to the UDB officer beside him.

Tyl would have hated to be bolted behind steel shutters below, where the sergeant major was arranging temporary billets for the troops. The windowed Consistory Room was the next best thing to being outside—

And headed *away* from this Lord-stricken place!

"Up here is where we learn what's happening,"Desoix said reasonably, nodding toward the elevator's ceiling. "Or at least as much as anyone in the government knows," he added with a frown which echoed the doubt in his words.

The car stopped with only a faint burring from its magnetic drivers. The doors opened with less sound even than that. Tyl strode into the Consistory Room.

He was Colonel Hammer's representative and the ranking Slammer on this continent. So long as he remembered that, nobody else was likely to forget.

There were fewer people in the big room than there had been in the morning, but their degree of agitation made the numbers seem greater. Marshal Dowell was present with a pair of aides, but those three and the pair of mercenaries were the only men in uniform.

The Chastain brothers smiled with frozen enthusiasm when Tyl nodded to them. They wore dark suits of conservative cut—and of natural off-planet fabrics that gave them roughly the value of an air car. Everyone else in the room was avoiding the Chastains. Backs turned whenever one of the twins attempted to make eye contact.

Berne, the City Prefect, didn't have even a twin for company. He huddled in the middle of the room like a clothes pole draped with the green velour of his state robe.

"Where are—" Tyl began, but he'd already lost his companion. Lieutenant Desoix was walking briskly toward the large-framed woman who seemed to be an aide to the President's wife. Neither the President nor Eunice Delcorio were here at—

Servants opened the door adjacent to the elevator. John

Delcorio entered a step ahead of his wife, but only because of the narrowness of the portal. Eunice was again in a flame-red dress. This one was demure in the front but cut with no back at all and a skirt that stretched to allow her legs to scissor back and forth as she moved.

Tyl hadn't found a sexual arrangement satisfactory to him on the freighter that brought him to Bamberia, and there'd been no time to take care of personal business since he touched down. He felt a rush of lust. It was a little disconcerting under the circumstances—

But on the other hand, it was nice to be reminded that there was more to life than the sorts of things that'd been going on in the past few hours.

"You there!" President Delcorio said unexpectedly. He glared at Tyl, his black eyes glowing like coal in a coking furnace. "Do you have to wear *that*?"

Tyl glanced down at where Delcorio pointed with two stubby, sturdy fingers together.

"This?" said the Slammers officer. His sub-machinegun hung from his right shoulder in a patrol sling that held it muzzle forward and grip down at his waist. He could seize it by reflex and spray whatever was in front of him without having to aim or think.

"Yessir," he explained. He spoke without concern, because it didn't occur to him that anyone might think he was offering insolence instead of information. "Example for the troops, you know. I told 'em nobody moved without a gun and bandolier—sleeping, eating, whatever."

Tyl blinked and looked back at the President. "Besides," he added. "I might *need it*, the way things are."

Delcorio flushed. Tyl realized that he and the President were on intersecting planes. Though the two of them existed in the same universe, almost none of their frames of reference were identical.

That was too bad. But it wasn't a reason for Tyl Koopman to change; not now, when it was pretty curst obvious that the instincts he'd developed in Hammer's Slammers were the ones most applicable here.

Eunice Delcorio laughed, a clear, clean sound that cut

like a knife. "At least there's somebody who understands the situation," she said, echoing Tyl's thought and earning the Slammers officer another furious glance by her husband.

"I think we can all agree that the situation won't be improved by silly panic," Delcorio said mildly as his eyes swept the room. "Dowell, what do you have to report?"

There had been movement all around the room with the arrival of the Delcorios' but it was mostly limited to heads turning. Major Borodin, who'd been present after all—standing so quietly by a wall that Tyl's quick survey had missed him—was marching determinedly toward his executive officer. Desoix himself was alone. His lady friend had left him at once to join her mistress, the President's wife.

But at the moment, everyone's attention was on Marshal Dowell, because that was where the President was looking.

"Yes, well," the army chief said. "I've given orders that a brigade be returned from Two as quickly as possible. You must realize that it's necessary for the troops to land as a unit so that their effect won't be dissipated."

"What about *now*?" cried the City Prefect. He stepped forward in an access of grief and rage, fluttering his gorgeous robes like a peacock preparing to fly. "You said you'd support my police, but your precious soldiers did *nothing* when those scum attacked the City Offices!"

One of Dowell's aides was speaking rapidly into a communicator with a shield that made the discussion inaudible to the rest of the gathering. The marshal glanced at him, then said, "We're still not sure what the situation over there is, and at any rate—"

"They took the place," Tyl said bluntly.

In the Slammers you didn't stand on ceremony when your superiors had bad data or none at all in matters that could mean the life of a lot of people. "Freed their friends, set fire to the building—hung at least some of the folks they caught. Via, you can see it from here, from the window."

He gestured with an elbow, because to point with his

full arm would have moved his hand further from the grip of his weapon than instinct wanted to keep it at present.

Perhaps because everyone followed the gesture toward the panels overlooking the courtyard, the chanted . . . *freedom* . . . echoing from that direction became suddenly audible in the Consistory Room.

Across the room, the concealed elevator suctioned and snapped heads around. The officer Desoix had nodded to downstairs, the CO of the Executive Guard, stepped out with a mixture of arrogance and fear. He moved like a rabbit loaded with amphetamines. "Gentlemen? he called in a clear voice. "Rioters are in the courtyard with guns and torches!"

Tyl was waiting for a recommendation—*do I have your permission to open fire?* was how a Slammers officer would have proceeded—but this fellow had nothing in mind save the theatrical announcement.

What Tyl didn't expect—nobody expected—was for Eunice Delcorio to sweep like a torch flame to the door and step out onto the porch.

The blast of noise when the clear doors opened was a shocking reminder of how well they blocked sound. There was an animal undertone, but the organized chant of "*Freedom!*" boomed over and through the snarl until the mob recognized the black-haired, glass-smooth woman facing them from the high porch.

Tyl moved fast. He was at Eunice's side before the shouts of surprise had given way to the hush of a thousand people drawing breath simultaneously. He thought there might be shots. At the first bang or spurt of light he was going to hurl Eunice back into the Consistory Room, trusting his luck and his clamshell armor.

Not because she was a woman; but because if the President's wife got blown away, there was as little chance of compromise as there seemed to be of winning until the brigade from Two arrived.

And maybe a little because she was a woman. "What will you have, citizens?" Eunice called. The porch was designed for speeches. Even without amplification, the modeling walls threw her powerful contralto out over the crowd. "Will you abandon God's Crusade for a whim?"

The uplifted faces were a blur to Tyl in the scatter of light sources that the mob carried. The crosses embroidered in white cloth on the left shoulders of their garments were clear enough to be recognized, though and that was true whether the base color was red or black. There was motion behind him, but Tyl had eyes only for the mob.

Weapons glinted there. He couldn't tell if any of them were being aimed. The night-vision sensors in his face shield would have helped; but if he locked the shield down he'd be a mirror-faced threat to the crowd, and that might be all it took to draw the first shots. . . .

Desoix'd stepped onto the porch. He stood on the other side of Eunice Delcorio, and he was cursing with the fluency of a mercenary who's sleep-learned a lot of languages over the years.

The other woman was on the porch too. From the way the UDB officer was acting, she'd preceded rather than followed him.

The crowd's silence had dissolved in a dozen varied answers to Eunice's question, all underlain by blurred attempts to continue the chant of "Freedom!"

Something popped from the center of the mob. Tyl's left arm reached across Eunice's waist and was a heartbeat short of hurling the woman back through the doors no matter who stood behind her. A white flare burst fifty meters above the courtyard, harmless and high enough that it could be seen by even the tail of the mob stretching across the river.

The mob quieted after an anticipatory growl that shook the panels of the doors.

There was a motion at the flagstaff, near where the flare had been launched. Before Tyl could be sure what was happening, a handheld floodlight glared over the porch from the same location.

He stepped in front of the President's wife, bumping her out of the way with his hip, while his left hand locked the faceshield down against the blinding radiance. The muzzle of his sub-machinegun quested like an adder's tongue while his finger took up slack on the trigger.

"Wait!" boomed a voice from the mob in amplified startlement. The floodlight dimmed from a threat to comfortable illumination.

"I'll take over now, Eunice," said John Delcorio as his firm hand touched Tyl's upper arm, just beneath the shoulder flare of the clamshell armor.

The Slammers officer stepped aside, knowing it was out of his hands for better or for worse, now.

President Delcorio's voice thundered to the crowd from roof speakers, "My people, why do you come here to disturb God's purpose?"

Through his shield's optics, Tyl could see that there were half a dozen priests in dark vestments grouped beside the flagpole. They had a guard of orderlies from the House of Grace, but both the man with the light and the one raising a bull-horn had been ordained. Tyl thought, though the distance made uncertain, that the priest half-hidden behind the pole was Father Laughlin.

None of the priests carried weapons. All the twenty or so orderlies of their bodyguard held guns.

"We want the murderer Berne!" called the bull horn. The words were indistinct from the out-of-synchronous echoes which they waked from the Palace walls. "Berne sells justice and sells lives!"

"Berne!" shouted the mob, and their echoes thundered BERNE*berne*berne.

As the echoes died away, Tyl heard Desoix saying in a voice much louder than he intended, "Anne, for the *Lord's* sake! Get back inside!"

"Will you go back to your homes in peace if I replace the City Prefect?" Delcorio said, pitching his words to make his offered capitulation sound like a demand. His features were regally arrogant as Tyl watched him sidelong behind the mirror of his faceshield.

The priest with the bull-horn leaned sideways to confer with the bigger man behind the flagpole, certainly Father Laughlin. While the mob waited for their leaders' response, the President used the pause to add, "One man's venality can't be permitted to jeopardize God's work!"

"Give us Berne!" demanded the courtyard.

"I'll replace—" Delcorio attempted.

GIVE*give*give roared the mob. GIVE*give*give. . . .

Eunice leaned over to say something to her husband. He held up a hand to silence the crowd. The savage voices boomed louder, a thousand of them in the courtyard and myriads more filling the streets beyond.

A woman waved a doll in green robes above her head. She held it tethered by its neck.

Delcorio and his wife stepped back into the Consistory Room. Their hands were clasped so that it was impossible to tell who was leading the other. The President reached to slide the door shut for silence, but Lieutenant Desoix was close behind with an arm locked around the other woman's waist. His shoulder blocked Delcorio's intent.

Tyl Koopman wasn't going to be the only target on the balcony while the mob waited for a response it might not care for. He kept his featureless face to the front—with the gun muzzle beneath it for emphasis—as he retreated after the rest.

———

CHAPTER FIFTEEN

"Firing me won't—" Berne began even before Tyl slid the door shut on the thunder of the mob.

"I'm not sure we can defend—" Marshal Dowell was saying with a frown and enough emphasis that he managed to be heard.

"Be silent!" Eunice Delcorio ordered in a glass-sharp voice.

The wall thundered with the low notes of the shouting in the courtyard.

Everyone in the Consistory Room had gathered in a

semicircle. They were facing the porch and those who had been standing on it.

There were only a dozen or so of Delcorio's advisors present. Twice that number had awaited when Tyl followed Eunice out to confront the mob, but they were gone now.

Gone from the room, gone from the Palace if they could arrange it and assuredly gone from the list of President Delcorio's supporters.

That bothered Tyl less than the look of those who remained. They glared at the City Prefect with the expression of gorgeously-attired fish viewing an injured one of their number . . . an equal moments before, a certain victim now. The eyes of Dowell's aides were hungry as they slid over Berne.

Eunice Delcorio's voice had carved a moment of silence from the atmosphere of the Consistory Room. The colonel of the Executive Guard filled the pause with, "It's quite impossible to defend the Palace from numbers like that. We can't even think of—"

"Yeah, we could hold it," Tyl broke in.

He'd forgotten his faceshield was locked down until he saw everyone start away from him as if he were something slime covered that had just crawled through a window. With the shield in place, the loudspeaker built into his helmet cut in automatically so they *weren't* going to ignore him if he raised his voice.

He didn't want to be ignored, but he flipped up the shield to be less threatening now that he had the group's attention.

"You've got what, two companies?" he went on, waving his left index finger toward the glittering colonel. All right, they weren't the Slammers; but they had assault rifles and they weren't exactly facing combat infantry either.

"We've got a hundred men," he said. "*Curst* good ones, and the troops the UDB's got here in the Palace know how to handle—"

Tyl had nodded in the direction of Lieutenant Desoix, but it was Borodin, the battery commander, who interrupted, "I have no men in the Palace."

"Huh?" said the Slammers officer.

"What?" Desoix said. "We have the offduty c—"

"I'm worried about relieving the crews with the, ah—" Borodin began.

He looked over at the President. The mercenary commander couldn't whisper the explanation, not now. "The conditions in the streets are such that I wasn't sure we'd be able to relieve the gun crews normally, so I ordered the reserve crews to billet at the guns so that we could be sure that there'd be a full watch alert if the enemy tries to take advantage of . . . events."

"*Events!*" snarled John Delcorio.

The door behind him rattled sharply when a missile struck it. The vitril held as it was supposed to do.

"John, they aren't after *me*," Berne cried with more than personal concern in his voice. He was right, after all, everybody else here must know that, since it was so obvious to Tyl Koopman in his first day on-planet. "You mustn't—"

"If you hadn't failed, none of this would be happening," Eunice said, her scorn honed by years of personal hatred that found its outlet now in the midst of general catastrophe.

She turned to her husband, the ends of her black hair emphasizing the motion. "Why are you delaying? They want this criminal, and that will give us the time we need to deal with the filth properly with the additional troops."

Vividness made Eunice Delcorio a beautiful woman, but the way her lips rolled over the word "properly" sent a chill down the spine of everyone who watched her.

Berne made a break for the door to the hall.

Tyl's mind had been planning the defense of the Palace of Government. Squads of the local troops in each wing to fire as soon as rioters pried or blasted off a flood shutter to gain entrance. Platoons of mercenaries poised to react as fire brigades, responding to each assault with enough violence to smother it in the bodies of those who'd made the attempt. Grenadiers on the roof; they'd very quickly clear the immediate area of the Palace of everything except bodies and the moaning wounded.

Easy enough, but they were answers to questions that nobody was asking any more. Besides, they could only hold the place for a few days against tens of thousands of besiegers—only long enough for the brigade to arrive from Two, if it came.

And Tyl was a lot less confident of that point than the President's wife seemed to be.

A middle-aged civilian tripped the City Prefect. One of Dowell's aides leaped on Berne and wrestled him to the polished floor as he tried to rise, while the other aide shouted into his communicator for support without bothering to lock his privacy screen in place.

Tyl looked away in disgust. He caught Lieutenant Desoix's eye. The UDB officer wore a bland expression.

But he wasn't watching the scuffle and the weeping prefect either.

"All right," said the President, bobbing his head in decision. "I'll tell them."

He took one stride, reached for the sliding door, and paused. "You," he said to Tyl. "Come with me".

Tyl nodded without expression. Another stone or possibly a light bullet whacked against the vitril. He set his faceshield and stepped onto the porch ahead of the Regiment's employer.

He didn't feel much just now, though he wanted to take a piss real bad. Even so, he figured he'd be more comfortable facing the mob than he was over what had just happened in the Consistory Room.

The crowd roared. Behind his shield, Tyl grinned—if that was the right word for the way instinct drew up the corners of his mouth to bare his teeth. There was motion among the upturned faces gleaming like the sputum the sea leaves when it draws back from the strand.

Something pinged on the railing. Tyl's gun quivered, pointed—

"Wait!" thundered the bull-horn.

"My people!' boomed the President's voice from the roofline. He rested his palms wide apart on the railing. He'd followed after all, a step behind the Slammers officer just in case a sniper was waiting for the first motion. Delcorio wasn't a brave man, not as a professional soldier came to appraise courage, but his spirit had a tumbling intensity that made him capable of almost anything.

At a given moment.

The mob was making a great deal of disconnected noise. Delcorio trusted his amplified voice to carry him through as he continued, "I have dismissed the miscreant Berne as you demanded. I will turn him over to the custody of the Church for safekeeping until the entire State can determine the punishment for his many crimes."

"Give us Berne!" snarled the bull-horn with echoing violence. It spoke in the voice of a priest but not a Christian; and the mob that took up the chant was not even human.

Delcorio turned and tried to shout something into the building with his unaided voice. Tyl couldn't hear him.

The President raised a hand for silence from the crowd. The chant continued unabated, but Delcorio and the Slammers officer were able to back inside without a rain of missiles to mark their retreat.

There was a squad of the Executive Guard in the Consistory Room. Four of the ten men were gripping the City Prefect. Several had dropped their rifles in the scuffle and no one had thought to pick the weapons up again.

Delcorio made a dismissing gesture. "Send him out to them," he said. "I've done all I can. Quickly, so I don't have to go out there—"

His face turned in the direction of his thoughts, toward the porch and the mob beneath. The flush faded and he began to shiver uncontrollably. Reaction and memory had caught up with the President.

There were only four civilian advisors in the room besides Berne. Five. A man whose suit was russet or gold, depending on the direction of the light, had been caught just short of getting into the elevator by Delcorio's return.

The Guards colonel was shaking his head. "No, no," he said. "That won't do. If we open a shutter, they'll be in and well, the way the fools are worked up, who knows what might happen?"

"But—" the President said, his jaw dropping. He'd aged a decade since he stepped off the porch. Hormonal courage abandoned him to reaction and remembrance. "But I *must*. But I promised them, Drescher, and if I don't—"

His voice would probably have broken off there anyway, but a bellow from the courtyard in thunderous synchrony smothered all sound within for a moment.

"Pick him up, then," said Eunice Delcorio in a voice as clear as a sapphire laser. "You four—pick him up and follow. We'll give them their scrap of bone."

She strode toward the door, the motion of her legs a devouring flame across the intarsia.

Berne screamed as the soldiers lifted him. Because he was screaming, no one heard Tyl Koopman say in a choked voice, "Lady, you *can't*—"

But of course they could. And Tyl had done the same or worse, checking out suspicious movements with gunfire, knowing full well that nine chances in ten, the victims were going to be civilians trying to get back home half an hour after curfew. . . .

He'd never have spent one of his own men this way; and he'd never serve under an officer who did.

Colonel Drescher threw open the door himself, though he stood back from the opening with a care that was more than getting out of the way of the President's wife.

Tyl stepped out beside her, because he'd made it his job, . . . or Hammer had made it his job . . . and who in blazes cared, he was there and the animal snarl of the mob brought answering rage to the Slammer's mind and washed some of the sour taste from his mouth.

The Guardsmen in azure uniforms and Berne in green made a contrast as brilliant as a parrot's plumage as they manhandled the prefect to the railing under the glare of lights. Floods were trained from at least three locations in the courtyard now, turned high; but that was all right, they needed to watch this, sure they did.

Eunice cried something inaudible but imperious. She

gestured out over the railing. The soldiers looked at one another.

Berne was screaming wordlessly. His eyes were closed, but tears poured from beneath the lids. He had fouled himself in his panic. The smell added the only element necessary to make the porch a microcosm of Hell.

Eunice gestured again. The Guards threw their prisoner toward the courtyard.

Berne grabbed the railing with both hands as he went over. His legs flailed without the organization needed to boost him back onto the porch, but his hands clung like claws of east bronze.

Eunice gave a furious order that was no more than a grimace and a quick motion of her lips. Two of the soldiers tried gingerly to push Berne away. The prefect twisted his head and bit the hands of one. His eyes were open now and as mad as those of a backward psychotic. Bottles and stones began to fly from the crowd, clashing on the rail and floor of the porch.

The Guardsmen drew back into a huddle in the doorway. The man who still carried his rifle raised it one-handed to shield his face.

A bottle shattered on Tyl's breastplate. He didn't hear the shot that was fired a moment later, but the howl of a light slug ricocheting from the wall cut through even the roar of the crowd.

"Get inside!" Tyl's speakers bellowed to Eunice Delcorio as he stepped sideways to the railing where Berne thrashed. Tyl hammered the man's knuckles with the butt of his submachinegun. One stroke, two—bone cracked—

Three and the prefect's screaming changed note. His broken left hand slipped and his right hand opened. Berne's throat made a sound like a siren as he fell ten meters to the mob waiting to receive him.

Tyl turned. If the Guardsmen had still been blocking the doorway, he might have shot them . . . but they'd fled inside and Eunice Delcorio was sweeping after them. Her head was regally high, and she was ignoring the streak of blood over one cheekbone where a stone had cut her.

Tyl turned for a last look into the courtyard. The rioters were passing Berne hand to hand, over their heads, like a bit of green algae seen sliding through the gut of a paramecium. There was greater motion also; the mob was shifting back—only a compression in the crowd at the moment, but soon to turn into real movement that would clear the courtyard.

They were leaving, now that they had their bone.

As the City Prefect was passed along, those nearest were ripping bits away. For the moment, the bits were mostly clothing.

Tyl stepped into the Consistory Room and slammed the door behind him hard enough to shatter a panel that hadn't been armored. He left his faceshield down, because if none of them could see his expression, he could pretend that he wasn't really here.

"Lieutenant Desoix," said Major Borodin. He wasn't speaking loudly, but no one else in the room was speaking at all. "Gun Three needs to be withdrawn. Will you handle that at once."

The battery commander's face looked like a mirror of what Tyl thought was on his own features.

"Nobody's withdrawing," said President Delcorio. He had his color back, and he stroked his hands together briskly as if to warm them. His eyes shifted like a sparkling fire and lighted on the Guards colonel. The hands stopped.

"Colonel Drescher," Delcorio said crisply. "I want your men on combat footing at once. Don't you have some other sort of uniforms? Like those."

One spade-broad hand gestured toward Tyl in khaki and armor. "Something suitable. This isn't a *parade*. We're at war. War."

"Well, I—" Drescher began. Everyone in the room was in a state of shock, hammered by events into a state that made them ready to be pressed in any direction by a strong personality.

For a moment, until the next stimulus came along.

"Well, get on with it!" the President snapped. While the squad of gay uniforms was just shifting toward the hall door,

Delcorio's attention had already flashed across the other faces in the Consistory Room.

And found very few.

"Where's—" Delcorio began. "Where's—" His voice rose, driven by an emotion that was either fury or panic—and perhaps had not yet decided which it would be.

"Sir," said one of the Chastains, stepping forward to take the President by the hand. "Thom and I will—"

"*You!*" Delcorio screamed. "What are you doing here?"

"Sir," said Thom Chastain with the same hopeful puppy expression as his brother. "We know you'll weather this—"

"You're spying, aren't you?" Delcorio cried, slapping at the offered hands as if they were beasts about to bite him. "Get out, don't you think I know it!"

"Sir—" said the two together in blank amazement.

The President's nephew Pedro stepped between the Chastain's and Delcorio. "Go on!" he snarled, looking like a bulldog barking at a pair of gangling storks. "We don't need you here. Get *out!*"

"But—" Richie Chastain attempted helplessly. Pedro, as broadly built as his uncle, shoved the other men toward the door.

They fled in a swirl of robes and words whimpered to one another or to fate.

"You there," the President continued briskly. "Dowell. You'll have the additional troops in place by noon tomorrow. Do you understand? I don't care if they have to loot shops for their meals, they'll be here."

Delcorio spoke with an alert dynamism. It was hard to imagine that the same man had been on the edge of violent madness a moment before, and in a funk brief minutes still earlier.

Dowell saluted with a puzzled expression. He mumbled something to his aides. The three of them marched out the hall door without looking backward.

If they caught the President's eye again, he might hold them.

"And *you*, Major Borodin, you aren't going to strip our city of its protection against the Christ-deniers," Delcorio said as he focused back on the battery commander.

The President should have forgotten the business of moving the gun—so much had gone on in the moments since. He hadn't forgotten, though. There *was* a mind inside that skull, not just a furnace of emotions.

If John Delcorio were as stupid as he was erratic, Tyl might have been able to figure out what in the Lord's name he ought best to be doing.

"*Do* you understand?" Delcorio insisted, pointing at the battery commander with two blunt fingers in a gesture as threatening as anything short of a gun muzzle could be.

"Yes sir," replied Major Borodin, his voice as stiff as the brace in which he held his body. "But I must tell you that I'm obeying under protest, and when I contact my superiors—"

"You needn't tell me anything, mercenary," the President interrupted without even anger to leaven the contempt in his words. "You need only do your job and collect your pay—which I assure you, your superiors show no hesitation in doing either."

"John," said Eunice Delcorio with a shrug that dismissed everything that was going on around her at the moment. "I'm going to call my brother again. They said they couldn't raise him when I tried earlier."

"Yes, I'll talk to him myself," the President agreed, falling in step beside the short woman as he headed toward the door to their private apartments. "He'd have nothing but a ten-hectare share-crop if it weren't for me. If he thinks he can duck his responsibilities now. . . ."

"Anne," Desoix said in a low voice as Eunice's aide hesitated. She looked from her mistress to the UDB officer—and stayed.

Pedro Delcorio raised an eyebrow, then nodded to the others as he followed his uncle out of the Consistory Room. There were only four of them left: the three mercenaries and Desoix's lady friend.

The four of them, and the smell of fear.

CHAPTER SIXTEEN

"Let's get out of here," Koopman said.

Charles Desoix's heart leaped in agreement—then bobbed back to normalcy when he realized that the Slammers officer meant only to get out of the Consistory Room, onto the porch where the air held fewer memories of the immediate past.

Sure, Koopman was the stolid sort who probably didn't realize how badly things were going . . . and Charles Desoix wasn't going to support a mutiny, wasn't going to desert his employers because of trouble that hadn't—if you wanted to be objective about it—directly threatened the United Defense Batteries at all.

It was hard to be objective when you were surrounded by a mob of perhaps fifty thousand people, screaming for blood and quite literally tearing a man to pieces.

They were welcome to Berne—he was just as crooked as the bull-horn had claimed. But. . . .

"What did you say, Charles?" Anne asked—which meant that Desoix had been speaking things that he shouldn't even have been thinking.

He hugged her reflexively. She jumped, also by reflex because she didn't try to draw further away when she thought about the situation. Major Borodin didn't appear to notice her to care.

The courtyard was deserted, but the mob had left behind an amazing quantity of litter—bottles, boxes, and undefinable scraps; even a cloak, scarlet and apparently whole in the light of the wall sconces. It was as if Desoix were watching a beach just after the tide had ebbed.

Across the river, fires burned from at least a score of locations. Voices echoed, harsh as the occasional grunt of shots.

Like the tide, the mob would return.

"We've got to get out of here," Desoix mused aloud.

"She'll leave," Anne said with as much prayer in her

voice as certainty. "If she stays, they'll do terrible things to . . . She *knows* that, she won't let it happen."

"Colonel wants me to hold if there's any chance to keep Delcorio in power," Koopman said to the night. There was a snicker of sound as he raised his faceshield, but he did not look at his companions as he spoke. "What's your bet on that, Charles?"

"Something between zip and zero," Desoix said. He was careful not to let his eyes fall on Anne or the major when he spoke; but it was no time to tell polite lies.

"'bout what I figured too," the Slammers officer said mildly. He was leaning on his forearms while his fingers played with a dimple in the rail. After a moment, Desoix realized that the dimple had been hammered there by a bullet.

"I don't see any way we can abandon our positions in defiance of a direct order," Major Borodin said.

The battery commander set his fingers in his thinning hair and squeezed firmly, as though that would change the blank rotation of his thoughts. He took his hands away and added hurriedly to the Slammers officer, "Of course, that has nothing to do with you, Captain. My problem is that I have to defend the city, so I'm in default of the contract if I move my guns. Well, Gun Three. But that's the only one that seems to be in danger."

"Charles, you'll protect her if we leave, won't you?" asked Anne in sudden fierceness. She pulled on Desoix's shoulder until he turned to face her worries directly. "You won't let them have her to, to escape yourself, will you?"

He cupped her chin with his left hand. "Anne," he said. "If Eunice and the President just say the word, we'll have them safely out of here within the hour. Won't we, Tyl?" he added as he turned to the Slammers officer.

"Colonel says, maybe just a week or two," Koopman said unexpectedly. When his index finger burnished the bullet scar, the muzzle of his own slung weapon chinked lightly against the rail. "Suppose Delcorio could hold out a week?"

"Suppose we could hold out five minutes if they come back hard?" Desoix snapped, furious at the infantryman's response when finally it looked as if there were a chance to clear out properly. There wasn't any doubt that Eunice Delcorio could bend her husband to her own will. She was inflexible, with none of John Delcorio's flights and falterings.

If Anne worked on her mistress, it could all turn out reasonably. Exile for Delcorio on his huge private estates; safety for Anne McGill, whose mistress wasn't the only one with whom the mob would take its pleasure.

And release for the mercenaries who were at the moment trapped in this place by ridiculous orders.

"Yeah," said Koopman with a heavy sigh. He turned at last to face his companions. "Well, I'm not going to get any of my boys wasted for nothing at all. We aren't paid to be heroes. Guess I'll go down and tell Jack to pack up to move at daylight."

The Slammers officer quirked a grin to Desoix and nodded to Anne and the major as he stepped toward the door.

"Tyl, wait . . ." Desoix said as a word rang echoes. "Can you . . . Major, how many men do you have downstairs still?"

Borodin shrugged out of the brown study into which he had fallen as he watched the fires burning around him. "Men?" he repeated. "Senter and Lachere is all. We're still short—"

"Tyl, can you, ah—" Desoix went on. He paused, because he didn't want to use the wrong word, since what he was about to ask was no part of the Slammers' business.

"I need to get down to the warehouses on the corniche," Desoix said, rephrasing the question to make the request personal rather than military. "All I've got here are the battery clerks and they're not, ah, trained for this. Could you detail a few men, five or six, to go along with me in case there was a problem?"

"Lieutenant," Borodin said gruffly. "What do—"

"Sir," Desoix explained as the plan drew itself in glowing lines in his mind, the alternative sites and intersecting fields of fire. "When we get Gun Five set up, we can move Three a kilometer east on the corniche and still be in compliance. Five on the outskirts of town near Pestini's Chapel, Three on Guizer Head—and we've got everything Delcorio can demand under the contract."

"Without stationing any of our men down. . . ." Borodin said as the light dawned. He might have intended to point toward the plaza, but as his gaze turned out over the city, his voice trailed off instead. Both UDB officers stared at Tyl Koopman.

Koopman shrugged. 'I'll go talk to the guys," he said.

And they had to be satisfied with that, because he said nothing more as he walked back into the building.

CHAPTER SEVENTEEN

Tyl's functional company had taken over the end of a second-floor hallway abandoned by the entourage of six noble guests of the President. The hundred troopers had a great deal more room than there'd been in the City Office billet—or any normal billet.

And, though they'd lost their personal gear when the office building burned, the nobles' hasty departure meant that the soldiers could console themselves for the objects they'd lost across the river. Jewelry and rich fabrics peeked out the edges of khaki uniforms as Tyl strode past the corridor guard and into the billeting area.

Too bad about Aunt Sandra's jelly, though. He could turn over a lot of rich folks' closets and not find anything to replace that.

Troopers with makeshift bedrolls in the hallway were jumping to attention because somebody else had. The heads that popped from doorways were emptying the adjoining guest suites as effectively as if Tyl had shouted, "Fall in!"

Which was about the last thing he wanted.

"Settle down," he said with an angry wave of his arm,

as if to brush away the commotion. They were all tight.
The troops didn't know much, and that made them rightly
nervous.

Tyl Koopman knew a good deal more, and what he'd
seen from the porch wasn't the sort of knowledge to make
anybody feel better about the situation.

"Captain?" said Jack Scratchard as he muscled his way
into the hall.

Tyl motioned the sergeant major over. He keyed his
commo helmet with the other hand and said loudly—most
of the men didn't have their helmets on, and only the senior
non-coms were fitted with implants—"At present, I'm
expecting us to get the rest of the night's sleep here, but
maybe not be around much after dawn. When I know
more, you'll hear."

Scratchard joined him. The two men stepped out of the
company area for the privacy they couldn't find within it.
Tyl paused and called over his shoulder, "Use a little
common sense in what you try to pack, all right?"

He glared at a corporal with at least a dozen vibrantly-
colored dresses in her arms.

The remaining six suites off the hallway were as empty
as those Scratchard had appropriated. He must have
decided to keep the troops bunched up a little under the
present circumstances, and Tyl wasn't about to argue with
him.

The doors of all the suites had been forced. As they
stepped into the nearest to talk, Tyl noticed that the richly-
appointed room had been turned over with great care,
although none of his soldiers were at present inside continuing their looting.

Loot and mud were the two constants of line service.
If you couldn't get used to either one, you'd better find
a rear-echelon slot somewhere.

"Talk to the Old Man?" Scratchard muttered when he
was sure they were alone in the tumbled wreckage.

Tyl shrugged. "Not yet," he said. "Sent an allclear
through open channels, is all. It's mostly where we left it
earlier, and I don't want Central" he wasn't comfortable

saying "Hammer" or even "the Old Man" "—thinking they got to wet nurse me."

He paused, and only then got to the real business. "Desoix—the UDB Number Two," he said. "He wants a few guys to cover his back while he gets a calliope outa storage down to the seafront. Got everybody but a couple clerks out with the other tubes."

The sergeant major knuckled his scalp, the ridge where his helmet rode. "What's that do for us, the other calliope?" he asked.

"Bloody zip," Tyl answered with a shrug. He was in charge, but this was the sort of thing that the sergeant major had to be brought into.

Besides, nothing he'd heard about Ripper Jack Scratchard suggested that there'd be an argument on how to proceed.

"What it does," Tyl amplified, "is let them withdraw the gun they got down by the plaza. Desoix doesn't like having a crew down there, the way things're going."

Scratchard frowned. "Why can't he—" he began.

"Don't ask," Tyl said with a grimace.

The question made him think of things he'd rather forget. He thumbed in what might have been the direction of the Consistory Room and said, "It got real strange up there. Real strange."

He shook his head to rid it of the memories and added, "You know, he's the one I finally raised to get us into here before it really dropped in the pot. None of the locals were going to do squat for us."

"Doing favors is a good way t' get your ass blown away," Scratchard replied, sourly but without real emphasis. "But sure, I'll look up five guys that'd like t' see the outside again."

He grinned around the clothing strewn about them from forced clothes presses. "Don't guess it'll be too hard to look like civilians, neither."

"Ah," said Tyl. He was facing a blank wall. "Thought I might go along, lead 'em, you know."

"Like hell," said the sergeant major with a grin that seemed to double the width of his grizzled face. "I might, except for my knees. You're going to stay bloody here, in charge like you're supposed t' be."

His lips pursed. "Kekkonan '11 take 'em. He won't buy into anything he can't buy out of."

Tyl clapped the non-com on the shoulder. "Round 'em up," he said as he stepped into the hall. "I'll tell Desoix. This is the sort of thing that should've been done, you know, last week."

As he walked down the hall, the Slammers officer keyed his helmet to learn where Desoix was at the moment. Putting this sort of information on open channels didn't seem like a great idea, unless you had a lot more confidence in the Bamberg army than Tyl Koopman did.

Asking for volunteers in a business like this was a waste of time. They were veteran troops, these; men and women who would parrot "never volunteer" the way they'd been told by a thousand generations of previous veterans . . . but who knew in their hearts that it was boredom that killed.

You couldn't live in barracks, looking at the same faces every waking minute, without wanting to empty a gun into one of them just to make a change.

So the first five soldiers Scratchard asked would belt on their battle gear with enthusiasm, bitching all the time about "When's it somebody else's turn to take the tough one?" They didn't want to die, but they didn't think they would . . . and just maybe they would have gone anyway, whatever they thought the risk was, because it was too easy to imagine the ways a fort like the Palace of Government could became a killing bottle.

They were Hammer's Slammers. They'd done that to plenty others over the years.

Tyl didn't have any concern that he'd be able to hand Desoix his bodyguards, primed and ready for whatever the fire-shot night offered.

And he knew that he'd give three grades in rank to be able to go along with them himself.

CHAPTER EIGHTEEN

The porch off the Consistory Room didn't have a view of anything Tyl wanted to see—the littered courtyard and, across the river, the shell of the City Offices whose windows were still outlined by the sullen glow in its interior. The porch was as close as he could come to being outside, though, and that was sufficient recommendation at the moment.

The top of the House of Grace was barely visible above the south wing of the Palace. The ghost of firelight from the office building painted the eyes and halo of the sculptured Bishop Trimer also.

Tyl didn't want company, so when the door slid open behind him, he turned his whole body. That way his slung sub-machinegun pointed, an "accident" that he knew would frighten away anyone except his own troopers—whom he could order to leave him alone.

Lieutenant Desoix's woman stopped with a little gasp in her throat, but she didn't back away.

"Via!" Tyl said in embarrassment, lifting the gun muzzle high and cursing himself in his head for the dumb idea. One of those dandies, he'd figured, or a smirking servant, . . . except that the President's well-dressed advisors seemed to have pretty well disappeared, and the flunkies also.

Servants were getting thin on the ground, too.

"If you'd like to be alone? . . ." the woman said, either polite or real perceptive.

"Naw, you're fine," Tyl said, feeling clumsy and a lot the same way as he had a few months ago. Then he'd been to visit a girl he might have married if he hadn't gone off for a soldier the way he had. "You're, ah—Lady Eunice's friend, aren't you?"

"That too," said the woman drily. She took the place Tyl offered at the railing and added, "My name's Anne McGill. And I believe you're Captain Koopman?"

"Tyl," the soldier said. "Rank's not form—" He gestured. "Out here."

She didn't look as big as she had inside. Maybe because he had his armor on now that he was standing close to her.

Maybe because he'd recently watched five big men put looted cloaks on over their guns and armor to go off with Lieutenant Desoix.

"Have you known Charles long?" she asked, calling Tyl back from a stray thought that had the woman wriggling out of her dark blue dress and offering herself to him.

He shook his head abruptly to clear the thought. Not his type, and he *sure* wasn't hers.

"No," he said, forgetting that she thought he'd answered with the shake of his head. "I just got in today, you see. I don't recall we ever served with the UDB before. Anyhow, mostly you don't see much of anybody's people but your own guys."

It wasn't even so much that he was horny. Screwing was just something he could really lose himself in.

Killing was that way too.

"It's dangerous out there, isn't it?" she said. She wasn't looking at the city because her face was lifted too high. From the way her capable hands washed one another, she might well have been praying.

"Out there?" Tyl repeated bitterly. "Via, it's dangerous *here*, and we can't anything but bloody twiddle our thumbs."

Anne winced, as much at the violence as the words themselves.

Instantly contrite, Tyl said, "But you know, if things stay cool a little longer—no spark, you know, setting things off . . . It may all work out."

He was repeating what Colonel Hammer had told him a few minutes before, through the laser communicator now slung at his belt again. To focus on the satellite from here, he'd had to aim just over the top of the House of Grace. . . .

"When the soldiers from Two come, there'll be a spark, won't there?" she asked. She was looking at Tyl now, though he didn't expect she could see any more of his face in the darkness than he could of hers. Firelight winked on her necklace of translucent beads.

The scent she wore brought another momentary rush of lust.

"Maybe not," he said, comfortable talking to somebody who might possibly believe the story he could never credit in discussions with himself. "Nobody really wants that kind a' trouble."

Not the army, that was for sure. *They* weren't going to push things.

"Delcorio makes a few concessions—he already gave 'em Berne, after all. The troops march around with their bayonets all polished to look pretty. And then everybody kisses and makes up."

So that Tyl Koopman could get back to the business of a war whose terms he understood.

"I hope . . ." Anne was murmuring.

She might not have finished the phrase even if they hadn't been interrupted by the door sliding open behind them.

Tyl didn't recognize Eunice Delcorio at first. She was wearing a dress of mottled gray tones and he'd only seen her in scarlet in the past. With the fabric's luminors powered up, the garment would have shone with a more-than-metallic luster; but now it had neither shape nor color, and Eunice's voice glittered like that of a brittle ghost as she said, "Well, my dear, I wouldn't have interrupted you if I'd known you were entertaining a gentleman."

"Ma'am," Tyl said, bracing to attention. Eunice sounded playful, but so was a cat with a field mouse—and he didn't *know* what she could do to him if she wanted, it wasn't in the normal chain of command. . . .

"Captain Koopman and I were discussing the situation, Eunice," Anne said evenly. If she were embarrassed, she hid the fact; and there was no trace of fear in her voice. "You could have called me.

Eunice toyed with the hundred millimeter wand that could either page or track a paired unit. "I thought I'd find you instead, my dear," she said.

The President's wife wasn't angry, but there was fierce

emotion beneath the surface sparkle. The wand slipped from her fingers to the floor.

Tyl knelt swiftly—you don't bend when you're wearing a ceramic back-and-breast—and rose as quickly with the wand offered in his left hand.

Eunice batted the little device out into the courtyard. It was some seconds before it hit the stones below.

"I told the captain," Anne said evenly, "that I was concerned about your safety in view of the trouble that's occurring here in the city."

"Well, that should be over very shortly, shouldn't it?" Eunice said. Nothing in her voice hinted at the way her body had momentarily lost control. "Marshall Dowell has gone to Two himself to expedite movement of the troops."

The technical phrase came from her full lips with a glitter that made it part of a social event. Which, in a manner of speaking, it was.

"Blood and Martyrs," Tyl said. He wasn't sure whether or not he'd spoken the curse aloud, and at this point he didn't much care.

He straightened. "Ma'am," he said, nodding stiffly to the President's wife. "Ah, ma'am," with a briefer nod to Anne.

He strode back into the building without waiting for formal leave. Over his shoulder, he called, "I need to go check on the dispositions of my troops."

Especially the troops out there with Desoix, in a city that the local army had just abandoned to the rebels.

CHAPTER NINETEEN

There were at least a dozen voices in the street outside, bellowing the bloodiest hymn Charles Desoix had ever heard. They were moving on, strolling if not marching, but the five Slammers kept their guns trained on the door in case somebody tried to join them inside the warehouse.

What bothered Desoix particularly was the clear

soprano voice singing the descant, "Sew their manhood to our flags. . . ."

"All right," he said, returning his attention to the business of reconnecting the fusion powerplant which had been shut down for shipping. "Switch on."

Nothing happened.

Desoix, half inside the gun carriage's rear access port, straightened to find out what was happening. Lachere, the clerk he'd brought along because he needed another pair of hands, leaned hopefully from the open driver's compartment forward. "It's on, sir," he said.

"Main *and* Start-up are on?" Desoix demanded. And either because they hadn't been or because a contact had been a little sticky, he heard the purr of the fusion bottle beginning to bring up its internal temperature and pressure.

Success. In less than an hour—

"The representative of Hammer's Regiment has an urgent message," said Control's emotionless voice. "Shall I patch him through?"

"Affirmative," Desoix said, blanking his mind so that it wouldn't flash him a montage of disaster as it always did when things were tight and the unexpected occurred.

Wouldn't show him Anne McGill in the arms of a dozen rioters, not dead yet and not to die for a long time. . . .

"We got a problem," Koopman said, as if his flat voice and the fact of his call hadn't already proved that. "Dowell just did a bunk to Two. I don't see the situation holding twenty-four hours. Over."

Maybe not twenty-four minutes.

"Is the Executive Guard . . ." Desoix began. While he paused to choose his phrasing, Koopman interrupted with, "They're still here, but they're all in their quarters with the corridor blocked. I figure they're taking a vote. It's that sorta outfit. And I don't figure the vote's going any way I'd want it to. Over."

"All right," Desoix said, glancing toward the pressure gauge that he couldn't read in this light anyway. "All right, we'll have the gun drivable in thirty, that's three-oh, minutes. We'll—"

"Negative. Negative."

"Listen," the UDB officer said with his tone sharpening. "We're this far and we're not—"

Kekkonan, the sergeant in charge of the detachment of Slammers, tapped Desoix's elbow for attention and shook his head. "He said negative," Kekkonan said. "Sir."

The sergeant was getting the full conversation through his mastoid implant. Desoix didn't have to experiment to know it would be as much use to argue with a block of mahogany as with the dark, flat face of the non-com.

"Go ahead, Tyl," Desoix said with an inward sigh. "Over."

"You're not going to drive a calliope through the streets tonight, Charles," Koopman said. "Come dawn, maybe you can withdraw the one you got down there, maybe you just spike it and pull your guys out. This is save-what-you-got time, friend. And *my* boys aren't going to be part a' some fool stunt that sparks the whole thing off."

Kekkonan nodded. Not that he had to.

"Roger, we're on the way," Desoix said. He didn't have much emotion left to give the words, because his thoughts were tied up elsewhere.

Via, she was *married*. It was her bloody husband's business to take care of her, wasn't it?

CHAPTER TWENTY

"Go," said Desoix without emphasis.

Kekkonan and another of the Slammers flared from the door in opposite directions. Their cloaks—civilian and of neutral colors, green and gray—fluffed widely over their elbows, hiding the sub-machineguns in their hands.

"Clear," muttered Kekkonan. Desoix stepped out in the middle of the small unit. He felt as much a burden to his guards as the extra magazines that draped them beneath the loose garments.

It remained to be seen if either he or the ammunition

would be of any service as they marched back to the Palace.

"Don't remember *that*," Lachere said, looking to the west.

"Keep moving," Kekkonan grunted. There was enough tension in his voice to add a threat of violence to the order.

One of the warehouses farther down the corniche—half a kilometer—had been set on fire. The flames reflected pink from the clouds and as a bloody froth from sea foam in the direction of Nevis Island. The boulevard was clogged by rioters watching the fire and jeering as they flung bodies into it.

Desoix remembered the descant, but he clasped Lachere's arm and said, "We weren't headed in that direction anyway, were we?"

"Too bloody right," murmured one of the Slammers, the shudder in his tone showing that he didn't feel any better about this than the UDB men did.

"Sergeant," Desoix said, edging close to Kekkonan and wishing that the two of them shared a command channel. "I think the faster we get off the seafront, the better we'll be."

He nodded toward the space between the warehouse they'd left and the next building—not so much an alley as a hedge against surveyors' errors.

"Great killing ground," Kekkonan snorted.

Flares rose from the plaza and burst in metallic showers above the city. Shots followed, tracers and the cyan flicker of powergun bolts aimed at the drifting sparks. There was more shooting, some of it from building roofs. Rounds curved in flat arcs back into the streets and houses.

A panel in the clear reflection of the House of Grace shattered into a rectangular scar.

"Right you are," said Kekkonan as he stepped into the narrow passage.

They had to move in single file. Desoix saw to it that he was the second man in the squad. Nobody objected.

He'd expected Tyl to give him infantrymen. Instead, all five of these troopers came from vehicle crews, tanks and combat cars. The weapon of choice under this night's conditions was a sub-machinegun, not the heavier, 2 CM semiautomatic shoulder weapon of Hammer's infantry. Koopman or his burly sergeant major had been thinking when they picked this team.

Desoix's sub-machinegun wasn't for show either. Providing air defense for frontline units meant you were right in the middle of it when things went wrong . . . and they'd twice gone wrong very badly to a battery Charles Desoix crewed or captained.

Though it shouldn't come to that. The seven of them were just another group in a night through which armed bands stalked in a truce that would continue so long as there was an adequacy of weaker prey.

The warehouses fronted the bay and the spaceport across the channel, but their loading docks were in the rear. Across the mean street were tenements. When Desoix's unit shrugged its way out of the cramped passage, they found every one of the windows facing them lighted to display a cross as large as the sashes would allow.

"Party time," one of the troopers muttered. Some of the residents were watching the events from windows or rooftops, but most of them were down in the street in amorphous clots like those of white cells surrounding bacteria. There were shouts, both shrill and guttural, but Desoix couldn't distinguish any of the words.

Not that he had any trouble understanding what was going on without hearing the words. There were screams coming from the center of one of the groups . . . or perhaps Desoix's mind created the sound it knew would be there if the victim still had the strength to make it.

A dozen or so people were on the loading dock to the unit's right, drinking and either having sex or making as good an attempt at it as their drinking permitted. Somebody threw a bottle that smashed close enough to Kekkonan that the sergeant's cloak flapped as he turned; but there didn't appear to have been real malice involved. Perhaps not even notice.

Party time.

"All right," Kekkonan said just loudly enough for the

soldiers with him to hear. "There's an alley across the way, a little to the left. Stay loose, don't run, . . . and *don't* bunch up, just in case. Go."

Except for Lachere, they were all veterans; but they were human as well. They didn't run, but they moved much faster than the careless saunter everybody knew was really the safest pace.

And they stayed close, close enough that one burst could have gotten them all.

Nothing happened except that a score of voices followed them with varied suggestions, and a woman naked to the waist stumbled into Charles Desoix even though he tried his best to dodge her.

She was so drunk that she didn't notice the contact, much less that she'd managed to grab the muzzle of his sub-machinegun for an instant before she caromed away.

The alley stank of all the garbage the rains hadn't washed away; somebody, dead drunk or dead, was sprawled just within the mouth of it.

Desoix had never been as eager to enter a bedroom as he was that alley.

"Ah, sir," one of the Slammers whispered as the foetor and its sense of protection enclosed them. "Those people, they was rag heads?"

The victims, he meant; and he was asking Desoix because Desoix was an officer who might know about things like that.

The Lord knew he did.

"Maybe," Desoix said.

They had enough room here to walk two abreast, though the lightless footing was doubtful and caused men to bump. "Landlords—building superintendents. The guy you owe money to, the guy who screwed your daughter and then married the trollop down the hall."

"But . . . ?" another soldier said.

"Anybody you're quick enough to point a dozen of your neighbors at," Desoix explained forcefully. "Before he points them at you. Party time."

The alley was the same throughout its length, but its

other end opened onto more expensive facades and, across the broad street, patches of green surrounding the domed mass of the cathedral.

Traffic up the steps to the cathedral's arched south entrance was heavy and raucous. The street was choked by ground vehicles, some of them trying to move but even these blocked by the many which had been parked in the travel lanes.

"Hey there!" shouted the bearded leader of the group striding from the doorway just to the left of the alley. He wore two pistols in belt holsters; the cross on the shoulder of his red cape was perfunctory. "Where 're *you* going?"

"Back!" said Kekkonan over his shoulder, twisting to face the sudden threat.

Even before the one syllable order was spoken, the torchlight and echoing voices up the alley behind them warned the unit that they couldn't retreat the way they had come without shooting their way through.

Which would leave them in a street with five hundred or a thousand aroused residents who had pretty well used up their local entertainment.

"Hey!" repeated the leader. The gang that had exited the building behind him were a dozen more of the same, differing only in sex, armament, and whether or not they carried open bottles.

Most of them did.

They'd seen Kekkonan's body armor—and maybe his gun—when he turned toward them.

"Hey," Desoix said cheerfully as he stepped in front of the sergeant. "You know us. We're soldiers."

He'd been stationed in Bamberg City long enough that his Spanish had some of the local inflections that weren't on the sleep-learning cube. He wouldn't pass for a local, but neither did his voice put him instantly in the foreign— victim—category to these thugs.

"From the Palace?" asked the leader. His hand was still on a pistol, but his face had relaxed because Desoix was relaxed.

Desoix wasn't sure his legs were going to hold him up.

He'd been this frightened before, but that was when he was under fire and didn't have anything to do except crouch low and swear he'd resign and go home if only the Lord let him live this once.

"Sure," he said aloud, marveling at how well his voice worked. "Say, chickie—got anything there for a thirsty man?"

"Up your ass with it!" a red-caped female shrieked in amazement.

All the men in the group bellowed laughter.

One of them offered Desoix a flask of excellent wine, an off-planet vintage as good as anything served in the Palace.

"You're comin' to the cathedral, then?" the leader said as Desoix drank, tasting the liquid but feeling nothing. "Well, come on, then. The meeting's started by now or I'll be buggered."

"Not by me, Easton!" one of his henchmen chortled.

"Come on, boys," Desoix called, waving his unit out of the alley before there was a collision with the mob following. "We're already late for the meeting!"

Thank the Lord, the troopers all had the discipline or common sense to obey without question. Hemmed by the gang they'd joined perforce, surrounded by hundreds of other citizens wearing crosses over a variety of clothing, Desoix's unit tramped meekly up the steps of the cathedral.

Just before they entered the building, Desoix took the risk of muttering into his epaulet mike, "Tyl, we're making a necessary detour, but we're still coming back. If the Lord is with us, we're still coming back."

CHAPTER TWENTY-ONE

The nave was already full. Voices echoing in debate showed that the gang leader had been correct about the meeting having started. Hospital orderlies with staves guarded the entrance—keeping order rather than positioned to stop an attack.

Bishop Trimer and those working with him knew there would be no attack—until they gave the order.

Easton blustered, but there was no bluffing the white-robed men blocking the doorway. One of the orderlies spoke into a radio with a belt-pack power source, while the man next to him keyed a hand-held computer. A hologram of the bearded thug bloomed atop the computer in green light.

"Right, Easton," the guard captain said. "Left stairs to the north gallery. You and your folks make any trouble, we'll deal with it. Throw anything into the nave and you'll all decorate lamp posts. Understood?"

"Hey, I'm important!" the gang boss insisted. "I speak for the whole Seventeenth Ward, and I belong down with the bosses on the floor!"

"Right now, you belong on the Red side of the gallery," said the orderly. "Or out on your butts. Take your pick."

"You'll regret this!" Easton cried as he shuffled toward the indicated staircase. "I got friends! I'll make it hot fer you!"

"Who're you?" the guard captain asked Charles Desoix. His face was as grizzled as that of the Slammers sergeant major; his eyes were as fiat as death.

If Desoix hadn't seen the platoon of orderlies with assault rifles rouse from the antechamber when the gang boss threatened, he would have been tempted to turn back down the steps instead of answering. He couldn't pick his choice of realities, though.

"We're soldiers," he said, leaving the details fuzzy as he had before. "Ah—this isn't official, we aren't, you see. We just thought we'd, ah . . . be ready ourselves to do our part. . . ."

He hoped that meant something positive to the guard captain, without sounding so positive that they'd wind up in the middle of real trouble.

The fellow with the radio was speaking into it as his eyes locked with Desoix's. The UDB officer smiled brightly. The guard captain was talking to another of his men while both of them also looked at Desoix.

"All right," the captain said abruptly. "There's plenty of

room in the south gallery. We're glad to have more con-
verts to the ranks of active righteousness."

"We shoulda bugged out," muttered one of the troopers as they mounted the helical stairs behind Desoix.

"Keep your trap shut and do what the el-tee says,"
Sergeant Kokkonan snarled back.

For good or ill, Charles Desoix was in command now.

Given the sophistication of the commo unit the orderly
at the door held, Desoix didn't dare try to report anything
useful to those awaiting him back in the Palace. He hoped
Anne would have had sense enough to flee the city before
he got back to the Palace.

Almost as much as another part of him prayed that she
would be waiting when he returned; because he was very
badly going to need the relaxation she brought him.

CHAPTER TWENTY-TWO

In daytime the dome would have floated on sunlight
streaming through the forty arched windows on which it
was supported. The hidden floods directed from light
troughs to reflect from the inner surface were harsh and
metallic by contrast, even though the metal was gold.

Desoix and his unit muscled their way to the railing of
colored marble overlooking the nave. It might have been
smarter to hang back against the gallery windows, but they
were big men and aggressive enough to have found a career
in institutionalized murder.

They were standing close to the east end and the
hemicycle containing the altar, where the major figures in
the present drama now faced the crowd of their supporters and underlings.

Between the two groups was a line of orderlies kneeling shoulder to shoulder. Even by leaning over the rail,
Desoix could not see the faces of those on the altar dais.

But there were surprises in the crowd.

"That's Cerulio," Desoix said, nudging Kekkonan to look at a sumptuously dressed man in the front rank. His wife was with him, and the four men in blue around them were surely liveried servants. "He was in the Palace an hour ago. Said he was going to check his townhouse, but that he'd be back before morning."

"Don't know him," grunted Kekkonan. "But that one, three places over—" he didn't point, which reminded Desoix that pointing called attention to both ends of the outstretched arm "—he's in the adjutant general's staff, a colonel I'm pretty sure. Saw him when we were trying to requisition bunks."

Desoix felt a chill all the way up his spine. Though it didn't change anything beyond what they had already determined this night.

The man speaking wore white and a mitre, so that even from above there could be no mistaking Bishop Trimer.

"—wither away," his voice was saying. "Only in the last resort would God have us loose the righteous indignation that this so-called president has aroused in our hearts, in the heart of every Christian on Bamberia."

One shot, thought Charles Desoix.

He couldn't see Trimer's face, but there was a line of bare neck visible between mitre and chasuble. No armor there, no way to staunch the blood when a cyan bolt blasts a crater the size of a clenched fist.

And no way for the small group of soldiers to avoid being pulled into similarly fist sized gobbets when the mob took its revenge in the aftermath. "Not our fight," Desoix muttered to himself.

He didn't have to explain that to any of his companions. He was pretty sure that Sergeant Kekkonan would kill him in an eye-blink if he thought the UDB officer was about to sacrifice them all.

"We will wait a day, in God's name," the Bishop said. He was standing with his arms outstretched.

Trimer had a good voice and what was probably a commanding manner to those who didn't see him from above—like Charles Desoix and God, assuming God was more than a step in Bishop Trimer's pursuit of temporal power. He could almost have filled the huge church with his unaided voice, and the strain of listening would have quieted the crowd that was restive with excitement and drink.

As it was, Trimer's words were relayed through hundreds of speakers hidden in the pendentives and among the acanthus leaves of the column capitals. Multiple sources echoed and fought one another, creating a busyness that encouraged whispering and argument among the audience.

Desoix had been part of enough interunit staff meetings to both recognize and explain the strain that was building in the Bishop's voice. Trimer was used to being in charge; and here, in his own cathedral, circumstances had conspired to rob him of the absolute control he normally exercised.

The man seated to Trimer's right got up. Like the Bishop, he was recognizable by his clothing—a red cape and a red beret in which a bird plume of some sort bobbed when he moved his head.

The Bishop turned. The gallery opposite Desoix exploded with cheers and catcalls. Red-garbed spectators in the nave below were jumping, making their capes balloon like bubbles boiling through a thick red sauce, despite the efforts of the hospital orderlies keeping the two factions separate.

All the men on the dais were standing with their hands raised. The noise lessened, then paused in a great hiss that the pillared aisles drank.

"Ten minutes each, we agreed," one of the faction leaders said to the Bishop in a voice amplified across the whole cathedral.

"Speak, then!" said the Bishop in a voice that was short of being a snarl by as little as the commotion below had avoided being a full-fledged riot.

Trimer and most of the others on the dais seated themselves again, leaving the man in red to stand alone. There was more cheering and, ominously, boos and threats from

Desoix's side of the hall. Around the soldiers, orderlies fought a score of violent struggles with thugs in black.

The man in red raised his hands again and boomed, "Everybody siddown, curse it! We're *friends* here, friends—"

When the sound level dropped minusculy, he added, "Rich friends we're gonna be, every one of us!"

The cheers were general and loud enough to make the light troughs wobble.

"Now all you know there's no bigger supporter of the Bishop than I am," the gang boss continued in a voice whose nasality was smoothed by the multiple echoes. "But there's something else you all know, too. I'm not the man to back off when I got the hammer on some bastid neither."

He wasn't a stupid man. He forestalled the cheers—and the threats from the opposing side of the great room—that would have followed the statement by waving his arms again for silence even as he spoke.

"Now the way I sees it," he went on. "The way *anybody* sees it—is we got the hammer on Delcorio. So right now's the time we break 'is bloody neck for 'im. Not next week or next bloody year when somebody's cut another deal with 'im and he's got the streets full a' bloody soldiers!"

In the tumult of agreement, Desoix saw a woman wearing black cross-belts fight her way to the front of the spectators' section and wave a note over the heads of the line of orderlies.

The black-caped gang boss looked a question to the commo-helmeted aide with him on the dais. The aide shrugged in equal doubt, then obeyed the nodded order to reach across the orderlies and take the note from the woman's hand.

"Now the Bishop says," continued the man in red, "'give him a little time, he'll waste right away and nobody gets hurt.' And that's fine, sure . . . but maybe it's time a few a' them snooty bastids *does* get hurt, right?"

The shouts of "yes" and "kill" were punctuated with other sounds as bestial as the cries of panthers hunting. It was noticeable that the front rank of spectators, the men and women with estates and townhouses, either sat silent or looked about nervously as they tried to feign enthusiasm.

While the red leader waited with his head thrown back and arms akimbo, the rival gang boss read the note he had been passed. He reached toward Bishop Trimer with it and, when another priest tried to take the document from his hand, swatted the man away. Trimer leaned over to read the note.

"Now I say," the man in red resumed in a lull, "all right, we give Delcorio time. We give the bastid as much time as it takes fer us to march over to the Palace and pull it down—"

The black-caped gang boss got up, drawing the Bishop's gaze to follow the note being thrust at the leader of the other street gang.

The timbre of the shouting changed as the spectators assessed what was happening in their own terms—and prepared for the immediate battle those terms might entail.

"The rightful President of Bamberia is Thomas Chastain," cried the black-caped leader as the cathedral hushed and his rival squinted at the note in the red light.

The man in red looked up but did not interrupt as the other leader thundered in a deep bass, "He was robbed of his heritage by the Delcorios and held under their guards in the Palace—but now he's escaped! Thom Chastain's at his house right now, waiting for us to come and restore him to his position!"

Everyone on the dais was standing. Some of the leaders, Church and gangs and surely the business community as well, tried to speak to one another over the tumult. Unless they could read lips, that was a useless exercise.

Desoix was sure of that. He'd been caught in an artillery barrage, and the decibel level of the bursting shells had been no greater than that of the voices reverberating now in the cathedral.

Bishop Trimer touched the gang bosses. They conferred with looks, then stepped back to give the Bishop the floor again. Though they did not sit down, they motioned their subordinates into chairs on the dais. After a minute or two, the room had quieted enough for Trimer to speak.

"My people," he began with his arms outstretched in benediction. "You have spoken, and the Lord God has made his will known to us. We will gather at dawn here—"

The gang bosses had been whispering to one another. The man in black tugged the Bishop's arm firmly enough to bring a burly priest—Father Laughlin?—from his seat. Before he could intervene, the red-garbed leader spoke to Trimer with forceful gestures of his hand.

The Bishop nodded. Desoix couldn't see his face, but he could imagine the look of bland agreement wiped thinly over fury at being interrupted and dictated to by thugs.

"My people," he continued with unctuous warmth, "we will meet at dawn in the plaza, where all the city can see me anoint our rightful president in the name of God who rules us. Then we will carry President Chastain with us to the Palace to claim his seat—and God will strengthen our arms to smite anyone so steeped in sin that they would deny his will. At dawn!"

The cheering went on and on. Even in the gallery, where the floor and the pillars of colored marble provided a screen from the worst of the noise, it was some minutes before Kekkonan could shout into Desoix's ear, "What's that mean for us, sir?"

"It means," the UDB officer shouted back, "that we've got a couple hours to load what we can and get the hell out of Bamberg City."

He paused a moment, then added, "It means we've had a good deal more luck the past half hour than we had any right to expect."

CHAPTER TWENTY-THREE

"We got 'em in sight," said Scratchard's voice through Tyl's commo helmet. The sergeant major was on the roof with the ten best marksmen in the unit. "Everybody together, no signs they're being followed."

Tyl started to acknowledge, but before he could Scratchard concluded, "Plenty units out tonight besides them, but nobody seems too interested in them nor us. Over."

"Out," Tyl said, letting his voice stand for his identification.

He locked eyes with the sullen Guards officer across the doorway from him, Captain Sanchez, and said, "Open it up, sir. I got a team coming in."

There were two dozen soldiers in the rotunda: the ordinary complement of Executive Guards and the squad Tyl had brought with him when Desoix blipped that they were clear again and heading in.

Earlier that night, the UDB officer had talked Tyl and his men through the doors that might have been barred to them. Tyl wasn't at all sure his diplomacy was good enough for him to return the favor diplomatically.

But he didn't doubt the locals would accept any suggestion he chose to make with a squad of Slammers at his back.

Sanchez didn't respond, but the man at the shutter controls punched the right buttons instantly. Warm air, laced with smoke more pungent than that of the omnipresent cigars, puffed into the circular hall.

Tyl stepped into the night.

The height and width of the House of Grace was marked by a cross of bluish light, a polarized surface discharge from the vitril glazing. It was impressive despite being marred by several shattered panels.

And it was the only light in the city beyond handcarried lanterns and the sickly pink-orange-red of spreading fires. Street lights that hadn't been cut when transformers shorted were tempting targets for gunmen.

So were lighted windows, now that the meeting in the cathedral had broken up and the gangs were out in force again.

Tyl clicked his faceshield down in the lighted courtyard and watched the seven soldiers jogging toward him with the greenish tinge of enhanced ambient light.

"All present 'n accounted for, sir," muttered Kekkonan when he reached Tyl, reporting because he was the senior Slammer in the unit.

"Sergeant major's got a squad on the roof," Tyl explained. "Make sure your own gear's ready to move, then relieve Jack. All right?"

"Yes *sir*," said Kekkonan and ducked off after his men. The emotion in his agreement was the only hint the non-com gave of just how tight things had been an hour before.

"Lachere, make sure Control's core pack's ready to jerk out," Desoix said. "We've got one jeep, so don't expect to leave with more than you can carry walking."

The clerk's boots skidded on the rotunda's stone flooring as he scampered to obey.

Desoix put his arm around Tyl's shoulders as they followed their subordinates through armored doors which the guard immediately began to close behind them. Tyl was glad of the contact. He felt like a rat in a maze in this warren of corridors and blocked exits.

"I appreciate your help," Desoix said. "It might have worked. And without those very good people you lent me, it would—"

He paused. "It wouldn't have been survivable. And I'd have probably made the attempt anyway, because I didn't understand what it was like out there until we started back."

"I guess . . ." Tyl said. "I guess we better report to, to the President before we go. Unless he was tapping the push. I guess we owe him that, for the contract."

They stepped together into the small elevator. It was no longer separately guarded. The Executive Guardsmen watched them without expression.

A few of the Slammers stationed in the rotunda threw ironic salutes. They were in a brighter mood than they'd been a few minutes before. They knew from their fellows who'd just come in that the whole unit would be bugging out shortly.

"You're short of transport too?" Tyl asked, trying to keep the concern out of his voice as he watched Desoix side-long.

"I can give my seat to your sergeant major, if that's what you mean," Desoix replied. "I've hiked before. But yes, this was the base unit they robbed to outfit all the batteries on Two that had to be mobile."

That was exactly what Tyl had meant.

The elevator stopped. In the moment before the door opened, Desoix added, "There's vehicles parked in the garage under the Palace here. If we're providing protection, there shouldn't be a problem arranging rides."

If it's safe to call attention to yourself with a vehicle, Tyl thought, remembering the fire trucks. Luxury cars with the presidential seal would be even better targets.

Tyl expected Anne McGill to be at the open door connecting the Consistory Room with the presidential suite, where she could be in sight of her mistress and still able to hear the elevator arrive. She was closer than that, arm's length of the elevator—and so was Eunice Delcorio.

The President was across the room, in silhouette against the faint flow which was all that remained of the City Offices toward which he was staring. His nephew stood beside him, but there was no one else—not even a servant—in the darkened room.

"Charles?" Anne said. Her big body trembled like a spring, but she did not reach to clasp her lover now, in front of Eunice.

Tyl let Desoix handle the next part. They hadn't discussed it, but the UDB officer knew more about things like this . . . politics and the emotions that accompany politics.

Desoix stepped forward and bowed to Eunice Delcorio, expertly sweeping back the civilian cape he still wore over his gun and armor. "Madam," he said. "Sir—" John Delcorio had turned to watch them, though he remained where he was. "I very much regret that it's time for you to withdraw from the city."

The President slammed the bottom of his fist against the marble pillar beside him. Anne was nodding hopeful agreement; her mistress was still, though not calm.

"There's still time to get out," Desoix continued. Tyl

marveled at Desoix's control. *He* wanted to get out, wanted it so badly that he had to consciously restrain himself from jumping into the elevator and ordering the unit to form on him in the courtyard.

"But *barely* enough time. The—they are going to anoint Thom Chastain President at dawn in the plaza, and then they'll come here. Even if they haven't gotten heavy weapons from one of the military arsenals, there's no possible way that the Palace can be defended."

"I knew the swine were betraying me," Delcorio shouted. "I should never have let them live, never!"

"We can cover the way out if you move fast enough," Tyl said aloud. "Ten minutes, maybe."

What he'd seen in the Consistory Room and heard from Desoix's terse report on the way back to the Palace convinced him that Delcorio, not Thom Chastain, was responsible for the present situation. But *why* didn't matter any more.

"All right," the President said calmly. "I've already packed the seal and robes of state. I had to do it myself because they'd all run, even Heinrich. . . ."

"No," said Eunice Delcorio. "*No!*"

"Eunice," begged Anne McGill.

"Ma'am," said Tyl Koopman desperately. "There's no way."

He was unwilling to see people throw themselves away. You learn that when you fight for hire. There's always another contract, if you're around to take it up. . . .

"I've been mistress of this city, of this planet," the President's wife said in a voice that hummed like a cable being tightened. "If they think to change that, well, they can burn me in the Palace first."

She turned to stare, either at her husband or at the smoldering night beyond him. "It'll be a fitting monument, I think," she said.

"And I'll set the fires *myself*—" whirling, her eyes lashed both the mercenary officers "—if no one's man enough to help me defend it."

Anne McGill fell to her knees, praying or crying.

"Madam," said Major Borodin, entering from the hall unannounced because there was no greeter in the building to announce him.

The battery commander looked neither nervous nor frustrated. There was an aura of vague distaste about him, the way his sort of officer always looked when required to speak to a group of people.

This was a set speech, not a contribution to the discussion.

"I urge you," Borodin went on, reeling the words off a sheaf of mental notes, "to use common sense in making personal decisions. So far as public decisions go, I must inform you that I am withdrawing my battery from the area affected by the present unrest, under orders of my commander—and with the concurrence of our legal staff."

"I said—" John Delcorio began, ready to blaze up harmlessly at having his nose rubbed in a reality of which he was already aware.

"No, of *course* we can defeat them!" said Eunice, pirouetting to Borodin's side with a girlish sprightliness that surprised everyone else in the room as much as it did the major.

"No, no," the President's wife continued brightly, one hand on Borodin's elbow while the other hand gestured to her audience. "It's really quite possible, don't you see? There's many of them and only a few of us—but if they're in the plaza, well, we just hold the entrances."

She stroked Borodin's arm and waved, palm up, to Tyl and Desoix. Her smile seemed to double the width of her face. "You brave lads can do that, can't you? Just the three stairs, and you'll have the Executive Guard to help you. The Bishop won't make any trouble about coming to the Palace alone to discuss matters if the choice is. . . ."

Eunice paused delicately. This wasn't the woman who moments before had been ready—*had* been ready—to burn herself alive with the Palace. "And this way, all the trouble ends and no one more gets hurt, all the rioting and troubles. . . ."

"No," said Major Borodin. His eyes were bulging and

he didn't appear to be seeing any of his present surroundings. His mental notes had been hopelessly disarrayed by this—

"Yes, yes, of *course!*" President Delcorio said, rubbing his hands together in anticipation. "We'll see how much Trimer blusters when he's asked to come and there's a *gun* at his head to see that he does!"

Tyl had pointed enough guns to know that they weren't the kind of magic wand Delcorio seemed to be expecting. He looked at Desoix, certain of agreement and hopeful that the UDB officer would be able to express the plan's absurdity in a more tactful fashion than Tyl could.

Desoix had lifted Anne McGill to her feet. His hand was on the woman's waist, but she wasn't paying any conscious attention to him. Instead, her eyes were on Eunice Delcorio.

"No," muttered Borodin. "No, no! We've got to withdraw at once."

Maybe it was the rote dismissal by the battery commander that made Tyl really start thinking, Colonel Hammer wanted Delcorio kept in power for another week—and no deal Trimer cut with the present government was likely to last *longer* than that, but a week . . . ?

Two hundred men and a pair of calliopes—blazes, maybe it *would* work!

"Of course," Tyl said aloud, "Marshal Dowell's on the other side, sure as can be, so the Guard downstairs . . . ?"

"Dowell isn't the Executive Guard," said the President dismissively. "He's nothing but a jumped-up shopkeeper. I was a fool to think he'd be loyal because he owed everything to me."

Like City Prefect Berne, Tyl thought. He kept his mouth shut.

"But the Guard, they're the best people in the State," Delcorio continued with enthusiasm. "They won't give in to trash and gutter sweepings now that we've found a way to deal with them."

"Lieutenant," said the battery commander, "I'll oversee the loading. Give the withdrawal orders as soon as you've determined the safest routes."

He pivoted on his left heel, rotating his elbow from Eunice's seductive touch. He stamped out of the room.

"Yes sir," Desoix said crisply, but he made no immediate motion to follow his superior.

"Well," said Tyl, feeling the relief that returned with resignation—it'd been a crazy notion, but just for a minute he'd thought . . . "Well, I better tell—"

"Wait!" Anne McGill said. She stepped toward her mistress, but she was no longer ignoring Charles Desoix. Halfway between the two she spun toward her lover and set a jewel-ringed hand at the scooped collar of the dress she wore beneath her cloak. She pulled fiercely.

The hem of lustrous synthetic held. White and red creases sprang out where the straps crossed her shoulders.

"Anne?" the President's wife called from behind her companion.

Anne wailed, "Mary, Queen of Heaven!" and tugged again, pulling the left strap down to her elbow instead of trying again to tear the fabric. Her breast, firm but far too heavy not to sag, flopped over the bodice which had restrained it.

"Is this what you want to give to them?" she cried. Her eyes were blind, even before she shut them in a vain attempt to hold back the tears. "Give the, the *mob*? I won't go! I won't leave Eunice even if you *are* all cowards?

"Anne," Desoix pleaded. "President Delcorio—the front row in the cathedral *was* the best people in the State. Some of them were here with you this morning. Colonel Drescher isn't going to—"

"How do you know until you ask him?" Eunice demanded in a voice like a rapier. Her arm was around Anne McGill now, drawing the dark cloak over the naked breast. Tyl couldn't say whether the gesture was motherly or simply proprietary.

This hasn't got anything t' do with . . . his surface mind started to tell him; but deeper down, he knew it did. Like as not it always did, one way or another; who was screwing who and how everybody felt about it.

"All right!" Desoix shouted. "We'll go ask him!"

"I'll go myself," said President Delcorio, sucking in his belly and adding a centimeter to his height by straightening up.

"That's not safe, Uncle John," said Pedro Delcorio unexpectedly. "I'll go with the men."

"Well . . ." Tyl said as the President's nephew gestured him toward the elevator. Desoix, his face set in furious determination, was already inside.

It was going to be cramped with three of them. "Via, why not?" Tyl said. It was easier to go along than to refuse to, right now. Nothing would come of it. He'd seen too many parade-ground units to expect this one to find guts all of a sudden.

But if just maybe it did work . . . Via, nobody liked to run with their tail between their legs, did they?

CHAPTER TWENTY-FOUR

Koopman's idiotic grin was just one more irritation to Charles Desoix as the elevator dropped.

"Bit of a chance you're taking, isn't it?" the Slammers officer asked. "Going against your major's orders and all?"

Desoix felt himself become calm and was glad of it. None of this made any sense. If Tyl decided to laugh— well, that was a saner response than Desoix's own.

"Only if something comes of it," he said, wishing that he didn't sound so tired. Wrung out.

He *was* wrung out. "And if I'm alive afterward, of course."

Pedro's eyes were darting between the mercenaries. His bulky body—soft but not flabby—would have given him presence under some circumstances. In these tight quarters he was overwhelmed by the men in armor—and by the way they considered the future in the light of similar pasts.

The car settled so gently that only the door opening announced the rotunda. Desoix swung out to the left side, noticing that identical reflex had moved Koopman to the right—as if they were about to clear a defended position.

Half a dozen powerguns were leveled at the opening door, though the Slammers here on guard jerked their muzzles away when they saw who had arrived.

The rotunda was empty except for Hammer's men.

"Where's the guards?" Koopman demanded in amazement.

One of his men shrugged. "A few minutes back, they all moved out."

He pointed down the corridor that led toward the Guard billets. "I called the sar'ent major, but he said hold what we got, he and the rest a' the company'd be with us any time now."

"Let's go, then!" said Pedro Delcorio, trotting in the direction of the gesture.

Desoix followed, because that was what he'd set out to do. He hunched himself to settle his armor again. When he felt cold, as now, he seemed to shrink within the ceramic shell.

"Carry on," Koopman said to his guard squad. As the Slammers officer strode along behind the other two men, Desoix heard him speaking into his commo helmet in a low voice.

The barracks of the Executive Guard occupied the back corridor of the Palace's south wing. It had its own double gate of scissor-hinged brass bars over a panel of imported hardwood, both portions polished daily by servants.

The bars were open, the panel—steel-cored, Desoix now noticed—ajar. Captain Sanchez and the squad he'd commanded in the rotunda stood in the opening, arguing with other Guardsmen in the corridor beyond. When they heard the sound of boots approaching, they whirled. Several of them aimed their rifles.

Charles Desoix froze, raising his hands and moving them out from his sides. He had been close to death a number of times already this night.

But never closer than now.

"What do you men think you're doing?" Pedro

demanded in a voice tremulous with rage. "Don't you recognize me? I'm—"

"*No!*" Sanchez snapped to the man at his side. The leveled assault rifle wavered but did not fire—as both Desoix and the Guards captain had expected.

"Wha . . . ?" Delcorio said in bewilderment.

"Rene, it's me," Desoix called in an easy voice. He sidled a step so that Sanchez could see him clearly past the President's nephew. Walking *forward* was possible suicide. "Charles, you know? We came to discuss the present situation with Colonel Drescher."

The words rolled off Desoix's tongue, amazing him with their blandness and fluency. Whatever else that scene upstairs with Anne had done, it had burned the capacity to be shocked out of him for a time.

Drescher stepped forward when his name was spoken. He had been the other half of the argument in the gateway. The lower ranking Guardsmen grounded their weapons as if embarrassed to be touching real hardware in the presence of their commander.

"Master Desoix," said Drescher, "we're very busy just now. I have nothing to discuss with you or any of John Delcorio's by-blows."

"*What?*" Pedro Delcorio shouted, able this time to get the full syllable out in his rage.

Koopman put a hand, his left hand, on the young civilian's shoulder and shifted him back a step without being too obvious about the force required.

Desoix walked forward, turning his spread arms into gestures as he said, "Sir, it's become possible to quell the rioting without further bloodshed or the need for additional troops. We'd like to discuss the matter with you for a moment."

As if Drescher's deliberate ignorance of his military rank didn't bother him, Desoix added with an ingratiating smile, "It will make you the hero of the day, sir. Of the century."

"And who's that?" Drescher said, waving his swagger stick in the direction of the Slammers officer. "Your trained dog, Desoix?"

Recent events had shocked the Guard Commandant into denial so deep that he was being more insulting than usual to prove that civilization and the rule of law still maintained in his presence. Charles Desoix knew that, but Tyl Koopman with a sub-machinegun under his arm—

"No sir," said the Slammers officer. "I'm Captain Koopman of Hammer's Regiment. My unit's part of the defense team."

"Sir," Desoix said in the pause that followed Koopman's response and sudden awareness of what the mercenary's response *could* have been. "The mob will have gathered in the plaza by dawn. By sealing the three exits, we can bring their, ah, leaders, to a reasonable accommodation with the government."

"The government of the State," said Drescher icily, cutting through Desoix's planned next phrase, "is what God and the people choose it to be. The Executive Guard would not presume to interfere with that choice."

"Colonel," Desoix said. He could feel his eyes widening, but he didn't see the Guardsmen in front of him. In his mind, a dozen men were raping Anne McGill while shrill-voiced women urged them on. "If they attack the Palace, there'll be a bloodbath."

"Then it's necessary to evacuate the Palace, isn't it?" Drescher replied. "Now, if you *gentle*—"

"Don't you boys take oaths?" Koopman asked curiously. There wasn't any apparent emotion in his tone. "Don't they matter to you?"

Colonel Drescher went white. "You foreign mercenaries have a vision of Bamberg politics," he said, "that a native can only describe as bizarre." His voice sounded as though he would have been screaming if his lungs held enough air. "Now get *away* from here!"

Charles Desoix bowed low. "Gentlemen," he murmured to his companions as he turned. "We have no further business here."

They didn't look behind them as they marched to where the corridor jogged and the wall gave them cover against a burst of shots into their backs. Pedro Delcorio was shaking.

So was Koopman, but it showed itself as a lilt in his voice as he said, "Well, they're frightened. Can't blame 'em, can we, Charles? And they'd not have been much use, just stand there and nobody who'd seen 'em in their prettiness was going to be much scared, eh?"

Adrenalin was babbling through the lips of the Slammers officer. His right hand was working in front of him where the Guardsmen couldn't see it, clenching and unclenching, because if it didn't move, it was going to find its home on the grip of his sub-machinegun. . . .

Anne was waiting around the corner. She looked at the faces of the three men and closed her eyes.

"Anne, we can't—" Desoix began. He was sure there had to be something he could say that would keep her from the suicide she'd threatened, at the hands of the mob or more abruptly here with a rope or the gun he knew she kept in her bedroom.

"Sure we can," said Tyl Koopman. His voice had no emotion, and his eyes had an eerie, thousand-meter stare.

"You've got a calliope aimed at both side stairs, sure, they won't buck that, one burst and that's over. And me and the boys, sure, we'll take the main stairs, those lock gates, they're like vaults, *no* problem."

"Then it's all right?" Anne said in amazement. Her beautiful face was lighting as if she were watching a theophany. "You can still save us, Charles?"

She touched her fingertips to his chest, assuring herself of her lover's continuing humanity.

"I—" said Charles Desoix. He looked at the Slammers officer, then back into the eyes of Anne McGill.

They'd have to do something about Major Borodin— literally put the old man under restraint. Maybe Delcorio still had a few servants around who could handle that.

"I—" Desoix repeated.

Then he squared his shoulders and said, "Certainly, darling, Tyl and I can handle it without the help of *those* fools."

It amazed the UDB officer to realize how easily he had

decided to ruin his life. The saving grace was the fact that there wouldn't be many hours of life remaining to him after this decision.

CHAPTER TWENTY-FIVE

Tyl watched the antenna of his laser communicator quest on the porch outside the Consistory Room, making a keening sound as it searched for its satellite. The link was still thirty seconds short of completion when his commo helmet said, "Four-six to Six, over."

Tyl jumped, ringing the muzzle of his sub-machinegun against the rail as he spun.

"Go ahead, Four-six," he said to Sergeant Major Scratchard when he realized that the call was on the unit push, not the laser link he'd been setting up. He was a hair late in his response, but nobody else knew the unexpected call had scared him like that.

"Sir," said Scratchard, "the Palace troops, they're all marching out one a' the side doors right now. Over."

Good riddance, Tyl thought. "Let 'em go, Jack," he said. "Six out."

"Six?"

"Go ahead, Four-six."

"Sir, should we secure the doors after them? Over."

"Negative, Four-six," Tyl snapped. "Ignore this bloody building and carry out your orders! Six out."

It hadn't been that silly a question. Jack was nervous because he didn't know much, because Tyl hadn't told him very much. The non-com was trying to cross all possible tees because he couldn't guess which ones would turn out to he of critical importance.

Neither could his captain. Which was the real reason Tyl had jumped down the sergeant major's throat.

A dim red light pulsed on the antenna's tracking head, indicating that the unit had locked on. Tyl switched modes on his helmet, grimaced, and said, "Koopman to Central, over."

Seconds of flickering static, aural and visual, took his mind off the cross dominating the skyline toward which the laser pointed. It was only an hour before dawn. The streets were alive with bands of men and women, ant-small at this distance and moving like foraging ants toward the plaza.

"Hold one," said the helmet. The screen surged into momentary crystal sharpness. Colonel Hammer glared from it.

He looked very tired. All but his eyes.

"Go ahead, Captain," Hammer said, and the static fuzzing his voice blurred his image a moment later as well, as though a bead curtain had been drawn between Tyl and his commander.

Tyl found that a lot more comfortable. Funny the things you worry about instead of the really worrisome things. . . .

"Sir," he said, knowing that his voice sounded dull—it had to, he couldn't let emotion get out during this report because he hadn't any idea of what emotion he'd find himself displaying. "I've alerted my men for an operation at dawn to bottle up the rioters and demand the surrender of their leaders. We'll be operating in concert with elements of the UDB."

There was no need to say "over," since the speakers could see one another—albeit with a lag of a few seconds. Tyl keyed the thumb-sized unit on his sending head, a module loaded with the street plan, routes, and makeup of the units taking part in the operation. The pre-load burped out like an angry katydid.

Hammer's eyes, never at rest, paused briefly on a point to the left of the pickup feeding Tyl's screen. A separate holotank was displaying the schematic, while Tyl's face continued to fill the main unit.

Hammer's face wore no expression as it clicked to meet Tyl's eyes again. "What are the numbers on the other side?" he asked emotionlessly.

"Sir, upwards of twenty kay. Maybe fifty, the plaza'd hold that much and more."

Tyl paused. "Sir," he added, "we can't fight 'em, we know that. But maybe we can face them down, the leaders."

People were moving in the courtyard beneath him, four cloaked figures slipping out of the Palace on their missions. Desoix and his two clerks to the warehouse and the calliope they'd set up only hours before. And. . . .

"How are you timing your assault?" the Colonel asked calmly. "If the ringleaders aren't present, you've gained nothing. And if you wait too long ?. . ."

"Sir, one of the women from the Palace," Tyl explained. "She's, ah, getting in position right now in the south gallery of the cathedral. There's a view to the altar on the seafront, that's where the big ones'll be. She'll cue us when she spots the ones we need."

He thought he was done speaking, but his tongue went on unexpectedly. "Sir, we thought of using a man, but a woman going to pray now—it's not going to upset anything. She'll be all right."

The Colonel frowned as if trying to understand why a line captain was apologizing for using a female lookout. It didn't make a lot of sense to Tyl either, after he heard his own words—but he'd been away for a long time.

And anyway, the only similarity between Anne McGill and the dozen females in Tyl's present command was that their plumbing was the same.

"What happens if they don't back down?" Hammer said in a voice like a whetstone, apparently smooth but certain to wear away whatever it rubs against, given time and will.

"We bug out," Tyl answered frankly. "The mall at the main stairs, that's where we'll be, it's got gates like bank vaults on all four sides. Things don't work out, Trimer ducks instead of putting his hands up and his buddies start shooting—well, we slam the plaza side doors and we're gone."

"And your supports?" Hammer asked. His mouth wavered in what might have been either static or an incipient grin.

"Desoix's men, they're mounted," Tyl said. It was an open question whether or not you could really load a double crew on a calliope and drive away with it, but that was one for the UDB to answer. "Worst case, there's going to be too much confusion for organized pursuit. Unless . . ."

"Unless the streets are already blocked behind you," said Colonel Hammer, who must have begun speaking before Tyl's voice trailed off on the same awareness. "Unless there's a large enough group of rioters between your unit and safety to hold you for their fifty thousand friends to arrive."

"Yes sir," said Tyl.

He swallowed. "Sir," he said, "I can't promise it'll work. If it does, it'll give you the time you wanted for things to hot up over there. But I can't promise."

"Son," said Colonel Hammer. He was grinning like a skull. "When you start making promises on chances like this, I'll remove you from command so fast your ears'll ring."

His face straightened into neutral lines again. "For the record," Hammer said, "you're operating without orders. Not in violation of orders, just on your own initiative."

"Yes *sir*," Tyl said.

Hammer hadn't paused for agreement. He was saying, "I expect you to withdraw as soon as you determine that there is no longer a realistic chance of success. Nobody's being paid to be heroes, and—"

He leaned closer to the pickup. His face was grim and his eyes glared like gun muzzles. "Captain, if *you* throw my men away because you want to be a hero, I'll shoot you with my own hand. If you survive."

"Yes *sir*," Tyl said through a swallow. This time his commander had waited for an acknowledgment.

Hammer softened. "Then good luck to you, son," he said. "Oh—and son?"

"Yes sir?"

The Colonel grinned with the same death's-head humor as before. "Bishop Trimer decided Hammer's Slammers weren't worth their price," Hammer said. "It wouldn't bother me if by the end of today, his Eminence had decided he was wrong on that."

Hammer touched a hidden switch and static flooded the screen.

"Four-six to Six," came Scratchard's voice, delayed until the laser link was broken. "We're ready, sir. Over."

"Four-six," Tyl said as he shrugged his armor loose over his sweating torso. "I'm on my way."

He left the laser communicator set up where it was. He'd need it again after the operation was over.

In the event that he survived.

CHAPTER TWENTY-SIX

"—gathered together at the dawn of a new age for our nation, our planet, and our God," said the voice.

Bishop Trimer's words had a touch of excitement remaining to them, despite being attenuated through multiple steps before they got to Tyl's helmet. Anne McGill aimed a directional microphone from the cathedral to the seafront altar, below her and over a kilometer away.

Trimer's speech was patched through the commo gear hidden between the woman's breasts, then shuttled by the UDB artificial intelligence over the interunit frequency to Tyl Koopman.

"We could shoot the bastard easy as listen to him," Scratchard said as he held out a shoulder weapon to his captain.

Only the two of them among the ninety-eight troopers in the rotunda had helmets that would receive the transmission. The other Slammers watched in silence as varied as their individual personalities: frightened; feral; cautious; and not a few with anticipation that drew back their lips in memory of past events. . . .

"Might break the back of the rebellion," Tyl said.

He had to will his eyes to focus on Scratchard's face, on anything as near as the walls of the big room. "Sure as blood that lot—" he touched his helmet over the tiny speaker "—they'd burn the city down to bricks 'n bare concrete. Might as well nuke 'em as that."

His voice didn't sound, even to him, as if he much cared. He wasn't sure he did care. He wasn't really involved with things that could be or might be . . . or even were.

"With dawn comes the light," the Bishop was saying. "With this dawn, the Lord brings us also the new light of freedom in the person of the man he has commanded me to anoint President of Bamberia."

"Jack, I don't need that," Tyl said peevishly. Sight of the 2 CM weapon being pushed toward him had brought him back to reality; irritation had succeeded where abstracts like survival and success could not. "I got a gun, remember?"

He slapped the receiver of the sub-machinegun under his arm, then noticed that the whole company was carrying double as well as being festooned with bandoliers and strings of grenades.

"UDB's weapons stores were here in the Palace," the sergeant major explained patiently. "Their el-tee, he told us go ahead. Sir, we don't got far t' go. And I swear, they all jam."

Scratchard grinned sadly. He lifted his right boot to display the hilt of his fighting knife, though with his hands full he couldn't touch it for emphasis. "Even these, the blade can break. When you really don't want t' see that."

"Sorry," said Tyl, glad beyond words to be back in the present with sweaty palms and an itch between his shoulder blades that he couldn't have scratched even if it weren't covered by his clam-shell armor.

"Blazes," he added as he checked the load—full magazine, chamber empty. "Here's my treatment a' choice anyhow. I'll take punch over pecka-pecka-pecka any day."

He looked up and glared around the circle of his troops as if seeing them for the first time. Pretty nearly he was. Good men, good soldiers; and just the team to pull the plug on Trimer and the bully boys who thought they owned the streets when the Slammers were in town.

"Thomas Chastain has mounted the dais," said Anne McGill. She sounded calm, but the distance in her voice was more than an electronic artifact. "Both Chastain brothers. The faction heads are present, and so are several churchmen, standing beneath the crucifix."

Tyl keyed the command channel while ducking through the bandolier of 2 CM magazines the sergeant major held for him.

"Orange to Blue Six," he said, using the code he and the UDB officer had set up in a few seconds when they realized that they'd need it. "Report."

"Blue Six ready," said Desoix's voice.

"Orange to Blue Three. Report."

"Blue Three ready," said a voice Tyl didn't recognize, the non-com in charge of the Gun Three near the east entrance to the plaza.

"Orange Six to Blue," Tyl said. "We're moving into position . . . now."

He cut down with his right index finger. Before the gesture ended, Sergeant Kekkonan was leading the first squad into the incipient dawn over Bamberg City.

CHAPTER TWENTY-SEVEN

"I figured they'd a' burned it down, the way they was going last night," said Lachere, blinking around the warehouse from the driver's seat.

"Tonight," he said, correcting himself in mild wonder.

"Senter, what's the street look like?" Desoix asked from the gun saddle. Beneath him the calliope quivered like a sleeping hound, its being at placid idle—but ready to rend and bellow the instant it was aroused.

Desoix couldn't blame his subordinate for thinking more than a few hours had passed since they first entered this warehouse. It seemed like a lifetime—

And that wasn't a thought Lieutenant Charles Desoix wanted to pursue, even in the privacy of his own mind.

"I don't see anybody out, sir," the other clerk called from

the half-open pedestrian door. "Maybe lookin' out a window, I can't tell. But none a' the big mobs like when we got here."

Reentering the warehouse without being caught up— or cut down—by the bands of bravos heading toward the plaza had been the trickiest part of the operation so far. Stealth was the only option open to Desoix and his two companions. Even if Koopman had been willing—been able, it didn't matter—to spare a squad in support, a firefight would still mean sure disaster for the plan as well as for the unit.

"All right, Senter," Desoix said. "Open the main doors and climb aboard."

Lachere was bringing the fans up to driving velocity without orders. He wasn't a great driver, but he'd handled air cushion vehicles before and could maneuver the calliope well enough for present needs.

The suction roar boomed in the cavernous room while Senter struggled with the unfamiliar door mechanism. The warehouse staff—manager, loaders, and guards—had disappeared at the first sign of trouble, leaving nothing behind but crated goods and the heavy effluvium of tobacco to be stirred into a frenzy by the calliope's drive fans.

The door rumbled upward; Senter scampered toward the gun vehicle. Desoix smiled. He'd been ready to clear their way with his eight 3 CM guns if necessary.

He had ordered control to lock the general frequency out of his headset. Captain Koopman was in charge of this operation, so Desoix didn't have to listen to the running commentary about what the mob in the plaza was doing.

If he listened on that frequency, he would hear Anne; and he would have to remember where she was and how certainly she would die if he failed.

"Ready, sir?" Lachere demanded, shouting as though his voice weren't being transmitted over the intercom channel.

Desoix raised a hand in bar. "Blue Six to all Blue and Orange units," he said. "We're moving into position—now."

He chopped his hand.

Lachere accelerated them into the street with a clear view of the plaza's south stairhead, two blocks away.

Metal shrieked as Lachere sideswiped the door jamb, but none of the calliope's scratch crew noticed the sound.

CHAPTER TWENTY-EIGHT

"I'm with you!' said Pedro Delcorio, gripping Tyl's shoulder from behind.

He was almost with the angels, because Tyl spun and punched the young noble in the belly with the weapon he'd just charged, his finger taking up slack.

"Careful, sonny," the Slammers officer said as intellect twitched away the gun that reflex had pointed.

Tyl felt light, as though his body were suspended on wires that someone else was holding. His skin was covered with a sheen of sweat that had nothing to do with the night's mild breezes.

Pedro wore a uniform—a service uniform, probably; though the clinking, glittering medals on both sides of the chest indicated that the kid still had something to learn about combat conditions. He also wore a determined expression and a pistol in a polished holster.

"You're doing this for my family," Pedro said. "One of us should be with you."

"That why we're doing it?" Tyl asked, marveling at the lilt in his own voice. Tyl wasn't sure the kid knew how close he'd come to dying a moment before. "Well, it'll do unless a better reason comes along. Stick close, boy, and leave that—" he nodded toward the gun "—in its holster."

He had a squad on the levee and a squad deployed to cover the boulevard and medians separating the Palace from the cathedral. The rest of the Slammers were moving at a nervous shuffle down the river drive bunched more than he liked, than anybody'd like, but they were going to need all the firepower available to clear the mall in a hurry. Those hydraulic gates were the key to the operation: the key to bare safety, much less success.

No one seemed to be out, but Tyl could hear occasional shouts in the distance as well as the antiphonal roars from the plaza—though the latter were directed upward, into the sulphurous dawn, by the flood walls. Litter of all sorts splotched the pavement, waste and shattered valuables as well as a few bodies.

One of the crumpled bodies jumped up ahead of them. The drunk tottered backward when his foot slipped on the bottle which had put him there in the first place.

Tyl's point man fired a ten-shot burst—far too long— at the drunk. The bolts splashed all around the target, cyan flashes and the white blaze of lime burned out of the concrete. None of the rounds hit the intended victim.

A sergeant jumped to the shooter's side and slapped him hard on the helmet. "Cop-head!" he snarled. "Cop-head! Get your ass behind me. And if you shoot again without orders, you better have the muzzle in your mouth!"

The drunk scrambled in the general direction of the cathedral, stumbling and rolling on the ground to rise and stumble again. The air bit with the odors of ozone and quicklime.

The company shuffled onward with a squad leader in front.

"Blue Six to all Blue and Orange units," said Tyl's commo helmet. Desoix sounded tight, a message played ten percent faster than it'd been recorded. "We're moving into position—now."

The point man paused at the base of the ramp to the mall and the plaza's main stairs.

"Check your loads, boys," said Sergeant Major Scratchard over the unit push. Jack was back with the three squads of the second wave, but Tyl didn't expect him to stay there long when the shooting started.

"Sir," reported the point sergeant, using the command channel, "the gates are shut on this side."

"Orange Six to all Blue and Orange," Tyl ordered as he

ran the ten meters to where the non-com paused. "Don't bloody move. We got a problem."

The gates separating the mall from the west river drive were as massive and invulnerable as those facing the plaza itself.

They were closed, just as the point man had said.

Tyl ran up the ramp, his bandoliers clashing against one another. The slung sub-machinegun gouged his hip beneath the flare of his armor. The gates were solid, solid enough to shrug away tidal surges with more power than a battery of artillery.

There was no way one company without demolition charges or heavy weapons was going to force its way through.

The small vitril windows in the gate panels were too scarred and dirty to show more than hinted movement, but there was a speaker plate in one of the pillars. Nothing ventured. . . .

Tyl keyed the speaker and said, "Open these gates at once, in the name of Bishop Trimer!"

The crowd in the plaza cheered deafeningly, shaking the earth like a distant bomb blast.

Shadows, colors, shifted within the closed mall. The plate replied in the voice of Colonel Drescher, "Go away, little lapdog. The Executive Guard is neutral, as I told you. And this is where we choose to exercise our neutrality."

The crowd thundered, working itself into bloodthirsty enthusiasm.

Tyl turned his back on the reinforced concrete and touched his commo helmet. His troops were crouching, watching him. Those who wore their shields down had saffron bubbles for faces, painted by the glow which preceded the sun.

"Orange to Blue Six," Tyl said. "We're screwed. The Guards 're holding the mall and they got it shut up. We can't get in, and if we tried we'd bring the whole bunch down on us. Save what you can, buddy. Over."

He'd forgotten that Anne McGill had access to the circuit. Before Desoix could speak, her voice rang like shards of crystal through Tyl's helmet, saying, "The river level has dropped. You can go under the plaza on a barge and come up beneath the altar."

The cross on the cathedral dome was beginning to blaze with sunlight. McGill's angle was on the seafront. She couldn't see any of the troops, Tyl's or the pair of calliopes, and she wouldn't have understood a *bloody* thing if she had been able to watch them. Bloody woman, bloody planet. . . .

Bloody fool, Captain Tyl Koopman, to be standing here. Nobody he saw was moving except Scratchard, clumping up the ramp to his captain's side. If Ripper Jack were bothered by his knees or the doubled load of weaponry, there was no sign of it on his expectant face.

"Tyl, she's right," Desoix was saying. "Most of the louvers are still closed, so there's no risk of drifting out to sea, but the maintenance catwalks lead straight up to the control house. The altar."

"Roger on the river level," the sergeant major muttered with his lips alone. He must've spoken to the non-com on the levee, using one of the support frequencies so as not to tie up the command push.

Tyl looked up at the sky, bright and clear after a night that was neither.

"Tyl, we'll give the support we can," Desoix said. Both officers knew exactly what the change of plan would mean. They weren't going to be able to *talk* to the mob when they came up into the plaza. Desoix was apparently willing to go along with the change.

Wonder what the Colonel would say?

Colonel Hammer wasn't here. Tyl Koopman was, and he was ready to go along with it too. More fool him.

"Orange Six to all Orange personnel," he said on the unit push. "We're going to board the nearest barge and cut it loose so we drift to the dam at the other end of the plaza. . . ."

CHAPTER TWENTY-NINE

Some of the men were still scrambling aboard the barge, the second of the ten in line rather than the nearest, because it seemed less likely to scrape the whole distance along the concrete channel. Tyl didn't hear the order Jack Scratchard muttered into his commo helmet, but troopers standing by three of the four cables opened fire simultaneously.

Arm-thick ropes of woven steel parted in individual flashes. The barge sagged outward, its stern thumping the fenders of the vessel to port. Only the starboard bow line beside Tyl and the sergeant major held their barge against the current sucking them seaward.

The vertical lights on the walls, faintly green, merged as the channel drew outward toward the river's broad mouth and the dam closing it. They reflected from the water surface, now five meters beneath the concrete roof though it was still wet enough to scatter the light back again in turn.

"Hold one, Jack," Tyl said as he remembered there was another thing he needed to do before they slipped beneath the plaza. He keyed his helmet on the general interunit frequency and said, "Orange Six to all Orange personnel. I am ordering you to carry out an attack on the Bamberg citizens assembled in the plaza. Anyone who refuses to obey my order will be shot."

"Via!" cried one of the nearer soldiers. "I'm not afraid to go, sir!"

"Shut up, you fool!" snarled Ripper Jack. "Don't you understand? He's just covered your ass for afterwards!"

Tyl grinned bleakly at the sergeant major. Everybody seemed to have boarded the vessel, clinging to one another and balancing on the curves of hogsheads. "Cut 'er loose," he said quietly.

Scratchard's powergun blasted the remaining cable with a blue-green glare and a gout of white sparks whose trails lingered in the air as the barge lurched forward.

Their stern brushed along the portside barge until they drifted fully clear. The grind of metal against the polymer fenders was unpleasant. Friction spun them slowly counterclockwise until they swung free.

They continued to rotate for the full distance beneath the widening channel. One trooper vomited over his neighbor's backplate, though that was more likely nerves than the gentle, gently frustrating, motion.

Light coming through the louvered flood gates was already brighter than the greenish artificial sources on either wall. It was still diffuse sky-glow rather than the glare of direct sun, but the timing was going to be very close.

The barge grounded broadside with a crash that knocked down anybody who was standing. Perhaps because of their rotation, they'd remained pretty well centered in the channel. Individually and without waiting for orders, the troopers nearest the catwalk jumped to it and began to lower a floating stage like the one on the dam's exterior.

"They must 've heard something," Tyl grumbled. The variety of metallic sounds the barge made echoed like a boiler works among the planes of water and concrete. But as soon as the barge had slipped its lines, Tyl had been unable to hear even a whisper of what he knew was a sky-shattering clamor from the crowded plaza. Probably those above were equally insulated.

And anyway, it didn't matter now. Tyl pressed forward to the pontoon-mounted stage and the stairs of steel grating leading up to the open hatch of the control room. Tyl's rank took him through his jostling men, but it was all he could do not to use his elbows and gun butt to force his way faster.

He had to remember that he was commanding a unit, not throwing his life away for no reason he could explain even to himself. He had to act as if there were military purpose to what he was about to do.

Only two men could stand abreast on the punched-steel stair treads, and that by pressing hard against the rails. The control room was almost as tight, space for ten men being filled by a dozen. Tyl squeezed his way in, pausing in the hatchway. When he turned to address his troops, he found the sergeant major just behind him.

It would have been nice to organize this better; but it would have been nicer yet for somebody else to be doing it. Or no one at all.

"Stop bloody pushing? Tyl snapped on the unit frequency. Inside the control room, his signal would have been drunk by the meter-thick floor of the plaza. No wonder sound didn't get through.

Motion stopped, except for the gentle resilience of the barge's fenders against the closed floodgates.

"There's one door out into the plaza," Tyl said simply. "We'll deploy through it, spread out as much as possible. If it doesn't work out, try to withdraw toward the east or west stairs, maybe the calliopes can give us some cover. Do your jobs, boys, and we'll come through this all right."

Scratchard laid a hand on the captain's elbow, then keyed his own helmet and said, "Listen up. This is nothin' you don't know. There's a lot of people up there."

He pumped the muzzle of his sub-machinegun toward the ceiling. "So long as there's one of 'em standing, none of us 're safe. Got that?"

Heads nodded, hands stroked the iridium barrels of powerguns. Some of the recruits exchanged glances.

"Then let's go," the sergeant major said simply. He hefted himself toward the hatchway.

Tyl blocked him. "I want you below, Jack," he said. "Last man out."

Scratchard grinned and shook his head. "I briefed Kekkonan for that," he said.

Tyl hesitated.

Scratchard's face sobered. "Cap'n," he said. "This don't take good knees. What it takes, I got."

"All right, let's go," said Tyl very softly. "But I'm the first through the door."

He pushed his way to the door out onto the plaza, hearing the sergeant major wheezing a step behind.

———

CHAPTER THIRTY

Anne McGill couldn't see the sun, but the edges of the House of Grace gleamed as they bent light from the orb already over the horizon to the northeast.

The crucifix on the seafront altar was golden and dazzling. The sun had not yet reached it, but Bishop Trimer was too good a showman not to allow for that: the gilt symbol was equipped with a surface-discharge system like that which made expensive clothing shimmer. What was good enough for the Consistory Room was good enough for God—as he was represented here in Bamberg City.

"Anne, what's happening in the plaza?" said the tiny phone in her left ear. "Do you see any sign of the, of Koopman? Over."

She was kneeling as if in an attitude of prayer, though she faced the half-open window. There were scores of others in the cathedral this morning, but no one would disturb another penitent. Like her, they were wrapped in their cloaks and their prayers.

And perhaps all of their prayers were as complex and uncertain as those of Anne McGill, lookout for a pair of mercenary companies and mistress of a man whom she had prevented from retreating with her to a place of safety.

"Oh Charles," she whispered. "Oh Charles." Then she touched the control of her throat mike and said in a firm voice, "Chastain is kneeling before Bishop Trimer in front of the crucifix. He's putting a—I don't know, maybe the seal of office around his neck but I thought that was still in the Palace. . . ."

The finger-long directional microphone was clipped to the window transom which held it steady and unobtrusive. UDB stores included optical equipment as powerful and sophisticated as the audio pickup; but in use, an electronic telescope looked like exactly what it was—military hardware, and a dead giveaway of the person using it.

She had only her naked eyes. Though she squinted she couldn't be sure—

"The Slammers, curse it!" her lover's voice snapped in her ear. Charles' tongue suppressed the further words, "you idiot," but they were there in his tone. "Is there any sign of them?"

"No, no," she cried desperately. She'd forgotten to turn on her microphone. "Charles, no," she said with her thumb pressing the switch as if to crush it. "Chastain is rising and the crowd—"

Anne didn't see the door beneath the altar open the first time. There was only a flicker of movement in her peripheral vision, ajar and then closed.

Her subconscious was still trying to identify it when a dozen flashes lighted the front of the crowd facing the altar.

For another moment, she thought those were part of the celebration, but people were sprawling away from the flashes. A second later, the popping sound of the grenades going off reached her vantage point.

Men were spilling out of the altar building. The bolts from their weapons hurt Anne's eyes, even shielded by distance and full dawn.

"Charles!" she cried, careless now of who might hear her in the gallery. "It's started! They're—"

The air near the seafront echoed with a crashing hiss like that of a dragon striking. Anne McGill had never heard anything like it before. She didn't know that it was a calliope firing—but she knew that it meant death.

Buildings hid her view of the impact zone at the west stairhead of the plaza, but some of the debris flung a hundred meters in the air could still be identified as parts of human bodies.

CHAPTER THIRTY-ONE

When the grenades burst, Scratchard jerked the metal door open again—a millisecond before a slow fuse detonated the last of their greeting cards. A scrap of glass-fiber shrapnel drew a line across the back of Tyl's left thumb.

He didn't notice it. He was already shooting from the hip at the first person he saw as he swung through the doorway, a baton-waving orderly whose face was almost as white as his robe except where blood spattered both of them.

Tyl's target was a meter and a half away from his gun muzzle. He missed. The red cape and shoulder of a woman beside the orderly exploded in a cyan flash.

The orderly swung his baton in desperation, but he was already dead. Jack Scratchard put a burst into his face before pointing his sub-machinegun at the group on the altar above and behind them. Trimer flattened, carrrying Thom Chastain with him, but blue-green fire flicked the chests of both gang bosses.

Tyl hadn't appreciated the noise. It beat on him, a pressure squeezing him into his armor and engulfing the usual *thump!* of his bolts heating the air like miniature lightning. He butted his weapon firmly against his shoulder and fired three times to clear the area to his right.

The targets fell. Their eyes were still startled and blinking, though the 2 CM bolts had scooped their chests into fire and a sludge of gore.

Tyl strode onward, making room for the troopers behind him as he'd planned, as he'd ordered in some distant other universe.

An army officer leaped from the altar with a pistol in his hand, either seeking shelter in the crowd or fleeing Scratchard's quick gun in blind panic. The Bamberg soldier doubled up as fate carried him past Tyl's muzzle and reflex squeezed the powergun's trigger.

Short range but a nice crossing shot. Tyl was fine and the noise, the shouting, was better protection than his helmet and clamshell. But there were too many of the bastards, a mass like the sea itself, and Tyl was all alone in a tide that would wash over him and his men no matter what they—

One calliope, then the other, opened fire. Not even

crowd noise and the adrenalin coursing through his blood could keep the Slammers officer from noticing that.

He stepped forward, his right shoulder against the altar building to keep him from slipping. Each shot was aimed, and none of them missed.

In a manner of speaking, Tyl Koopman's face wore a smile.

CHAPTER THIRTY-TWO

The bollards at the stairhead were hidden by the units on guard, thugs wearing the colors of both factions and a detachment of hospital orderlies

There were at least fifty heavily armed men and women in plain sight of Desoix's calliope—and it was only a matter of moments before one of them would turn from the ceremony and look up the street.

There weren't many options available then.

"Is there any sign of them?" Desoix shouted to—at his mistress as she nattered on about what Trimer was using as he swore in his stooge as President.

Lachere was twisted around in the driver's saddle, peering back at his lieutenant and chewing the end of a cold cigar, a habit he'd picked up in the months they'd been stationed here. He didn't look worried, but Senter had enough fear in his expression for both clerks as he stared at Desoix's profile from his station at the loading console.

"Charles!" cried the voice he had let through to him again for necessity. "It's—"

Desoix had already heard the muffled exclamation points of the grenades.

"Blue Six to Blue Three," he said, manually cutting away to the unit frequency. "Open fire."

As his mouth voiced the final flat syllable, his right foot rocked forward on the firing pedal. Traversing left to right,

Desoix swept the stairhead clear of all obstructions with the eight ravening barrels of his calliope.

The big weapon was intended for computer directed air defense. Under manual control, its sights were only a little more sophisticated than those of shoulder fired powerguns: a hologrammatic sight picture with a bead in the center to mark the point of impact.

Nothing more was required.

Several of the guards turned when the grenades went off, instinctively looking for escape and instead seeing behind them the calliope's lowered muzzles. One of the orderlies got off a burst with his sub-machinegun.

The bullets missed by a hundred meters in the two blocks they were meant to travel. Concrete, steel, and flesh—most particularly flesh—vaporized as the calliope chewed across the stairhead in a three-second burst.

Desoix switched to intercom with the hand he didn't need for the moment on the elevation control and said, "Lachere, advance toward the stair-head at a—"

Faces appeared around the seawall just north of where the bollards had been before the gun burned them away. The high-intensity 3 CM ammunition had shattered concrete at the start of the burst before Desoix traversed away. His right hand rolled forward on the twist-grip, reversing the direction in which the barrel array rotated on its gimbals.

More of the wall disintegrated in cyan light and the white glare of lime burned free of the concrete by enormously concentrated energy. Most of the rioters had time to duck back behind the wall before the second burst raked it.

The wall didn't save them. Multiple impacts tore it apart and then flash-heated the water in their own bodies into steam explosions.

Beneath Desoix, the skirts of the calliope's plenum chamber dragged the pavement. Air had enough mass to recoil when it was heated to a plasma and expelled from the eight tubes as the gun fired. Lachere drove forward, correcting inexpertly against the calliope's pitch and yaw.

Gunfire was a blue-green shield against the roar from

the plaza, but in the moments between bursts the mob's voice asserted itself over the numbness of ringing breech blocks and slamming air. The stairhead was now within a hundred meters as the gun drove onward. There was a haze over the target area—steam and dust, burnt lime and burning bodies.

Desoix's faceshield protected him from the sun-hot flash of his guns. Events, thundering forward as implacably as an avalanche, shielded him from awareness that would have been as devastating to him as being blinded.

With no target but the roiling haze, Desoix triggered another burst when they were ten meters from the stairhead. Fragments blown clear by the impacts proved that there had been people sheltering beneath eye level but accessible to the upper pair of gun tubes.

"Sir?" a voice demanded, Lachere slowing and ready to ground the vehicle before they lurched over the scars where the bollards had been and their bow tilted down the steps.

"Go!" Desoix shouted, knowing that the plenum chamber would spill its air in the angle of the stair treads and that their unaided fans would never be able to lift the calliope away once they had committed.

Koopman and his company of Slammers weren't going anywhere either, unless they all succeeded in the most certain and irrevocable way possible.

The stench of ozone and ruin boiled out from beneath the drive fans an instant before the calliope rocked forward. Gravity aided its motion for an instant before the friction of steel against stone grounded the skirts. The plaza was a sea of faces with a roar like the surf.

Bullets rang off the hull and splashed the glowing iridium of one port-side barrel. The doors of the mall at the head of the main stairs were open toward the plaza. Men there were firing assault rifles at the calliope. Some of them were either good or very lucky.

Desoix rotated his gun carriage.

"Sir!" Senter cried with his helmet against the lieutenant's. "Those aren't the mob! They're the Guard!"

"Feed your guns, soldier!" said Charles Desoix. The open flood gates filled his sight hologram.

He rocked the firing pedal down and began to traverse his target in a blaze of light.

CHAPTER THIRTY-THREE

Tyl's index finger tightened. The gunstock pummeled his shoulder. The center of his faceshield went momentarily black as it mirrored away the flash that would otherwise have blinded him.

A finger of plastic flipped up into his sight picture, indicating that he'd just fired the last charge in his weapon. He reached for another magazine.

A hospital orderly stopped trying to claw through the mass of other panicked humans and turned to face Tyl. He was less than ten meters away and held a pistol.

Tyl raised the tube of 2 CM ammunition to the loading gate in the forestock and burned the nail and third knuckle of all the fingers on his left hand. He'd already put several magazines through the powergun, so its barrel was white hot.

He dropped the magazine. The orderly shot him in the center of the chest.

There was no sound any more in the plaza. Tyl could see everything down to the last hair on the moustache of the orderly collapsing around a bolt from somebody else's powergun. His armor spread the bullet's impact, but it felt as if they'd driven a tank over his chest. Maybe if he didn't move. . . .

The calliope which was canted down the west staircase opened fire again.

Only three of the eight barrels were live at the moment. Individual bolts made a thump as ionized air ripped from the barrel; they crossed the plaza a few meters over Tyl's head as a microsecond *hiss!* and a flash of light so saturated that it seemed palpable.

Everything the bolts hit was disintegrated with a crash sharper than a bomb going off, solids converted to gas and plasma as suddenly as the light-swift bursts of energy had snapped through the air. The plaza's concrete flooring gouted in explosions of dazzling white—

But the crowd was packed too thickly for that to happen often. The calliope's angle allowed its crew to rake the mob from above. Each 3 CM bolt hit like the hoof of a horse galloping over soft ground, hurling spray and bits of the footing in every direction before lifting to hammer the surface again.

Bodies crumpled in windrows. Screaming rioters climbed the fallen on their way toward the main stairs, already packed with their fellows. The guns continued to fire.

"If I can hear, I can move," Tyl said, mouthing the words because that *was* his first movement since the bullet hit him.

He knelt to pick up the magazine he had dropped. The pain that flooded him, hot needles being jabbed into his whole chest, made him drop the empty gun instead.

He couldn't breathe. He didn't fall down because his muscles were locked in a web of flesh surrounding a center of pulsing red agony.

The spasm passed.

Tyl's troopers were spread in a ragged semicircle, centering on the building from which they'd deployed. He was near the east stairs; the treads were covered with bodies.

Rebels had been shot in the back as they tried to run from the soldiers and the blue-green scintillance of hand weapons. If they reached the top of the stairs, Gun Three on the seafront hurled them back as a puree and a scattering of fragments.

The west stairs were relatively empty, because the mob had time to clear it in the face of the calliope staggering toward them. They died on the plaza floor, because they'd run toward the debouching infantry; but the steps gleamed white in the sunlight and provided a pure contrast to the bodies and garments crumpled everywhere else in muddy profusion.

Tyl left the 2 CM weapon where he'd dropped it; he
raised his sub-machinegun. It felt light by contrast with
the thick iridium barrel of the shoulder weapon, but he
still had trouble aiming.

It was hot, and Tyl was as thirsty as he ever remembered being. Ozone had lifted all the mucus away from
the membranes of his nose and throat. The mordant gas
was concentrated by shooting in the enclosed wedge of the
plaza. The skin of Tyl's face and hands prickled as if sunburned.

He aimed at a face and missed high, the barrel wob-
bling, sending the round into the back of somebody a
hundred meters away on the main stairs.

He lowered the muzzle and fired again, fired again, fired
again.

Single shots, aimed at anyone who looked toward him
instead of trying to get away. Second choice for targets were
the white robes of orderlies, most of whom had been
armed—though few enough had the discipline to stand in
chaos against the mercenaries' armor and overwhelming
firepower.

Third choice was whoever filled the sight picture next.
None of the mercenaries were safe so long as one of the
others was standing.

The calliope opened up again. Desoix had unjammed
and reloaded six of the barrels. A thick line staggered
through the mob like the track of a tornado across a corn
field.

Tyl fired; fired again; fired again. . . .

CHAPTER THIRTY-FOUR

It was very quiet.

Desoix watched the men from Gun Three's doubled crew
as they picked their way across the plaza at his orders. Sergeant Blaney was leading the quartet himself. They were

carrying their sub-machineguns ready and moving with a gingerly awkwardness, trying to avoid stepping in the carnage.

Nobody could get down the east stairs without smearing his boots to the ankles with blood.

"They could hurry up with the water," Lachere muttered.

"They didn't see it happen," Desoix said. He lay across the firing console, his chin on his hands and his elbows on the control grips he no longer needed to twist.

He closed his eyes for a moment instead of rubbing them.

Desoix's hands and face, like those of his men, were black with iridium burned from the calliope's bores by the continuous firing. The vapor had condensed in the air and settled as dust over everything within ten meters of the muzzles. Rubbing his eyes before he washed would drive the finely-divided metal under the lids, into the orbits.

Desoix kept reminding himself that it would matter to him some day, when he wasn't so tired.

"They just shot when somebody ran up the stairs and gave them a target," he continued in the croak that was all the voice remaining to him until Blaney arrived with the water. "It wasn't like—"

He wanted to raise his arm to indicate the plaza's carpet of the dead, but waggling an index finger was as much as he had need or energy to accomplish. "It wasn't what we had, all targets, and it. . . ."

Desoix tried to remember how he would have felt if he had come upon this scene an hour earlier. He couldn't, so he let his voice trail off.

A lot of them must have gotten out when somebody opened the gates at either end of the mall. Desoix had tried to avoid raking the mall and the main stairs. The mercenaries had to end the insurrection and clear the plaza for their own safety, but the civilians swept out by fear were as harmless as their fellows who filled the sight picture as the calliope coughed and traversed.

There'd been just the one long burst which cleared the mall of riflemen.

Cleared it of life.

"Here you go, sir," said Blaney, skipping up the last few steps with a four-liter canteen and hopping onto the deck of the calliope.

"Took yer bloody time," Lachere repeated as he snatched the canteen another of the newcomers offered him. He began slurping the water down so greedily that he choked and sprayed a mouthful out his nostrils.

Senter was drinking also. He hunched down behind the breeches of the guns he had been feeding, so that he could not see any of what surrounded the calliope. Even so, the clerk's eyelids were pressed tightly together except for brief flashes that showed his dilated pupils.

"Ah, where's Major Borodin, sir?" Blaney asked.

Desoix closed his eyes again, luxuriating in the feel of warm water swirling in his mouth.

Gun Three had full supplies for its double crew before the shooting started. Desoix hadn't thought to load himself and his two clerks with water before they set out.

He hadn't been planning; just reacting, stimulus by stimulus, to a situation over which he had abdicated conscious control.

"The Major's back at the Palace," Desoix said. "President Delcorio told me he wanted a trustworthy officer with him, so I commanded the field operations myself."

He didn't care about himself any more. He stuck to the story he had arranged with Delcorio because it was as easy to tell as the truth, . . . and because Desoix still felt a rush of loyalty to his battery commander.

They'd succeeded, and Major Borodin could have his portion of the triumph if he wanted it.

Charles Desoix wished it had been him, not Borodin, who had spent the last two hours locked in a storeroom in the Palace. But his memory would not permit him to think that, even as a fantasy.

"Blaney," he said aloud. "I'm putting you in command of this gun until we get straightened around. I'm going down to check with Captain Koopman." He nodded toward the cluster of gray and khaki soldiers sprawled near the altar.

"Ah, sir?" Blaney said in a nervous tone. Desoix paused after swinging his leg over the gunner's saddle. He shrugged, as much response as he felt like making at the moment.

"Sir, we started taking sniper fire, had two guys hurt," Blaney went on. "We—I laid the gun on the hospital, put a burst into it to, you know, get their attention. Ah, the sniping stopped."

"Via, you really did, didn't you?" said the officer, amazed that he hadn't noticed the damage before.

Gun Three had a flat angle on the south face of the glittering building. Almost a third of the vitril panels on that side were gone in a raking slash from the ground floor to the twentieth. The bolts wouldn't have penetrated the hospital, though the Lord knew what bits of the shattered windows had done when they flew around inside.

Charles Desoix began to laugh. He choked and had to grip the calliope's chassis in order to keep from falling over. He hadn't been sure that he would ever laugh again.

"Sergeant," he said, shutting his eyes because Blancy's stricken face would set him off again if he watched it. "You're afraid you're in trouble because of *that*?"

He risked a look at Blaney. The sergeant was nodding blankly.

Desoix gripped his subordinate's hand. "Don't worry," he said. "Don't. I'll just tell them to put it on my account."

He took the canteen with him as he walked down the stairs toward Tyl Koopman. Halfway down, he stumbled when he slipped on a dismembered leg.

That set him laughing again.

CHAPTER THIRTY-FIVE

"Got twelve could use help," said the sergeant major as Tyl shuddered under the jets of topical anesthetic he was spraying onto his own chest.

Scratchard frowned and added, "Maybe you too, hey?"

"Via, I'm fine," Tyl said, trying to smooth the grimace that wanted to twist his face awry. "No dead?"

He looked around sharply and immediately wished he hadn't tried to move quite that fast.

Tyl's ceramic breastplate had stopped the bullet and spread its impact across the whole inner surface of the armor. That was survivable; but now, with the armor and his tunic stripped off, Tyl's chest was a symphony of bruising. His ribs and the seams of his tunic pockets were emphasized in purple, and the flesh between those highlights was a dull yellow-gray of its own.

Scratchard shrugged. "Krasinski took one in the face," he said. "Had 'er shield down too, but when your number's up. . . ."

Tyl sprayed anesthetic. The curse that ripped out of his mouth could have been directed at the way the mist settled across him and made the bruised flesh pucker as it chilled.

"Timmons stood on a grenade," Scratchard continued, squatting beside his captain. "Prob'ly his own. Told 'em not to screw with grenades after we committed, but they never listen, not when it gets . . ."

Scratchard's fingers were working with the gun he now carried, a slug-firing machine pistol. The magazine lay on the ground beside him. The trigger group came out, then the barrel tilted from the receiver at the touch of the sergeant major's experienced fingers.

Jack wasn't watching his hands. His eyes were open and empty, focused on the main stairs because there were no fallen troopers there. They'd been his men too.

"One a' the recruits," Scratchard continued quietly, "he didn't want to go up the ladder."

Tyl looked at the non-com.

Scratchard shrugged again. "Kekkonan shot him. Wasn't a lotta time to discuss things."

"Kekkonan due another stripe?" Tyl asked.

"After this?" Scratchard replied, his voice bright with unexpected emotion. "We're *all* due bloody something, sir!"

His face blanked. His fingers began to reassemble the

gun he'd picked up when he'd fired all the ammunition for both the powerguns he carried.

Tyl looked at their prisoners, the half dozen men who'd survived when Jack sprayed the group on the altar. Now they clustered near the low building, under the guns of a pair of troopers who'd been told to guard them.

The soldiers were too tired to pay much attention. The prisoners were too frightened to need guarding at all.

Thom Chastain still wore a gold-trimmed scarlet robe. A soldier had ripped away the chain and pendant Tyl remembered vaguely from earlier in the morning. Thom smiled like a porcelain doll, a hideous contrast with the tears which continued to shiver down his cheeks.

The tears were particularly noticeable because one of the gang bosses beside Thom on the altar had been shot in the neck. He'd been very active in his dying, painting everyone nearby with streaks of bright, oxygen-rich blood. The boy's tears washed tracks in the blood.

Bishop Trimer and three lesser priests stood a meter from the Chastains—and as far apart as turned backs and icy expressions could make them.

Father Laughlin was trying to hunch himself down to the height of other men. His white robes dragged the ground when he forgot to draw them up with his hands; their hem was bloody.

The prisoners weren't willing to sit down the way the Slammers did. But *nobody* was used to a scene like this.

"I never saw so many bodies," said Charles Desoix.

"Yeah, me too," Tyl agreed.

He hadn't seen the UDB officer walk up beside him. His eyes itched. He supposed there was something wrong with his peripheral vision from the ozone or the actinics—despite his faceshield.

"Water?" Desoix offered.

"Thanks," Tyl said, accepting the offer though water still sloshed in the canteen on his own belt. He drank and paused, then sipped again.

Where the calliope had raked the mob, corpses lay in rows like flotsam thrown onto the strand by a storm.

Otherwise, the half of the plaza nearer the sea front was strewn rather than carpeted with bodies. You could walk that far and, if you were careful, step only on concrete.

Bloody concrete.

Where the plaza narrowed toward the main stairs, there was no longer room even for the corpses. They were piled one upon another . . . five in a stack . . . a ramp ten meters deep, rising at the same angle as the stairs and composed of human flesh compressed by the weight of more humans—each trying to escape by clambering over his fellows, each dying in turn as the guns continued to fire.

The stench of scattered viscera was a sour miasma as the sun began to warm the plaza.

"How many, d'ye guess?" Tyl asked as he handed back the canteen.

He was sure his voice was normal, but he felt his body begin to shiver uncontrollably. It was the drugs, it *had* to be the anesthetic.

"Twenty thousand, thirty thousand," Desoix said. He cleared his throat, but his voice broke anyway as he tried to say, "They did, they . . ."

Desoix bent his head. When he lifted it again, he said in a voice as clear as the glitter of tears in his eyes, "I think as many were crushed trying to get away as we killed ourselves. But we killed enough."

Something moved at the head of the main stairs. Tyl aimed the sub-machinegun he'd picked up when he stood. Pain filled his torso like the fracture lines in breaking glass, but he didn't shudder any more. The sight picture was razor sharp.

An air car with the gold and crystal markings of the Palace slid through the mall and cruised down the main stairs. The vehicle was being driven low and slow, just above the surface, because surprising the troops here meant sudden death.

Even laymen could see that.

Tyl lowered his weapon, wondering what would have happened if he'd taken up the last trigger pressure and spilled John and Eunice Delcorio onto the bodies of so many of their opponents.

The car's driver and the man beside him were palace servants, both in their sixties. They looked out of place, even without the pistols in issue holsters belted over their blue livery.

Major Borodin and Colonel Drescher rode in the middle pair of seats, ahead of the presidential couple.

The battery commander was the first to get out when the car grounded beside the mercenary officers. The electronic piping of Borodin's uniform glittered brighter than sunlight on the metal around him. He blinked at his surroundings, at the prisoners. Then he nodded to Desoix and said, "Lieutenant, you've, ah—carried out your orders in a satisfactory fashion."

Desoix saluted. "Thank you, sir," he said in a voice as dead as the stench of thirty thousand bodies.

Colonel Drescher followed Borodin, moving like a marionette with a broken wire. The flap of his holster was closed, but there was no gun inside. One of the Guard commander's polished boots was missing. He held the sole of the bare foot slightly above the concrete, where it would have been if he were fully dressed.

President Delcorio stepped from the vehicle and handed out his wife as if they were at a public function. Both of them were wearing cloth of gold, dazzling even though the cat's fans had flung up bits of the carnage as it carried them through the plaza.

"Gentlemen," Delcorio said, nodding to Tyl and Desoix. His throat hadn't been wracked by the residues of battle, so his voice sounded subtly wrong in its smooth normalcy.

Pedro Delcorio was walking to join his uncle from the control room beneath the altar. He carried a pistol in his right hand. The bore of the powergun was bright and not scarred by use.

The President and his wife approached the prisoners. Major Borodin fluffed the thighs of his uniform; Drescher stood on one foot, his eyes looking out over the channel.

President Delcorio stared at the Bishop. The other

priests hunched away, as if Delcorio's gaze were wind-blown sleet.

Trimer faced him squarely, The Bishop was a short man and slightly built even in the bulk of his episcopal garments, but he was very much alive. Looking at him, Tyl remembered the faint glow that firelight had washed across the eyes of Trimmer's face carven on the House of Grace.

"Bishop," said John Delcorio. "I'm so glad my men were able to rescue you from this—" his foot delicately gestured toward the nearest body, a woman undressed by the grenade blast that killed her "—rabble."

Father Laughlin straightened so abruptly that he almost fell when he kicked the pile of communications and data transfer equipment which his two fellows had piled on the ground. No one had bothered to strip the priests of their hardware, but they had done so themselves as quickly as they were able.

Perhaps the priests felt they could distance themselves from what had gone before . . . or what they expected to come later.

"Pres . . ." said Bishop Trimer cautiously. His voice was oil smooth—until it cracked. "President?"

"Yes, very glad," Delcorio continued. "I think it must be that the Christ denying elements were behind the riot. I'm sure they took you prisoner when they heard you had offered all the assets of the Church to support our crusade."

Laughlin threw his hands to his face, covering his mouth and a look of horror.

"Yes, all Church personalty," said Trimer. "Except what is needed for the immediate sustenance of the Lord's servants."

"All assets, real and personal, is what I'd heard," said the President. His voice was flat. The index finger of his right hand was rising as if to make a gesture, a cutting motion.

"Yes, personal property and all the estates of the Church outside of Bamberg City itself," said Bishop Trimer. He thrust out his chin, looking even more like the bas relief on the shot scarred hospital.

Delcorio paused, then nodded. "Yes," he said. "That's what I understood. We'll go back to—"

Eunice Delcorio looked at Tyl. "You," she said in a clear voice, ignoring her husband and seemingly ignoring the fact that he had spoken. "Shoot these two."

She pointed toward the Chastains.

Tyl raised his sub-machinegun's muzzle skyward and stepped toward the President's wife.

"Sir!" shouted Ripper Jack Scratchard, close enough that his big hand gripped Tyl's shoulder. "Don't!"

Tyl pulled free. He took Eunice's right hand in his left and pressed her palm against the grip of the sub-machinegun. He forced her fingers closed. "Here," he said. "You do it."

He hadn't thought he was shouting, but he must have been from the way all of them stared at him, their faces growing pale.

He spun Eunice around to face the ramp of bodies. She was a solid woman and tried to resist, but that was nothing to him now. "It's easy," he said. "See how bloody easy it is?

"*Do you see?*"

A shot cracked. He *had* been shouting. The muzzle blast didn't seem loud at all.

Tyl turned. Scratchard fired his captured weapon again. Richie Chastain screamed and stumbled across his twin; Thom was already down with a hole behind his right ear and a line of blood from the corner of his mouth.

Scratchard fired twice more as the boy thrashed on his belly. The second bullet punched through the chest cavity and ricocheted from the ground with a hum of fury.

Tyl threw his gun **down. He turned** and tried to walk away, but he couldn't see anything. He would have fallen except that Scratchard took one of his arms and Desoix the other, holding him and standing between him and the Delcorios.

"Bishop Trimer," he heard the President saying. "Will you adjourn with us, please, to the Palace." There was no question in the tone. "We have some details to work out, and I think we'll be more comfortable there, though my servant situation is a—"

Tyl turned.

"Wait," he said. Everyone was watching him. There was a red blotch on the back of Eunice's hand where he'd held her, but he was as controlled as the tide, now. "I want doctors for my men."

He lifted his hand toward the House of Grace, glorying in the pain of moving. "You got a whole hospital, there. I want doctors, *now*, and I want every one of my boys treated like he was Christ himself. Understood?"

"Of course, of course," said Father Laughlin in the voice Tyl remembered from the Consistory Meeting.

The big priest turned to the man who had been wearing the commo set and snarled, "Well, get *on* it, Ryan. You heard the man!"

Ryan knelt and began speaking into the handset, glancing sometimes up at the hospital's shattered facade and sometimes back at the Slammers captain. The only color on the priest's face was a splotch of someone else's blood.

Trimer walked to the air car, arm in arm with President Delcorio.

Borodin and Drescher had already boarded. Neither of them would let their eyes focus on anything around them. When Pedro Delcorio squeezed in between them, the two officers made room without comment.

Father Laughlin would have followed the Bishop, but Eunice Delcorio glanced at his heavy form and gestured dismissingly. Laughlin watched the car lift into a hover; then, sinking his head low, he strode in the direction of the east stairs.

Tyl Koopman stood between his sergeant major and the UDB lieutenant. He was beginning to shiver again.

"What's it mean, d'ye suppose?" he whispered in the direction of the main stairs.

"Mean?" said Charles Desoix dispassionately. "It means that John Delcorio is President—President in more than name—for the first time. It means that he really has the resources to prosecute his crusade, the war on Two, to a successful conclusion. I doubt that would have been possible without the financial support of the Church."

"But who *cares*!" Tyl shouted. "D'ye mean we've got jobs for the next two years? Who bloody cares? Somebody'd 've hired us, you know that!"

"It means," said Jack Scratchard, "that we're alive and they're dead. That's all it means, sir."

"It's *got* to mean more than that," Tyl whispered.

But as he looked at the heaps and rows of bodies, tens of thousands of dead human beings stiffening in the sun, he couldn't put any real belief into the words.

CHAPTER THIRTY-SIX

The Slammers were gone.

Ambulances had carried their wounded off, each with a guard of other troopers ready to add a few more bodies to the day's bag if any of Trimer's men seemed less than perfectly dedicated to healing the wounded. Desoix thought he'd heard the sergeant major say something about bivouacking in the House of Grace, but he hadn't been paying much attention.

There was nothing here for him. He ought to leave himself.

Desoix turned. Anne McGill was walking toward him. She had thrown off the cloak that covered her in the cathedral and was wearing only a dress of white chiffon like the one in which she had greeted him the day before.

Her face was set. She was moving very slowly, because she would not look down and her feet kept brushing the things that she refused to see.

Desoix began to tremble. He had unlatched his body armor, but he still had it on. The halves rattled against one another as he watched the woman approach.

There was nothing there. There couldn't be anything left there now.

It didn't matter. That was only one of many things which had died this morning. No doubt he'd feel it was an unimportant one in later years.

Anne put her arms around him, crushing her cheek against his though he was black with iridium dust and dried blood. "I'm so sorry," she whispered. "Charles, I—we . . . Charles, I love you."

As if love could matter now.

Desoix put his arms around her, squeezing gently so that the edges of his armor would not bite into her soft flesh.

Love mattered, even now.

Afterword to
Counting the Cost

HOW THEY GOT THAT WAY

I gained my first real insight into tanks when I was about eight years old and the local newspaper ran a picture of one, an M41 Walker Bulldog, on the front page.

The M41 isn't especially big. It's longer than the Studebaker my family had at the time but still a couple feet shorter than the 1960 Plymouth we owned later. At nine feet high and eleven feet wide, the tank was impressive but not really out of automotive scale.

What was striking about it was the way it had flattened a parked car when the tank's driver goofed during a Christmas Parade in Chicago. That picture proved to me that the power and lethality of a tank are out of all proportion to the size of the package.

I learned a lot more about tanks in 1970 when I was assigned to the 11th Armored Cavalry Regiment in Viet Nam.

Normally, interrogators like me were in slots at brigade level or higher. The Eleventh Cav was unusual in that each of its three squadrons in the field had a Battalion Intelligence Collection Center—pronounced like the pen—of four to six men. After a week or two at the rear echelon headquarters of my unit, I requested assignment to a BICC. A few weeks later, I joined Second Squadron in Cambodia.

Our BICC had a variety of personal and official gear— the tent was our largest item—which fitted into a trailer about the size of a middling-big U-Haul-It. We didn't have a *vehicle* of our own. When the squadron moved (as it generally did every week or two), the trailer was towed by one of the Headquarters Troop tracks; and we, the personnel, were split up as crew among the fighting vehicles.

The tanks were M48s, already obsolescent because the 90 MM main gun couldn't be trusted to penetrate the armor of new Soviet tanks. That wasn't a problem for us, since most of the opposition wore black pajamas and sandals cut from tire treads.

M48s have a normal complement of four men, but that was exceptionally high in the field. In one case, I rode as loader on a tank which would have been down to two men—driver and commander—without me. The Eleventh Cav was at almost double its official (Table of Organization) strength, but the excess personnel didn't trickle far enough from headquarters to reach the folks who were expected to do the actual fighting.

While I was there, a squadron in the field operated as four linked entities. Squadron headquarters (including the BICC) was a firebase, so called because the encampment included a battery of self-propelled 155 MM howitzers—six guns if none were deadlined.

Besides How Battery, the firebase included Headquarters Troop with half a dozen Armored Cavalry Assault Vehicles— ACAVs. These were simply M113 armored personnel carriers modified at the factory into combat vehicles. Each had a little steel cupola around a fifty caliber machinegun and a pintle-mounted M60 machinegun (7.62 MM) on either flank.

There were also a great number of other vehicles at the firebase: armored personnel carriers modified into trucks, high-sided command vehicles, and mobile flamethrowers (Zippos); maintenance vehicles with cranes to lift out and replace engines in the field; and a platoon of combat engineers with a modified M48 tank as well as the bulldozers that turned up an earthen berm around the whole site.

Apart from these headquarters units, the squadron was made up of a company of (nominally) seventeen M48 tanks; and three line troops with twelve ACAVs and six Sheridans apiece. The Sheridan is a deathtrap with a steel turret, an aluminum hull, and a 152 MM cannon whose ammunition generally caught fire if the vehicle hit a forty pound mine.

Either a line troop or the tank company laagered at the firebase at night for security. The other three formed separate night defensive positions within fire support range of How Battery.

I talked with a lot of people in the field, and I got a good firsthand look at the way an armored regiment conducts combat operations.

When I got back to the World, I resumed my hobby of writing fantasies. I'd sold three stories to August Derleth in the past; now I sold him a fourth, set in the late Roman Empire. Mr. Derleth paid for that story the day before he died.

With him gone, there was no market for what I was writing: short stories in the heroic fantasy subgenre. I kept writing them anyway, becoming more and more frustrated that they didn't sell. (I wasn't real tightly wrapped back then. It was a while before I realized just how screwy I was.)

Fortunately, writer friends in Chapel Hill, Manly Wade Wellman and Karl Edward Wagner, suggested that I use Viet Nam as a setting. I tried it with immediate success, selling a horror fantasy to F&SF and a science fiction story to Analog.

I still had a professional problem. There were very few stories that someone with my limited skills could tell which were SF or fantasy, and which directly involved the Eleventh Cav. I decided to get around the issue by telling a

...that was SF because the characters used ray guns ...stad of M16s . . . but was otherwise true, the way it had been described to me by the men who'd been there.

The story was "The Butcher's Bill," and for it I created a mercenary armored regiment called Hammer's Slammers.

The hardware was easy. I'd spent enough time around combat vehicles to have a notion of their strengths and weaknesses. Hammer's vehicles were designed around the M48s and ACAVs I'd ridden, with some of the most glaring faults eliminated.

All the vehicles in the field with the Eleventh Cav were track laying; that is, they had caterpillar treads instead of wheels. This was necessary because we never encamped on surfaced roads. Part of any move, even for headquarters units, was across stretches of jungle cleared minutes before by bulldozers fitted with Rome Plow blades.

The interior of a firebase was also bulldozed clear. Rain turned the bare soil either gooey or the consistency of wet soap. In both cases, it was impassable for wheeled vehicles. Our daily supplies came in by helicopter.

Tracks were absolutely necessary; and they were an absolute curse for the crewmen who had to maintain them.

Jungle soils dry to a coarse, gritty stone that abrades the tracks as they churn it up. When tracks wear, they loosen the way a bicycle chain does. To steer a tracked vehicle, you brake one tread while the other continues to turn. If the tracks are severely worn, you're certain to throw one.

If they're not worn, you may throw one anyway.

Replacing a track in the field means the crew has to break the loop; drive off it with the road wheels and the good track while another vehicle stretches the broken track; reverse onto the straightened track, hand feeding the free end up over the drive sprocket and along the return rollers; and then mate the ends into a loop again.

You may very well throw the same track ten minutes later.

Because of that problem (and suspension problems. Want to guess how long torsion bars last on a fifty ton tank bouncing over rough terrain?) I decided my supertanks had to be air cushion vehicles. That would be practical only if fuel supply weren't a problem, so that the fans could be powerful enough to keep the huge mass stable even though it didn't touch the ground.

I'm a writer, not an engineer. I didn't have any difficulty in giving my tanks and combat cars (ACAVs with energy weapons) the fusion power plants without which they'd be useless.

Armament required the same sort of decision. Energy weapons have major advantages over projectile weapons; but although tanks may some day mount effective lasers, I don't think an infantryman will ever be able to carry one. I therefore postulated guns that fired bolts of plasma liberated—somehow—from individual cartridges.

That took care of the hardware. The organization was basically that of the Eleventh Cav, with a few changes for the hell of it.

The unit itself was *not* based on any US unit with which I'm familiar. Its model was the French Foreign Legion; more precisely, the French Foreign Legion serving in Viet Nam just after World War Two—when most of its personnel were veterans of the SS who'd fled from Germany ahead of the Allied War Crimes Commission.

The incident around which I plotted "The Butcher's Bill" was the capture of Snuol the day before I arrived in Cambodia. That was the only significant fighting during the invasion of Cambodia, just as Snuol was the only significant town our forces reached.

G, one of the line troops, entered Snuol first. There was a real street, lined with stucco-faced shops instead of the grass huts on posts in the farming hamlets of the region. The C-100 AntiAircraft Company, a Viet Cong unit, was defending the town with a quartet of fifty-one caliber machineguns.

A fifty-one cal could put its rounds through an ACAV the long way, and the aluminum hull of a Sheridan wasn't much more protection. Before G Troop could get out, the concealed guns had destroyed one of either type of vehicle.

The squadron commander responded by sending in H Company, his tanks.

The eleven M48s rolled down the street in line ahead. The first tank slanted its main gun to the right side of the street, the second to the left, and so on. Each tank fired a round of canister or shrapnel into every structure that slid past the muzzle of its 90 MM gun.

On the other side of Snuol, they formed up to go back again. There wasn't any need to do that.

The VC had opened fire at first. The crews of the M48s didn't know that, because the noise inside was so loud that the clang of two-ounce bullets hitting the armor was inaudible. Some of the slugs flattened and were there on the fenders to be picked up afterwards. The surviving VC fled, leaving their guns behind.

There was a little looting—a bottle of whiskey, a sack of ladies' slippers, a step through Honda (which was flown back to Quan Loi in a squadron helicopter). But for all practical purposes, Snuol ceased to have human significance the moment H Company blasted its way down the street.

The civilian population? It had fled before the shooting started.

Not that it would have made any difference to the operation.

So I wrote a story about what wars cost and how decisions get made in the field—despite policy considerations back in air-conditioned offices. It was the best story I'd written so far, and the first time I'd tackled issues of real importance.

Only problem was, "The Butcher's Bill" didn't sell.

Mostly it just got rejection slips, but one very competent editor said that Joe Haldeman and Jerry Pournelle were writing as much of that sort of story as his magazine needed. (Looking back, I find it interesting that in 1973 magazine terms, the stories in *The Forever War*, *The Mercenary*, and *Hammer's Slammers* were indistinguishable.)

One editor felt that "The Butcher's Bill" demanded too much background, both SF and military, for the entry-level anthology he was planning. That was a good criticism, to which I responded by writing "Under the Hammer."

"Under the Hammer" had a new recruit as its viewpoint character, a kid who was terrified that he was going to make an ignorant mistake and get himself killed. (I didn't have to go far to find a model for the character. Remember that I hadn't had advanced combat training before I became an ad hoc tank crewman.) Because the recruit knew so little, other characters could explain details to him and to the reader.

I made the kid a recruit to Hammer's Slammers, because I already had that background clear in my mind. I hadn't intended to write a series, it just happened that way.

"Under the Hammer" didn't sell either.

I went about a year and a half with no sales. This was depressing, and I was as prone as the next guy to whine "My stuff's better 'n some of the crap they publish."

In hindsight, I've decided that when an author doesn't sell, it's because:

1) he's doing something wrong; or
2) he's doing something different, and he isn't good enough to get away with being different.

In my case, there was some of both. The two Hammer stories were different—and clumsy; I was new to the job. Most of the other fiction I wrote during that period just wasn't very good.

But the situation was very frustrating.

The dam broke when Gordy Dickson took "The Butcher's Bill" for an anthology he was editing. It wasn't a lot of money, but I earned my living as an attorney. This was a sale, and it had been a long time coming.

Almost immediately thereafter, the editor at *Galaxy* (who'd rejected the Hammer stories) was replaced by his assistant, a guy named Jim Baen. Jim took the pair and asked for more.

I wrote three more stories in the series before Jim left

to become SF editor of Ace Books. One of the three was the only piece I've written about Colonel Hammer himself instead of Hammer's Slammers. It was to an editorial suggestion: tell how it all started. Jim took that one, and though he rejected the other two, they sold elsewhere. The dam really had broken.

I moved away from Hammer and into other things, including a fantasy novel. Then Jim, now at Ace, asked for a collection of the 35,000 words already written plus enough new material in the series to fill out a book. Earlier I'd had an idea that seemed too complex to be done at a length a magazine would buy from me. I did it—"Hang Man"— for the collection and added a little end-cap for the volume also—"Standing Down."

To stand between the stories, I wrote essays explaining the background of the series, social and economic as well as the hardware. In some cases I had to work out the background for the first time. I hadn't started with the intention of writing a series.

Hammer's Slammers came out in 1979. That was the end of the series, so far as I was concerned. But as the years passed, I did a novelet. Then the setting turned out to be perfect for my effort at using the plot of the *Odyssey* as an SF novel (*Cross the Stars*). I did a short novel, *At Any Price*, that was published with the earlier novelet and a story I did for the volume. . . .

And I'm going to do more stories besides this one in the series, because Hammer's Slammers have become a vehicle for a message that I think needs to be more widely known. Veterans who've written or talked to me already understand, but a lot of other people don't.

When you send a man out with a gun, you create a policymaker. When his ass is on the line, he will do whatever he needs to do.

And if the implications of that bother you, the time to do something about it is before you decide to send him out.

Dave Drake
Chapel Hill, N.C.

The Interrogation Team

The man the patrol brought in was about forty, bearded, and dressed in loose garments—sandals, trousers, and a vest that left his chest and thick arms bare. Even before he was handed from the back of the combat car, trussed to immobility in sheets of water-clear hydorclasp, Griffiths could hear him screaming about his rights under the York Constitution of '03.

Didn't the fellow realize he'd been picked up by Hammer's Slammers?

"Yours or mine, Chief?" asked Major Smokey Soames, Griffiths' superior and partner on the interrogation team— a slim man of Afro-Asian ancestry, about as suited for wringing out a mountaineer here on York as he was for swimming through magma. Well, Smokey'd earned his pay on Kanarese. . . .

"Is a bear Catholic?" Griffiths asked wearily. "Go set the hardware up, Major."

"And haven't I already?" said Smokey, but it had been nice of him to make the offer. It wasn't that mechanical interrogation *required* close genetic correspondences between subject and operator, but the job went faster and smoother in direct relation to those correspondences. Worst of all was to work on a woman, but you did what you had to do. . . .

Four dusty troopers from A Company manhandled the subject, still shouting, to the command car housing the interrogation gear. The work of the firebase went on. Crews were pulling maintenance on the fans of some of the cars facing outward against attack, and one of the rocket howitzers rotated squealingly as new gunners were trained. For the most part, though, there was little to do at midday, so troopers turned from the jungle beyond the berm to the freshly-snatched prisoner and the possibility of action that he offered.

"Don't damage the goods!" Griffiths said sharply when the men carrying the subject seemed ready to toss him onto the left-hand couch like a log into a blazing fireplace. One of the troopers, a non-com, grunted assent; they settled the subject in adequate comfort. Major Soames was at the console between the paired couches, checking the capture location and relevant intelligence information from Central's data base.

"Want us to unwrap 'im for you?" asked the non-com, ducking instinctively though the roof of the command car, cleared his helmet. The interior lighting was low, however, especially to eyes adapted to the sun hammering the bulldozed area of the firebase.

"Listen, me 'n my family *never*, I swear it, dealt with interloping traders!" the York native pleaded.

"No, we'll take care of it," said Griffiths to the A Company trooper, reaching into the drawer for a disposable-blade scalpel to slit the hydorclasp sheeting over the man's wrist. Some interrogators liked to keep a big fighting knife around, combining practical requirements with a chance to soften up the subject through fear. Griffiths thought the technique was misplaced: for effective mechanical interrogation, he wanted his subjects as relaxed as possible. Panic-jumbled images were better than no images at all; but only *just* better.

"We're not the Customs Police, old son," Smokey murmured as he adjusted the couch headrest to an angle which looked more comfortable for the subject. "We're a lot more interested in the government convoy ambushed last week."

Griffiths' scalpel drew a line above the subject's left hand and wrist. The sheeting drew back in a narrow gape, briefly iridescent as stresses within the hydorclasp readjusted themselves. As if the sheeting were skin, however, the rip stopped of its own accord at the end of the scored line. "What're you doing to me?"

"Nothing I'm not doing to myself, friend," said Griffiths, grasping the subject's bared forearm with his own left hand so that their inner wrists were together. Between the thumb and forefinger of his right hand he held a standard-looking stim cone up where the subject could see it clearly, despite the cocoon of sheeting still holding his legs and torso rigid. "I'm George, by the way. What do your friends call you?"

"You're drugging me!" the subject screamed, his fingers digging into Griffiths' forearm fiercely. The mountaineers living under triple-canopy jungle looked pasty and unhealthy, but there was nothing wrong with this one's muscle tone.

"It's a random pickup," said Smokey in Dutch to his partner. "Found him on a trail in the target area, nothing suspicious—probably just out sap-cutting—but they could snatch him without going into a village and starting something."

"Right in one," Griffiths agreed in soothing English as he squeezed the cone at the juncture of his and the subject's wrist veins. The dose in its skin-absorbed carrier— developed from the solvent used with formic acid by Terran solifugids for defense—spurted out under pressure and disappeared into the bloodstreams of both men: thrillingly cool to Griffiths, and a shock that threw the subject into mewling, abject terror.

"Man," the interrogator murmured as he detached the subject's grip from his forearm, using the pressure point in the man's wrist to do so, "if there was anything wrong with it, I wouldn't have split it with you, now would I?"

He sat down on the other couch, swinging his legs up and lying back before the drug-induced lassitude crumpled him on the floor. He was barely aware of movement as Smokey fitted a helmet on the subject and ran a finger up and down columns of touch-sensitive controls on his console to reach a balance. All Griffiths would need was the matching helmet, since the parameters of his brain were already loaded into the database. By the time Smokey got around to him, he wouldn't even feel the touch of the helmet.

Though the dose *was* harmless, as he'd assured the subject, unless the fellow had an adverse reaction because of the recreational drugs he'd been taking on his own. You could never really tell with the sap-cutters, but it was generally okay. The high jungles of York produced at least a dozen drugs of varying effect, and the producers were of course among the heaviest users of their haul.

By itself, that would have been a personal problem; but the mountaineers also took the position that trade off-planet was their own business, and that there was no need to sell their drugs through the Central Marketing Board in the capital for half the price that traders slipping into the jungle in small starships would cheerfully pay. Increasingly-violent attempts to enforce customs laws on men with guns and the willingness to use them had led to what was effectively civil war—which the York government had hired the Slammers to help suppress.

It's a bitch to fight when you don't know who the enemy is; and that was where Griffiths and his partner came in.

"Now I want you to imagine that you're walking home from where you were picked up," came Smokey's voice, but Griffiths was hearing the words only through the subject's mind. His own helmet had no direct connection to the hushed microphone into which the major was speaking. The words formed themselves into letters of dull orange which expanded to fill Griffiths' senses with a blank background.

The monochrome sheet coalesced abruptly, and he was trotting along a trail which was a narrow mark beaten by feet into the open expanse of the jungle floor. By cutting off the light, the triple canopies of foliage ensured that the real undergrowth would be stunted—as passable to the air-cushion armor of Hammer's Slammers as it was to the locals on foot.

Judging distance during an interrogation sequence was

a matter of art and craft, not science, because the 'trip'—
though usually linear—was affected by ellipses and the subject's attitude during the real journey. For the most part,
memory was a blur in which the trail itself was the major
feature and the remaining landscape only occasionally
obtruded in the form of an unusually large or colorful
hillock of fungus devouring a fallen tree. Twice the subject's
mind—not necessarily the man himself—paused to throw
up a dazzlingly-sharp image of a particular plant, once a
tree and the other time a knotted, woody vine which stood
out in memory against the misty visualization of the trunk
which the real vine must wrap.

Presumably the clearly-defined objects had something
to do with the subject's business—which was none of
Griffiths' at this time. As he 'walked' the Slammer through
the jungle, the mountaineer would be mumbling broken
and only partly intelligible words, but Griffiths no longer
heard them or Smokey's prompting questions.

The trail forked repeatedly, sharply visualized each time
although the bypassed forks disappeared into mental fog
within a meter of the route taken. It was surprisingly easy
to determine the general direction of travel: though the
sky was rarely visible through the foliage, the subject
habitually made sunsightings wherever possible in order to
orient himself.

The settlement of timber-built houses was of the same
tones—browns, sometimes overlaid by a gray-green—as the
trees which interspersed the habitations. The village glowed
brightly by contrast with the forest, however, both because
the canopy above was significantly thinner and because the
place was home and a goal to the subject's mind.

Sunlight, blocked only by the foliage of very large trees
which the settlers had not cleared, dappled streets which
had been trampled to the consistency of coarse concrete.
Children played there, and animals—dogs and pigs, probably, but they were undistinguished shadows to the subject, factors of no particular interest to either him or his
interrogator.

Griffiths did not need to have heard the next question

to understand it, when a shadow at the edge of the trail sprang into mental relief as a forty-tube swarmjet launcher with a hard-eyed woman slouched behind it watching the trail. The weapon needn't have been loot from the government supply convoy massacred the week before, but its swivelling base was jury-rigged from a truck mounting.

At present, the subject's tongue could not have formed words more complex than a slurred syllable or two, but the Slammers had no need for cooperation from his motor nerves or intellect. All they needed were memory and the hard-wired processes of brain function which were common to all life forms with spinal cords. The subject's brain retrieved and correlated the information which the higher centers of his mind would have needed to answer Major Soames' question about defenses—and Griffiths collected the data there at the source.

Clarity of focus marked as the subject's one of the houses reaching back against a bole of colossal proportions. Its roof was of shakes framed so steeply that they were scarcely distinguishable from the vertical timbers of the siding. Streaks of the moss common both to tree and to dwelling faired together cut timber and the russet bark. On the covered stoop in front, an adult woman and seven children waited in memory.

At this stage of the interrogation Griffiths had almost as little conscious volition as the subject did, but a deep level of his own mind recorded the woman as unattractive. Her cheeks were hollow, her expression sullen, and the appearance of her skin was no cleaner than that of the subject himself. The woman's back was straight, however, and her clear eyes held, at least in the imagination of the subject, a look of affection.

The children ranged in height from a boy already as tall as his mother to the infant girl looking up from the woman's arms with a face so similar to the subject's that it could, with hair and a bushy beard added, pass for his in a photograph. Affection cloaked the vision of the whole family, limming the faces clearly despite a tendency for the bodies of the children to mist away rather like the generality of trees along the trail; but the infant was almost deified in the subject's mind.

Smokey's unheard question dragged the subject off abruptly, his household dissolving unneeded to the answer as a section of the stoop hinged upward on the end of his own hand and arm. The tunnel beneath the board flooring dropped straight down through the layer of yellowish soil and the friable rock beneath. There was a wooden ladder along which the wavering oval of a flashlight beam traced as the viewpoint descended.

The shaft was seventeen rungs deep, with a further gooseneck dip in the gallery at the ladder's end to trap gas and fragmentation grenades. Where the tunnel straightened to horizontal, the flashlight gleamed on the powergun in a niche ready to hand but beneath the level to which a metal detector could be tuned to work reliably.

Just beyond the gun was a black-cased directional mine with either a light-beam or ultrasonic detonator—the subject didn't know the difference and his mind hadn't logged any of the subtle discrimination points between the two types of fuzing. Either way, someone ducking down the tunnel could, by touching the pressure-sensitive cap of the detonator, assure that the next person across the invisible tripwire would take a charge of shrapnel at velocities which would crumble the sturdiest body armor.

"Follow all the tunnels," Smokey must have directed, because Griffiths had the unusual experience of merger with a psyche which split at every fork in the underground system. Patches of light wavered and fluctuated across as many as a score of simultaneous images, linking them together in the unity in which the subject's mind held them.

It would have made the task of mapping the tunnels impossible, but the Slammers did not need anything so precise in a field as rich as this one. The tunnels themselves had been cut at the height of a stooping runner, but there was more headroom in the pillared bays excavated for storage and shelter. Flashes—temporal alternatives, hard to sort from the multiplicity of similar physical locations—showed shelters both empty and filled with villagers crouching against the threat of bombs which did not come. On one image the lighting was uncertain and could almost have proceeded as a mental artifact from the expression of the subject's infant daughter, looking calmly from beneath her mother's worried face.

Griffiths could not identify the contents of most of the stored crates across which the subject's mind skipped, but Central's data bank could spit out a list of probables when the interrogator called in the dimensions and colors after the session. Griffiths would do that, for the record. As a matter of practical use, all that was important was that the villagers had thought it necessary to stash the material here—below the reach of ordinary reconnaissance and even high explosives.

There were faces in the superimposed panorama, villagers climbing down their own access ladders or passed in the close quarters of the tunnels. Griffiths could not possibly differentiate the similar, bearded physiognomies during the overlaid glimpses he got of them. It was likely enough that everyone, every male at least, in the village was represented somewhere in the subject's memory of the underground complex.

There was one more sight offered before Griffiths became aware of his own body again in a chill wave spreading from the wrist where Smokey had sprayed the antidote. The subject had seen a nine-barrelled powergun, a calliope whose ripples of high-intensity fire could eat the armor of a combat car like paper spattered by molten steel. It was deep in an underground bay from which four broad 'windows'—firing slits—were angled upward to the surface. Preparing the weapon in this fashion to cover the major approaches to the village must have taken enormous effort, but there was a worthy payoff: at these slants, the bolts would rip into the flooring, not the armored sides, of a vehicle driving over the camouflaged opening of a firing slit. Not even Hammer's heavy tanks could survive having their bellies carved that way. . . .

The first awareness Griffiths had of his physical surroundings was the thrashing of his limbs against the sides of the couch while Major Soames lay across his body to keep him from real injury. Motor control returned with a hot rush, permitting Griffiths to lie still for a moment and pant.

"Need to go under again?" asked Smokey as he rose, fishing in his pocket for another cone of antidote for the subject if the answer was 'no.'"

"Got all we need," Griffiths muttered, closing his eyes before he took charge of his arms to lift him upright. "It's a bloody fortress, it is, all underground and cursed well laid out."

"Location?" said his partner, whose fingernails clicked on the console as he touched keys.

"South by southeast," said Griffiths. He opened his eyes, then shut them again as he swung his legs over the side of the couch. His muscles felt as if they had been under stress for hours, with no opportunity to flush fatigue poisons. The subject was coming around with comparative ease in his cocoon, because his system had not been charged already with the drug residues of the hundreds of interrogations which Griffiths had conducted from the right-hand couch. "Maybe three kays—you know, plus or minus."

The village might be anywhere from two kilometers to five from the site at which the subject had been picked up, though Griffiths usually guessed closer than that. This session had been a good one, too, the linkage close enough that he and the subject were a single psyche throughout most of it. That wasn't always the case: many interrogations were viewed as if through a bad mirror, the images foggy and distorted.

"Right," said Smokey to himself or the hologram map tank in which a named point was glowing in response to the information he had just keyed. "Right, Thomasville they call it." He swung to pat the awakening subject on the shoulder. "You live in Thomasville, don't you, old son?"

"Wha . . . ?" murmured the subject.

"You're sure he couldn't come from another village?" Griffiths queried, watching his partner's quick motions with a touch of envy stemming from the drug-induced slackness in his own muscles.

"Not a chance," the major said with assurance. "There were two other possibles, but they were both north in the valley."

"Am I—" the subject said in a voice that gained strength as he used it. "Am I all right?"

Why ask us? thought Griffiths, but his partner was saying, "Of course you're all right, m'boy, we said you would be, didn't we?"

While the subject digested that jovial affirmation, Smokey turned to Griffiths and said, "You don't think we need an armed recce then, Chief?"

"They'd chew up anything short of a company of panzers," Griffiths said flatly, "and even *that* wouldn't be a lotta fun. It's a bloody underground fort, it is."

"What did I say?" the subject demanded as he regained intellectual control and remembered where he was—and why. "Please, please, what'd I say?"

"Curst little, old son," Smokey remarked. "Just mumbles— nothing to reproach yourself about, not at all."

"You're a gentle bastard," Griffiths said.

"Ain't it true, Chief, ain't it true?" his partner agreed. "Gas, d'ye think, then?"

"Not the way they're set up," said Griffiths, trying to stand and relaxing again to gain strength for a moment more. He thought back over the goose-necked tunnels; the filter curtains ready to be drawn across the mouths of shelters; the atmosphere suits hanging beside the calliope. "Maybe saturation with a lethal skin absorbtive like K3, but what's the use of that?"

"Right you are," said Major Soames, tapping the console's preset for Fire Control Central.

"You're going to let me go, then?" asked the subject, wriggling within his wrappings in an unsuccessful attempt to rise.

Griffiths made a moue as he watched the subject, wishing that his own limbs felt capable of such sustained motion. "Those other two villages may be just as bad as this one," he said to his partner.

"The mountaineers don't agree with each other much

better'n they do with the government," demurred Smokey
with his head cocked toward the console, waiting for its
reply. "They'll bring us in samples, and we'll see then."

"Go ahead," said Fire Central in a voice bitten flat by
the two-kilohertz aperture through which it was transmitted.

"Got a red-pill target for you," Smokey said, putting one
ivory-colored fingertip on the holotank over Thomasville
to transmit the coordinates to the artillery computers.
"Soonest."

"Listen," the subject said, speaking to Griffiths because
the major was out of the line of sight permitted by the
hydorclasp wrappings, "let me go and there's a full three
kilos of Misty Hills Special for you. Pure, I swear it, so
pure it'll float on water!"

"No damper fields?" Central asked in doubt.

"They aren't going to put up a nuclear damper and warn
everybody they're expecting attack, old son," said Major
Soames tartly. "Of course, the least warning and they'll turn
it on."

"Hold one," said the trooper in Fire Control.

"Just lie back and relax, fella," Griffiths said, rising to
his feet at last. "We'll turn you in to an internment camp
near the capital. They keep everything nice there so they
can hold media tours. You'll do fine."

There was a loud squealing from outside the interrogators' vehicle. One of the twenty-centimeter rocket howitzers was rotating and elevating its stubby barrel. Ordinarily
the six tubes of the battery would work in unison, but there
was no need for that on the present fire mission.

"We have clearance for a nuke," said the console with
an undertone of vague surprise which survived sideband
compression. Usually the only targets worth a red pill were
protected by damper fields which inhibited fission bombs
and the fission triggers of thermonuclear weapons.

"Lord blast you for sinners!" shouted the trussed local,
"what is it you're doing, you blackhearted devils?"

Griffiths looked down at him, and just at that moment
the hog fired. The base charge blew the round clear of
the barrel and the sustainer motor roared the shell up in

a ballistic path for computer-determined seconds of burn. The command vehicle rocked. Despite their filters, the vents drew in air burned by exhaust gases.

It shouldn't have happened after the helmets were removed and both interrogator and subject had been dosed with antidote. Flashback contacts did sometimes occur, though. This time it was the result of the very solid interrogation earlier; that, and meeting the subject's eyes as the howitzer fired.

The subject looked so much like his infant daughter that Griffiths had no control at all over the image that sprang to his mind: the baby's face lifted to the sky which blazed with the thermonuclear fireball detonating just above the canopy—

—and her melted eyeballs dripping down her cheeks.

The hydorclasp held the subject, but he did not stop screaming until they had dosed him with enough suppressants to turn a horse toes-up.